The Season of Lost Children

karen Blomain

PEARLSONG PRESS
NASHVILLE, TN

Pearlsong Press
P.O. Box 58065
Nashville, TN 37205
1-866-4-A-PEARL
www.pearlsong.com
www.pearlsongpress.com

Original trade paperback ISBN: 9781597190282
Ebook ISBN: 9781597190299

Book & cover design by Zelda Pudding.
Cover photo & author photo © Michael Downend—ASMP.

Library of Congress Cataloging-in-Publication Data

Blomain, Karen, 1944–
The season of lost children / Karen Blomain.
    p. cm.
ISBN 978-1-59719-028-2 (original trade pbk. : alk. paper)—ISBN
978-1-59719-029-9 (ebook)
 I. Title.
PS3552.L6363S43 2011
813'.54—dc22
                                        2011003294

FOR MICHAEL, FOREVER.

Acknowledgments

Kielty Turner, Dan Grippo, Leslee Becker, Andi Mitnick, and Michael Downend for their good eyes and good advice

and

The Ragdale Foundation, The Virginia Center for the Creative Arts, The F. Lamot Belin Arts Scholarship, and Anam Cara Artists Retreat, for the space and time to dream this book into life.

The law of chaos is the law of ideas,
Of improvisations and seasons of belief.

WALLACE STEVENS
"Extracts from Addresses to the Academy of Fine Ideas"

Chapter 1
1955

Ellie had readied the bath. Sister Thomas Mary clasped her arms close to her sides, refusing to undress. "Talcum. Sprinkle," she said, gesturing across the tub. "No. No. Don't look at the body. Body. Blue. Body. Body…" Finally when Ellie had wrestled free the layers of the blue serge and soiled underthings from arms and legs ribboned with thick blue veins, the old nun's large loose rump puddled toward her knees as she stood rigid beside the tub. Eyes squeezed shut; face held aloft as if she had not removed the stiff collar that prevented her from looking down, the nun recited a litany, "Body. Blue. Powder. Smell. Bad. Bad. Don't look…"

Holding the old nun's arm—the ancient skin mottled bluish-gray and pleated unevenly like used crepe paper—steady, Ellie anointed the waiting water with talcum and swished it until nothing could be seen beneath its cloudy surface. Careful not to rush, she helped one immense leg then the other clear of the edge and guided her charge to a seated position into the deep tub. "In, in, in, in." The scent of baby powder swirled around them.

Maybe the old ones were right: it was impossible to reassume innocence once you started with the body. "Cracked vessel." Once loosed, passion and longing can't be restrained. Ellie had first fallen in love with Father Edward Roderi's scent. In the convent dining room resplendent with china and flowers and the products of three days of baking, Mother Arthurian had introduced all the professed nuns in the order of seniority, then the postulants and the novices, Ellie among them, to the new chaplain. Throughout the long recitation of names, he smiled attentively and mingled easily. Monsignor Young, who the young priest would replace, walked him to the dessert table. After a few minutes, Mother Arthurian drew the older man away and Ellie, whose job it was to keep the table stocked and freshened, was left standing next to Father Roderi.

"Nice spread," he said, looking pleased with the dishes of sweets and tiny triangular sandwiches. "Do you know if there's a liturgical cookbook with recipes for priestly visits, the first rule of which is whatever you do, make sure the bread is crust free?"

Ellie shrugged. "Maybe," she said, hoping someone would join them. In the six months she'd been in the convent, the only men she'd spoken to were the elderly Monsignor Young and Dr. Grady. "Care of the body and soul, that's all we need them for," one of the newly professed sisters had jokingly advised the postulants. Ellie, who had always been uncomfortable with men, silently agreed. This young priest was a disquieting presence in the convent.

"I'm joking," he said. 'Don't look so serious."

She read in his gaze around the room an astonishing, affronting confidence. "I'm not," Ellie said. "Taking it seriously." She felt her face redden. *I'm a fool. Can't even keep up a simple conversation. Of course,* she thought, *in the seminary he'd probably been taught how to communicate with anyone.* Across the room Sister Gloria fussed with the tea things. Ellie willed her friend toward them, to save her from his attention, but Gloria bustled off. Ellie couldn't simply walk away and leave the guest of honor alone holding a crustless sandwich. From the depth of her being she summoned words, "I think the dark bread are more substantial. Egg salad."

"Will you be in my liturgy class?"

"Yes. All the postulants," she answered.

Father Roderi reached across to the table and plucked two brown bread sandwiches and placed one on her plate and popped the other into his mouth. In the slight breeze of his movement, she smelled him. Indefinable. Comforting. A scent both real and enduring, like the deep woods where the light didn't fully penetrate and the ferns grew to waist height.

That was the beginning.

And here she was only six weeks later planning to run off with her confessor and chaplain. She knew Father Edward Roderi and she were doing something very wrong. Her mind raced with terror: now that she had touched him, she was never without thinking of how his skin felt. Her legs went watery and weakened when she recalled the pressure of something thick and magical, something that drew a sharp twitch from her pelvis as he leaned against her, his breath feathering her cheek.

"Warm, warm, warm," the nun said, drawing Ellie back to the present. Then, "Stella Maris." *Just enough sense to it,* Ellie thought as she realized that Sister Thomas Mary's verbal wanderings had connected the bath water with the sea. "Stella Maris—" she clawed Ellie close and pointed across the room to the small window above the row of sinks. Steam shrouded the panes. "Stella Maris—" finally almost a laugh as she watched Ellie register the joke: Stella Maris, the name of the motherhouse where the postulants, novices and retired nuns lived. *Star of the sea.* Sister Thomas Mary had been pointing to the dark sky and the small seam of morning starlight visible in the crack where Ellie had propped a stick against the sill to admit some cool air.

The effort of bending to have her back washed caused Sister Thomas Mary to murmur, an odd babyish *ma, ma, ma* sound. Working in the retirement convent was no different than babysitting—wrestling the same fears, the need to invent a game around resistance. Or was it Ellie's special penance that she, having given birth and given away her own baby, would find in convent life, in her service to this old woman, so many odd and hurtful reminders?

Handing the lathered washcloth to Sister Thomas Mary, she pointed with a circular scrubbing motion down into the water. "Now your coolie," she said. The old nun smiled back, vacant gums closed coquettishly around her outstretched tongue. "My coolie." She swiped at the triangle between her legs, the loose skin of her arm swaying with each inept swipe.

The ancient breasts lay like two scant sacks of sand against the rib cage. Ellie lifted them to wash beneath. After she shampooed Sister Thomas Mary's sparse hair, she filled a plastic bowl with clean water and dribbled it over the bent head. "Again. Again. Rain. Cry. Blue—" smiling, the old nun closed her eyes and leaned back against the young, strong arm. The room was abruptly silent. The incessant vocalizing stilled by some shift.

"That's good," Ellie crooned. "Very, very good. Such a good girl, Maureen." For Ellie knew by the silence that the old nun was no longer present. She had become a young girl before the name imposed and taken to replace her own, before her body gained its bulk and then began to lose it, before the thought of God or religion or the dark garb she would wear every day for sixty-seven years, before she ushered her first group of students into the classroom, before the feelings she had denied so long but couldn't escape.

"That's good. So good," Ellie said, stretching out the words, almost singing them. "It feels so gooood to be nice and clean." The heavy limbs relaxed and stretched with pleasure. "Mumm-mumm," Maureen crooned back.

If there had been sunshine at the window, Ellie would have laid Sister Thomas Mary fresh washed and naked in front of it to let the air play over all the tatters and folds of skin, to let the light caress the scars on her wide veiny belly, the surprisingly pinkened nakedness, the babyish bald mound and the slack gash of her fallow sex. But by the time dawn arrived they would be finished with the bath and seated in chapel. Flexing her elbows and knees, Ellie grasped the nun's arms and levered her to a standing position.

As soon as the opaque water coursed away in a loud shower, the old nun regretted the pleasure of her bath. Recalling the sins of the body, she hated it again. Ellie had all she could do to get her charge safely from the tub and into the waiting towels, a wild copious wrapping tolerated only if Ellie kept crooning "That's right. Good girl. One more minute."

Even before she was dry the nun grabbed at the bundle of fresh clothing. Unassisted, Sister Thomas Mary donned the complicated habit, the same one, fumblingly at first, Ellie would learn to wear if she professed and received her white veil at the end of her second year in the novitiate. Twittering through folds and sashes, the ancient hands hoisted the capacious undergarments, poked her head through the heavy slip and dark blue panels, and wound the sash below her breasts. Complete, the gown shrouded the body. She wrenched the white collar, its sharp edge settling into the ridge in her doughy chin, and tugged the celluloid bib in place, twined the wooden rosary at her waistband and attached the veil. Once encased, her face looked squeezed, as the sides of her bonnet obscured peripheral vision. Here and there, the knotty knowing fingers adjusted and straightened. Forbidden mirrors, the nuns learned to dress by rote and to check the rightness of their habit by feel. The skill never left Sister Thomas Mary, even when prayer cascaded into the syllables of reckless blather.

Can I do it? Ellie thought. *Can I dress each day and never think again of the way my body blossoms at his touch?*

Once clothed, Sister Thomas Mary curled the golden earpieces of her heavy bifocals around her ears. When she plucked her dripping dentures from the waiting cup and thrust them into her mouth, her face shifted and assumed again its powerful presence.

Asked to bathe Sister Thomas Mary as part of her service, Ellie had nodded obedience, accepting the task even though she recoiled at the aged, yellowing flesh. At night in her cell, she prayed to fulfill her duties without anyone, especially the old sister, recognizing her disgust. Slowly she began to accept the complicated feelings she had about her own willful, unsettled body, recalling fingertips moving like flame against her skin, the hazy torture of childbirth, the weak aftermath. The guilt and shame her family had showered on her. And now Father Roderi. Was her still evil body drawing them into sin?

How could torture and pleasure be so close? Ellie prayed to accept the work she had been given, even the baths—to do it lovingly and gratefully and to make her effort beautiful in God's sight. Later, she would think her prayers had been answered; as the days went by, she grew to enjoy the bath ritual. Inside Sister Thomas Mary, Maureen— who enjoyed the pleasure of warm water and soap on her skin—was still alive and could be summoned.

In the large white bathroom with Maureen McGarity's help, Ellie accepted the power of her own body. She understood that what had happened to her had not been her fault. The past and its mistakes had nothing to do with loving Father Roderi. The body. Her body. She would use it to explore the world.

That night in chapel, the last rays through the stained glass bled away and only the mobile light from the sacristy lamp and winking candles lit the feet of statues. The chapel closed around her. Like every other night, she removed the short, burnt sticks and pried the spent metal bases from the votive cups; she wiped the smudged glass chimneys and polished them clear. She placed a votive candle in each holder, then raked the sand tray free of charred sticks. Her short habit whispered against the wood as she knelt, and the loops of beads at her waist ticked softly against each other. Aware of every gesture, every smell, even the feeling of the worn velvet *prie dieu* she knelt on, she waited for something to push her forward or pull her back. Around her the warm holy air of the chapel held its breath.

The odor of chrysanthemums—the sharp, slightly acrid scent, mixed with incense lingering from the consecration— pushed her to the edge of tears. How could she give up this place? Yet what they were doing—despite their daily feverish resolutions and infinite pain, could not help themselves from doing—had already made them unworthy. She remembered how the baby had latched itself to the side of some secret chamber, grown inside her without her permission, and waited till it was ready to propel itself out. And now this.

One night when their mouths felt blue and pulpy and thick from kissing, when they pulled air like spirit back and forth between them, opening their hearts to each other, he slipped his hand under the front panel of her habit and touched her breasts. "See," he said, as her nipples hardened. He lifted her short veil away from the back of her neck and bent his face to the small ribbon of bare skin above her collar. "This is what is leading us into our future."

After six weeks of meeting in the back of the chapel, fumbling at each other, starting with each creak, never having enough of those kisses they'd surprised each other with, Father Edward's tongue slipping like a melting fragment of something sacred between her lips, she knew that the passion between them was not going to wane. When they put their bodies together, their faces inches apart, their hands exploring the unseen territory of each other's shoulders and thighs and armpits, their pulses joined in one common need, she knew they would eventually make love.

Everything in the universe argued for it. The rest would be cancelled out. Ellie would never become a nun. The convent, its security, the ritual of her work, the beloved hours of study and prayer, the quiet walk into the chapel six times during the day and night, the bright blossoming light of certainty—all of it would be left behind. But would she be able to forgive herself the past? Having confessed and been forgiven, she would continue to try to put the birth of her child behind her. She had told him about it in the confessional, though technically she did not have to, as she had confessed it before to her pastor while she was still carrying the baby. But she wanted him to know. And to know that she wished never to speak of it again.

Loving Father Edward had nothing to do with her past. Being with him—obeying the needs of their bodies and minds—was not a sin. They would have a life together and their lovemaking would be holy in God's sight, too.

One day, after weeks of trying to figure out how he could arrange a car, he slipped a note inside the Latin grammar book, the one on the top of the stack. As usual, she entered the classroom before the others. She took the book and slid into her seat, second row nearest the window. Finally, he looked up and nodded a brief correct greeting. "Tonight. After chapel," she read from the paper cupped in her hand. Her face reddened, despite her attempt at control, as she slipped the note into her pocket.

Because of her cleaning duties, no one thought it odd that she lingered in chapel. The motherhouse grew quiet; the other sisters murmured in their cells as they fell asleep. Missing. Mother Arthurian would rouse the house and call the chaplain when she found Ellie missing. Then they would discover that Father Roderi was gone as well.

As she crept along the dark hallway, heart pounding, Ellie paused to listen for any sound—the footsteps of Sister Jane opening the pharmacy for medicine for one of the ailing sisters, the swish of a habit along the corridor. Somewhere in the basement a scurry of rats seeking out the grains stored there. The refectory tables stood set for breakfast, white cups upended on saucers, folded napkins. She thought of Sister Gloria squeezing her hand under the table that morning to suppress the giggles as the reading dragged on and eggs congealed on their plates. She felt a stab of grief at what she was giving up, but there was no way back to the innocence of her life in the convent before Father Roderi arrived.

She slipped out the scullery door and across the wooden porch, treading quietly as not to wake Sister Agatha's sleeping shepherd,

Scout, who patrolled the grounds. Through the lattice she glimpsed the beautiful, almost new Buick. Eddie was waiting at the back door with the headlights off, the car idling quietly.

In the basement of the huge brick edifice a switch clicked and the small worm that fed the stoker turned and pushed coal toward the waiting flame. On the top floor Sister Thomas Mary flopped onto her back, her mouth forming words for the vibrant pictures in her mind. Sibilant joy gurgled in her throat, pictures of cows and hillsides, images she'd brought across the water from her Irish childhood.

Father Edward slid across the seat and opened the door. She dove down the steps and into the car. A glint of light from his glasses startled Ellie. She felt herself shiver with fear and longing. "I've been waiting to do this," he said, drawing her into the car. She lifted her face to his. Lightly, he ran his fingertips across her cheek. He traced her lips and eyebrows. Digging his fingertips under the band holding the short veil to her head, he pulled the veil away and fluffed the chopped hair around her face.

In the faint light, Eddie's intense gaze frightened her. *"Mirabale visu,"* he said, moving both his hands through the dark thatch of hair shorn unevenly close to her head since the day of her profession. He turned her face, straining to see her in the sliver of light. His eyes glazed with tears, "Yes, yes," he whispered, "yes," as if she had asked him a complex and difficult question.

Chapter 2

Chasing a moon as useless as a dab of milk dried on a black plate, the priest and the young nun drove all night. Rain tittered the window. *What am I do-ing, what am I do-ing, what am I do-ing*, pulsed the wipers, echoing the terror surging in his heart. He imagined that she would have changed from her habit before she left the convent. But how? No street clothes were allowed in the novitiate. Hadn't she asked him to bring a pair of his khaki trousers and a white shirt? When Ellie slipped from the shadowed edge of the porch and opened the door, he realized he had been lost in a fantasy. The night veered from his dream version of their elopement, carrying reality into the car on a cool breeze. Her habit, her veil were indistinguishable against the interior. Still, when he felt the close, dark cloud of her hair, his body throbbed with joy and longing. Had he spoken? Language evanesced in the air. Within the folds of dark clothes her body, warm and alive, thrummed in response to his touch.

In three short months, Father Edward Roderi had morphed from a priest strictly observant of his vow to a man at the mercy of his own lust, tormented and helpless before his cravings for this young woman he was in love with. Now he was responsible not only for his own damnation, but hers as well. The clash between his beliefs and his behavior forced him to consider, not for the first time as he worked the car into gear and drove without headlights down the long brick driveway and away from the convent, that he had been bewitched.

The attendant at the ESSO station in Scranton slouched against the back fender holding the pump casually and nodding to his buddies inside to check out the nun. He whistled "Sweet Butterfly" through his teeth as he ragged the windshield then waited at the driver's door to be paid. "Nice buggy," he said, his glance sweeping the length of the car. "53 V-8, right?"

"Right." Though Father Edward didn't really know what that meant. The car, borrowed from his brother, was as unfamiliar in his hands as a woman. He looked inside the bright rectangle of glass where three other young men elbowed a counter, smoking and looking out into the illuminated rectangle of blacktop, waiting for whatever the spring evening might bring.

A nun? He saw it register as Ellie passed them on her way to the restroom clutching the paper bag containing his clothes. Perhaps one of them would later hear through the congregational grapevine about the nun and the priest who had run away together and make the connection.

"Seen them," he could hear the boy whistle through his teeth. "Last Wednesday they came inta the grage, late."

"In Scranton?"

"A looker. Except for the hair cut funny."

"They chop off all their hair."

"Saw him too. He only got out of the car for a second. Older guy."

"A priest?"

"Dark suit. Maybe."

He watched as Ellie, empty-handed, emerged from the bathroom looking like a kid from an *Our Gang* movie—pants rolled above her dark oxfords and white shirttails hanging almost to her knees. Father Edward felt his face redden with the realization that she would have to walk past the boys again. To his surprise, she stopped and said something. There was a general nervous shifting. He opened the door of the car and shot out. He took two strides around the pump, fists clenched at his sides, furious with himself. How could he have let her go in there alone? Didn't he know the simplest thing about being with a woman—that protective instinct felt by every sixth grade boy with his first crush? God help him. He wasn't up to having a wife.

Ellie paused just inside the door, her hand on the glass, and pointed to the restroom. Hoots of laughter came from inside the station and he felt his own shame and worry derided. Head thrown back, she joined the young men in laughter. Had she ever laughed like that with him? Not likely in the quiet cloistered world they inhabited—their swift, furtive meetings. As she walked toward him, Father Edward felt his legs weaken with a flood of relief. He had so much to learn about her, about himself, about what life outside vocations might be.

"What happened in there?" He noticed that his hand was trembling as he guided her into the car. Through his cotton shirt, so much thinner than the thick serge habit she'd removed, he fingered the small ridge of her shoulder, the scapular, the tiny, discrete bones of her neck. Beneath the drape of cloth she had been so little, her bones thin and frangible.

"I knew they saw me go in with the habit. I could feel them watching. Even in 1955 in Scranton you don't see a nun at night. When I came out dressed in your clothes, they turned to look." Her eyes rounded in imitation of their consternation. "Guess I gave them a shock."

"They might have hurt you. And I just sat here."

"They're just kids. They didn't mean anything."

"But laughing? Practically doubled over. What did you say?"

A squeaky giggle escaped her, another sound new to him. It was as if leaving the convent and removing the habit allowed her access to the music of her youthfulness, her candor and warmth. He registered the change in her. "I told them the first one inside the restroom could have my habit."

She examined his face and realized that he had suffered something. She patted his hand. "I wish we could stick around to see if any of them take me up on it. But we're off, aren't we?"

"Ellie," he said, a catch in his throat.

"No. Not Ellie. Not ever again." Her voice was firm, as if she had rehearsed something important. "From now on, Ellie is gone. I'm Eleanor. And you, Father Edward, are just plain Eddie."

"Eleanor."

"Drive, Eddie, drive." She giggled again. Then reached up and touched his cheek. "Yes, Eddie. Tonight we *both* become new people. "

Later as she slept on the seat beside him, her head nudging his shoulder, he remembered how she looked laughing with the young men in the ESSO. Instead of feeling, as he had since he entered the priesthood, that he was young and strong and smart—therefore powerful—he realized that he was almost twice as old as Eleanor. Thirty to her seventeen. Next to the problems of their respective vows, the need for secrecy, the formation of a plan that might allow them to be together, her youth had seemed almost unimportant. Now it was a larger thing than he would have thought possible. She had already suffered so at the hands of those who should have loved and nurtured her. He felt a protective rush unlike anything he had experienced before. In truth, that night he became an old man, the caretaker, the husband, bent by loving so vastly that even the thought of loss or damage could kill him.

Chapter 3
1995

Conscious of the late August air, the dry heat of the store, the fragrance of bananas turning brown in their fragile skins, the swirl of dust around her legs as the cooler compressor hummed on, Eleanor Roderi stood at the counter of Wescott's General Merchandise and Dry Goods. Thunderclouds formed against the Crystalle ridge and a low grumble introduced a storm. She closed her eyes and dipped her hand into the pocket of her sweater to touch the smooth cool beads.

On any ordinary day, Eleanor prayed many times. But this special day she had already begun to storm heaven with regret and repentance; knuckling fiercely along the beads as she observed the Sorrowful Mysteries and asked for a sign that she had been forgiven. Forty years before to the day—she had given away her baby. She tried to make this dread and sorrow disappear through prayer. To no avail. Frenetically she fussed about the counter of the empty store, hoping someone would come and ask something of her. When no one did, she ate a Milky Way.

At last, a small brass bell rang sharply as the door opened. The note hung in the air. Eleanor held her breath. How she realized that the person about to enter Wescott's would set in motion a sequence of events that would answer her prayers can't be known, but her eyes swam with inexplicable gratitude and anticipation.

Eleanor knew a thing or two about secrets. Her own of forty years—

she and Eddie alone knew about that long ago baby—and other secrets of the townspeople of Fenston. Often people in moral anguish, recalling that Eddie had been a priest, sought out his counsel. Sometimes, when he could bear the solitude of those confidences no longer, he told Eleanor, an act he considered a weakness, a violation of the trust that had been placed in him. Unable to prevent himself from telling his wife, he swore her to secrecy—a confidence well placed. Even when she found out her best friend's husband was a bigamist, she kept silent. But she had also come to understand that secrets always return.

Instead of looking up, she studied the credit wall above the register and finally settled her gaze on the floor. Her visitor, Clem Tompkins, Fenston's policeman, portly and officious, lifted two fingers to the brim of his hat in salute. "Wicked hot out there." He nudged his sunglasses down the length of his nose and looked over them at Eleanor.

She withdrew her hand from her pocket and answered, "What's up with the siren? How many times already today?" She fluffed ropes of gray-black hair away from her face and tried to look busy. He poured himself coffee from the pot on the table beside the counter and flicked a quarter into a small basket.

"That's another department. But I think the fire company planned an emergency drill." The way he looked past her and to the back of the store where Will Wescott normally presided over the meat counter annoyed Eleanor in the way that much about Clem did, particularly his penchant for stating the obvious. "Minding the store?"

"Will and Athena are in Binghamton. Stocking."

"Wednesday. Right. I forgot." He stood still until he seemed to realize he was holding the cup of coffee. He took a short, thoughtful sip.

"Back tonight," she said. She emptied the basket of grounds into a paper towel and removed the pot from the burner, pointedly swirling the sludgy residue around the glass bottom. "Noon. I'm about to close up."

He stared at the pot. "Good timing. Came to see you. I just left Eddie. He said you were the one to talk to."

"About?" Clem's deep lugubrious nods, as if his badge exacted a thousand pounds of worry, annoyed her as well. Refusing to react on cue, just because he rubbed his face in that world weary, seen-it all-and-then-some air he had, she waited.

"We got a situation on our hands."

"Our hands?" She waited.

Leaning his hip against the counter, he breathed in. Eleanor knew a lengthy recitation would follow, one in which Clem Tompkins featured as local hero. Preparing herself, and just a bit pleased for the distraction from her own sad thoughts, she crossed her arms against her prodigious silk polka dot covered chest and raised herself on tiptoe to perch on Athena's counter stool.

"Doc Pryal got the surprise of his life this morning," Clem launched into a preamble. Eleanor realized that he had already begun writing the day's script. She nodded the merest interest, just enough to keep him going.

"Went out back to that old trailer behind his kennel where he stores feed and supplies. Door busted open. First he thought some animals. But the bed was made up and there was food. Pryal never saw lights or anything. He used his head and called me. I staked it out. Could have been anyone. Someone on the run." He paused, giving her the chance to imagine various dangerous scenarios.

She knew the place well—the old silvery humpback trailer, blistery and faded, squatting in a nest of ashy gravel, the front window replaced by cardboard. Inside, a peeling naugahyde banquette served as bed and chair. Old linoleum curled at the edges, and thin strips of sun-eaten yellow curtains hung across the front window.

She hadn't been there since she and Millie Pryal gave up making maple syrup. They'd build a fire in the pit next to the trailer and sit inside playing cards and waiting out the long boil. If she thought hard, she could recall the mishmash of crockery, the feel of the scabby oil-cloth under her elbows, the taste of their thermos coffee as they sat in sweaters warming themselves and passing time.

"Turned out to be a kid." Clem brought the recitation to an abrupt climax. Lowering his tone a notch, he continued, "Must have been living there a while."

"And this involves me?"

"He won't talk. Won't even give his name."

"And…"

"You know how kids are—" A complaint more than a comment.

"I still don't understand—"

"My only official choice is to haul him to juvie custody. They'll toss him into the foster system. The kid seems scared. And small."

Behind the bluster and ego Eleanor caught the sincerity in Clem's face and started to pay attention. "Then he'd really be lost. Juvie's no place for a kid." The irony seemed lost on him.

"And," Eleanor answered, but her tone had softened.

"Well, I thought before I dumped him into that—maybe you and Eddie might—try to find out where he belongs."

Averting her face, she slipped down from her stool, picked up the coffee pot and turned to the sink to wash it. "Eddie sent you over here?" She scoured any trace of interest from her face or voice. It would do no good to let Clem sense the thread of—what was it—excitement, challenge—no, joy—she felt joy as she listened.

"Said it's up to you. If you felt you could nurture this child," Eleanor heard her husband's precise diction, the exact wording so completely Eddie's that it sounded artificial as Clem rendered it, "he said he's willing to participate."

"Why us?"

"Who else?" After a moment, he said, "Who else around here would do it?" Were they, in Clem's mind, a kind of court of last resort for all the misfits he could round up? He exhaled with a tone of angry befuddlement, as if he thought there should be others. At the same time he betrayed his understanding of the untidy, bookish, brilliant, and strange Roderi clan. And his admiration. "It's your specialty, isn't it? Taking care of people."

Eleanor shrugged her disregard for his opinion. "I'm about to close. Give me a few hours. Bring him over toward dinner time."

"He's outside."

"You left him in the squad car?"

"Air's on," he said apologetically.

She exhaled. "You mean you left some kid sitting locked in the car all this time wondering what you were going to do to him?"

Clem's florid face darkened and Eleanor glimpsed his flinty edge. He looked her straight in the eye, drew in a deep breath, released it in an exasperated loud huff and said, a thread of official steel in his tone, "That's exactly right. Instead of heading over to the county seat and turning him in to the sheriff and being done with him hours ago like

I should have and on to the rest of my work, I've been driving around all morning trying to figure out something better. And in order to do that, I had to keep him in custody."

Refusing to be bullied, Eleanor looked up as if unaware of the dynamic of the exchange with Clem and smiled her nicest little lady smile, "Well now that you figured it out, you'd best bring him in."

The boy watched through the front window of the store as the cruiser pulled away. Eleanor poked a few of loaves of bread into a straight row, pulled the lever on the old-fashioned cash register, lifted her bib apron over her long hair and hung it on a peg behind the counter.

"Take me five minutes to close up, then we'll be off." He could tell by her skittery voice that she was nervous. Maybe frightened. He noticed the long tangle of gray hair, bare arms wound with silver bracelets, the big dotted blouse, her strange, thick-strapped sandals.

As they settled in the car, she made small talk—the weather, the apple crop, the busy store, "people in and out like a fiddler's elbow." Eventually, when he didn't respond, her voice trailed off and they drove in silence, the ancient pink Cadillac floating along the road. She was going so slow that he probably could have jumped from the car. Was that it: did she want him to run? He gripped the cracked upholstery, peering through the open window, as they turned off the main road.

The first floor of the farmhouse was one immense room: kitchen, parlor, workshop—archways instead of walls between. Clutter glittered everywhere, piles of magazines listed from the seats of chairs, and a tower of books leaned precariously in one corner. A stuffed squirrel clutching a nut stood ready to scamper along a branch strung over a windowsill. Opposite, a bobcat displayed its large claws, and along a third wall an entire family of deer heads listened attentively, their soft, trusting eyes glistening.

The boy blinked. To the right of the sink, a museum poster luffed away from the wall. Small bits of scribbled notepaper were tacked to the wall next to the table. A ladder hung parallel to the ceiling; threaded through it a complex web of philodendron formed the warp and woof of a jungle canopy. From the chair rail around the room dangled tarnished copper-bottom pots, old cooking implements and dozens of baskets, filled with dried flowers, herbs, garlic and onions.

Next to an unlit modern gas stove, a coal cook stove glowed warmly. The kitchen was unbearably hot. And fragrant. Three loaves of bread, covered with a tea towel, cooled on a breadboard. Rockers clustered in an alcove for the view of a deck, a meadow and apple trees. In the distance, the sun played against the surface of objects hidden in the woods.

A formal dining table covered with a jumble rope of colored lights, a bale of wire and carpentry implements, and a sideboard bearing dozens of photos in ornate frames of all sizes dominated one part of the room. A sewing machine and bolts of fabric filled another corner. A bookshelf, open baby grand piano and an old fashioned record player hunkered in the others. The boy assumed the loud waves of music were coming from a recording, but then he sensed movement behind the open top of the piano and saw the crown of a bent head.

"Eddie's practicing," Eleanor said proudly, pointing the boy into an orange crushed velvet easy chair near the piano.

Lowering his ear to within a foot of the keys, the man smiled vaguely in his direction, nodded and uttered one word: Chopin. His hands leapt around the keyboard lightly but decisively. Eddie gave the impression of a large powerful body just beyond sturdy, shoulders sloping slightly downward to his surprisingly delicate hands. As he played the woman stood transfixed, and the boy's attention drifted around the room. On a small stand by the piano the tense body of a dusty red fox waited beneath a shelf displaying a coiled erect rattlesnake. The eyes of the snake and the fox, like those of the animals in the kitchen, watched him intently.

The boy closed his eyes and allowed the mind pictures bidden by the music. He yawned. He felt his body quake then lighten, falling away as he entered the flow of music. He tried to concentrate on figuring out how he was going to get away from these people, how he would find Tina. His sister's face swam in closer to him, bringing the warm scent of something he'd lost, remembered only in bits and wafts. He hoped she would not be angry with him for following her. Things at home had become even worse since she left and he finally just couldn't stand it.

When the boy awakened Eddie was standing over him. "I'm glad you enjoyed the music," he said, his face settling into the creases of a smile so satisfied and genuine it didn't seem to require an answer. The boy's eyes raced about as he tried to make some sense of his surroundings. Shame, that most familiar emotion, filled him. But Eddie was smiling and his eyes twinkled with humor and acceptance as he jerked his head, indicating that the boy should follow him into the kitchen. Eleanor carried a heavy covered tureen to the table and lifted the lid. The aroma of meat and cabbage, the blending scents of tart and sweet made the boy's mouth water as she heaped his plate then handed him a basket of bread. "Eddie's special whole wheat," she smiled.

"Chopin was our grace, El," Eddie said. "Let's just eat."

Through dinner Eleanor and Eddie talked, looking at him from time to time to include him in the conversation. They spoke of their lives, their work on the farm, their neighbors. Interrupting each other and smiling, Eddie described the scene of their elopement so clearly that Billy understood their fear of discovery by the mother superior. He could imagine them lurching down the long driveway behind the convent as Eddie mastered the intricacies of the new stick shift car. But why were they telling him about their lives? "We've been happy ever since," Eddie crowed. "Good thing, too. They don't give errant priests and nuns a second chance."

They seemed to require nothing from him. He relaxed into the chair, his leg stopped jiggling. He drew in a breath between bites and let his thoughts wander away from their talk and into his own concerns. He'd find Tina. She'd take care of him. They'd take care of each other.

As Eleanor and Eddie cleared the table, the boy studied the family photos lined up on the breakfront. Eleanor moved quickly to his side, drawing his attention to pictures of the Roderi children, explaining their lives and whereabouts. "Cute?" she asked, handing him a photo of a little girl. "Chrissie." Eleanor's voice softened around her grandchild's name. "The twins—Shirley, now married and Chrissie's mom. They live in New Hampshire now." Eleanor sighed. "Here's Sharon—in France now—graduate school. Twins, they could not be more different. And here's our baby, Robbie." She handed him a photo of a young man in a cap and gown. Eleanor kissed her fingertips and rubbed them lightly over the photo. 'The house feels empty. Thanksgiving—we'll all be together for the first in a long time."

Something hard rose in him, looking for a way out. The boy's eyes again swept the rows of photos. He still hadn't said a word. And he didn't intend to.

Eleanor and Eddie believed they lived their lives from sign to sign—waiting for whatever messages the universe might send. And often enough to support their theory, it gave them something they found promising enough to work with. Throughout the evening as they talked, Eleanor's mind had obsessively darted to the birth of her first child so long ago. The appearance of the boy on the 40th anniversary of that birth triggered something seismic in her. She recalled the premonition she'd had before Clem entered the store. Mysteriously, something long dormant had awakened that very morning. The years she carried the secret of her first child's existence fell on her like an immense weight; she had to regain her balance or it would crush her. She wished that she and Eddie in one of their million deep conversations had talked about that long ago baby. Still, when she thought about it, she realized she had fended off any discussion of it and Eddie had, reluctantly at first, taken her lead. Inchoately, she sensed there was a connection between this boy and that old pain. He was a sign. But what was she to read in it beyond more suffering for the sin of abandoning her child?

Eleanor carried the dishwater to the back door and stepped out onto the stoop. Smacking the bottom of the pan, she flung the water into the marigolds and pansies. Then she took a deep breath of the cool evening and sighed a quick prayer that she might help this boy and, in helping him, she might begin to heal the old rent that had once again burst open inside her.

Chapter 4

"Binghamton seems closer every week," Will Wescott said the next day as they unloaded the back of his van.

"Why's that?" Eleanor asked.

"Used to be miles of empty land between here and there. Now it's built up almost the whole way, strip malls appearing like mushrooms."

"Like what?"

In the background, the pop music station played softly. Athena, who prided herself on knowing all the hits, sang with Foreigner, "I Want To Know What Love Is."

The Roderi/Wescott/Darling friendship was part of the fabric of Fenston and the interconnection of three families. Will and Athena had come to Fenston in the early 50s and bought the general store, set on enjoying small town life, so different from New York City where they had both grown up. Hattie Beste, unmarried and the only child of the biggest landowner in the area, soon became Athena's closest friend. Afternoons, during the slow hours, Athena left the store in Will's care and the two young women drove the back country roads, Athena marveling at every vista. One day they saw that the tattered, sun-bleached For Sale sign had been removed from the lane leading to the long vacant Flynn farm, a place so run-down and long-abandoned that the locals took bets on whether it would be sold or collapse first.

"What fools would take that on?" Athena wondered aloud. Hattie grinned in agreement. Turning the corner, they noticed that the fallen tree limbs that had crisscrossed the drive had been pulled to one side.

Eleanor and Eddie Roderi were dragging their belongings into the old house. Stacked on the buckling porch were boxes of crockery, old chairs and rolled carpets and more books than either Hattie or Athena had ever seen before. The couple stopped and waved as if they had been expecting Hattie and Athena. Summoned by his wife, Will closed the store and pitched in, unloading the heavier items with Eddie.

By late afternoon, the truck was empty and the five sat warming themselves, their legs dangling from the edge of the porch. Maybe Eddie and Eleanor Roderi hadn't been so foolish, after all. The house was situated perfectly to catch the afternoon sun. The overgrown yard promised seasons of flowers and fruit. "We've come to paradise," Eddie said, sweeping his arms across the horizon. "All it will take is a bit of elbow grease," Eleanor added.

With Athena and Hattie's help, she spent the first week cleaning and readying the house, haphazardly painting a room a day. All summer she and Eddie slept on the sun porch on a mattress positioned so that they could look out into the sunny side yard where they would build an arbor. The private porch became the afternoon gathering spot for Will, Athena and Hattie. Just like that, Eddie and Eleanor, despite their odd bookish and untidy ways, were clasped close to Fenston's bosom.

Later that summer Eddie's brother Len, recently discharged from the Marines, visited Fenston accompanied by one of his service pals, Ben Darling. Hattie and Ben fell in love at a dance in the Chaplin Lake Pavilion. When Ben and Hattie were married in her family home with Athena and Will, Eddie and Eleanor as their attendants, the circle of five opened just enough for Ben to slip in. Partway.

"Give me that." Eleanor wrested a large carton of toilet paper from Will. "What did you see?"

Athena laughed when she realized what Will was referring to. "You wouldn't be talking about that outfit in the old service station in Wiggins, would you?"

"Flea market? Antique shop?" Eleanor suggested.

"Wishful thinker."

"What then?"

"You wouldn't believe it," Athena added.

"Something for the guys for a change," Will offered broadly, await-ing Athena's reaction. "Classy Acts: A Gentleman's Club."

"What's that?" Eleanor looked from one to the other, recognizing a private joke acted out for her benefit.

"Not sure. Guess Eddie and I'll have to take a run over there to find out."

"Will Wescott. If you even think…"

"Exotic dancers, according to the sign," Will continued.

"In Wiggins?" Eleanor snorted as her friends broke into laughter.

"Wait till Grace and her morality squad get wind of this." Eleanor added.

"I'd have to be automatically on the opposite side from them on any issue," Athena said. "Even this one. But I don't think we need that kind of thing around here. When they find out nobody's interested, they'll close down anyway."

"Who said nobody'd be interested?" Will put another carton on the counter. "I think you'll be surprised." Then he put up his hands as if in surrender or innocence, "Not me. That's for sure." He kissed the air over Athena's head. "You're all the exotic I need. He turned to Eleanor. "Did Eddie get that computer yet?"

"Don't change the subject," Athena said.

"No, but he's reading up on them. I suspect one of these days…"

"Maybe he should. He can put it down in that shelter he built that time when he thought the bombs would be flying any day."

Eleanor ignored the sarcasm in Will's voice. She knew that even their close friends, though they outwardly admired Eddie's intelligence, thought her husband was a dreamer. She bristled. It was all right for her to ride Eddie for his impracticality, but she wouldn't let anyone else do it. "Guess he's just so far ahead of the rest of the world, we'll never catch up."

"When he gets it, I want him to ask it how to sell all this stuff we get talked into stocking." Will nodded to the crates strewn around the front of the store.

Unpacking the boxes, the women worked together silently with a practiced economy of motion. Athena wore her usual costume of old blue jeans and a white broadcloth shirt, her halo of graying blonde hair tied back with a leather shoelace. Small and limber, she climbed onto the counter to restock the top shelves. Looking like a gypsy queen in a flared skirt and white blouse with gold stitching along the collar and cuffs, an outfit she was proud to have made herself—copying the embellishments from a photo of Russian stitchery—Eleanor, a woman of sturdier construction, stood beneath, unpacking the boxes and handing cans up to Athena.

As they worked, Eleanor told Athena about Clem and the boy he had found, trying to keep her voice casual.

Athena shook her head, shrugged and continued to count the large cardboard boxes on the floor, checking them against an invoice. "You really are the earth mother. Just let some needy person come within two miles of you and you're in heaven. I wish I knew what motivated you."

"Two miles? That's more credit than I deserve." Eleanor laughed. Pretending that her life was so simply defined was easy when she was with others. Although she and Athena had been friends for almost a lifetime and knew each other intimately, Eleanor's deepest secret, the fountain of all her sorrow, was not part of that friendship. A million times in their days together, Eleanor had almost confessed the birth then loss of her child. But something held her back.

"What are friends for?" Finished with her task, Athena put the paper and pencil on the counter and gazed at her friend. All humor had disappeared from her face. "Why?"

Eleanor waited so long to answer that Athena tapped her fingers on the counter as if to get her attention. "Good question. One I don't think I can answer. Other than to say it just seemed like the right thing. Okay?" Was that why she had never told Athena about the child? One question would lead to another and then another and she was not willing to expose that much of her pain, even to herself. Even people who loved you could not be counted on not to scrape away beyond the level you could tolerate.

"Okay?"

"Okay!"

"Who is he?"

"Don't know yet. Hasn't said a word. No identification. About twelve, I'd say. Could be older and just small."

"What else? How does he act?"

"Docile. Clem explained to him that it was either stay with us, causing no problems, or off to juvenile hall. Meanwhile, Clem is making inquiries into runaways within a day's distance."

"Did he understand?"

"Seemed to. He could have run off again. We don't lock the doors or keep a watch over him. But he didn't."

"So far," Athena interjected with her usual practicality.

"So far. I got together some clothes Robbie'd long outgrown and put them in the room for him. One good thing about being a packrat, I guess, I always have something that will work. He ate. We just keep talking to him. Mostly about us. But we told him he was safe and not to worry. Eddie gives me the hairy eyeball when I start to question him."

"Where is he now?"

"At the house. With Eddie."

"I don't know, El. All the things you read about kids doing drugs and going haywire. I'm worried this might backfire on you."

Eleanor seemed not to be listening. When she turned, Athena was surprised to see her eyes brimming with tears. "I can't turn him away."

"Oh, honey—not if you feel that way." Athena's tone was warm and soothing.

Athena often simply didn't understand her friend. She knew Eleanor had been a nun. Maybe that accounted for her good-heartedness when good sense would serve her better. Athena just couldn't figure out why Eleanor had the compulsion to care for every strange and wayward soul she met and to see every fork in the road as a moral decision.

"I wish Hattie were here," Eleanor sighed, echoing Athena's exact thought. Usually when there was a problem the three friends gathered and put their heads together. While Athena was all common sense, Eleanor turned spiritual and mystic, while Hattie was the leavening agent that could make sense of both sides of any issue.

But Hattie had become an enigma. For the first forty-five years of her life, she'd hardly left Fenston. People hadn't heard of agoraphobia back then, and chalked Hattie's odd ways up to her upbringing—a lonely only child. While Ben was working the New England territory for Precision Tools, she just sat up in her big house on the hill and waited for him to come home. Ironically, after Ben died she started to travel and hadn't stopped since.

"No telling when she'll be back."

"She's missing some really fine weather," Athena remarked. They both turned to look out into the morning light.

"And some classy acts." Eleanor ratcheted up the volume on the radio, wiggled her prodigious curvy butt, threw back her head. The two woman bumped hips and shimmied. Their laughter could be heard out into the intersection, causing Grace Morgan to slow her car. She stopped at the blinker light and watched the animated silhouette of Eleanor and Athena inside Wescott's General Merchandise and Dry Goods.

"Old witches," she muttered.

Chapter 5

The silent, undemanding presence of the boy who sat huddled in a chair in the living room leafing through an old Scientific American unsettled Eddie as he went about his morning chores. Like Eleanor, he wanted to help the boy, if he could figure out how. Had someone asked him what his life's work was, Eddie would answer: to love Eleanor, to help others, and to learn about the world. Here in the form of this young man was an opportunity to do all three. Eleanor was happiest when she had someone to fuss over. The kid obviously was in need. But something about his silence, his flat blank look, as if the world could neither interest nor disappoint him, bothered Eddie. He recognized it as the look he'd seen on the faces of much older men—often among the prisoners that Eddie counseled and befriended. It was the expression of someone who was giving up hope.

As Eddie tidied the kitchen and folded *The New York Times* to the crossword puzzle, he glanced toward the boy. He printed *inept* where "maladroit" indicated and then put down his pen. How could he help when he himself felt so tense? "I'll be in my workshop, if you need me," he said, nodding toward the basement door.

At the bottom of the stairs, Eddie flipped on a dim light and shook his head as if to clear it before beginning the work of reconstructing the cunning face of a female opossum. In the clutter of their farmhouse, only Eddie's work surface was always clear. At the rear of the table sat a small wooden box containing glass cruets with water and shellac, salt and beeswax, a crock of nippers, scrapers, knives, scissors, forceps and files.

He removed the specimen from the refrigerator and lit a candle. The light embraced the animal's waiting bones, the defining shadows rendering the creature more beautiful and vulnerable than it had been in life. Eddie peeled back the animal's pelt and lifted the small pads of flesh away, cutting and scraping with such intensity and precision that he flinched with each tearing sound. With excelsior and clay, cotton, wax and paper mache, slowly and patiently he made the animal whole again, allowing memory and imagination to guide him in devising the expression and attitude for its final incarnation.

Eddie's bent face was shadowed as he worked. His hands moved deftly, touching the scooped out shell of bone and plying it again with substance and form. Each movement of his hands brought the visage closer to life. The quiet chill of the dark room and the salvific gestures called Eddie back into his old habitual listening. Sibilant, the Latin words, the whispering vowels floated out of him into the air, causing him to tremble with a sense that things, however bad, can be righted.

As his fingers coaxed the tiny body on the table closer to a state of wholeness, he shuddered briefly and sighed as the damp, cool air carrying the merest hint of musk and rot and incense passed over him, alerting him to the opening door. The boy who'd crept down the stairs stood silently watching the ritual.

When Eddie tilted the small animal upright, the body assumed the integrity of motion suspended. If he was aware of the boy watching, his attention never flickered from his task. His lips continually moving, Eddie fingered through a small basket at the back of his worktable, slowly hefting, examining, discarding, and balancing again and again. Satisfied at last, he held two identical glittering brown convex discs. Leaning close, he shook them back and forth like dice in the palm of his hand where they gathered and refracted light.

The candle hissed out. The room devoured its ragged sulfuric scent. Both Eddie and the boy held their breath as Eddie lifted the small puckered vacant lids and thrust the brilliant eyes into the waiting sockets.

Eddie was scrubbing his hands with the intensity of a surgeon at the kitchen sink when the question came. "What were you doing down there?" the boy asked, his adolescent voice wavered between high and low. Eddie did not betray any surprise when the boy spoke. Slowly, he dried each finger and then began taking vegetables from the refrigerator as he spoke. "It's called taxidermy. Been at it on and off for years. You take an animal or bird, and—"

"Stuff it?"

"Roughly, yes. But not exactly. There's a science of making it look real and alive. As if caught in the middle of ordinary life."

"Do you kill them?"

"Never," Eddie said softly but emphatically. "Mostly, I find them in the woods or on the road. Sometimes people bring them to me. But I'd never harm something deliberately."

"Why?"

"Because they know I'm interested."

"I mean why do you do it?"

"Occasionally, because I'm asked. Someone needs to have the physical representation of an animal they love or fear."

The boy thought about it. "Like they kill something and want to keep it?"

"Some. But I don't do trophies. Seems wrong. I like to preserve things that were beautiful. People don't want to let go of things they love. Take Roy Rogers, for instance."

Billy looked mystified.

"Roy Rogers?"

Billy shook his head.

"An old cowboy. From the movies."

"Yeah, I guess I heard of him."

"He had this horse, Trigger. His constant companion. The story goes that old Roy was so broken up when Trigger died that he had him stuffed. He's in the cowboy museum out west. An enormous horse, a star in all those movies." Eddie paused and placed a cutting board and knife on the table in front of him. Then he began to dice vegetables. "You like soup, don't you?"

The boy nodded.

"Back to our discussion. Why do I do it? That, my friend, is what you'd call an existential question. I'll answer it with another question: Why does anyone do anything?"

"Because they want to?"

"Very good. And that's called begging the question. We do things because we want to. But the choices we make reveal important information about us. In other words, we have to wonder why one thing appeals to us and another doesn't."

The boy looked intent but confused.

"Take you, for instance. It's clear that you can speak, but until now have preferred not to. You are curious. The only way to satisfy your curiosity is to ask questions. To do that, you must speak. Right? You must weigh two wants or needs and decide which is more important. We see by your speaking which won. But what causes the curiosity you want to satisfy?"

A shrug.

Eddie continued, "If I'm curious about you—and I am—I have to ask myself why you chose silence to begin with. Everything, and I do mean everything, we do or don't do means something."

The boy nodded to indicate he was following Eddie.

"Could mean that you were afraid to talk."

The boy's expression revealed nothing.

"So I'm assuming it has something to do with trust. You watched us, Eleanor and me, and figured you could trust us. By the way, your instinct is good--you're right about that." Eddie stopped working and looked at the boy. "You already know a great deal about me, including my name and what I do on Tuesday afternoons while El is out and about."

"My name is Billy Fallon." He held Eddie's gaze.

Eddie dried his hand on the tea towel he wore around his middle and offered it. "And, Billy Fallon, what brings you to Fenston?"

By the time Billy had haltingly explained his abusive stepfather and timid mother and his quest for his sister Tina who had left home a year earlier, the room filled with the aroma of vegetable soup. While Billy spoke, Eddie's face reflected complete interest and empathy. "I'm trying to find Tina. My mom got a postcard from her. From Fenston. She didn't know I saw it, but I did. So I came looking for her."

"She's here, in Fenston?"

"She sent the card last month."

"Shouldn't be hard to find. The town's not very big."

"When I planned it, I figured it'd be easy to find her."

"Like magic," Eddie added.

Billy nodded. "But when I got here, I didn't have a clue. Didn't know what to do next. Then I saw that old trailer."

"You thought it was abandoned."

"I figured no one would care."

"Right."

"Even though I didn't find Tina, it wasn't too bad. I was away from him. I had enough money for a while." Eddie heard the swagger behind the words. "Then that cop came and…" The words poured out of Billy's mouth and Eddie could read the relief in the boy's face that he had at last found someone who would listen and maybe even help.

Silently, Eddie listened as he cut and buttered slabs of bread and ladled the steaming soup into two bowls.

Chapter 6

Dressed for summer in an untamable canopy and skirt of vegetation, Fenston, like other small towns in the Pennsylvania mountains, seemed on the verge of returning to the wild. During the night, weeds along the berm of the road shot up full of leaping insects. The air was restless and people asked a neighbor to trim their yards if they expected to be away for more than a few days.

At the edge of gardens, asparagus fern rallied and trumpet vine and periwinkle climbed any surface offering the slightest purchase. The kind of summer when things multiply, a delicate war between wild growth and judicious containment, deer leapt into headlights and were frozen in tableau by porch light. The bullfrogs in the swamp at the end of the lake harangued the tree frogs and peepers who countered in their own register.

Coyotes boldly strode out of the woods and congregated under the streetlights at the side of the road. When the fire whistle blew, they sat back on their tails, raised their pointy heads and retorted. People came out onto their porches to locate the unusual sound and went back in scratching under their chins. The August air thickened with pollen. Children skimmed it from their wading pools and wrote their names on the surfaces of windows and cars. Even those indoors with the television on loud knew it was an exceptional summer.

The doldrums were upon them, vexing and soporific. Eleanor in her worry and confusion attempted to distract herself with the care of Billy Fallon and a flurry of other activities. Thursday night, it was the summer auction. Athena settled herself on the scabby leather seat of the pink Cadillac Coupe de Ville Eleanor had bought almost new secondhand fifteen years earlier from the New York champion Mary Kay cosmetic saleswoman who preferred her green Volvo wagon. The dashboard had long since sun bleached to the color of tea roses and the dark pink carpeting had grayed and matted beyond recognition, but the Mary Kay decal on the side door was bright as the first day Eleanor picked up the car in Binghamton and drove it regally through the awed lanes of Fenston.

Athena asked, "What's up over at your place?"

"Eddie's getting ready for canning season. Jars everywhere."

Athena laughed. "Didn't he notice all the jars you didn't use last year?"

"That's not the point with him. He enjoys doing it. He said this year he'll donate what he cans to that shelter Gloria started in Scranton."

"Harmony House."

"She can use the help."

"Do you think they'll take home canned stuff?"

"From Eddie. Sure. She'd never turn anything down from him."

"Married to their staunchest volunteer. I wouldn't think so."

Eleanor sighed. "I wish we could do more than help out from time to time and donate food."

"I meant what's up with the kid?"

"He's talking, at least. And not the condensed version. He and Eddie have been at it for hours. Frankly, I was glad to get out of the house."

"I got the picture. Meanwhile, Eddie's teaching him how to can?"

"How did you guess?"

Something in Eleanor's voice must have betrayed her real feelings beneath her flippant tone, for as they enjoyed a laugh at Eddie's expense, Athena glanced quickly in her direction. "You okay?"

Eleanor needed to talk but couldn't bring herself to do it. How she envied Billy Fallon the catharsis of telling his story to a willing listener. She simply could not find her way into the place where she could revisit her own painful past. "I'm fine," she said. She blinked at the road in front of her. "We'd better hurry."

The auction at the Crystalle Hose Company was the highlight of late summer. Eleanor and Athena arrived in time to get a number in the double digits, put their cushions on good seats in the third row, and look over the offerings. Eleanor pawed through a cardboard box of old fabric remnants, tablecloths, curtains and sheets, inspecting a bit of lace. "Nothing much here," she said to Athena, who was upending a crock looking for a date or signature.

"Thought this might be a McCoy. No such luck," Athena said with uncharacteristic listlessness. The auction, for the first time in memory, failed to hold their attention. Athena sat back, fanning herself with her cardboard number. "There's not one thing up there I'd care to tote home. Will's right. We have way too much stuff already."

"Never bothered us before."

"I know it. But after all these years, why bother?"

Still, they waited through the first half of the auction. Eleanor went to the snack bar and came back carrying a food tray made of the bottom of a cardboard box. She handed Athena a hot dog and coffee. When the second auctioneer, the young guy with the straw hat and the faster pace, stepped up and held aloft a Hummel figurine with a chipped hand, Eleanor leaned over and said, "I'm ready if you are."

Silent, studying the road in front of them, they realized, almost simultaneously, that they were in Wiggins. "Certainly has changed since Hattie was the bookkeeper for Wiggins Dairy," Athena said with a loud laugh. The air in the car seemed to lighten; as if they had left whatever else they were tired of behind at the auction. "Feel like stopping for ice cream?"

"Not after stuffing myself back there."

As they rounded the curve, a neon roadside marquee blinked:

CLASSY ACTS: A GENTLEMEN'S CLUB
TONITE: WHAT MAKES MOANA LISA SMILE?
KANDY KOTTON AND THE KUPCAKES

"Shall we see what all the fuss is about?" Abruptly, Eleanor pulled into the parking lot.

"What are you doing?" Athena gasped.

"We're here. And we like music." Eleanor gave Athena a mischievous look.

More like her old self, Athena thought.

"What's the harm in a little diversion?"

"The things you get me into. Can't say I'm not curious," Athena confessed.

Eleanor glanced at the crowded parking lot. "Quite a turnout."

They parked between a gold Lincoln Continental with *The Italian Stallion* stenciled in large spidery lettering on the faux spare tire cover and a deluxe Ford van with black windows and an EAT MY DUST bumper sticker. "I think that's somebody we know." Athena nodded to a fancy late dark sedan nestled demurely between the two.

"Looks familiar, but I can't say who."

Even before they opened the car doors, Eleanor and Athena could feel the bass thrumming in the air. Athena shook her frizzy hair free of the rubber band that held it back in a ponytail and tried to tame it behind her ears. She swiped a strawberry Chapstick across her mouth. Eleanor flipped down the visor, looked in the mirror, straightened her collar, fluffed her long, graying curls and lamely vamped a pout. "Are they ready for us?"

"We'll see about that."

"What's the joke Tom Miller tells about turning in a forty for two twenties. Guess we'd we worth two and a half."

"Are we crazy?" Athena laughed. The women breathed air now infected with possibility and adventure.

Eleanor zipped the jacket of her shiny purple running suit and looked across at Athena's white cotton shirt and denim slacks. "Not exactly dressed for it, are we? But we're this far."

"Does gentlemen's club mean no women allowed?"

"We'll find out."

A fiftyish fellow with an immense bib of gold chains and a molar-sized diamond earring stood inside the entrance. He stretched an arm thickly forested with wiry gray curls across the doorway in front of the women. "This ain't ladies night. Gotta pay the cover like everybody else," he said, pointing to a sign: *10$ per person. No acceptions.*

Eleanor fished a twenty out of her pocket. He took the money with an amused glance. "Enjoy yourselves, ladies. Four-girl review's over. Star feature starts in ten minutes." He handed them each a large light coin imprinted with the likeness of a naked woman and the words *Moana Lisa.*

"Ten dollars," Athena mused, looking around the crowded bar. "Must be a good—" she broke off as Eleanor tugged at her arm and nodded toward the back bar where a young woman, the only other female in the place, dressed in glittery high heels, a pink bandanna tied around her neck, hot pink dots where her nipples should be and a sparkly pink triangle of fabric at her crotch, squatted talking to some men at the bar. All they could see of the men was the underside of their chins.

"Seats here." Behind the bar, a young man dressed in a ruffled shirt and bow tie pointed at two empty stools at the square bar. The music was deafening, but they made out the last part of his next question; "—getcha?"

"Beers," Eleanor mouthed.

The bartender waved away the bills Eleanor pulled from her pocket. "Tokens?"

"Sure." Athena said, sliding the almost weightless coin across the bar.

Ruffles took one. "Two beers or one mixed—" before the next wave of music crashed over their heads.

"Let's see if we can spot The Stallion." Athena practically had to howl to make herself heard.

Eleanor's eyes veered left to a young man in tight jeans; a turquoise silk shirt and a silver belt buckle large as a personal pizza.

"Maybe. Or—" Just the slightest crook of Athena's index finger as she lifted her beer directed Eleanor to the end of the bar where a middle-aged man sporting a white straw hat and dark glasses pouted around a cigar the size of a chair leg.

The music slid from pounding pelvic disco to an equally loud, but slowly winding version of something they almost recognized. Suddenly applause flittered around the bar and the woman, sans bandanna, appeared to their left from behind a red silk curtain. She moved slowly, walking along the inside ledge of the bar, her feet flawlessly avoiding spilling drinks, stopping here and there for a little engagement with the music. Her hips slipped around the notes, pulling them toward her, rhythmically teasing them back and forth with her knees and hands.

Her young high breasts glowed as the fractured light from a suspended disco ball reflecting the colored beams aimed at it from the corners of the room. But it was the smile. Lips closed in some personal silent secret. Just the slightest lift of something working the edges, she hinted at a deep knowledge of a world beyond. Eleanor wondered what smart and/or smarmy entrepreneur had seen the promise of that smile and bestowed the name.

At the end of the bar Moana spun around, took her breasts in her hands, cradled them, offering them as if they were small pets she wanted the audience to admire. Her body argued with the music, pushing it farther and farther away, then begging it to come back, tricking it with slow then sudden movements. Moana's demure close-mouthed smile flickered with a dimple in her cheek. She looked at Eleanor and let her in on a secret: she was somewhere far away and the distance made her tolerant of the blur of faces, their slurpy chewing sounds diminished by the music of her own thoughts. After she teased the last slow note back into silence, she waved, shook her body, and with a coy little smirk disappeared. Two other girls hopped onto tiny circular stages hung over the bar where they paid lazy homage to the music.

Halfway through the second beer, Eleanor realized she had to pee. She motioned the bartender over. Before she could ask, he pointed to a short corridor off the opposite side of the room. Wondering whether Ruffles recognized a special need-to-go look or he understood the effect of two beers on the bladder, reluctantly she headed for the bathroom.

Eleanor shook her head as if to empty it of leftover notes. Gratefully, she realized that she hadn't once thought about her lost baby while she was there. One of the two stalls was free. Squatting in an effort not to make contact with the toilet seat, she glanced to the floor and saw glittery high heels and trim ankles in the next stall. Moana Lisa was peeing a tiny bright-sounding river. They finished at the same moment and bumped elbows as they came together at the two vanity sinks.

"Whoops. Sorry," Eleanor said.

"My fault."

"What was that song?"

"Beg pardon?" The old-fashioned phrase hung in the air.

"The music?"

As a shy smile uncovered painfully buckteeth, the woman echoed,

"The music?" Close up, Eleanor thought Moana looked tired, her face pale under a thick paste of rouge. The girl lifted her hand to her mouth as if to shield the offensive teeth from view. Her long auburn hair, a slightly lighter color than the brown fringe at her temples, was attached to a small headband of the same color.

"The song you just danced to."

"Oh, that. I don't know. Jocko, the owner, the guy at the door, he picks the tapes."

Suddenly enlightened, Eleanor asked, "The Stallion?"

Moana snorted when she laughed. "He wishes." Her long pink nails scratched along her wrist at a cluster of little blisters. They both looked at the rash on her arm.

"Yellow soap," Eleanor commented.

"What?"

"Best thing for poison ivy. Wash it good every hour or two with yellow soap. Let it air dry. Clear it up in a few days."

"Thank you."

"I keep trying to remember the name of that song."

"Sorry." Moana looked as if she actually were.

"I'll be humming it for days—until I figure out what it was."

"I hate that. When you get a song in your head and it won't give up. Happens to me sometimes with commercials. I'm walking along and catch myself singing about cat food or Roto-Rooter. The stupidest stuff, really."

"Me too," Eleanor commiserated.

Moana leaned nearer the mirror to examine the shiny pink discs attached to her breasts. Closing her lips over her protruding teeth, she smiled at herself in the mirror, then grimaced. She stood on one leg, kicked off a shoe and put her foot up on the vanity to remove a corn plaster from the side of her pinkie toe. "God, these shoes are murder."

Noticing that a bit of pink sparkling dust from Moana's costume had rubbed off on her sleeve, Eleanor remembered where she was, snapped a paper towel from the dispenser, dried her hands and said, "See you."

As she returned to the bar, Eleanor spotted Eldon Questor, the local undertaker, hunched at the opposite side, right where Moana had been squatting when they came in. His toupee was askew and his navy jacket appeared to have a sprinkling of that same fairy dust across the shoulders.

Athena leaned over and shouted in her ear, "You were gone long enough. I've had it." Her two almost full beers sat before her. "What about you?"

Eleanor nodded. "Isn't that the science guy from the college? The one who gives tree lectures?"

"Del Ray. Yeah. And look—" Athena's whisper was so loud Ruffles looked down the bar at them. "Isn't that Bob Morgan? Who'd ever suspect he'd show up in a place like this?"

"Mr. Clean Cut. Married to Mrs. Morality."

"You never know about people, do you? Hattie would have gotten a kick out of this."

"For once, when she comes back and asks what's new, we'll have a good story." Athena put a five-dollar bill on the bar.

"I talked to Moana in the bathroom."

Athena looked up sharply in surprised. "And?"

"She seemed nice. Not like you'd think. Real young."

"I'll never be able to listen to "Smoke Gets In Your Eyes" again without the image of her sashaying her naked butt along that bar."

"That's it."

"That's what?"

"The song. Thank you."

Slightly askew, the Cadillac's headlights inched along 101 toward Fenston, Eleanor pitched slightly forward over the pink velour covered steering wheel. After the adventure of Classy Acts, the women were tired and silent as they headed for home. It was 11 p.m., later than they usually stayed out, even if the auction was exciting.

"Do you think we should tell Will and Eddie where we were?" Athena mused.

"Don't see why. They'll only kid us about it."

"You're right."

"Let's keep our sociological outings to ourselves."

"You don't suppose Questor or Del Ray or Bob will spread it around, do you?"

"Seems to me they wouldn't be eager for folks to know where they spent this evening either."

Chapter 7

The morning trembled and blazed in the streets of Warsaw. Smog and clatter. Kasia Darling thought of her city as the ringing of bicycle bells, the sweet, floury interior of Muha's Bakery, the neighbors' backyard garden. As they drove, she looked out on the passing streets. *Please let me remember. I don't want to lose these years in the same careless way I misplaced the first part of my life.* But thoughts of what she was about to do and the touch of her uncle's hand lightly on her shoulder distracted her. Suddenly they were at the airport and she had missed her last July morning in the city she had come to as a child. She felt a great heave of her breath as she swallowed tears. *This was your own idea,* she admonished herself, reading her uncle Piotr's look.

She had approximated the garb of American college students: jeans, black T-shirt, bush jacket and black boots, an enormous duffle bag at her feet. Kasia hefted the ultimate identifier of those in the know, the army surplus backpack, ordered by mail and lovingly embellished with embroidery and patches. Outfitted according to the magazines she'd pored over for months, Kasia struggled not to cry. Leaving Poland turned out to be more than simply finding an escape route her uncle couldn't object to. Now that she had achieved her goal, a nine month separation seemed impossible. He had been everything to her in the years since her mother's death and her father's disappearance. Now by her own choice, she was leaving.

Puffing with effort, Piotr bent to reposition her bag as they moved in line. "When I get home, I expect to find the television missing, that and my old shoes and the canned goods from the cupboard. Maybe all the books in the house. What else could account for this?" He joked as he had nightly for the past month when he came into her room to kiss her forehead, to say *kolorowych snow,* bright dreams, and survey the growing pile of her belongings readied to go to America with her. He'd moan, "Will there be a few slices of bread and my old coat left when you finish packing? Now his teasing sounded forced and somehow too loud, though no one in the Okecie Airport seemed to be paying any attention to them.

He was testing her, gauging her nervousness, her sadness. She frowned and struggled for a retort that would set him at ease. "You have too many shoes already. Besides, I took only half of them—the left, if you insist on details."

Piotr pretended to study the flight schedule and consult his watch. "Lots of time," he remarked. "Shall I take off my left shoe now and hand it over?"

"You don't have to wait with me," she said, reading fatigue and sadness in his voice. "This queue could take an hour."

"What else have I to do except go home and polish my shoe? Besides, now that I have you all packed and ready, I want to make sure you get on the plane."

Kasia knew what her leaving meant to him, even though he teased her about how blessedly quiet the house would be without her loud music. Over the years she had tried to get her uncle to take her back to the states. He could not be budged. Determined, she had found her own way. The day her acceptance to Hapwell College came signaled liberation. Steadfastly, they shuffled along the queue. As they neared the *passengers only* sign, she slid her backpack to the floor. He nudged it in closer with the side of his foot. "You must be alert at all times."

"Certainly," she said, as she bent to readjust the pack. "Don't worry."

"It is easy to become confused. Distracted. People will watch and take advantage.

Normally, she would have bristled at the advice; instead, she smiled. "I'll be careful. I promise."

They were next. His arms surrounded her and pulled her toward him in a bear hug. Nuzzling into his chest, she inhaled the comforting scent of his green cardigan, the same sweater she'd deplored as old-fashioned just weeks earlier. *"Malutka,"* he whispered, using the pet name of her childhood. *"Malutka.* I'm proud of you. You are smart and strong. Make good choices."

She thought he was going to say something more, but his voice faltered. He held her at arms length and tried to smile, "Remember. No tattoos. Understood?" Thumbing through one of her magazines, he had been shocked at a photo of young women decorated with tattoos.

"Okay. Now you promise to let Sophie clean the house once in a while. I don't want to have to dig my way through with a snow plow when I get back."

"I promise."

As she passed through the boarding gate, Kasia Darling turned and looked back at the substantial, slightly balding man whose shoulders had been her only refuge for the last ten years. He gazed back at her with an expression of sorrow and hope so painful that she gave a quick wave, pasted a bright smile on her face, and turned to hide the tears filling her eyes.

Kasia slid past two people arguing about whether they should put their jackets in the overhead. An older woman and a man in his thirties, they had the same hairline and eyes. The woman smiled when Kasia took the seat next to her and confided in Polish that her son was taking her to his home in the states for a visit. The old pain shot through her. She actually felt it in her heart. Whenever she saw a mother and child, even such an old and cranky duo, her body remembered her loss. She revisited that little girl who lived inside her, the one whose parents suddenly were no more. She was small and sad. Kasia sometimes pretended that she was her own older sister, telling her smaller self that they would learn how to be safe and happy. To feel loved.

The son explained to Kasia that he had lived in New Jersey for ten years. The mother's quick, fluent Polish punctuated the young man's rusty pronunciation. "I noticed your bags and your father. Heading to college?"

She nodded, not wanting to clarify her relationship to Piotr. "That was me. I left at your age. Rutgers."

"And you stayed?"

"I didn't intend to. I just had the opportunity, and—" He looked at his mother, who had busied herself arranging her pillow and adjusting her seat belt.

"I didn't know at the time what a big step it was. Paul Smaljewski." He extended his hand.

"Kasia Darling. I'm going to Pennsylvania. Hapwell College." She formed the English words carefully, trying to gauge his assessment of her fluency. Even though her teachers in Warsaw marveled at her perfect pronunciation, she wondered whether she still sounded like a native speaker. Whenever she had the chance to talk with an American, she felt herself shift into those unfamiliar vowels, her tongue reaching around in her thoughts as if searching for something she hadn't known she'd lost. Speaking American English was one way of connecting to her life, the life she had before going to Poland with Piotr. The image of him standing behind the gate came to her and brought with it a welling up of tenderness and sorrow.

"Darling?" he asked.

"American father. I was born in the states."

"So you're going home, then." He looked appraisingly at her. "No wonder your English is perfect.

kasia fought the dream. Spindles of light, as if she were walking up a flight of stairs, thrown across her path. In the light, shifting back and forth, sometimes too quickly for her to register them, were the images she had of her father and mother. They were sitting at the table in the kitchen, or standing in the yard. Snow and then flowers behind them. They threw back their heads in laughter. Her father removed the training wheels from her pink bike. They walked in from the backyard, carrying a basket full of greens. The scent of lavender. Then her mother was sobbing, lying on the bed. Medicine bottles in the cupboard, all the labels facing out. Hattie was there. Pale curtains fluffed out in the air at the top of the stairway. The tantalizing scent of these persistent dreams. Flowers drove the emotion or the dream. She felt herself at the edge of tears. Then the smell before rain. Ribbons of light again. The overheard lights in the cabin switched on just as she struggled out of the familiar chaos of those dreams that been with her as long as she could remember.

Forcing herself awake, Kasia realized her bladder was full, but the line for the restrooms snaked down the aisle. Although she was still drowsy, she willed her mind to stay in the present. She had thought she was too excited to rest, but no matter how excited or rested she was, any length of time spent in motion lulled her to sleep. Before he began teaching her to drive, Piotr would say half-jokingly that he feared she'd fall asleep at the wheel. She glanced around; the other passengers were in the pre-landing mode—repositioning their belongings, sweeping their teeth with their tongues, and patting their hairdos back into shape after the long flight. She fingered the grid marks the nubbly surface of the bag she had used as pillow had imprinted on her cheek. *Great, now I'm going to look like a waffle when I meet the others.* She took a warm, moist towel from the steward and rubbed away the indentations and other traces of sleep. The family behind her began discussing how long it would take them to reach their home in Metuchen.

Once on the ground the passengers stood, some of them with their heads bent at an uncomfortable angle under the luggage compartments She sat back and pulled her new Walkman from her bag but didn't start the tape. She watched those at the front of the plane get off. A man who had pushed his way from a seat in the rear of the plane was stalled in the aisle next to them. A wary, almost wolfish expression about his eyes made her register the silky running suit, the expensive American sneakers, a gold link bracelet.

The same man waited next to Kasia at the luggage carousel. After a warning bleat and several buzzers, a maw opened and bags disgorged onto the chute. When her large duffle shot down the incline, she bent to get it, sliding her backpack to the floor at her feet. She sensed the man shift. At first she thought he was trying to help her balance the bag on the lip of the conveyor. His hand moved lightly against her. In one motion, he lifted her backpack to his shoulder and shifted it easily to the other side of his body. It happened so quickly Kasia wasn't sure what she'd seen. She scanned the floor. Her backpack was gone.

Prickles of sweat beaded her neck. In the next instant, she dropped the duffle back into the tray and said, "Stop." And then more loudly, "Help! He has my bag."

The man bolted. She spun in pursuit, pushing off with her left foot where she had placed it for leverage to get her bag and sprinted after him.

As she started to run, nudging her way through the crowd, she heard a high-pitched voice yell, "Police. Stop." She tailed the thief down a wide corridor. For a moment she lost sight of him. At a corner she spotted him again, hugging her motley backpack incongruously against his side. He walked as fast as he could without actually running. Determined to catch him and get her property back, she broke into a run. People stared after her in mild interest. "He's got my bag," she said, pointing ahead.

One woman reached out as if to ask a question.

"He stole my bag," Kasia said as she passed.

"I'll call—" The woman's face and words were lost.

Ahead Kasia saw the customs stations, manned and waiting for the next group of travelers to present their baggage. Would her English fail her? The explanation raced through her head.

Suddenly, the silk suit vanished. He couldn't have gotten through the customs line already. How could she have lost him? Out of the corner of her eye, she saw the door to the men's room closing. Rushing up to one of the customs booths, she slowed her breath enough to gasp, "A man stole my backpack. I think he's in the men's room."

The customs officer pressed a button. Immediately, two policemen appeared at her side. She pointed. They moved toward the door.

What if her bag was gone—her passport, money, the information about who was picking her up and where they were to meet? Then she thought of the journal. That would be lost too. Without it, she would never be able to search out the people and places she had waited so long to find. Her past, her parents, the life she'd traveled so far to claim would be wrenched from her forever. The irony stung.

She realized she was choking back sobs. A customs matron handed her a tissue. "Don't worry, honey. They'll get him."

It seemed like a long time before the men's room door opened and one of the policemen came out, his arm clasped to the thief's shoulder. "You're mistaked," he stammered angrily, alternating between Polish and broken English, "You're mistaked. I did not steal. I made mistaked. I thought it was my—"

The officer led him away.

The second officer emerged carrying Kasia's backpack. The zipper was open. Her passport in his other hand, he examined the photo and looked at Kasia. "He had this in his pocket." He handed Kasia her things and said, "Better check to make everything's there, Miss."

Kasia's fingers shook as she groped through the bag. "Yes. Everything's here," she said, opening her wallet and feeling around for the journal and her travel information papers. "Thank you. I didn't know what to do. I couldn't follow him into the men's room." She felt herself blushing.

The gentle-eyed policeman hardly older than Kasia laughed, "You didn't have to. You had him pretty well cornered. All we had to do was pick him up."

Kasia looked back down the long hallway to the luggage carousel, now nearly deserted. She blurted, "I was trying to get my bag. I guess I wasn't paying attention to my backpack. I put it on the floor. Foolish."

"Can't blame yourself. Guys like that have figured out when people will be vulnerable. They prey on people who are preoccupied." Piotr's exact words.

"He was on the same plane. I saw him before."

"He probably saw you too. Figured you for young, first time away from home."

"I must have seemed stupid."

He smiled at Kasia. "Seems to me, he picked on the wrong person. You were smart to start yelling. That's what we teach in our self-defense classes." Kasia blushed when she realized he was flirting with her. "Enjoy your stay," he said. Her mood plummeted when she realized he thought she was a foreigner.

Kasia hoped she looked confident, but walking back to the luggage claim her legs seemed rubbery and weak. She felt off balance, almost as if she were staggering. Her bladder was so full she imagined the sensation of relief—just peeing right where she was. Why not? Nobody knew her here. Even if they did, who would blame her? She'd been robbed. She felt as if every eye in the airport was on her. She had a mental image of herself standing in the middle of a growing puddle of pee, feeling the gush. The relief. She started to laugh. Then with her knees clamped tightly together she ran.

Finally, a ladies room. An empty stall. Sitting on the toilet, she put her head in her hands and tried to slow her breathing. Prickles of adrenaline coursed along her neck. She forced herself to breathe deeply. Around her she heard conversations and flushing and the taps and door opening and closing. She sat, unable to force herself to resume her journey. She shuffled through her backpack again, reorganizing and reexamining everything inside. According to the packet of information she'd received from Hapwell, she was to gather with the other international students at the information desk in terminal C, wherever that was.

Fifteen minutes in the states and she'd already gotten herself into trouble. Had she called misfortune down on herself? Piotr had tried to warn her, but no, she hadn't listened. In the future, she would have to be aware that she was no longer in the small, sheltering world of her Warsaw neighborhood, where people watched out for each other. This was America. She must learn to take care of herself.

On the other hand, maybe the young policeman was right. She might have looked like an easy target, but she stood up for herself. She was the one who actually caught the thief. Heartened by that thought, she went to the sink and washed her hands and face. Though refreshed, she still had the odd sensation of being off balance. Her right foot— something was wrong. She tested it with her weight. Yes. Definitely strange. Had she broken a bone? Nothing hurt. But she could not walk without effort. She hobbled over to the mirror area where the light was better. She examined her foot. She bent to slip off her shoe when she noticed that the heel was missing. Wonderful! She'd make a great first impression on the other students. She pictured herself hobbling up to a crowd of gawking strangers. Her new shoes, an important part of her college student costume, were ruined.

Hers was the lone bag pirouetting on the metal conveyor. Her heart pounded with relief. At least she hadn't lost her luggage. She slipped the straps of her backpack over either arm and hiked the duffle to her shoulder. *You can do this.* Her plan had worked. No matter what else, here she was. She had made it to America.

Kasia Darling rose to her full height of five feet two inches, looked around and smiled. She staggered slightly under the weight of so much hope as she hobbled off in pursuit of terminal C.

Chapter 8

Mary Turkelson, Hapwell College's International Student Coordinator, was a bulldog of a woman dressed in baby doll clothes, a short flouncy blue skirt appliquéd with apples, and a white peasant blouse, ruffled at the shoulders. Twenty or so silver bangle bracelets jangled up her chubby forearm. A black nylon fanny pack freed her hands for the COLLEGE INTERNATIONAL STUDENTS WELCOME sign she held aloft. Blonde curls springing with every step, she bounded toward the small group of tired, nervous and hungry international students. Up close, Kasia smelled lilacs and registered the contradiction between Mary's no-nonsense tone and the laugh lines around her eyes and mouth. Instead of a barrage of questions, she greeted them with her assessment of their condition. "Tired isn't in my vocabulary. And nervous, nothing but time'll help that. But hungry, now you're talking. Let's get these bags in the car and head for the Greco-Roman Diner. Best chow for a hundred miles."

"Chow?" The new word slid into their receptive mental files. Like imprinted ducklings, the gaggle of young people trailed her out of the airport and onto the shuttle. No one seemed to notice Kasia's altered gait. No one spoke.

Even though she had lived in America for her first eight years, Kasia found everything suddenly confusing. Why had she wanted to come? Why couldn't she have stayed in Warsaw where everything was familiar and easy? She could only imagine what the others were feeling. The two Japanese guys bowed, almost knocking into each other. Motioning vaguely, they hopped into the van and claimed the back seat. Before she could stow her bag in the back and hoist herself up, the other two girls, France and Germany, had claimed the second seat next to a large blonde guy. Mary patted the front passenger spot and leaned toward Kasia. "Best view in the house," she said. "Controls the radio and the air. Now that's real power."

At the large table in the back room of the ornate diner just off Route 80, swirls of artificial ivy dangling from pots along the ceiling and classical nude statuary swathed discretely in white fabric reflected in the gold and black flecked mirrors against the back wall. Three of the students slid into the corner banquette bench and the others clustered around the outside of the table. A wagon wheel light fixture cast its spoked glare down on them.

Without consulting anyone, Mary ordered the typical cuisine preferred by American college students. It took a raft of Texas wieners, Buffalo wings, a vat of french fries and something called a blooming onion, three rounds of Cokes and numerous slices of pie to loosen the tongues of the students headed for Hapwell College. No one wanted to be the first to speak, as they all imagined the others capable of emitting flawless American English.

Irrepressibly interested, especially in their reactions to blooming onions, Mary kept the talk and the food coming. Finally Gunnar, the Swede, his gray blue eyes magnified by round silver glasses, peered at Mary and queried nervously, "Buffalo. Yes. I've seen the picture. Big furry heads. Like cows. Right? But where are growing the wings?" The table erupted in laughter, gratitude, and admiration. He had broken the spell by admitting he didn't already know everything American.

Yvette chimed in with a funny account of the terrible traffic jam on the way to Orly. She had almost missed the plane. "Imagine. I expect to arrive two hours before. Then I am running for the plane instead," she said, moving her tiny, perfectly manicured hand to augment her description of the line of cars and wagging her curly head to demonstrate her increasing frustration. "And the blankets, they were used. All the way on the plane, I was freezing." Kasia scanned Yvette's skimpy tank top and the tiny skirt that barely covered her petite rear.

Each student had a tale of travel woe. Gudrun, the girl from Frankfurt, pointed to a red stain along the sleeve of her white blouse: "This man sitting next to me, drinking many wine. He fells asleep and the wine fell on me." Yo and Wenji, the Japanese guys—who met for the first time on the plane—had waited at the wrong carousel for their luggage for more than an hour. Yo mimed the antics of the children seated in front of him. His face, assuming the petulance of a maniacal three-year-old, reduced them all to laughter.

When it was her turn, Kasia recounted her stolen bag adventure. Realizing her English was at least as good as anyone else's, she warmed to her tale, embellishing the story with little details like a description of the felon's clothing and how silly he looked with her backpack on his shoulder. Gudrun had seen Kasia running in the airport. "You were brave," she said. The others nodded, imagining themselves in her predicament. Diners came and went at the other tables.

In their travel misadventure sweepstakes she was the first prize winner. Her heelless boot, which they insisted on inspecting, a badge of courage. Suddenly she did feel brave. Piotr would have been proud. Recalling the young cop's approving glance, she felt pretty too. More tales—the packing predicament, the leave-taking of home—and the gaiety continued until tears rolled down the chubby cheeks of Mary Turkelson, who had without their even realizing it rendered them all special and interesting and ready for the challenge of college life. Between the lines of all the others' stories Kasia felt a bond forming with her group of international students and understood that they were all as nervous and eager to fit in as she. They would help each other.

By the time they left the diner and headed west on Route 80, traffic was light and the conversation begun in the restaurant subsided. In the dark van they were quiet, but this time it was a comfortable silence. They had passed the first hurdle of their new life. They had arrived. And now they had friends. They would not, as each of them imagined on their worst days, be eating in a big cafeteria alone at an enormous table, or walking alone to and from classes and their dorm rooms. The lights from oncoming cars illuminated their fatigued faces with little beams of comforting light.

Kasia looked out the side window into the woods along the highway, wondering how long it would take her to find Hattie—where to go first in her search. She felt around in her backpack for the journal.

Now ten years old, the battered notebook contained the account of the year her life changed. Kasia had been given the journal by the social worker assigned to her at the Webster School in Hartford, Connecticut, to help her record her feelings and thoughts during the traumatic time, the year her father disappeared and her mother died. There was nothing anyone could do to mitigate those facts. Mrs. Neville had helped her understand that her fears were understandable, and most of all that what had happened was not her fault.

Kasia had written faithfully each day. On Wednesday afternoons when she visited the guidance office and sat in the flower-scented, soft green room amid the plants and posters picturing happy children, she and Mrs. Neville talked. There she tried to explain what she was feeling, using the journal as a guide. Dated in the upper right-hand corner, each page contained a few sentences of tight curling script that slanted upward. There were misspellings and cross outs, neither of which bothered Mrs. Neville. Kasia was to write whatever came into her head and it didn't matter if it was neat or spelled correctly. Some of the pages had been turned in on themselves, as Mrs. Neville had instructed her to do if there was something she didn't want to share.

The book had grown smaller as Kasia's hands grew larger. What seemed like volumes when she wrote it was merely a few paragraphs rendering the events of her life in the vague language of an eight-year-old. By the time her Uncle Piotr had arrived from Poland, she had realized that her father was not just away on one of his long business trips. Mrs. Neville helped Kasia talk about her father's absence and her mother's illness. Together they drew pictures of Kasia's family and house as they talked. Except for the journal, the only physical touchstone, the last months in Hartford were a blur in her memory.

When Piotr had emptied and sold the house on Gordon Street, he got rid of everything that spoke to him of his sister's disastrous life. He threw out all the old photos and anything else that might have helped Kasia remember those years. When she realized that her uncle was bent on obliterating her past, Kasia crept into the living room, took the photo of her family from its frame on the hall table and pasted it inside the front cover of her journal. Afraid he would discard her journal as well, Kasia hid it. Countless times in the past ten years she had studied the photo in an attempt to remember her parents. She needed to know for sure that they had loved each other and her. Each time she was disappointed. But that did not stop her from reexamining the picture, hoping each time to find a clue.

She had read each entry in the journal so often she knew them by heart. Yet she returned to it again and again, searching for something she had previously overlooked, a line, a phrase, an inference that would help her understand what had happened to her family. Until she was eight, her life had been so happily ordinary that, like the streets of Warsaw she was already missing, she had not even thought to notice it.

For comfort, Kasia closed her eyes and tried to imagine the reunion with Hattie Beste, the woman who had been her friend in that sad time. Shortly after her father left, Hattie had moved into their house in Hartford as a boarder. Hattie taught her pick-up sticks and math, filling in with nurturing, support and love as her mother became sicker.

In one lucid ribbon of memory, Hattie and her mother were at the kitchen table. Hattie had said something Kasia couldn't recall. Her mother answered, "He sent me here. He didn't care what I wanted then. Why would he care what happens to me now—"

"Think of Kasia," Hattie said, her voice slow and warm. "She needs to know there's someone."

Hattie had risked her friendship with Kasia's ailing mother by insisting that they contact the brother she'd not spoken to in ten years. When Anya agreed, Hattie had found Piotr in Poland and made him come. She had been the miracle worker of Kasia's childhood. The only miracles her friend couldn't perform were the ones Kasia wanted most: her father's return and her mother's health.

Whenever Kasia thought over those days, so many questions came to her. She knew so little about her parents. Piotr refused to speak of them. That left Hattie. Could she perform one more miracle and restore Kasia to wholeness—if not a child with parents, at least a child with a history? Could Hattie provide a sense of who her parents were and how they'd loved each other and her? Could Hattie reassure her that her parents would never, ever have left her if the choice had been theirs?

Shortly after Piotr arrived and just as suddenly as she had appeared on Gordon Street, Hattie left. Kasia never saw her again. Kasia recalled their last evening together, analyzing every detail to solve the mystery of

Hattie's departure. There had been a letter from her daughter. But that was weeks earlier. Nothing urgent. They had settled into a routine to keep the household going. Anya had been in bed for weeks. That final night, Hattie and Piotr washed the dinner dishes while Kasia worked on math story problems at the kitchen table. As usual, they looked over her homework and talked, but she knew instinctively something was different. Piotr kept clearing his throat and Hattie had a determined, distracted look that focused just to the right of Kasia's face.

The scene played itself out like a silent film. Every detail of the kitchen of their old house on Gordon Street was clear—her name printed on the frosted window, the shelf of her mother's plates she and her uncle had later packed for the Goodwill, the cuckoo clock over the sink, the chrome ridges along the edge of the table, her math home-work half finished, her Brownie uniform pressed and hanging over the back of a chair. She could see Hattie and Uncle Piotr's lips moving and the kind melancholy look on their faces. But no words. She could only imagine that Hattie was explaining why she was about to leave.

Her father's disappearance and Hattie's leaving were the central mysteries of Kasia's life. He had gone without a word—no, worse than that, he had said he would be back soon. *A promise,* his face crinkled around a smile. Then he would stay with them forever. He left and then Hattie left and then her mother died. Long after she should have given up hope, she still imagined that her father would come for her. When Piotr said they would go to Poland to live, her first thought was that her father would not be able to find her. How foolish she had been even to hope. Eventually she had given up the dream of her father.

When Piotr's brickworks flourished after Glasnost and they had some money, she begged him to take her back to the states to find Hat-tie. A mixture of sadness and determination on his face, he said, "Hat-tie knows where we are if she wants to see us. Otherwise, we leave her alone. She lent herself to us at a very sad time. We are grateful for that. But we have no claim on her." Then his expression changed to the one Kasia understood to mean no more discussion.

Even if she got to the states, how would she find Hattie? Although her memories tried to convince her that if she returned to Gordon Street in Hartford, Hattie would be sitting on the porch waiting for her to come down the block, Kasia knew Hattie had left Hartford even before they did. And gone where? Hattie had told her many things about the town in the mountains. "Nothing like Hartford. A little smudge of a place surrounded by woods."

"Are there wild animals in the wood?"

Hattie laughed. "You mean like bears and deer and snakes?"

Kasia nodded.

"Yes. But they won't bother you. In fact, you almost never see them. They're very shy and run away as soon as they hear someone coming."

"What else?" Kasia asked, greedy for tales of another place.

"Much cooler, I can tell you that." Hattie wiped her face on a paper towel. "Wouldn't we just relish a swim in the pond today. Even on the hottest days, the water is cool and refreshing," she said wistfully. They had been at the kitchen table struggling with soggy oak tag and construction paper, their hands so sweaty that the color imprinted on their fingers. Hattie was helping Kasia make a map of her neighborhood for a Brownie project. The memory was tantalizingly clear.

But where in Pennsylvania?

One day when she was thirteen or so while Kasia was leafing through her journal the word Fenston appeared on the screen of her thoughts. Immediately, she knew it had come from some secret hidden place in her mind where everything she had forgotten was locked away. Fenston. Then Fenston, Pennsylvania. She put the words together and the sound blew across her thoughts with the cool clear promise of forests and water. She could hear them in Hattie's warmest voice, "Fenston, Pennsylvania."

In the next instant, a plan formed. She jumped up from the library table where she had been daydreaming and asked the librarian for a map of the United States. She puzzled out the lines on the small page and found Pennsylvania. But not Fenston. A more detailed map was located. Finally, she saw the blue dot that was Fenston, Pennsylvania. Just saying the words thrilled her.

She took a sheet of tracing paper and copied the map, the outline of the county where Fenston stood between Crystalle and Wiggins, right along the bold line of Route 81, the line that intersected with Route 84 moving toward Connecticut. She folded the paper and put it in the back of her journal. It waited there for three years, a clue, one she didn't yet understand. But little by little, more things Hattie had told her resurfaced. The year she was sixteen, suddenly she knew the map could help. The director of her gymnasium came into their class to discuss their education plans, the possibility of going to university in another country. She retrieved the paper. The next step, finding the closest college to Fenston with an international student program, was easy.

Now, just hours away from Fenston, Kasia leaned back into the seat, adjusted her seat belt, slipped on her earphones and smiled a little self-congratulatory smile—great planning. With Mary at the wheel, she was on her way.

Fleetingly, she visualized the town Hattie had rendered so clearly for her. Wescott's Store, Chaplin Lake, the dairy where they made their own ice cream. She visualized Hattie putting her hands to her face in pleasure and surprise when she opened the door to find Kasia. Wouldn't she be pleased to know that Kasia had remembered her all this time?

For a while, she thought about writing in advance to let Hattie know she was coming. But she relished the idea of a surprise. She knew Hattie would be amazed that she had come all this way to talk to her, knowing she could count on her for the truth.

Kasia realized that Hattie might have changed a little in the ten years. But in her thoughts, Hattie looked the same. Her auburn hair combed back from her face, she wore slacks and a green silk blouse—the one she had worn often to work. What a wonderful reunion lay ahead of them. Hattie did not speak. Instead, Kasia heard the strains of a song she associated with her childhood. In a high, clear voice Hattie was singing *Que Sera Sera*.

Chapter 9

Kasia unpacked her English/Polish dictionary, pens and tablets, her Walkman and tapes, a book called *College: A Survival Guide for Students*, the photo of her parents, one of Piotr and another of her group of friends taken after their last class. In the bottom of her suitcase amid her socks and pajamas she found a tiny bundle she didn't recall packing. Kasia unwound a length of old quilting and found the one thing she had from her mother's childhood, the doll that had been her constant companion during the early years in Poland. Her eyes brimmed with tears as she lifted her beloved Lulu from the bag. Kasia sighed and ran her cheek across the mottled, sparse-haired head. Pinned to Lulu's red skirt was a note in Piotr's old-fashioned writing: *I thought I'd be too lonely without you, so I came to college too.*

Even with her familiar things in place, the room felt empty. Kasia's hands shook. She had nothing to do for two days until the international student orientation classes started except to sit listening to creatures knocking around in the woods outside her window. A city girl, she imagined birds and wild animals and strange vines creeping toward her as she slept. Beneath all the outside noises, she thought she heard water running and someone walking around on the next floor.

She looked at the other bed. What kind of roommate would she get? She hoped someone who would be easy and accommodating. She'd try her best to fit in. She wanted to learn whatever necessary to assume her rightful place as an American. In the meantime, she'd go downstairs to see what Yvette was doing.

After a few minutes of tapping lightly on the door, Kasia realized that Yvette could not hear her over the music. She banged hard and the door opened. Dressed in a short white terry robe, her dark fringe of hair pulled back in a band, Yvette smiled and waved Kasia into the room.

Walking on her heels, her toes a few inches off the floor, Yvette slowly made her way back to the edge of her bed. She stretched her legs out in front of her and bent at the waist to reposition wads of cotton between her toes. With the small brush from bottle of brown nail polish on the nightstand she dabbed at her smeared nails. "Whitney Houston," Yvette nodded to the tape player on the dresser, moving her birdlike body to the music. "This is a good color. Don't you think?" She spoke with a decidedly British accent.

"Very nice."

"Help yourself."

Kasia shook her head.

Engrossed in the task, Yvette pursed her lips into a little bow and applied another coat. Kasia looked around the room, the twin of her own except for the clothes piles, the heaps of combs, brushes, hair ornaments and jewelry on the dresser, and the posters of Madonna and Prince over the bed. Yvette's room looked as if she'd lived in it for years. And she had found time to shower and wash her hair.

How had Yvette crammed all this stuff in her luggage?

"Use what you like," Yvette nodded to a case containing a dozen or so colors of nail polish.

Kasia hesitated. She was not sure whether she'd be steady enough to manage the tiny brush without making a mess. "Maybe some other time," she said, mentally comparing her own primitive Soviet-made cosmetics, their simple colors and clunky applicators, to Yvette's treasure trove of exotic French supplies. Had all the other students come prepared for glamour and high fashion? Kasia inventoried the things she had just put away in her room, clothing and accessories she thought lovely when she bought them. Suddenly, next to Yvette's belongings everything she brought might have come from the gulag. She resolved to take the S.A. van to the mall that weekend; the shopping list forming in her mind included new tapes, cosmetics and some real jeans.

"Want a doobie?" Yvette offered. Kasia tried unsuccessfully not to look confused. "You know—" Yvette pointed with a world-weary air to a small tray with six neatly rolled joints. "I'll be dry in a minute." She lifted her feet in the air and inspected the polish job.

"Thanks. But not really," Kasia replied. "Makes me sleepy. But I'd love a Coke. Want to walk over to the snack bar?"

"I have to wait for Gunnar. He's stopping by after he unpacks."

Kasia recalled the scene at the diner, Yvette and Gunnar, sitting next to each other. "Are you two—?"

"Silly." Yvette smirked.

"Not that I'd blame you," Kasia hastened to add.

"Cute, don't you think? He'd like to. But I prefer to play the field. It's tempting. He's so sexy and it would be easy. But I didn't come all this way to get involved with another foreign student. I want to find myself an American. What about you?" This was Yvette's third trip to the U.S. and she was determined to stay.

"I'm American already." Kasia added quickly. "Born here. That makes me a citizen."

"Lucky you."

The easy retort caused Kasia to wince. If Yvette, who bragged constantly about her indulgent parents, had the real story of Kasia's past, she'd know there was nothing to envy. Kasia resolved that she would keep her problems to herself.

"Are you looking or trying to be faithful to some guy at home, Kasia?"

For the first time, she realized guys had been far from her thoughts. Decidedly unlike her. She was so focused on getting to Fenston that she hadn't gone past noticing which ones were cute. "Nu-uh. Still looking," she said.

Yvette bent and plucked the ribbon of cotton from between her toes. She stretched and yawned and leaned to the mirror to inspect her eyebrows. Then she began a lengthy toilette and Kasia got bored watching her shade and pluck and sharpen. "Maybe I'll see you later," Kasia said, as she picked her way through the bright piles of expensive French clothing on the floor of Yvette's room.

Every minute of the international students' day was a learning experience engineered by Mary Turkleson. Even the cafeteria workers had been asked to name each food as they served it. A woman at the head of the line smiled at Kasia, "hot dogs, tomato soup." The next server said, "cabbage salad, scalloped potatoes, Jello." Kasia already knew the names of the dishes the others struggled with. She smiled and chose her food quickly, tuning out the recitation.

As Kasia passed down the line one morning, she heard "Oatmeal? French toast? Did you know there are Darlings who live around here?" The sunny voice was loud, enunciating every word precisely. It took Kasia a few minutes to realize that the woman leaning across the counter with an outstretched ladle had read her nametag and was speaking to her.

"Excuse me?" she answered.

"Oh, you're American. I thought only the foreign students were on campus." The woman shifted to an ordinary tone.

Kasia preened. "I'm both. My family lived in Connecticut until I was eight, then I moved to Poland."

The woman said, putting a scoop of gray goo in Kasia's dish, "Then you wouldn't be."

"What?"

"Related to the local Darlings."

"Don't think so."

"Funny. I didn't know Darling was a Polish name."

"My father was American," Kasia said. The anxious and courteous Japanese students wanting their breakfast so they could get to class on time jostled ever so slightly behind her. Kasia smiled, but the woman had already returned to her task of filling the next student's bowl. "Oatmeal," she said slowly.

In addition to classes during the day, every evening Mary had something planned to help them assimilate. During the first night's obligatory round of self-introduction, as nervous and soft-spoken as the others, Kasia explained that she preferred the KA-SHE-AH pronunciation of her name rather than the KAT-SHE-AH. The other students formed their mouths in imitation of hers. They listened attentively as she explained her interest in psychology and education, her desire to become a child psychologist. The students had been taking notes and were expected to ask questions of each other. This could be the tricky part. While one could write out and rehearse the self-introduction, the questions had to be answered spontaneously. Yvette asked Kasia the question they had agreed upon—whether she had taken a psychology class before. Kasia answered at length. Then Wenji asked what people had influenced her in her career choice. It was a question Kasia had never even asked herself before. But suddenly Mrs. Neville's face came to her. She explained that had known someone who had the job she wanted, helping people through the difficult periods in their life.

Kasia smiled and blushed at the applause of her peers as she resumed her seat. In the evenings films, games, role-playing and talks on study habits and something called transcultural exploration absorbed her attention. Except for the lack of transportation, everything about being back in the States pleased her. More than ever, she was aware that Poland had never really been her home. As much as she loved her uncle, like Yvette, she would find a way to stay in America. She was biding her time until she got acclimated and then she would visit Fenston. In the meantime, she was content with the life of a college student. Hapwell, chosen for its proximity to Fenston, was more than satisfactory for its own sake.

After all the manipulating and planning it took to convince her uncle to let her attend college in the States, the research and thought to locate the right school, Kasia, certain that the rest would fall automatically into place, was disconcerted to discover that rural Pennsylvania was without metros, bus service or taxis. Fenston was only an infuriating thumbspan away on the map, but she could not figure out how to get there. The final twelve miles to her goal would take as much work as the first forty-two hundred. Undaunted, Kasia resolved to figure out something. She'd start at the top.

Dressed in a red and white checked jumper and black high top sneakers, Mary Turkelson sat at her massive, orderly desk. When Kasia entered, she grinned. "Looks like next semester we'll have students from Russia with us. How's your Russian?" she asked.

"Basic conversation. That's about it. Of course we studied it in school. It was required. And my uncle took me to Moscow on his business trips a few times."

"Impressive."

"But I'm hardly fluent."

"Better than anyone else around here. Before these students arrive, I'll have to find someone to work with them."

"I could, how do you say, brush up, right?" Kasia blushed with pleasure at recalling the correct expression. "Then I could help."

"You could. But it might interfere with your other studies. Anyway, why would you? I can't pay you, you know. International students are not eligible for campus work first semester."

"You wouldn't have to pay me. It would be good for me."

"What's the scoop?"

"Scoop?"

"Why would you want to?"

"Just to be helpful." Kasia glanced at Mary, a plea on her face. "But I do have a small favor."

"Shoot."

"Shoot?"

"Tell me."

"I need to have a car."

"No soap, Kasia. You know the rule. Only students on a varsity team can have cars freshman year." Mary lifted the Hapwell College student handbook from her bookshelf, thumbed through the pages to the section on vehicles and handed it to Kasia.

"Not fair," Kasia argued.

"Granted, but the rule is the rule." Mary had returned to her drill sergeant demeanor. "No way I can make an exception for you or for anyone else."

"But why? I don't understand."

"That's the way with rules. Some are hard to figure out. This one I'm not sure about. Maybe the Dean of Students and whoever else wrote the handbook thought a car would be too much of a distraction for first year students. The policy hasn't changed since Hector was a pup. I've been here five years now and it was in place when I came."

"It's not fair. What about responsible people who want to get around? Who ever heard of a place that doesn't have a bus or train?" Kasia wailed.

"Beats me. I'm from Philly—grew up on a train."

"It's not fair."

"Now simmer down. And that's an order." The smile in Mary's voice and face contradicted her stern words. "It's not like you're stuck out here in the middle of nowhere. The S.A. transport van will take you anywhere you want to go—the mall, the movies, a dentist appointment, wherever. All you have to do is sign up at the desk."

Kasia shrugged her shoulders and gave Mary a frustrated frown.

"How about a Toll House and a cuppa joe?" Mary pointed to the corner of her desk, the coffee pot and box of cookies. Even delivering bad news, Mary was hard to dislike. "We can make a plan for whatever you've got in mind."

For one warm moment Kasia thought about telling Mary the whole story—the past—the real reason she was in northeastern Pennsylvania. Mary was the kind of person who could be trusted. Kasia tried to open her mouth and force the words out. Instead she felt the deep well of shame open inside her. And she was the little kid again, bereft and feeling as if what had happened was her fault. Foolish as it seemed, she thought that if anyone found out about her life, they'd look down on her. Or pity her. She wanted neither.

She'd keep her own counsel and figure it out. She had always been able to be strong that way. Eventually she'd manage to get to Fenston. But Kasia's fantasy plan, her reunion with Hattie, didn't include seven students in various hues and languages waiting outside in a van on their way to the record store at the mall. She left Mary's office muttering to herself, "No soap? Cup a joe. And who is Hector?"

Chapter 10

Two weeks later, dragging duffle bags, a boom box, hockey stick over her shoulder, Kasia's roommate looked around the room with a 100-watt smile, dumped her things on the unoccupied bed and said, "Lucked out. I was thinking they'd stick me in an empty room at the end of a long creepy corridor. I'm B.J. Mitchell. Please tell me I didn't miss dinner?"

"Hi. My name is Kasia Darling." She reddened at how awkward and foreign she sounded. In Poland it was easy to think of herself as an American, but when she heard herself in conversation, she realized how much fluency she had lost. Determined to re-Americanize herself, Kasia smiled and forced herself to continue. "I was just about to walk over."

"Let's do it." B.J.'s energetic smile forced one from Kasia.

The dining room clattered and hummed like a huge machine ratcheting up after a long pause. Teams of fall athletes reporting to the campus for practice had joined the international students. Now ten of the large round tables buzzed with conversation. Students shouted greetings as B.J. entered. She led Kasia through the room, stopping to joke with other hockey players. "Say hi to Kasia, my roommate." Kasia felt her face blush in the welcome from B.J.'s teammates.

When the evening's movie, *The Jerk,* was over, the roommates walked down the path to the back campus together. B.J. switched back and forth between characters from the film, imitating their voices. Kasia collapsed in laughter when B.J. tried to explain why Steve Martin could only dance to certain music and the difference between shit and Shinola. Under a streetlight she stopped to demonstrate how you spit on a cloth and wiped the Shinola on your shoes.

"So that's the comparison," Kasia asked. "They both go on shoes?"

B.J. snorted a laugh.

After they had turned out the light, an owl screeched in the tree outside their window. Eased by darkness, Kasia told a little about her childhood in Warsaw, the political changes, her uncle. She recounted her decision to come to a small school like Hapwell and her experiences since she arrived. "What you said about being alone in a room at the end of a creepy hall. That's how it was until you showed up. I was spooked. Spooked—is that the right word?"

"Yeah. Spooked."

"And walking through the woods at night alone. Whoo! I kept thinking some wild animal had followed me and would hide under my bed."

As the night drew close around them, B.J. recounted her high school field hockey triumphs and the thrill of being named outstanding freshman player at Hapwell. Suddenly, she paused mid-sentence. "God, I feel like the talking heads over here. Why didn't you stop me?"

"It's so interesting. I didn't know about hockey. And I'm not tired at all." Kasia burrowed into her covers. B.J.'s American friendly and forthcoming self-confidence thrilled Kasia. Here was just the roommate she had hoped for. And the way she talked—Kasia determined to listen closely so she could learn the college dialect, that curious version of American English. *Yes,* she thought, *yes. I'm finally back where I belong. All the years of waiting and working and now I'm home.*

B.J. described her sisters and the pressure she felt as the oldest in the family and the first ever to make it to college. Her parents had been *cool* too about her wanting to go to Hapwell, even though she'd gotten a much better deal from Penn State. Despite the heavy training and game schedule, she managed to get good grades. Her parents were proud of her.

Voice softer and lower, the words farther and farther apart as the roommates started to drift off to sleep, B.J. talked about her parents— "cool except for that lapse when I was born and they named me Billie

Jean. God, can you imagine? My mom was watching television when she was in labor. I guess it was hyped up hugely and the whole country was glued to the television. This woman, Billie Jean King, beat some guy in a famous tennis match. My mom even put a newspaper clipping in my baby book—'The Battle of the Sexes.' Did you ever hear anything so lame? Then they decided to nickname me B.J."

"I guess it could have been worse," Kasia said.

"Think so? Guess they don't have them in Poland."

"Nicknames?" Kasia replied, a little annoyed.

"B.J.s. You know."

"I don't," Kasia admitted.

"Blow jobs."

"We do have it. We just have a different name. You mean they call it B.J. here?" Kasia held her hand over her mouth to stifle a laugh. "Oh, God. You poor thing." She gulped back another giggle.

"Don't worry. You can laugh. I'm used to it. But my parents. What were they thinking?"

"Maybe they didn't know about such things back then."

"I don't dwell on that part. Skieves me out to just think about them having sex, never mind that."

"Yeah," Kasia replied, mentally filing *skieve* as verb—to disgust. They were silent for a minute, then Kasia giggled again. B.J. chortled. Each time one of them would stop laughing, the other would try to stop only to have it burst out of both of them again. Kasia was gasping for breath and holding onto Lulu with all her might.

"Knowing them, I wouldn't have escaped a weird name even if I had been a boy. They probably would have named me Engelbert after their favorite singer. Or O.J. My dad wanted a boy—a football dream—you know how that goes. Instead he got five girls. I think they named me Billie Jean hoping that at least I'd be a jock. Guess it worked. The parents, they're pretty cool though. They roll with most stuff. Best of all," she whispered across the dark room to Kasia, waking her completely with the answer to the dilemma that had plagued her since she arrived at Hapwell, "the day I came back to school they gave me a car."

The bedside clock winked 2:15. Kasia winked back. A canny smile crossed her face.

Chapter 11

Eleanor watched the car arrive. The driver took her time searching for the parking brake. Hidden from Eleanor's view momentarily by the lettering on the window, the driver stood, stretched, and looked up at the store's façade. Then a long gold braid whipped around and snaked down a bare white shoulder. The young woman's lovely face came into view as she bent and slipped on a pair of thong sandals and lifted an odd little burlap purse to her shoulder.

"Great. I knew I could find the store. You're Athena?" the girl asked, leaning on the counter, a nascent smile working the edges of her mouth. Her eyes did not meet Eleanor's. Instead, they roamed the shelves. She placed her hand on the counter as if to prove it tangible. Her nails were short, painted a pale peach. On the middle finger of her right hand she wore an ornate old-fashioned ring, a thickly set blue stone.

"Not here today." Eleanor tried to keep the odd gravity she felt out of her voice. She watched the girl without looking directly at her. The girl looked exactly like someone Eleanor knew.

A terrible thought flashed across Eleanor's mind. The right age. And the accent. Polish. Could it possibly be? Ben had told Eddie the woman he became involved with was European—? Eleanor lifted her eyes and looked into the face of the young woman leaning at the counter. Absolutely certain, Eleanor forced herself to look away from Alice's small double. Jesus, Mary and Joseph, why did everything have to happen on Wednesday when she was minding the store?

Without responding, the young woman glided to the back of the store fondling things as she went—the chrome handle on the milk cooler, the wire rack of Tastykakes, the slanted glass of the meat counter. She trailed her fingertips along a row of canned vegetables. Her voice came from the dim interior, and Eleanor was forced to follow it with her eyes. "It's how I thought it would be," the girl said.

Eleanor made a kind of a sound, an inquiring, encouraging "eeeh." She dropped the Rosary to finger the tangle of silver necklaces she wore.

"The store. Exactly how I imagined it."

Again Eleanor was aware of the sweet smell of the place, the musty, the familiar. How did the child know about Wescott's? Had Ben told the other woman about Fenston?

"Nothing much changes around here," Eleanor flushed. The lie's stale taste lingered on her tongue.

Hattie, Eleanor thought. Where was she and how would she handle this? She had always been fragile, easily distressed. For years all but housebound, fearful of driving in a car or traveling to Scranton. After Ben's death she had emerged from her agoraphobia to worry her friends by disappearing for several months. As unexpectedly as she left, she came back. But she had changed. Something profound had happened, even though Hattie took up the thread of her life in Fenston.

In a cycle they grew accustomed to, every two years or so, Hattie disappeared for weeks. Some locals conjectured that she had a bit of romance stashed somewhere. Eleanor doubted that. But Hattie refused to explain her absences, providing them with one silly scenario after another. One time she insisted she was going to a monastery for a long retreat. The next disappearance occurred after she told them she'd booked a bird watching safari. Then she'd gone for a facelift, though there was no evidence to back up her claim. Finally they'd given up asking and simply accepted her protracted absences and her insistent silences about them.

The girl withdrew her hand almost reluctantly from amid stacked loaves of Wonder Bread, turned suddenly and clasped her eyes directly on Eleanor's, trapping them, daring her to lie again. "And Hattie?"

Eleanor tensed. Was the girl reading her mind?

"I'm actually looking for Hattie."

Dear God. Had the girl found out about Ben? What could she want with Hattie? Money? Revenge? "She's away on a long trip."

The girl hid her disappointment. "I'd hoped to see her. I've come a long way."

Eleanor felt the heat drain from her face. She was absolutely certain who this girl was. She wanted to reach across the counter and grab the beautiful long braid and pull the girl's face close to hers and say, "Get out of here. You don't want to know." Instead, she shrugged. The coward's gesture. Wishing she could retreat to her kitchen and forget everything she knew about Ben Darling's secret, she looked away to hide the emotion in her face.

What was her duty as Hattie's friend? Should she tell the girl what she knew? Should she give her false information to mislead her onto another path? How would that help? Eleanor felt the future and its sorrows rushing toward them, heedless as a freight train. The inevitable, once set in motion, would come soon enough. Still, Eleanor Roderi would not be the person to tell this beautiful young woman that she was someone else's sin.

"Athena will be back tomorrow."

Just beyond the blinker light, slivers of Chaplin Lake winked through the trees, even more inviting and beautiful than Hattie had described it. Then the road curved and began climbing out of the valley toward the college on the hill. Thick woods formed a broken canopy overhead. Kasia drove through the rippling light thinking about Athena's store and the joy she felt to finally be in Fenston. Seeing all the places that Hattie had rendered so vividly that they had lived in her imagination, Kasia wondered which driveway, at what mailbox, behind which thick stand of trees she'd find the old Beste house and Hattie. One more delay, one more stumbling block. Kasia gripped the wheel as if the strength of her will could force the world to offer up what she most wanted. But she felt a curious calm as well. She was where she needed to be. The rest would fall into place eventually. Even if she had to wait for Hattie to return, their meeting was certain.

Suddenly, B.J.'s car started to chug and sputter, losing power. Pulling to the side of the road, she flicked on the hazard lights and noticed the gas gauge on the dashboard on E. Kasia tried to calculate how far she had driven from Fenston, where she recalled seeing a gas station. *"Cholera jasna,"* she groaned, and slammed the door. "Cursing in Polish, no good." Gathering up her purse and the car keys, she began to walk. "Okay, shit, shit, shit."

A hundred or so yards down the road a pickup truck appeared at the end of a drive in front of her. A young man leaned out the window and said, "Don't get much foot traffic out this way." Dark brown hair curled up at the edges around his baseball cap. Even with the squint his brown eyes were full of humor, and the arm resting on the driver's side door was tan and well-muscled.

Kasia sighed. "An involuntary pedestrian. Out of gas."

"Figured something like that. Saw you from up there." He nodded toward the driveway to a large old house almost hidden by bushes. Beyond it, a ladder leaned against a half-painted barn. "You're supposed to walk facing traffic, not with your back to it. You might end up roadkill. Have to go to the Texaco in Fenston for the gas. Hop in." He spoke quickly, as if he didn't need to breathe between sentences.

By the time they pulled into the station Kasia had noticed earlier at Fenston Corners, Nick Morgan, a junior at Hapwell himself, had recounted his day's activities, his summer job, and the current family squabble over whether to paint the barn white again or switch to red, therefore requiring more than one coat. "Figures—the ones who want red are not the ones climbing the ladder," he laughed good-naturedly.

Nick hefted two gas cans out of the truck bed, filled them himself and went into the station. He emerged carrying two bottles of Pepsi and a bag of potato chips.

Halfway back to the disabled car, Nick looked over and finally asked, "New in Fenston?"

"Kasia Darling. Just started at Hapwell. Borrowed my roommate's car to do an errand and didn't check the gas gauge." Her clipped answer belied the amused look on her face.

"Related to the Fenston Darlings?"

"Not that I know of. You're the second person who asked me that. What are they, famous or something?"

Nick laughed again, an effortless, pleasing sound, "People around here keep up with each other. Not much else to do."

"Sounds like you'd rather be somewhere else."

"Doesn't matter what I'd rather. When I graduate I'll leave. Just like everybody else. No jobs. For the record, I'd rather stay put."

Nick expertly tipped the gas can into the tank of B.J.'s car, then announced, "If you're in the mood for a little picnic, I can show you the best view in town." When she smiled and nodded, he picked up the sodas, bag of chips and a blanket and pointed to a break in the vegetation at the other side of the road. Suddenly quiet, he cleared his throat. He looked at her shyly.

Duh, Kasia thought, realizing Nick was being more than just a Good Samaritan. She glanced at her reflection in the car window—her hair shone in the summer light and she did look pretty. She paused, knowing that she shouldn't follow even a cute stranger into the woods. But what was the harm. He was practically a classmate. She smiled. "You must be a mind reader. I'm thirsty."

A few feet in from the road they began to climb sharply. During orientation the school nurse had warned them about poison ivy, a ground plant with three shiny leaves that caused a terrible skin rash. Here and there along the path, Kasia thought she spotted such a plant. Following closely behind Nick's work boots, she kept her eyes on her sandaled feet picking her way around any suspicious foliage. When he stopped, she nearly ran into his back. As he turned his arm brushed hers.

Her first day away from Hapwell and she'd already broken two of her uncle's cardinal rules about strangers: Don't talk to them, never take a ride. Now here she was breaking a rule that Piotr hadn't even thought to make—hiking off into the woods with someone she hardly knew. Relieved to see a small clearing, she asked, "Here?" Her voice sounded small and weak.

"Just a little farther." He shifted the blanket to his other arm and scrambled up another rise. He reached back to tug her up a high step.

She wondered if she had locked B.J.'s car. Was it safe on the side of the road? By the time they reached the crest of the hill, she was angry. They must have been walking for ten minutes. The soda was probably already lukewarm.

Then she thought of Nick's kindness, climbing down from his ladder to try to help a stranded traveler. Despite Uncle Piotr's cautionary tales, she had trusted this young man immediately. She wanted to believe in her instincts about people. That she was mature enough to judge situations. Nick turned, smiled encouragingly as she stepped up the last steep rise, and wordlessly spread his other arm across the valley below.

Chapter 12

Beneath them the town of Fen-
ston looked like an illustration in a travel magazine, streets branching
away from the center—the blinker light, Wescott's, the Texaco, and
the post office. Driveways like tributaries ran here and there connecting farmhouses and barns. Haloed by evergreens, Chaplin Lake lay
blue and serene. Stone fences, hay bales and brown and white cows
speckled the hillside of this postcard vista. "This should answer why I'd
rather stay," he said proudly. Kasia found his openness, his innocence
refreshing.

"Oh, my," Kasia said involuntarily, recognizing that she had uttered
Hattie's expression of pleasure. She could visualize Hattie putting her
hands to her cheeks in delight as she said it.

Nick opened the sodas and chips and shook the blanket. It settled at
their feet. "Good a place as any for our picnic."

Kasia sank down near the edge. "I didn't know we'd come so high.
What's that?" she pointed to a dark jut on the opposite hillside.

"Roderi's quarry. My old man calls it Eddie's Folly. Hasn't been
worked for years."

She grew nervous again and wondered if he had moved his hand
closer to her unconsciously.

"This is where I always take strangers. If they're brave enough to follow me," he said in a mock scary voice, as if he had read her thoughts.

"I'm glad I was. It's beautiful."

"Might as well get the whole lay of the land. Anyway, gives me an excuse to come up here. I like it here. Not that I've been very far. Not like you." He looked away shyly.

"If you love it, how can you think about leaving when you graduate?"

"Reality 101. What would I do around here? Can't make a living farming. A college degree and I'd end up pumping gas at the Texaco or driving an hour each way to work at a desk in Scranton or Binghamton, if I could even get a job."

"It's sad to think that work makes our decisions."

"Like I said. Reality."

After a few deft questions, Nick had succeeded in learning about Kasia. "You'll like Hapwell." And then, music to Kasia's ears, "And you'll fit right in."

They sat admiring the view. They both grew quiet. In the silence, the sound of the birds calling to each other somewhere in the woods made Kasia feel at peace. When Nick lay back on the blanket, she did too. After a long day full of curious events, she was enjoying a moment to reflect. Kasia stared up at the clouds breaking apart and reforming overhead. She began to imagine the shapes as portents of her new life.

A persistent tickling woke her. She looked down to see a blade of grass moving along her wrist and forearm. "Most guys would be insulted if they brought a girl to their special place and she fell asleep." His tone was gentle as he continued to tickle the inside of her wrist. "But I'll forgive you if you'll go to the Labor Day Picnic with me?"

"That's a long way off. Lots could happen between now and then." Kasia felt pleased that she could joke so easily.

"I'd ask you out sooner, but tomorrow I'm leaving for the shore for two weeks. Family vacation before school starts. So it'll have to be the picnic."

Kasia smiled and stretched—demurely, she hoped. "What is this picnic?"

"You'll see."

She glanced at her watch. She'd been gone for three hours. "I have to get back. B.J. needs the car. She's driving to a hockey clinic."

"There's a shortcut." They folded the blanket and he set off straight down the hill, tromping through underbrush and gullies. He turned to make sure she was behind him and pointed to a loose piece of barbed wire along a stone fence. "Careful here. Don't want any surprises."

"Snakes? Poison ivy?" She sounded alarmed.

"More like loose dirt. Careful you don't slip."

At the end of a shady thicket, dark and moist underfoot, about halfway down the hill another clearing opened. Blinking, they stepped onto a level plain awash in sunlight. Surrounded by a high white ruffle of Queen Anne's lace and dotted with chickory, rows of tombstones and a few raw mounds of earth strewn with withering flowers lay before them.

Kasia shuddered. "A cemetery. That's the shortcut?"

"They won't mind." Nick smiled at her and threaded a row of graves

Nick stopped to wait for her. She looked across the grid of markers, pausing in front of one and bent to try to read the weathered inscription. "Here lies—Wife of—can't make out the names. But the date is 1862. Some of these stones are pretty old," she said.

"Guess so. Old as Fenston."

"Everyone's buried here?"

"Uh-huh."

"Like *Our Town,*" she said.

"What's that?"

"A play we had to read last year. American writer, so I was interested. It's about the people in a cemetery talking about life in their town. 'Our town,' get it?"

"Sounds weird." Then quickly, "In a good way."

"I liked it. They were always making us read stuff they insisted every American student knew by heart."

"One of those motivational tricks teachers use."

They stood for a moment, wondering what to say next. Kasia smiled.

"Hey, want to visit your American relatives?" He looked around. "I think I can find a Darling."

"Sure."

He walked slowly and Kasia followed, looking at the names as they passed. The Nelsons lay between the Johnsons and the Lyntons, and beyond them, the Quinns and the Romas in well-tended plots with a fresh bouquet on each marker. They passed a pedestal bearing aloft two little stone angels with puckered lips and missing fingers that marked the resting place of newborn twins—Wilfred and Patterson Jenkins—

and on past the heavily padlocked tomb where the Morris family rested in isolated Gothic splendor.

Kasia stopped by a flag to read the inscription on the brass honor plaque above the tomb of Gordon Wescott, a seventeen year old hero in Vietnam: BELOVED SON: SUN, MOON, WORLD. Kasia felt tears and turned her face so Nick wouldn't see. Too late. "The people from the store."

"Their son." He shrugged as if there were nothing else to say.

"Young—" she stared to say. Then felt her breath catch.

"Over here," he said, motioning for her.

Kasia turned again to look at the grave of Gordon Wescott, younger at his death than she was now.

She joined Nick in front of a small plot surrounded by a white metal fence, the posts like small twisted swords aimed skyward, the gate fastened with a iron slide clasp. Inside lay five generations of Bestes in demure rows. Surprise and wonder lit her face. How had Nick known she was looking for Hattie Beste?

He waited. As if in introduction, he extended his hand.

"Hattie Beste?" A chill shot through Kasia. What if Hattie had died? What if she'd come all this way—But no. The woman in the store would have told her.

Nick smiled and pointed beyond the Bestes. "There it is. See?"

And she did.

A whooshing sound filled her ears. It was the noise of stars working their way out of order, of music playing itself on the skulls of dead children, of the edge of a blackness she had never imagined, of fate's evil laughter. Blind, Kasia took a few steps, then staggered. Nick caught her by the arm and righted her.

A sob.

"Hurt?" she thought he'd asked. She shook her head. Her mother's gesture—she put her hand to her mouth and coughed. Her chest felt as if it had sealed itself against her breath. Air, she needed air.

Blackness wove itself into whole cloth in front of her eyes. She blinked it away. Confusion washed over her as she tried to make sense of what lay before her. She forced herself to concentrate.

There, at the end of the hummocks of grass, at the edge of the family plot, two centuries of a family—births and deaths fading away as though lost in memory—it stood. A modest, roseate stone, adorned with double hearts and birds. Ivy, trailing from their beaks, encircled the two etched legends:

BENJAMIN STUART DARLING
HUSBAND AND FATHER
JUNE 1, 1927–MAY 13, 1982

HATTIE BESTE DARLING
WIFE AND MOTHER
APRIL 4, 1936–

Chapter 13

She dived into the oasis of her bed and hugged her knees to her chest as if to protect her heart. Emotion flooded through her. She had to think. But as soon as she did, she either burst into tears or the numbing orange haze descended. Finally, when she had wept and screamed into the pillow and was spent, she went over what she had seen and thought about what it meant.

There was a Ben Darling buried on a hillside in the next town. He had the same birthday and middle name as her father. The day of the hillside Ben's death was, to her best recollection, just about the time that her father had disappeared from their life in Hartford. Next to Ben's grave was another grave, awaiting his wife. The birth date was there but not the death date. The name was the same as the woman who had appeared in Hartford shortly after Kasia's father had disappeared.

The facts. What had she seen? Her father and the hillside Ben were the same person. Her father was a bigamist.

Suddenly, it all seemed so clear. His long absences. His mysterious job. That's what had kept him away from home all those times when she wanted him there. How else could what she'd seen be interpreted?

Hattie? The woman she'd come all this way to find was her father's other wife. Hattie had tricked them. Why had she come to Hartford? Why had she made Kasia believe in her? Why had she befriended Anya and cared for them? Why had she insisted on locating Piotr and staying with them until he arrived?

When Kasia closed her eyes, she saw the hillside again, the orderly stones marching up the incline. She had felt her world shift on its axis. How had she been able to keep her composure while she said goodbye to Nick? Had she thanked him? What had she said? She must have seemed all right because he smiled and waved as she got into the car and drove away.

"*Vajdak.*" Kasia spit the word across the room as if it were venom she had sucked from a snakebite. Her father had been nothing more than a philandering creep. All those months while he was away, months when she and her mother missed him so much, he was with another woman. Married to her. What fools she and her mother had been. The years of longing for her father through her birthdays and Christmases and lost teeth while he was away—working. Those nights dreaming of a re-union with him. Longing for any bit of information about him and her mother, she had come all this way to find out he was a common *vajdak?* And Hattie? Kasia didn't even want to guess what had motivated her.

As she calmed down, she tried to sort through every alternative, every possible event that might explain the tombstone. She got out a pad and pencil and made lists, jotting down the scenarios as they came to her: WHY?? She crumpled the paper and tossed it, missing the basket. Another sheet: Why hadn't Hattie told them who she was? Could there possibly be two Hatties? Filling the page, she tried to make sense of what she knew. Exhausting her tablet and her patience, everything but the truth seemed just too far-fetched. Her father had another wife all the time. That's why he was away so much; that's why he was constant-ly enveloped in mystery. It was not, as he had told her mother, a secret government job. Anya, trusting Anya, a foolish young immigrant when they met. She must have seemed such easy prey to that sophisticated older man.

Preoccupied and depressed, Kasia cut classes, skipped meals and spent her time lying on the bed going over every detail Hattie had told her about her life. She tried to recall anything about Hattie's husband who had died suddenly, at about the same time that her father had disappeared. Conflicting emotions wore deep paths toward and away from each other, then back again. Feeling angry, tricked and foolish, she wanted to hate her father and Hattie. As soon as she felt settled in that idea, another part of her mind focused on how much her father had loved her and her mother. The look on her father's face the day he left—loving, hopeful, concerned—floated before her. And how kind Hattie had been to them. Surely neither Ben nor Hattie would have been capable of such treachery. But how else to explain what had happened?

Kasia forgot about the mandatory talk on self-defense Mary had scheduled for that evening in preparation for the trip to New York City the following week. Instead, she lay immobilized by the plethora of explanations for the hillside graves—none of which, she knew in her heart of hearts, would add up to anything except that her adored father had been a cheat, a liar, and worse, a bigamist.

Chapter 14

Head down, impervious to the small rustlings in the underbrush, Kasia walked the path from the front campus to her dorm. The woods surrounding Hapwell began to tarnish into the full dapple of late summer. Kasia didn't notice. The summer school work for international students that she had reveled in became an impediment to her obsessing on what must have happened and what it meant. One moment she convinced herself that she was jumping to some hysterical conclusion and that there was some very real explanation for what she had seen in the cemetery, an explanation that would exonerate her father and Hattie: Maybe because she had just been at Wescott's store she had unconsciously superimposed the names, misreading what she had seen. In the very next moment, she was certain that she had seen what was there, that her father and Hattie were liars and cheats.

Knowledge had fallen upon her like a dark musty blanket, tainting everything else in her life with its suffocating density. If Kasia could only sleep, maybe then she could think. Finally she visited Yvette, who had occasionally offered Kasia drugs. Kasia got some neatly rolled joints and a few Valium and Ambien tablets. She hadn't used drugs often, though they were as easily available in Warsaw as at Hapwell. In both cultures, people were sharply divided into two camps. Her own natural inclination for order, clarity and self-control alone would have placed her in the anti-drug camp, but having B.J., who despised the campus druggies, as a roommate had further influenced Kasia. But now that her life was crumbling in front of her eyes, she reasoned why not take whatever comfort she could get.

With B.J. away, Kasia didn't need to worry about smoking in the room. She lay on her bed in the dark, lit up and waited to feel better. But the marijuana only magnified her worst thoughts and kept her from focusing on a solution to her problems. As she struggled to clear her head, she kept hearing the words to a song her father used to sing: "Doe, a deer, a female deer. Ray, a drop of golden sun—"

She began to sing softly, stopping to blow her nose. If only she hadn't come to the States. If only she had been smart enough to let the past be the past. She heard that refrain in Piotr's voice.

If only she could sleep.

Out in the hall students were returning from a concert. Someone kicked the wall and made farting sounds. Then laughter. Isolated, depressed, out of touch with what the other students cared about, she felt her life derided and ridiculed, as if they were standing outside her door laughing at her. Kasia realized that the grass had only deepened her depression. She felt tears leaking from her eyes. She put the pillow over her head to block out sound, but her thoughts were harder to deflect.

Why hadn't she stayed in Poland? She was not American. She was as much a stranger here as any of the other foreign students. She had tricked Piotr into letting her come, even when she knew he didn't want her to. So far, she had resisted the urge to confess to Piotr that she had selected Hapwell because she wanted to find Hattie. Her fear that he would be angry and make her return to Poland before she found Hattie stopped her. But now, what did she have to lose? Tomorrow she'd write. It would be easier than telling him over the phone; she could explain everything without having to hear the disappointment in his voice.

Kasia got up and drank a warm Coke that had been on the windowsill for two days. Light leapt out of the little refrigerator when she opened it. She blinked, grabbed the jar of Jif Extra Crunchy and slammed the door. Stopping at her desk for a spoon, she opened the jar and shoved a large glob of peanut butter into her mouth. She was hungry. Hungrier than she'd been in a long time. She lay on the bed again, chewing greedily. She realized she'd not eaten anything since the day before when she inhaled three packages of Krimpets. Even her favorite junk food didn't make her happy.

She got up and took a Valium. Slowly she began to feel better. After all, she had met Nick. She had a great roommate. Her classes were stimulating. She had been doing very well. Maybe things weren't so bad. She'd just force her thoughts away from her parents and Hattie and concentrate on being happy. The drug had made her mellow, as Yvette, thinking that Kasia was overwhelmed with schoolwork, promised it would. She would listen to music. She put on the Madonna tape Yvette had lent her and lay back, forcing her mind into blankness as she let the music touch her. She felt tears ready behind her lids.

Kasia sat up and put the empty peanut butter jar on her nightstand. She reached under her pillow. The old journal flipped open to November 23, 1982: *Uncle Piotr came yesterday. He is tall. Mom came downstairs. He brought me Lulu her old doll from when she was little. And he bought me a fur hat. We are going to make the turckey together. Maybe Hattie will have to help with pelling the potatoes.*

With the journal as a prompt, she let herself slip back into the memories of the fall she realized that her mother was sick. She remembered when her uncle arrived. He sat in the big green chair in the living room holding out something to her—what was it? What was he saying? He was asking her about school, noticing her Brownie uniform. Hattie was standing by the kitchen door smiling. She had sensed Hattie's relief when Piotr arrived. Soon Hattie would go upstairs to see if Anya was awake. Kasia wanted to recall what she and Piotr had talked about, but all she could think of was the way he held his hands down at his sides as if they were torn paper, useless and indecipherable.

Kasia slept through to morning. Sunday bells from the First Primitive Methodist Church on the hill behind the college pulled her from a dream of Piotr coming toward her hand-in-hand with Hattie. They were walking atop ocean waves and stopped and kissed each other. Hattie whispered something in Piotr's ear. Suddenly his face darkened and he turned and walked away. The dream made Kasia angry. She sat up and ran her fingers through her dirty, knotted hair. Her gritty mouth tasted salty. In her sleep she had drooled, and her pillow was stained with dried tan saliva. The room smelled like peanut butter and sweat.

Her psychology book talked about dream interpretation. She lay there, afraid to move lest the dream evaporate, taking with it whatever clues it contained. At first nothing occurred to her. She tried switching her thoughts from Hattie to Piotr when suddenly she realized that the dream was telling her that Piotr had known everything. About Ben and Hattie—that explained why he wouldn't allow her to speak of her father. Or Hattie. For a time, Hattie and Piotr had spent every minute together. She thought she remembered seeing them touch and look at each other with loving secret faces. She hadn't been wrong about that. But she had never seen them kiss.

Abruptly, inexplicably, Hattie left. Piotr must have found out who she was. Or maybe Hattie told him, thinking he'd be on her side, thinking she was somehow the injured one. That's why he refused to try to find her or to allow Kasia to contact her. Piotr had known all along about her father's double life. And he had kept it from her. He called her his little princess. He indulged her every whim, surrounding her with gifts, love. And lies.

Her fury had found its focus. Piotr. Like Hattie, he had deceived her. Everyone she had ever loved and trusted had left her or lied to her? When she felt the world completely against her, she thought of one more thing: Maybe her mother had known, too. Was that why she finally gave up the struggle with her illness? She'd been sick before and had always gotten better. Then Hattie appeared and her mother died.

Her father and mother were gone. But Hattie and Piotr—she would make them pay.

Chapter 15

"Something bothering you, El?"
Athena handed her friend the cup of tea.

Unsurprised at the question, as they often read each other's moods, Eleanor asked, "Why?

"Just something about the way you laughed before. Nervous or worried, I'd say."

Eleanor shrugged.

"Just spit it out," Athena advised.

Eleanor moved closer, her face darkening. "Would you know how to get in touch with Hattie, if you had to?" She tried to keep her voice casual.

Athena shook her head.

"Would Alice?"

"Don't think so. They're not exactly on the best terms lately."

"Lately?" Eleanor laughed.

Athena gave an exasperated smile.

"You mean to tell me even her daughter doesn't know where Hattie went? What if there's an emergency?"

"Is there?"

"Maybe something she'd want to know."

"About?"

"This girl came into the store yesterday afternoon looking for Hattie."

"So. Did you tell her Hattie's away? Why would someone come into the store for her anyway?"

"Something about knowing about the town. She heard about the store."

"We're famous, huh?" Athena smiled.

Despite her own upset and the worry about what would happen, Eleanor paused, took a deep breath, then said, "Little Polish girl. Right out of the blue, and announces she's looking for Hattie."

"Who was it?" Athena asked—too casually, Eleanor thought. "How old? A friend of Alice?"

Clearly, Athena knew about Ben and the other woman and child. Hattie must have told her. It galled Eleanor to think that her two best friends had kept a secret from her. True, she herself had kept the same secret from them, but that was because she had sworn to Eddie. She would never break the seal of the confessional.

"The weirdest thing: This girl looks exactly like Alice."

"Really?"

"Wanted to know where she could find Hattie Beste." Eleanor kept her voice flat and non-committal.

"Sure you don't have the names confused? How would she know Hattie's maiden name?"

"She's pretty definite about who she is looking for."

"First the boy who won't speak and now some mystery person looking for Hattie. Things do seem to happen when you're here, Eleanor."

"That they do."

"And folks say nothing ever goes on in a town this small. We're just the tiniest dot on the map."

"Stranger still, the girl said her name is Kasia Darling."

In the silence that followed, each woman tried to think of a plan. All well and good to have a serves-you-right attitude, Eleanor admonished herself, but now they would have to pull together if they were going to try to avert disaster. Hattie and Alice needed their protection. And the girl too—what she might discover would be devastating. They simply could not let that happen. She hoped Athena would think of something; she herself was at a loss to figure out how to put this particular genie back in the bottle.

"Something happened a long time ago—" Athena spoke tentatively.

Full of shame and guilt and a tinge of triumph, Eleanor paused a second before her loyalty to Eddie fell away and she blurted, "Don't bother explaining. I know. Ben had this other woman, even married her when she got pregnant. In Connecticut, I think it was. Years ago. He told Eddie all about it. That girl must be—"

"Why?"

"Who knows why men stray. Excitement. Or maybe—"

"I mean why did he tell Eddie?"

"Guilt, maybe. Someone to talk to. I don't know. Lots of people confide in Eddie." Eleanor's voice had just an edge of huffiness, as if she felt Athena didn't give Eddie enough credit.

"What makes you think there's any connection?"

"The timing is right. And she looks like a miniature Alice. The girl said Hattie was with them in Hartford years ago. Then I remembered that time Hattie left, right after Ben died. Somewhere in New England. I think you even went up to see about getting her to come home."

"You knew all along." Athena was incredulous.

Eleanor nodded.

"Even before Ben died?"

"I did."

"And you didn't tell?"

Eleanor shrugged.

"Why?"

"Couldn't. Swore to it. Besides, what good would have come of my telling? Wasn't like he was asking permission. He'd already gone ahead and done it."

"How could you even look at him, acting like nothing was wrong?" Athena studied Eleanor's face as if seeing it for the first time.

"Not that it didn't cause me sleepless nights. I just tried to put it out of my mind. Told myself it was not my doing, nor mine for the fixing." Eleanor paused. "What does that matter now? Seems like we should be trying to figure out how to cause the least hurt."

"Enough hurt to go around twice over. We never really said it outright, but I know you'd agree Hattie's been—well, just not herself ever since. Something broke in her when she found out about Ben. Then she got so attached to the little girl. And the woman, too. A regular soap opera. The uncle shows up and she falls in love with him."

"What?" Eleanor thought she knew it all. Now this new bit of information.

"According to Hattie, she did. And nothing could come of it without causing more hurt."

"I'm sure you warned her?"

"Oh, God, I tried." Athena's voice was low and her face slackened with worry. "That's why I followed her up there. No matter what I said to her on the phone, I couldn't talk her out of seeing the thing through. I don't think Hattie ever let on to them who she was."

"How could she?"

"At first she intended to. She wanted the other woman to suffer. But then she realized that Anya didn't know anything about Ben's life. If anything, she was even less aware than Hattie. Hattie grew to really care for her. And especially the little girl. Then all hell broke loose. Turns out Anya was very ill. She died and the little girl went to Poland to live with the uncle. End of story."

"Don't we wish."

"I think Hattie got her heart broken for the second time. She hated to lose them but couldn't figure any way out of her own deceit by that time."

"She'd gotten in too deep."

"She put herself right in the same position as Ben. She came home and thought that'd be the end of it."

"Wrong as she could be about that."

"Wishful thinking."

"I figured eventually you'd tell me about it. But you didn't." Eleanor's voice trembled with the slight she still felt. "You and Hattie went right on as if nothing had happened. So I never said anything either."

"We never really spoke about it again. I hoped it was done and over with. An episode best forgotten."

"Some secrets have a way of coming back." Eleanor felt the thread of sorrow and regret tug at her heart as she recalled her own secret.

"Clearly, this is one."

Eleanor wiped her cheek on the napkin.

"What did she say? What does she want? How did she get here?"

Eleanor was not to be rushed. "Sweet girl. Long blonde braid—so much like Alice it would take your breath away. But not as sturdy.

Small-boned. Quick. A bright face. Seems Hattie made a big impression on her. Knowing Hattie's way with kids, I don't doubt it."

"Gotta give Kasia credit," Athena said. "It's a long way to come to find someone."

"That's the other thing that'd remind you of Alice. You know how she gets when she's determined. This one had that same look: Don't cross me, world."

"What did you tell her?" Athena studied the remaining boxes as if she didn't know what to do next and mumbled, "Why do things always happen when I'm not here?"

"I said Hattie was gone on a very long trip. Right? And that you were away for the day, not expected back until late last night."

"You didn't tell her where Hattie lives, did you?"

"Absolutely not. She didn't ask."

"That's a relief. Imagine Alice opening the door to find herself face-to-face with a half-sister she didn't even know existed."

"Knowing how contrary Alice can be, maybe she'd be sympathetic," Eleanor said.

"That's it? She left? Was she upset?" Athena's voice had the same relief in it that Eleanor had felt when Kasia turned to leave the store.

"Not exactly upset." Eleanor paused, recalling the proud look on the girl's face. Then she tried to imitate the unfamiliar accent and the slang expression she'd used, to give Athena the news verbatim. "When I told her I didn't know how long Hattie'd be away, she turned to go. The she stopped and looked back. 'No problem,' she said. 'I'm a freshman at Hapwell College. I'll just keep checking in until she gets home.'"

Chapter 16

After her conversation with Athena, Eleanor thought about the way people bleed into each other's lives. Hattie had gone to Connecticut without even knowing about Ben's other family. When she discovered what he'd done and that the woman was gravely ill, she moved in with his other wife and the child. Without meaning to, she wound her life around theirs. Ten years and a half a world away, Kasia had been pining for Hattie.

Eleanor moved beyond Kasia's quest to her own long ago loss; suddenly, like a flash of grace, she understood the large blank page a human being's absence represented. Of course Kasia needed to find Hattie. The child had grown up thirsting for the reflection she would see in the eyes of those who have loved her. A psychiatrist might be able to do it, or a priest. Might. But Kasia was looking for Hattie, not Ben. How much did she know about Hattie's life? If Athena was right, Kasia didn't even know that Hattie and Ben had been married.

And what about that other child, the one she should have been responsible for and had abandoned. What longings had filled that child's dreams?

Children. How often we fail them.

Eddie and Billy had settled into the routine of watching the eleven o'clock news before bed. In the darkened bedroom, Eleanor, clad in pajamas, robe and slippers, knelt beside the bed as she had every night since childhood. She prayed in a whisper, explaining about Kasia Darling and the way Ben's secret life had come back.

Eleanor asked for guidance: How could she avert—or failing that, minimize—the disastrous outcome of Kasia's arrival? The boy, too, was in her thoughts. She prayed that she and Eddie could guide Billy and make the world a safe enough place that he could grow strong. Eleanor touched the painful lack of knowledge about her own lost child. Her guilt at abandoning her baby. Somehow she would redeem herself. First Billy, then the girl foreshadowed her own deliverance. She prayed now for that release—that the time had arrived and she would be strong enough to bear whatever came.

So fatigued that she had to grip the spread to draw herself to her feet, she sat on the edge of the bed fingering the rosary she lacked the concentration to complete. She lay down and closed her eyes before Eddie came into the room to report the latest mayhem in the world.

When he slipped in next to her, she asked, "Billy's asleep?"

"Exhausted. We did some yard work."

"Eddie, there's something. That girl from Poland—Ben's girl with that woman in Connecticut."

"I'd almost forgotten about that."

"No chance."

"Why? What's—"

"She came into the store. Looking for Hattie. Seems she's a student at Hapwell."

"How things do come home to roost. Even after all these years."

"What'll we do?"

"Nothing at the moment. We'll wait and see."

"Could be Alice's double. But smaller. A delicate little thing."

Eddie exhaled into the still night. "First Billy. Now Ben's girl. Must be the season of lost children."

Eleanor was rent by her husband's words. She wondered if he had forgotten about her own lost child. Was she the only one still thinking of that baby?

"Lost children," she echoed.

"Let's hope we have the wisdom to help them," Eddie said and touched her wet cheek. "Darling, don't let yourself grieve for what cannot be helped," he counseled.

Hours later, she awoke and listened to the night sounds. She smelled the dirt Eddie and Billy had turned in the beds under their window, the humid, dense decadence of late summer. She lay still, summing up the time since Clem entered Wescott's and this parade of characters began.

She cupped the palm of her right hand and imagined the heft of a baby's head. Then she recalled the girl's face. So familiar. The wide, blue eyes. The golden mane thick as a man's wrist. So like Alice.

Eleanor was certain that she must act; she must help Billy and somehow make the inevitable meeting between Hattie's worlds easier. And then she would make her own world right again.

Eventually she fell into a sound, dreamless sleep.

Chapter 17

"Are you sure?" Athena whacked the pie dough onto the floured board and began to flatten it with the rolling pin, making long, thin swaths of pale crust. An enormous basket of apples sat on the end of the counter and a large bowl of sliced apples waited next to her work surface. "Eddie with those trees. I don't know whether to be thrilled or annoyed. As soon as Al and Gary find out that I have apples, all they can think about is pies. Surprising how many visits I've had from my son and grandson lately."

"Rome apples make the best pies, don't you think?"

"Rome or Empire." Athena paused. "Absolutely certain?"

"I'm sure. Don't forget, I stood next to her in the ladies room. The hair was a little different color. But nobody could mistake those teeth?"

"Lots of people have buckteeth."

"Not like those."

"What did he say?"

"We had just stopped picking. He'd been in the tree next to me. Talking two-forty. Hard to believe that just days before you couldn't get a word out of him. His home life was horrific. On and on. The stereotype of the cruel stepfather and weak, wimpy mother. The sister had taken off a few months after she hit eighteen."

Athena folded the crust in half and lifted it carefully onto the waiting pie tin, where she unfolded it. "And he showed you the picture?"

"'Here's Tina,' he said—a high school grad shot, but there is no doubt in my mind. It's her. I thought I'd swallow my tongue."

"The stripper's name is Moana."

Eleanor rolled her eyes in exasperation. "Do you think they use their real names? Moana Lisa just happens to have Kandy Kotton and Honey Buns working with her. Use your head. It's her, I tell you."

"Assuming it is?"

Eleanor paused. "We have to find her for him."

"You don't mean you're going to let anyone know we went to Classy Acts?"

"How else can we get them together?"

"I thought we agreed: Our secret."

"That was before there was anything else to consider."

"I can't believe we did such a damn fool thing."

"So what?"

"There's something brewing about that place. Darleen Newberry and Grace Morgan were in here yesterday, waving around a petition to shut it down."

"So Darlene's finished picking out sofa fabric and has moved on to being guardian of the public morals?"

"Guess so. Judging by the number of names she's collected, she really hit a nerve. Must be fifty people signed so far."

"Who, for instance?"

"Half the town."

Something in Athena's tone drew a sharp look from Eleanor. "You didn't—"

Athena looked away.

"You did. You signed. Oh my God. You signed?"

"Not me. I just ignored it."

But Eleanor read something more in Athena's expression. "Will?"

Athena nodded.

"I can't believe it."

"Didn't have much of a choice. She traipsed in here during our busy time and started getting everyone worked up about what that kind of a place can do to a community."

"I can just hear her."

"That's why you should leave this alone."

"I see. Billy should suffer because people around here are squeamish about naked bodies," Eleanor said. She gave her butt a shake for emphasis.

Athena said, "I—we—" then broke off. "Anyway, what makes you think this Moana or Tina or whatever her name is wants to be found?"

"If you could have seen his face when he started talking about her. I think this is the last straw for him. He needs her."

"But does she need him? Wouldn't he be better off in foster care or something, rather than with someone like that? Besides, if Darleen and her group get their way, Moana or whatever her name is and the rest of them won't be around long." Athena scraped the mixture of apple slices, flour, sugar and cinnamon, lemon juice and salt into the waiting crust.

"Maybe. But she seemed nice. At least we should talk to her. Tell her about him being here."

"We?" Eleanor was silent.

"You want us to traipse over there and find that girl and tell her?"

Eleanor nodded and blinked, sure that she'd not gotten her way quite yet.

"Maybe we could disguise ourselves as protesters. Darleen and Grace are planning to picket outside whenever the club is open—carrying signs and taking pictures of anyone who goes inside. I can just see us sashaying through that door with half the town jeering."

Eleanor looked dejected. "Please."

"No. Absolutely not."

"But how else can we get them together? It's her brother, for God's sake."

Athena stared at the ceiling. "You're not going to let this go, are you?"

"No." Eleanor's voice was firm.

"Maybe we can find out where she's staying and see her there." Athena's voice softened.

"Are you worried about what Will's going to say when he finds out we were there?"

"No." Athena unfolded the top crust flawlessly over the filling and crimped it around the edges with her thumb and forefinger.

"You are, aren't you?" Eleanor looked incredulously at her friend.

"He'll be upset that I didn't tell him."

"I'd keep you out of it, if I could. But Eddie would hardly believe I went alone."

"Never mind. If you're set on doing this, they'll just have to get over it."

"I tried to find out where she's staying. Even talked to Clem. Figured he'd know, if anyone would." She snickered.

"You didn't tell him?"

Eleanor fluffed her hair over her shoulder in exasperation. "What kind of fool do you take me for? Anyway, he flat refused."

"Probably thought you're part of the morality police. Afraid you'd head over there and cause trouble."

"People make such snap judgments."

"You mean just because you were a nun doesn't automatically mean you're against strippers." Athena's voice was playful.

"I'm not the one who signed the petition," Eleanor responded archly.

Athena ignored the remark, but her eyes suddenly lit with a small epiphany. "And Clem's not the only person in town who knows where everyone lives—"

"Tom." Eleanor exhaled the word. "Of course. But will—"

"Just leave that part up to me." Athena winked as she picked up the paring knife, poked slits in the top of the pie, smoothed a handful of milk over the crust, and sprinkled it with sugar and cinnamon. "Guess I better get busy baking. Nothing puts people in a chatty mood like fresh apple pie."

The row of little boxes, fronted with old-fashioned dial combination locks for patrons to access the mail Tom Miller had slotted—the whole untidy range of news, bills, woe and joy for the residents of Fenston—divided the ten by twenty foot room. Opened, each box provided a tiny window into the inner workings of the Fenston Post Office.

The day's mail sorted and the early morning rush of selling stamps and weighing packages over, Tom sat heavily at the table in the back office where he would spend the rest of the day, his thoughts and reading interrupted, all too infrequently for his taste, by a customer.

Tom was about to consult his horoscope in the paper when Athena Wescott tapped at the door from the lobby. A red bandana held her wild hair back from her face. A fresh white Oxford shirt, sleeves rolled to the elbows, was tucked into worn Levis. Her Dr. Scholl's sandals clacked on the linoleum. A brown willow basket containing something covered with a blue cloth hung from the crook of her arm.

A warm sweet scent wafted from the basket, making Tom's mouth pucker in pure longing. When he saw Athena's bandana, he said, "You look just like Little Red Riding Hood today."

"Thought it was time you could use a pick-me-up," Athena said, as if she habitually delivered a coffee break to everyone in Fenston. "Just made the pies."

She uncovered a big, sweet smelling wedge and put it in front of him. She poured him a cup of coffee from a thermos, then peeled the wax paper from a thin slice of cheddar cheese and put it on top of the pie. Settling herself into the chair facing him, Athena watched him devour the treat.

"Any word when Hattie'll be back? Must be gone a couple of weeks now," Tom said between bites. He nodded to an immense pile of mail in a box on the floor.

"She didn't say. But I have a feeling she'll be along anytime."

Tom chewed thoughtfully when she asked him about the women who worked at Classy Acts.

"Sure, I know them. Getting mail here off and on for six weeks or so. General delivery," Tom said as he scrunched the tines of his fork across the few remaining crumbs of his treat. "The teeth. Soon as you mentioned those teeth, I knew who you meant."

"Hard to miss. Poor kid. Braces would have fixed them up long ago."

"When she smiles she tries to keep her lips closed. Makes her look mysterious or something."

Athena wondered whether Tom had actually seen Moana in action. "Too bad. She would have been really beautiful—"

"Maybe that's why she does it? How she got into that life." Tom stopped as if lost in the wonder of how buckteeth could cause a young woman to be drawn into a life of dancing naked in front of a bunch of strangers.

Eleanor watched his expression. "You ever go over there?"

"Lord, no. That stuff's not for me."

Athena waited.

Finally, Tom added, "They seem like kids. Darleen and Grace have been trying to locate the same people. A witch hunt, if you ask me. I feel sorry for the girls. Somehow they found themselves in that mess—"

"I need to find her, the one with the teeth."

Immediately, Tom's hackles went up. "You know better than ask me that. The post office is confidential. I'm sworn not to give out addresses no matter who the person is or what the occupation. It's the rule."

"Don't get all Clem and official on me. I'm not part of Darleen's gang. I just wanted to return something the girl left in the store the other day."

Tom's look softened.

"Her glasses. She came in and bought up a bunch of stuff. When she left I found a pair of glasses on the counter. Have to be hers."

"Wish I could help. But look at it this way: Would you want me giving out your address to anyone who inquired?"

"Our name is right there across the street on front of the store in big letters."

"Still, it's the rule. I just can't give out addresses."

"Post office has lots of rules?" Athena's voice carried the conversation into safer territory. "Must be hard to remember them all sometimes."

Tom nodded his agreement with someone who finally took the time to understand the complexity of his work.

"Probably all kinds of rules even about the inside of the post office."

Then he began to look slightly worried as if the conversation might be going somewhere he'd rather not visit.

"Like who has to stay in the lobby. And who is allowed to be back here. Back where all the mail—"

In the silence between them they could hear someone in the lobby of the post office opening one of the boxes. A hand reached in and captured the waiting mail. But the box stayed open and two eyes witnessed the short impasse between Tom and Athena and its resolution. The little chamber amplified their conversation.

"I need to know where those girls from Classy Acts are staying. And you are going to tell me. Or else," Athena said, her voice low and steely.

"Or else? Are you threatening me?"

"Are you refusing to do this little favor for me?"

The two glared at each other. Tom's face was a mask of resignation as he lifted his hand to his mouth and burped softly. "Pardon," he said.

She held his gaze.

"I think you'll find your party—the whole gang of them—over with Edwina Phipps." His voice was contrite and resolute at the same time.

The box closed silently and someone crept out of the post office.

Athena smiled and slid her hand into the basket and withdrew another parcel and placed it in Tom Miller's hands. "For later," she said. Through the foil, he could smell the heat of the sweet dough and apples, the bittersweet heft of failed duty warm in his hand.

Chapter 18

The next day, Eleanor and Athena told Will and Eddie that they were going to the Viewmont Mall to browse the end of summer sales. When pressed, Athena cited the flyer for colorful bed sheets and Eleanor wondered at lunch with Eddie and Billy, who had planned to spend the afternoon watching some game on television, whether she could find one of those new atomizers for olive oil she'd seen in the expensive kitchen catalogs.

When Athena drove up, Eleanor, never someone to whom the word understatement applied, appeared at the door wearing black stretch pants and a bright red silky, flowing shirt. Her hair arranged in a coronet of twists and tucks, she had obviously taken pains to complete the picture with triangular dangling earrings and a multi-colored straw bag capacious enough for a three day supply of clothing and essentials. She slipped into the car and looked across at Athena. "Ready," she said.

"Don't ask how I let you draw me into—"

"Never mind. We're in it together."

"Sharing the blame."

"Sharing the glory." Eleanor almost giggled. For the first time in days, she felt happy. The dark cloud of dread and guilt had dissipated, as it always had before.

It was a cycle: She'd grieve her lost baby, suffer endless torment—almost to the point of suicidal thoughts. Weeks would go by. Suddenly, inexplicably her grief and guilt would lift. And the world as she knew it would come back into focus. Color and sound and scent would return; the fog would blow away and she'd be left quivering with relief and awe that she was once again able to take her place in the world.

It was not as if she ever forgot about the baby. The pain and confusion were there, but she was able to muse to herself about it in a way that made sense. She had been young. It had not been her fault. She had no choice. She had confessed and atoned. The child had been placed with a loving family. When she was herself, engaged in her real life, it made a kind of sorrowful sense to her. Until the fog rolled in again and with it the raging torment of emotion.

Good, Athena thought, glancing at Eleanor. Whatever'd been the problem had passed. She was her old beautiful, kooky self, right down to her purple Birkenstocks—ready to put herself through any fool thing to take care of someone else. Athena just hoped that when they found this Tina, it would work out. Billy could use a few breaks. Lucky for him that he had wandered into Eleanor's exquisite caring world.

If only Edwina would have gotten her to the phone," Eleanor said, reviewing the forced, silly conversation during which she tried to impress upon a reluctant Mrs. Phipps that she did not care who stayed where or what their occupation, but that she simply wanted to give Tina a message from a family member. "Imagine, treating me like I was a reporter from *The New York Times* or something. She mimicked the simpery voice of an old woman. "You're mistaken. There's no Moana or Tina here."

"Edwina's a nitwit. Always has been. And holier than thou. Do you think for a second she'd want anyone to know she was putting up a troupe of exotic dancers? Not the way she darts to the front pew of the Methodist every Sunday. I wonder whether Grace brought the petition to services?"

"And whether Edwina signed it with her usual flourish," Eleanor testily finished the thought.

"I am surprised she'd let rooms, frankly."

"Probably needs the money. The house is about to fall down around her ears."

"Lots of places like that. Remember the shape ours was in? Still, I wonder how she got mixed up with this crowd?" As they neared the property, Athena flicked on her turn signal. Then suddenly she nudged it off and continued without turning.

"You chickening out?"

Athena gave her an exasperated look. "Just had a thought that we might be better off parking somewhere else." She circled around the long country lane and parked in an access road seventy or so feet away from the Phipps' driveway.

"Didn't know I was in for a hike," Eleanor complained, then added, "You might be right to keep the car out of sight."

"Regular Nancy Drews—that's us. All we need are little gray feathers in our caps and a snappy roadster."

"Silly. We're making such a big deal about all this."

"All we want is to find the woman and let her know her brother's in town looking for her."

"Who's convincing whom?"

Eleanor pushed the car door open and clomped through the tall grass at the edge of the road. They walked single file along the berm and turned into the overgrown walkway. Across the front yard, they could hear music pulsing in the air.

"Crazy For You." Like a contestant on *Name That Tune*, Athena identified the song. "Maybe they're practicing?" she wondered aloud and raised her arms, swinging her butt around in imitation of the show at Classy Acts.

Eleanor laughed. Athena stood behind her as she jabbed the doorbell three times. Then, keeping time with the music, three thrusts of her hips: *ba, ba, ba*—three more.

The music stopped. For a moment, there was silence. Then the lace curtain at the window beside the door moved and a face appeared. Not Moana. Or Edwina Phipps. Under a thick parenthesis of brow, the eyes that peered out were deep-set, glossy black buttons; the saucer-sized face brown and angular with cheekbones like tennis balls. The mouth opened on an expansive pink fleshy interior and an astonishing panoply of orangish gums and khaki teeth. A pristine sailor cap canted along the right side of the head. The creature seemed to hang in mid-air and stared straight at Eleanor.

Startled, she lurched backward, crashing into Athena and almost sending the two of them off the porch. Eleanor lost her grip and the contents of her straw bag spilled. Coins and scraps of paper, rosaries, makeup and, inexplicably, a handful of marbles and dice tumbled around. Had Athena's feet not been firmly planted, she could not have caught Eleanor's flailing arms and they both would have toppled into the unruly mock orange bushes, now well past blooming.

"Dear Jesus," Eleanor squeaked, as she clutched her friend's shoulder. "Did you see that?"

"What was it?" Athena squatted, collecting the contents of the bag and handing them to Eleanor.

"I don't know. Some kind of dwarf, I think. A brown one."

Athena lifted her eyebrows at the impossibility of a dwarf in Edwina Phipps' parlor. But then, she reasoned, who would have expected to find exotic dancers there either? "You sure?"

"Not really. But something. I only got a glimpse." Eleanor shivered.

Suddenly the door opened and a young woman stepped out. Hanging from her neck, one long arm slung across her chest, a monkey rode her hip. He gleamed a bright smile of welcome at Athena and Eleanor. The young woman blinked twice as she inspected them. "Mrs. Phipps is not at home," the girl recited in a breathless voice.

Eleanor's attention was riveted on the monkey, whose response was to play peekaboo, covering his eyes with surprisingly long thin fingers.

Athena looked the woman up and down, taking in the bare feet, toenails a screaming mauve, the bare midriff and stretchy halter, the blonde hair drooping into amazingly keen eyes. *Sixteen,* she thought. *Couldn't be a day older.*

In the week since Billy Fallon had come to stay with them, Eleanor was happy and her house hummed with energy and life. Eddie noted the shift. He was all too familiar with the dark, quiet periods that came on her unexpectedly.

She had just emerged from a bad one—days on end when Eddie witnessed her torment. He had seen many spiritual struggles; sometimes he had been able to help. But during those bleak times Eleanor closed herself off from him. What was the use of his life, his training and study, if he could not even help his own wife through a crisis?

Still, Eleanor staunchly refused to discuss her cares with him, even to the point of insisting there was nothing wrong. The first sign that she was returning from the dark place was her renewed interest in domesticities. He'd see a line of sopping sheets hanging in the backyard or a new piece of cut cloth covered by the tissue of pattern paper on her work table and breathe a sigh of relief that her demons, whatever they were, had been vanquished.

Eddie knew when they took in the boy that Eleanor would provide sustenance, guidance and comfort, but he would provide the day-to-day companionship. Much of the time, Eleanor was away from home, delivering Meals on Wheels, working at Wescott's or wandering the countryside in search of the right Fiestaware pitcher or a patch of wild swamp irises. When she was busy, she was happy.

She announced her shopping excursion and that she would leave them to their enjoyment as the Yankees took on the Angels in Yankee Stadium on the television in the den. She had laid out a lunch of salad and blueberry cobbler and iced tea on the coffee table. He and the boy had eaten companionably in front of the television.

The game interested Eddie because he had followed the story of the pitcher, Tommy John, who amazed everyone when the operation, which took a tendon from his right arm and attached it around his left elbow, had made a comeback. "Not bad for an old guy of 44," Eddie advised the boy. Where had she said she was going? Her car was in the driveway. Had Athena picked her up? He wished he had paid closer attention.

Eddie enjoyed hearing Billy's commentary, peppered with unfamiliar jargon; "Trash 'em," the boy urged his team when Tommy pitched a sinker. Eleanor had not reappeared by the time the game had ended.

Eddie sensed the boy growing restless. Holding out the magazine he was reading to show the boy the photo of a computer, Eddie said, "Imagine. It used to take a room to hold the memory this has." Eddie'd been following the growth, or rather the shrinkage, of computers for years.

The boy looked politely befuddled. "What's it for?"

"A computer. Soon every house will have one. Like a television."

"I've heard of them. But what will you do with it?"

"Information," Eddie answered, still looking at the page.

Billy glanced at the clock. "About what?"

"Anything. It's all there. You tell it what you want—" Eddie heard his own voice and stopped trying to explain. His thoughts raced with possibility. Unfortunately, no matter how hard he tried he hadn't been able to bring anyone else along on his mental journey.

The boy stood and walked to the window and looked out. The sun had shifted and the back of the house was cooled by a light breeze. A flutter of annoyance, or maybe apprehension, caught Eddie off guard. It was so unlike his lovely wandering Eleanor to tarry this close to the dinner hour.

He would not have cared, if only she had told him she'd be gone so long. Soon, if she didn't return, he'd go into the kitchen and switch on the light and root around in the fridge for something to feed the boy and himself. A pleasant enough prospect, the unrestricted access to things she considered bad for him.

"Let's make a Dagwood sandwich?" He motioned the boy toward the kitchen.

"It's a question of architecture," Eddie said. Hoping Eleanor's arrival would not coincide with this gustatory infraction, he smacked his lips with relish as he laid the salami, ham, provolone, sweet and hot peppers, tomato, lettuce, onion, basil leaves, mayo, ground mustard, black and green olives, and catsup on the counter. He took a loaf of his homemade Italian bread and cut it lengthwise and doused it with olive oil. "A good base is important," he demonstrated, "a sprinkling of balsamic" to construct a meal, inviting Billy to invent his own concoction.

"Peanut butter?" the boy asked. Eddie stood back in awe as Billy slathered it on the bread and then applied a thin coat of catsup before applying the meat, cheese and garnishes.

The kid's a natural, Eddie thought.

They sat hunched at the table, the juice from their sandwiches rivering down their forearms, a roll of paper towel and a bag of Wise potato chips ripped open between them. They devoured their creations, washing them down with swigs of root beer.

Billy opened the last few bites of his sandwich and arranged potato chips atop the lettuce and tomato layer, then reapplied the top crust. Eddie stood and got the jar of peanut butter and applied a dab to the edge of his sandwich, while Billy, expectant as a celebrity chef, waited for confirmation of his skill and taste. Eddie chewed evaluatively and smiled. "Next time," he said.

Disposing of the evidence of their debauchery, including an ice cream container they'd emptied, digging their spoons deep into the velvety-cratered mint-chocolate chip interior—"No use dirtying any more dishes," Eddie said—Eleanor still hadn't arrived. Eddie felt a twinge of edginess as well as a small shoot of discomfort in the vicinity of his gallbladder.

He blew the dust off his chess set, unused except for the infrequent visits of Paul Myers since their son Robbie left home. "Play?" he asked. And the boy nudged aside newspapers to make room for the board.

When he realized it was chess and not checkers, Billy tried to hide his disappointment. Eddie insisted he could teach him quickly. Billy was soon engrossed in finding his way around the board, imagining the various outcomes of each move and calculating the infinite number of ways he could go.

The boy shoved his piece forward decisively, but kept his hand on it for a few seconds. Eddie lingered over the table long enough in response to allow for it to seem a good move. Indeed it was, for someone only an hour into learning the game of a lifetime. He sighed deeply and scratched his cheek with the back of his knuckles as the boy watched. Where was Eleanor?

"Good job," Eddie said, and explained just what the move had done to thwart his own goal. The boy exhaled in relief. "Yes indeedy. Fine work," Eddie continued as he passed his hand tentatively above the pieces, exhaling too. He had learned early on in life to listen to the breath of a person and let that direct the exchange. In addition to small comforting hand movements, he often matched his own breathing tempo and sometimes his posture to the other person's to foster trust and understanding between people, a silent communication more important than conversation. It always worked.

He did not let the boy win, but had allowed the loss of a number of his own pieces. Billy was trying to reset the board, recalling where each piece belonged, when the phone rang.

"She's fine, Eddie, don't worry on that account. Athena too. But you'd better come over to the station." Clem's tone was official bordering on lugubrious.

Eddie drew in his breath to ask what was going on when he heard the click.

Chapter 19

The single cell was empty, but along the outer wall of the ten feet square room a thousand watts of brightness shown down on a desk, a phone, an overstuffed filing cabinet and a cranky and bedraggled group of women sitting on a church pew bench and staring ahead as if waiting for the service to begin. One of the women cradled a monkey in her lap.

When Will entered the Fenston Borough Building, the women leapt into action as a cacophony of angry voices, led by Athena, tried to elucidate various versions of what had happened at Edwina Phipps' house. Then Eddie, Billy right behind him, dashed into the room, followed by Jeff Newberry, Bob Morgan and a fellow wearing cowboy boots, a silk shirt and an enormous glittery belt buckle.

"Minding our own business on our day off. Relaxing and listening to a few tunes and they barge in," the young woman with the purple nails said, her eyes flashing as she glared at Darleen and Grace.

"We don't want your type here," Darleen said, her face darkening with fury. "Get out of Fenston."

"This is a family town. Take your trash someplace else," Grace added.

"I had no idea—" Edwina's dissembling was obvious even to Eddie. "I thought they were in town with that new supermarket in Crystalle." Her words were lost in a snarl of competing voices.

Clem pulled Eddie aside. "Worse than herding cats, trying to get

them over here. Hadda call up Tom for a second car. Even so, the problem was figuring out who could ride with who. They were crammed in
pretty tight."

Eddie tried to visualize the transport of Edwina, Darleen, Grace,
Eleanor and Athena, as well as the other women and the monkey.
Knowing how Eleanor and Athena felt about Darleen and Grace, the
combination was problematic.

"And a monkey to boot." Clem leaned against the corner of the
door post and moved back and forth, scratching his shoulder along
the edge. Eddie started at the little humanoid features, the wise alert
expression on the monkey's face as it darted its head this way and that.
Smiling. Wearing a jaunty nautical jacket and cap, the monkey was the
only one present who seemed to be enjoying himself.

"Sailor," cried the unidentified cowboy who had wormed his way to
the front of the room. He grabbed the monkey away from the woman
it clung to and inspected the tiny paws and face. "Good pal! Are you
okay, little buddy?" he said, as the monkey emitted a word in squeak
language and wrapped its arms around the man's neck, burying his face
in the shoulder.

The young woman snarled as she peeled the monkey's hands away
and wrested it free from the man, turning her back to him and nuzzling
into the animal's furry pelt. "Fuck off, Al, you know he's mine."

"Not till you make up whatever this little gig is going to cost you,"
he said, his face a mask of unrestrained fury as he dodged around her
trying to snatch the animal back.

"That's not what the magistrate said. Full custody to me. Read the
papers."

"Don't I know you two?" he questioned Athena and Eleanor.

Completely flummoxed, Eddie tried to figure out what had happened. How were Eleanor and Athena involved in this brouhaha with
Edwina and the other women? What did a monkey have to do with it?
He looked at Eleanor for an explanation, but she was too engrossed in
the tussle over the monkey to notice his questioning expression.

The monkey's woman wore a short tie-dyed dress and lace up sandals, her hair parted primly in the middle and pulled back from her
face. Next to her was a younger doll-like woman, obviously terrified,
her gaze fixed on Clem's scowl. "Don't call my parents," she begged, her

face crumbling into little girl blubbering.

Suddenly Billy darted past Eddie into the throng. "Tina," he shouted, and headed for the third young woman, the one who had been hidden by the taller girl's shoulder.

A confused expression on her face, Moana looked around at the sound of her real name. Her hand darted to her pocket; she flicked on a pair of glasses and looked anxiously toward the door.

"Tina!" Billy lurched forward, catching his foot on the strap of Eleanor's huge straw bag, causing the contents for the second time that day to disgorge onto the floor. Without stopping to notice what had tripped him, he lurched forward again.

The woman with the glasses elbowed her way toward him. Her lips parted and for a moment stretched to cover her ugly protruding teeth. Then she surrendered to a wide smile, whereupon Eddie recognized her at once from Billy's photograph. The boy dove into her arms and she closed them around him; her face lowered to his—both draped by a curtain of her long rusty hair.

Everyone, even Darleen, stopped talking. The room was a still frame of amazement as the stripper and the young boy stood locked in a tight embrace. There was an immense choking sob followed by a long moan. "Billy," she said. "Oh my Billyboy. How did you get here?" Her long fingernails traced his back, as if to verify his solidity.

Billy looked over toward the Roderis. Eddie tried again to catch his wife's eye, but she was transfixed by Billy and Tina's reunion. When she looked up to catch his gaze she winked.

So *that*, thought Eddie, *is what kept Eleanor away through suppertime.*

Chapter 20

Sleeves rolled up past the elbow of his surprisingly strong forearms, a rack of sterilized mason jars and a bushel of ripe fruit next to him, Eddie stood at the sink paring apples. The sugar bin lay on its side and little hills of sugar dotted the linoleum floor and the counters. In the corner, the compost overflowed with slick peels and cores. The hot sweet air of the kitchen hummed with industry.

Before he fell in love with Eleanor, Eddie had lived a lonely, priestly life; after, he relished marriage like a parched traveler drinks his first long draft of water, enthusiastically though not neatly. The ramshackle farmhouse they had eloped to had been enhanced by many labors of love in the form of home improvements in all stages of completion and abandon. Recently, Eddie had begun to leave the heavier tasks for the visits of their son, Robbie, and to concentrate on more sedentary activities like canning applesauce.

Turandot played softly on the kitchen radio. Eddie sang along, obscuring the sound of Eleanor's approaching footsteps. She stood at the door watching her husband and wondering how all that time had passed and she had never noticed that when her husband stood he listed slightly to the right, his left foot toeing out like a ballet dancer. Eddie's voice. The rich sad music and the sight of Eddie blanching apples brought tears to Eleanor's eyes. She crunched across the sugary kitchen floor and put her hand on Eddie's shoulder.

Eddie turned, surprise evident on his thick, still handsome face. "You're up," he said, quickly running his hands under the kitchen tap.

Eleanor looked around at the disarray of her kitchen. "Quite the mess you've got going for yourself."

"I'll clean up after," Eddie said.

"Sure you will," she replied, a little more archly that she had intended.

"Aren't you just aggravated about last night?"

"Why shouldn't I be? I should be outraged. Athena too. We went out of our way to find out where Billy's sister was staying on the Q.T. to avoid just such a scene. We were hardly there two minutes, trying to convince the one with the monkey that we had legitimate business with Tina so she would wake her up, when Darleen and Grace and the Morality Minion showed up, waving their placards and causing a racket."

"That's not the same tale as the others tell."

"Meaning?"

"There are other versions."

"What makes you think I'm not telling you the real story?"

"I'm only trying to find out what happened. What was Clem saying then about you and Athena at Edwina's with those girls? Were you and Athena and those young women consuming alcohol together and dancing?"

"He blew it all out of proportion. Kandy offered us a beer while she went to get Tina out of bed. It was so hot. We were thirsty. So, yes. We drank a beer. A federal crime?"

"And the dancing?" Eddie struggled to keep a straight face.

"We weren't dancing. Not really. They were playing Athena's new favorite, 'One More Chance.' Every time it comes on the radio, she stops everything to listen. She's a fool for Madonna. I guess we were kind of shuffling from side to side with the beat. You know how Athena and I love to dance."

"I do." Eddie paused to allow the mental picture of Eleanor in her flowing garb and Athena with her oxford shirt tucked tidily into her jeans dancing with the two young strippers.

"We didn't want to seem snobby or anything."

"Of course not. Anybody'd do the same, except, of course, Darleen."

"The nerve of them. Coming right up on Edwina's porch and look-ing in the window. Spying on us like we were common felons."

"Did they follow you?"

"I don't think so."

"But how did she know where they were staying?"

"Who knows?"

"How did *you* find them?"

"Promise not to tell?"

"Certainly."

"Athena talked Tom into telling her."

"Why would he do a damn fool thing like that?"

"Had to do with Athena's apple pie."

"Something still does not add up. I get why you went there. But I still don't understand how you made the connection between those women and Billy." Eddie looked perplexed.

"Doesn't matter."

"It matters to me, El. Especially when I think there's something you're keeping from me."

"Now what? You're going to start the third degree."

"You're defensive. What do you have to hide?" Eddie asked.

Suddenly Eleanor shot out the door into the soak and pelt of sum-mer afternoon rain, her violet shirtwaist plastering itself to her body, her feet squishing slowly through the sopping, gluey grass.

Head down, without thinking where she was going, she found herself back at the far end of their acreage—the old quarry, carrying with her the pain she'd masked and ignored and bargained with each day since Billy Fallon appeared. His desperation to find someone who belonged to him, his stories about his stepfather's treatment, his shut, quiet look, drew Eleanor again and again to the thought of what had happened to that baby she had given birth to so long ago and abandoned.

Eddie's question, "What do you have to hide?" registered. How could she have lived her regular life all these years without knowing what had become of that child? She had masked, denied, bargained, and worked through her pain, but it always came back.

With Billy in the house, there had been little time to dwell on her own problems. Now that he and Tina were at Harmony House in the care of Sister Gloria, the future seemed gloomy and endless.

The edges and cliffs of the quarry lay raw fifteen years after the last groan and scrape and rumble tore away at them. The seams of rock, carved and bitten and chewed, stood waiting for the next assault. Nothing Eleanor told herself about how young she had been, how afraid, how unlikely it was that she could have found the child even if she looked, how impossibly small her will had been in the face of her grandmother's fury, nothing had been able to erase the guilt she felt. Forty years of hiding the truth from everyone except Eddie would not take it away. She was as raw as the gashes on the bluestone, a thing ripped and marked, a thing that could not be whole again. All the years between had been sham and deceit, no less so because she had wanted only to forget.

She stumbled. Reflexively pulling away from the lip of the quarry, grabbing backward involuntarily, she caught her hand on the brambles of wild blackberries. Losing her balance, she fell back into the briar and felt through the thin wet cotton of her dress the gash of a thousand tiny arrows.

The skin along the back of her head felt wet and prickly. She twisted, attempting to free herself, and for just that moment the pain left her. She heard Eddie say "Don't fight the bush, push toward it to free yourself." Yet who could deliberately force herself farther into the path of pain?

When the stinging returned, she thought of the trap she had laid for herself with the secret she'd held so many years. The impossibility of release lay before her. Still pinioned by the briars, she writhed in the muddy gravel, her feet skidding awkwardly away from any purchase. How could she live for one more moment with the secret thorn she'd worn so close to her heart? She couldn't bear it. Nor could she imagine after all these years letting go of the secret, the constant companion and source of grief and longing, terror and regret.

Now she knew that however it pained her there was no way out but to push herself deeper into the grief in order to be finally free of it. But how?

The rain intensified, slashing against her face and body as she tried to extricate herself from the bramble, to stand upright and pull away. At each effort, just as she felt she was almost out, she'd feel the sharp tentacle grabbing against some virgin part of her body. Sobbing, blinded by her long wet hair, she scrambled on hands and knees, heedless of the thorns grinding into her skin with the slightest pressure. In the struggle she had lost everything but the will to get out. Her bloody hands and legs, her face, a large three-tiered scrape across her cheek and chin, were washed clean by the rain only to have pinpricks of blood reappear immediately.

Exhausted, Eleanor paused, knowing that she had only the strength for one final attempt. She felt in her pocket for the rosary, but found it missing. Furious, she prayed anyway, her words coming thick and clotted with fury and fear. As the dense arms of bramble tore at her, she pulled the hem of her dress up around her left arm to cover her face. Using her right arm to push herself to standing, she lurched up and through the thicket with as much momentum as she could muster. Later she would say that the branches parted like the Red Sea—quick and inexplicable and the answer to a prayer. Even she would relish the irony of her enormous unnecessary lunge, a self-propelled thrust that drove her not only out of the blackberry patch but beyond and across the path.

Shocked at her unimpeded speed, she lowered her violet cotton shield and opened her eyes in time to see the clouds breaking up across the chasm, a small seam of baby blue winking amid the white and gray. She grabbed at the long fronds at the opposite edge of the path, pulling a handful of weeds and black-eyed Susans and flocks with her, a little decorative bouquet clutched to her chest. Her face wore a small smirk of surprise and awe as she cleared the stubbled edge and tumbled down the embankment past the various hues of stone and dirt. Bumping against a little outcropping of grass and daisies and pebbles, she fell fifteen feet into the waiting crater of the quarry.

"It's a miracle you weren't killed," Eddie said after Clem left.

"I'm okay. Except for feeling foolish." She touched the scratches on her cheek.

"Imagine falling off the roof of the barn. That's how high up you were. You could have—"

"I did what you said—when I knew I was falling, I didn't struggle."

Eddie continued to bathe her cuts with warm water. "You look like the loser in a cat fight."

"I'm fine. Really."

"You could still be lying there hurt and nobody'd know what happened."

"I was just dazed. Resting a bit before I tried to walk home."

"Look at your poor hand," and they both did. Long scratches covered her right forearm, wrist and hand.

"Just a few scratches."

"Good thing Clem was on patrol and saw you tumble."

"Clem's a snoop. Using binoculars to scan our land. What did he expect to find? Rustlers?"

Eddie laughed softly. "Still, he saved you."

"I appreciate that. But he goes overboard. I can't believe he got an ambulance and crew up here for that. I just fell, for God's sake, I didn't die. Nothing broken, not even a sprain."

"I'm grateful to him. Told him so."

"Don't encourage him. After twenty years of being the chief, you think the shine'd be off the apple. I guess old voyeurs never quit."

Eddie studied his wife's face and smiled in relief. Beyond the scratches, she looked unscathed. "Could have been much worse. Dashing out of here like that. What's gotten into you, El?" His tone was light but probing.

Eleanor looked at him and her face darkened. She drew in a long breath, then she looked away. Eddie reached for the knob on the stereo atop the refrigerator. The bright voices leapt back into the little machine. Eleanor felt her courage shrivel in the quiet of Eddie's gaze. She leaned her face on his chest and inhaled deeply of his scent—the peace and security that emanated from him—to steady herself. She took both of his hands and drew him to the kitchen table to sit at his place across from hers. Before she recognized the words forming in her mind, she blurted out, "It's about that baby, the baby I had before I met you."

"The baby?"

"Did you forget?"

"Of course not. But—"

"I've been tortured thinking—"

"You've never spoken of it before."

"Doesn't mean it didn't weigh on me."

Eddie searched her face. "I thought you were trying to forget, so I didn't mention it. I've thought of it many times."

Her eyes fastened onto the fruit on the drain board and she could not move them back to look at her husband. She felt as if a large undigested wad of something putrid was forcing itself out of her mouth. She almost gagged as she continued, "My grandmother made me. They gave away my baby. I wanted it, but they gave it away and wouldn't tell me where. They didn't believe anything I told them. I always said I wanted to go to the convent. She got a good laugh out of that. 'A slut like you in the convent. They wouldn't take you on a bet.' But she was wrong. They took me." She sobbed quietly for a few minutes.

"You don't have to tell me anything you don't feel like talking about, darling. This is about how you feel."

She quieted and gathered her resolve. For once, she wanted to say it all. "He said he'd hurt me, if I told. They believed him and not me. My uncle—" As her eyes closed, Eleanor seemed to gradually deflate and her voice grew more faint. At the end, she spoke so softly that Eddie had to lean across the table to hear, "It was so long ago—" Her voice broke into the kind of long, wrenching sobs he had never heard from his wife. "—but it tears at me all the time."

Eddie held her until her cries subsided. "You mean all these years you were thinking about it and you didn't tell me? El? Why?" His voice was soft too, uncertain as he waited for her to speak again. "Did you think I wouldn't want to share this with you. To listen?"

"I don't know. In the beginning when you were Father Edward, I didn't want you judging me. I'd confessed and did penance. Once I told you about it I wanted to be free. I thought if I didn't talk about it, my sorrow would go away. I would forget."

He looked at her with love and concern. Her sobbing resumed as he came around the table and with great effort knelt in front of her and drew her toward him. "So long ago, darling. Before we were together. I hardly remember life before you. Little bits and pieces that float into view from time to time, that's all." He drew his hands softly through her hair, petting her and soon her shoulders were still. "I love you."

"Here, you'll hurt yourself. Your joints will be killing you all night." They stood, their faces inches apart.

Eddie shifted his weight as if his legs had already started to throb, but he stood facing her. Eleanor led him into the parlor where they sat on the couch. She needed Eddie beside her while she talked. She wanted him to hold her hand and occasionally for his scent to reach her. Like the old days of the dark box at the back of the chapel, she wanted to avert her face while she spoke about the years of torment she'd endured. Eddie listened with his heart and absorbed her awful sadness. By the time she finished talking, cars had begun to switch on their lights and floated like lightning bugs along the ridge to Crystalle.

"The worst part is that Billy found us on August 10." Eleanor began to sob again, halting between words, hardly able to catch her breath. "On that day every year, wherever I was, whatever I was doing, I wanted to die. My child's birthday. Forty years and the pain was worse than ever. Some years it was so bad, I had all I could do to stop myself from driving off the overpass into the river."

Eddie sat up and looked at her sharply. "In the quarry? Did you?"

"No." She said quickly. "No. That was an accident. I just fell."

When she was quiet for a time and Eddie thought she had finished, he bent his lips to her ear. Instead of the Latin phrases of comfort which often came unbidden, he kissed her over and over, her face, her chin, her eyelids, the deep cuts across her cheek, her forehead, her throat, and began one of the most mysterious rituals of healing—slowly, tenderly he made love to his wife.

Neither of them slept. Before dawn, Eddie piled a blanket in the wheelbarrow. He found Eleanor in the living room, watering her plants, and suggested they walk into the woods to watch the sun rise. The air had a whisper of chill and the hills were ribboned with a light fog. The gold of late summer intensified. Fat, resplendent roses thrashed their way through the weed-choked borders and clung to every purchase. The fields beyond the garden, hayed for the final time only the week before by Bob and Nick Morgan, were alive in the early sunlight.

The timeline of the Roderi family reflected in the overgrown pasture behind the barn, where every car they had ever owned squatted in the sun. The imposing presence of the oldest models, a red '52 Ford sedan and a glorious '59 turquoise and white Mercury convertible, a faux wood-sided Country Squire wagon, and a GMC pickup, rusted impressively in a nest of waist-high milkweed. The more recent additions were less metallic, grand and romantic: the '78 Ford Bronco and the '84 Dodge Omni. Behind the cars, a shell of a stock car bore the number 23 and the name EDDIE's EDGER near where a school bus labeled SUPERIOR COACH, LIMA, OHIO had waited years for conversion to a family travel bus, its seats a cozy home for animals. Scrub brush sprouted from the roof and its broken windows held distorted images of the encroaching woods.

In silence, they stopped and sat on the blanket, watching the sun begin its faithful round along the ridge behind the quarry, until its first warm fingers pointed them toward home. They folded the blanket and ambled back. Even the house and barn, both in need of paint, looked substantial and lovely in the scrollwork patina of wisteria and bindweed. Eddie hoped that if he could remind his wife of the beauty of their life, she would be able to put the past behind her. Part of him knew it would not be enough. She would have to find out what had happened to her child in order to put it to rest.

Outside the kitchen door, Eleanor stooped to gather a handful of mint, absently lifting the fragrant greens to her face. Lost in separate contemplations, they sat at the table quietly eating cinnamon toast and drinking mint tea laced with Eddie's honey. The silence with its sense of shared worries and the comfort of each other alive within the same hopes gladdened them more than words.

Looking across at his wife in the shifting light, Eddie saw all the stages of their life reflected in her face: the young postulant flushed with the confusion of their unexpected love, the disappointment of her barren years, the joy of motherhood, the building and growing together. The layers of time showed in her face and the softening slope of her heavy body. Love beyond anything he had ever felt surged through him. She was his world. All the years he had imagined he was her protector and comfort; she had hid her suffering from him. The world spun away from them every day, joining them only in the miraculous elasticity of love. Now that he knew his wife had suffered so, he had no choice.

Chapter 21

Even when they'd prefer not to, people leave their mark. Some like the ephemeral afterglow of a firefly, some with the panache of a jet trail; still others with the viscosity of a slug's path. Finally, Eddie understood those odd, detached moments, times when Eleanor seemed to be listening to something very far away, her face so full of sorrow and resignation that it brought tears to his eyes. The stain thrown across her life had imprinted her, bent her early on, forced her to lean a certain way as if expecting the weight of obsession to fall into her arms.

Edward had been the golden boy at the seminary, brilliant, studious and eager to please his superiors. They had spoken of his abilities, his vocation, in hushed tones. Alerted to his promise, the bishop had posted him to Stella Maris, the prized assignment, as the little work involved in being the resident chaplain was pleasant enough and the sisters easy to minister. In those quiet quarters he would have adequate time to study doctrine and learn Italian before the next step for a gifted young priest, a term in Rome.

During their brief, strange courtship, those furtive hours imploding under the weight of joy, passion and fear, they had had little time for the usual getting-to-know you conversations. Thinking back, Eddie could not recall her mentioning one person, one moment from her life before the convent—except for that one statement, very soon after they had begun to meet secretly, "I had a baby and gave it away." It came as a simple fact, delivered in a tone that warned him away from further inquiry. In the time he had known her in the convent, she never had a single visitor. Even after they left Stella Maris, Eleanor didn't speak of her family, beyond saying she'd been raised by her grandmother in Harley. Shortly after they were married, Eddie tried for rapprochement with her family. "They'll forgive you, darling. Don't you think you should let them know where you are?" Instead of answering, she'd take a handful of her dark hair and flick it over her shoulder, a gesture he came to identify with her thinking about something unpleasant then dismissing it.

Imagining that she feared her family's judgment, their anger at her leaving her vows, he didn't bring it up again until they had been in Fenston for a year. He had inherited enough money to buy the old farm. Little by little, they were refurbishing it according to their own energy and taste. For the first time in his life he was working with his hands, as together they caulked windows, hammered shingles and hefted sheetrock.

Late afternoons, they admired their day's work and then swam and played. The summer air was still and hot as they picked their way along the path to the pond at the back of the property. They had spent the late spring pulling weeds and clearing debris so that they would have their own swimming hole away from everything. When they emerged from the woods at the edge of the pond, Eddie tugged at his wife's dark hair, freeing it from the kerchief she'd worn against the dust of their work. In the bower of a willow tree, they undressed each other slowly. They dove into the cold spring-fed pond from the edge of the dock they'd made from wooden pallets and metal barrels. They embraced underwater—Eleanor wrapping her legs round Eddie's waist. When they surfaced, Eddie floated on his back and Eleanor treaded water at his side while they kissed, enjoying the clean, fishy smell of the water and the feel of each other's silky skin.

Later as they lay on the dock, talking and laughing, Eddie suggested again that it was time for Eleanor to contact her family. "They might be worried. Just let them know that you're all right. Happily married and all," he said, running his hand along her sun-freckled shoulder "to a man who adores you."

"That again?" she said, irritation inching into her voice. Without moving, Eleanor seemed to pull her body away from his.

"Why not?"

"I don't want to, that's why."

"But they must be worried?"

"With all the Roderi doting you're used to, I know it's hard for you to understand, but no, they're not worried."

"How do you know?"

"If they wanted to find me, how hard could it be? They know I left with you. We didn't even leave the state."

"But—"

"Please, leave it alone. You're projecting your family onto mine. It's just not the same thing."

He rolled onto his back and encircled his young wife with his arm. Running his fingers lightly from her navel to her chin, he studied every inch of her skin, every texture, every sun-washed pore. Her dark thick hair shimmered blue-black against her creamy skin. "If you're counting my freckles," she said, shading her deep blue eyes to peer up at him, "you'll be here all day and half the night." It was true. The sun had dappled her; Eddie thought he had never seen anything so beautiful, so perfect in his life. Sometimes when he woke first, he lay quietly admiring her face and body. How could it be that this magnificent young woman loved him?

Eddie had studied the mirror long enough to know he was not handsome, not even ordinary. His forehead wore deeply into his dark hair, and a large crooked nose and deeply notched chin dominated his face. His teeth—even, strong and white, were his best feature, but a smile had never come easily. The misfit, the brain, the egghead, the dreamer—in a culture that appreciated brawn; he knew how people thought of him and had made his peace with that particular loneliness. The status of the priesthood had changed all that.

As Father Edward he had enjoyed the parish work and his short time at the motherhouse. The day after his welcome reception, he had gone to the convent to teach the new postulants Latin. While the other novices were struggling with the first lesson he had prepared for them, Ellie raced through the week's work. She smiled over the top of her book when he asked her if she had any questions and then spent an hour discussing proposed changes in the liturgy and the political impulse behind them. Suddenly he understood the poetry of the shared mind. And he knew that he would have this brilliant, beautiful woman for his own.

His family, though disappointed in his choice to leave the priesthood—his aunt Margaret going so far as to say she was glad his parents were dead and didn't have to know what he had done—had rallied around the newlyweds. The farmhouse filled with hand-me-down furniture, new curtains, the warm smell of tomatoes and basil and the latest family gossip. Eventually, a small stipend from the family's import business began to appear monthly as Eddie and Eleanor's defection paled in comparison to the cousin who was readying for a trip to Sweden pending the outcome of the first sex change operation.

As the newlyweds, alternating between sheepish and defiant in their attitude, drove the two hours to command performances in Newsome, where the Roderi clan gathered three or four times a year, Eddie proclaimed the distance "just far enough," knowing that he and Eleanor would have family support and yet the privacy they wanted. A few months later, as they drove along Rt. 81, Eddie pointed out the sign for Harley. He suggested that in fairness they should stop and just surprise her family. Surely, enough time had passed for their anger to dissipate.

"It's not anger," Eleanor said, not taking her eyes from the road in front of them.

"Then what? What are you afraid of?"

"I'm not afraid. You don't know anything about it."

"This isn't like you. Why don't you want to see them?"

"I have nothing to say. Not to them. And not to you, if you persist in meddling."

"Is it because of—? Do you feel guilty?"

Her eyes darkened with fury. "Don't psychoanalyze me. There's nothing to understand. I didn't belong there. It wasn't a family like you think of family. I left. They weren't sorry and neither was I."

An uncommon cool silence fell between them. Eddie noted the defiant turn of Eleanor's head. Feeling sorry for upsetting her but confused by her anger, he waited.

She looked out across the pond as she spoke. "At Stella Maris—when some of the others would cry with homesickness, I didn't even know what they meant. Away from home, I was happier than I'd ever been. Isn't that enough for you? Can we just drop it?"

Her lost baby came to mind. Eddie wondered if she would ever get over the anger and rejection she had suffered. But he knew his wife well enough to realize further discussion would be frustrating and fruitless. She was as pliant as a lily pad in most situations, but if she felt strongly about something, she had the tenacity of the lily's root. Besides, something told Eddie not to force the issue. He tried to ignore the thread of curiosity—no, more than curiosity, fear—he felt when he thought of Eleanor's life before him. He wondered, too, about his own motives for not asking more questions earlier on. Was he afraid of what he might find out? Had he tried to block out her previous sexual experiences rather than face them? Now who was he analyzing?

That night as Eleanor slept, he walked alone in the woods; he prayed for her safety and happiness. Suddenly he visualized his young wife walking along a path, her dress torn by ever thickening briar bushes— little dots of blood blooming on her bare legs and arms. Above her, a dark bird threatened, swooping down toward her face—closer and closer—and then retreating.

Chapter 22

"Wanna talk about it?" B.J. asked. "Are you sick?" B.J. sat on the edge of her bed and scanned her new friend with concern. Kasia looked like she hadn't slept or showered in days. Her eyes were ringed with purple shadows and her cheeks were sallow.

"I'm okay. Just a flu or something."

"The nurse's in the clinic today. I'll call."

"Don't. Really. I'll be fine in a day or two. I get this sometimes. Maybe from some food that doesn't work for me."

"Flu? Food poisoning? Both possible. Let me know if you need anything, okay?" B.J. began dumping the contents of her duffle bag onto the floor. From amid the pile of musty clothing she extracted a toothbrush, a stick of deodorant, a large bag of peanut M&Ms, two textbooks, and her Week At A Glance appointment book. "Whoa," she said, relief evident in her voice. "I couldn't remember what I did with this. My ass would be grass if I lost it. Might as well lose my mind."

She settled herself on the floor. Using the dirty laundry as a pillow, she lay back and crunched a handful of M&Ms. Then she began leafing through the calendar, planning the tasks ahead of her. She shoved the bag of candy toward Kasia. "So?"

"Nothing, really," Kasia said in response to B.J.'s earlier question. But she was thinking about whether she should tell her roommate about her misadventures in Fenston. She imagined herself beginning the long tale, but the words wouldn't come. Exhausted from her own thoughts, she was incapable of the effort it would take to explain. Maybe the pain would scab over if she slept. She needed sleep. The hole in her life was too raw and painful yet to allow anyone else near it. The comfort she imagined in sharing her problems with B.J. would have to wait. For the time being, Kasia would shoulder them alone. Besides, she reasoned, looking down at B.J. nested in her own dirty laundry, who needs somebody else's psychodrama?

When Kasia had cut all her classes for a week, the college's early intervention system in the person of Mary Turkelson kicked in. Clad in a fringed denim skirt and matching bolero jacket and shod in red cowboy boots, Mary clattered down the third floor corridor of Mitchell Hall and banged on Kasia's door. "Open up right now," she barked in a voice that would have frightened Marine recruits.

Nothing.

"Give it up. I know you're in there."

A slight shuffling sound. Then nothing.

"If I have to get the janitor to take this door off the hinges, there'll be hell to pay." Students, worried that they were somehow the object of Mary's tirade, opened doors. All but 228. Mary banged again. "To the count of ten," she roared and began, "One, two—"

At six, Kasia yanked the door open and Mary stomped in. She opened the blinds and looked around the room, then at Kasia. "You got yourselves quite the pigpen," Mary said as she started to pick up the clothes B.J. had disgorged from her duffle bag five days earlier, the soda cans and empty pizza box from the floor. "And you, kiddo, look like you've been rode hard and put up wet."

When Kasia didn't respond, Mary continued, "Better knock up your cotton. Your uncle filed an MIA. Seems in addition to cutting classes and generally goofing off, you've stopped returning his calls. Just what I need—hysterical calls from Poland. What kind of game are you playing?"

Before she left Poland, they had worked out a system: Piotr would call Kasia before he went to bed at night—around 11. She'd plan to be in her room the hour before dinner to get the call. If she missed it, he'd leave a message and call back the next night at the same time. At first, they'd talked every three days. For the past eight days since figuring out his part in the conspiracy of silence, keeping her in the dark about her parents' situation, she had not answered the phone or written or read any of Piotr's letters. Eight added to the three days before—yes, he was worried. *Good,* Kasia thought. He was already beginning to suffer. *Good,* she smiled to herself. *He deserves it.*

"D'ya think I've got nothing better to do than hike over here to give you what for?" Mary's voice had softened.

Despite her funk, Kasia felt herself beginning to smile at the notion of Piotr's suffering. She turned away so Mary wouldn't see.

"Don't pull this crap on me, young'un, if you know what's good for you. If there's a problem let's hash it out. Otherwise, shape up or ship out. Understood."

Kasia turned to face Mary and nodded.

It was just the opening she needed. She softened her expression and lowered her voice to a sweetly sympathetic tone. "Okay. You were doing great and then suddenly *kaboom.* What gives?"

"Just homesick, I guess." Kasia fell back on the predictable.

"Horsefeathers," Mary barked, returning to her original register. "If you were homesick you'd be all over those calls from your uncle." Realizing that she had not intimidated Kasia as she had hoped, Mary looked exasperated. "I don't have all day. You're not doing drugs, are you?"

Kasia shook her head, guiltily recalling her Yvette-fueled spree.

"Love problems? What?"

Kasia stood mute, looking down at the floor.

"A psych major no less—you should know no matter what it is, we have people trained in helping."

Please God, let her go away, Kasia prayed. *There's no way I'm telling her or the campus shrink anything.*

"Just a slump," Kasia said.

"Don't want to tell me, huh?"

"A slump." Kasia liked the way the word sounded—predictable, reversible, temporary, something like the weather. A slump was what ordinary people with ordinary problems suffered, a little delay in life's progress. Something fixable. A condition that could be rectified with the right attitude. Of course, Kasia didn't think of her own situation that way. Hers was irreparable. Damaged, broken long ago. And now all she could do was try to figure out how to punish those responsible and put them out of her life. Maybe then she could salvage some bit of normalcy. She sure wasn't going to let Mary in on any of it. "Just a little slump. I'll get over it."

"Up to you, if you don't want help. But you better snap out of it or you'll blow this ballgame. Whatever got into you thinking you can lay around and do nothing, get that right out of your head."

Kasia nodded.

"Better do more than nod your head or you'll be on the next slow boat to Poland."

Kasia nodded again, struggling against the giggle she felt rising. How was it that no matter what the situation, Mary was able to make Kasia laugh? Mary walked over and shoved her face into Kasia's. "Agreed."

But Kasia had not been lying around doing nothing. She'd been making a plan. She had every intention of going back to her classes. She would work hard to catch up. But she would not write to or speak to Piotr. And she would find a way to make Hattie suffer too. The notion of their misery made her spiteful heart glad.

"Agreed," she snapped back, thinking, *Rode hard and put up wet. Hash it out. Young'un.* Was the woman really speaking English?

Chapter 23

"Looked for you all over campus."
Nick Morgan stood outside her dorm room door, his face betraying frustration. Kasia noticed his blue oxford shirt neatly pressed and tucked into his worn khakis. Then he smiled, his eyes crinkled pleasingly. "Hi!" And he looked cool despite the brutal September weather.

"Bet you didn't look in the library. That's where I am most of the time."

"Aren't you the excellent student?" he teased.

"Excellent. That would be the air-conditioning." Kasia was enjoying the exchange, proud of her ability to banter so easily with a native speaker. Nick shuffled from foot to foot before her. As she had kept to her resolve about returning to her schoolwork, the fits of depression that followed her discovery had lessened every day. Working hard, she had easily caught up with her studies. Her determination did not extend to tidying her room, which was still in shambles. Regretting the piles of clothes she was readying for the wash and the sloppy sweats she wore, she opened the door. "You might as well come in for a soda. I owe you one."

Nick smiled again and ambled into the room, stepping over the clothes and taking the only chair. "You should see *my* room," he said, as if in answer to her unspoken apology. His frame seemed to take up all the available space between her desk and the bed. Kasia noticed his large hands, clutching a notebook, textbook and pen, the right index finger stained blue along the inside of the tip.

"Can't stay. Bio in ten minutes. Can't cut. I already missed the first class for our family vacation. Just came by to confirm for Saturday."

"Saturday?" Her voice betrayed her confusion.

Nick looked at her in mock dismay. "I know I've been away for a few weeks, but you can't have forgotten."

She had. Of course she had. At his words, their conversation before she drove away from the graveyard came back to her. Had she agreed to a date? She would have said yes to anything, just to get out of there and as far away from that hillside as she could get. Kasia tried to keep the other events of that day out of her thoughts, forcing away the mental picture of those graves, her father's name etched on the headstone. She had tried to rid herself of every thought of that day, every detail. "I didn't know it was Saturday." Had she noticed before the way he held his shoulders as if he were carrying something balanced equally across them? Or the way his nose crinkled when he made a remark he thought funny?

"Four. If we leave then, we won't have to walk miles to the car."

"I don't know," she said. Even if every time she saw Nick she didn't automatically recall that terrible afternoon, he was from Fenston. There was just too much there to contend with emotionally. In her own best interest, she knew she should avoid him and anything to do with Hattie's town.

"No question about it," Nick replied. "A promise is a promise. Wear jeans and sneakers—the hayride can be rough on nice clothes. Four. I'll pick you up outside." He spoke sternly, then smiled. The door shut behind him; the air in the room whirled in his wake.

When the door opened again, B. J., clad in her plaid hockey uniform, rushed to her dresser. "Forgot my socks." She opened the top drawer and started pulling unmatched socks out one by one, obviously hunting for a specific pair. "Was that Neanderthal coming out of here?"

"Yes. Nick Morgan." Kasia felt her face flush as she said his name. "He's okay. The guy that saved me when I ran out of gas with your car."

B.J. stopped and looked back at her. "Yah. So."

"He invited me to go with him to a picnic Saturday. In Fenston." Inexplicably, Kasia felt herself walking on mined territory. Just saying the word Fenston made her feel jittery and off balance.

"And you're going?"

"I guess. Might be fun. Something new."

"A kind of sociological experience?" B.J. triumphantly held up a matching pair of socks. "Eureka."

Somehow feeling like she needed to defend Nick, Kasia said, "He's very nice." But her words sounded trite and unconvincing. She bent to pick up a pair of jeans from the floor beside her bed. Then she dropped them and sat heavily on the side of the bed.

"Just be *careful.*" B.J. exaggerated the word as if putting it in italics, as Kasia might have predicted she would.

"What does that mean?" Kasia was getting a little tired of B.J.'s behaving like an older, wiser sister. She felt them edging toward an argument. It would be their first.

But really, why did B.J. think she was the authority on guys when she hadn't had a date the whole time they'd been roommates? She didn't even talk about guys when all the girls gathered in the television lounge to complain about teachers and homework and dates and to stuff themselves with popcorn and contraband Rolling Rock. And here she was telling Kasia what was good for her. "It *means*"—again the italics—"he just might be one of the local Tarzans."

"Please translate for me?" Kasia's words were icy. "You know us Polish girls are kinda dumb. Especially the blondes."

"Come off it, Kasia. You know what I mean. The kind of guy, I'm sure they have them in Poland and even Connecticut, not just in Pennsylvania hick towns—Tarzan, the kind of guy who has a girl stashed in every settlement of the jungle. Know the type?"

Kasia's reply surprised them both: She burst into tears.

Chapter 24

In the small white lights hung along the path between stalls at the Fenston Hose Company Picnic the night glowed gauzy and full of promise. Nick walked confidently, greeting his friends and neighbors. At his side, Kasia inspected the booths: scouts making candy apples, the sausage and fried dough concession, the ring toss, the big wheel and other games of chance.

Occasionally, Nick's hand brushed hers as they walked. She was trying to heed B.J.'s admonition, but everything Nick did disputed the Tarzan label. When he helped her down from the truck, his touch seemed tentative, almost timid. Kasia was aware of the way men directed their gaze to her ample chest and the slight curve of her narrow hips. In comparison, Nick focused on her face, studying her words and expressions. He referred to things she had told him about her life in Poland. Apparently, he remembered their initial conversation better than she did. The telling sign of real engagement for Kasia was whether people asked questions. If they just listened, they could be thinking of a million other things, waiting their turn to talk. Nick was full of follow-up: What had her high school been like? What were some Polish foods? They chatted and walked along the midway.

The small dark-eyed guy wearing a faded navy shirt bearing the image of a cartoon character above the legend EVERYTHING MATTERS handed Nick a ball. While Nick took aim at the pyramid of bottles, Kasia wondered whether the shirt displayed a bit of wisdom or folly.

If everything does matter, does it matter to the same extent? Does her loss of belief in everyone she loved matter more than Nick's loss at the game? How could anyone live day by day with the weight of so many things mattering? She would force herself to put it all out of her mind—her father, Hattie, Piotr. Maybe the good parts of her new life—her work at Hapwell, B.J's friendship, Nick's kindness and honesty—were enough to make the bad parts fade away.

The Big 6 Wheel ticked someone's luck and someone's loss as the bettors held their breath. Nick was the latter. At the coin toss he won her an immense Tweetie Bird, then led Kasia to a table in the pavilion. "You two sit here," he said, propping the bird on the table between them. Then he disappeared and returned with chili dogs and, as if to make her feel at home, two dishes of pierogi, though the doughy dumplings heavy with butter and fried onions didn't at all resemble the light tangy potato, cheese and onion pies of Warsaw. Even so, she felt a little pang of homesickness for Piotr, who she had dubbed the sloppiest pierogi maker in Poland. For the millionth time she forced herself to banish her uncle from her thoughts.

Insisting that they couldn't even say they'd been to the picnic unless they had a piece of homemade pie, Nick tugged her toward the Chaplin Lake Ladies Auxiliary pie tent, where they studied the list posted on a sheet of butcher paper over the counter. Raspberry and peach were already crossed out. As they were deciding, one of the women working in the tent took a marker and drew a line through coconut custard. "Better think fast," Nick said.

"Blueberry," Kasia responded.

"That'll be two blueberries, Mrs. Welbert."

"Sure you won't mind the blue teeth?"

"Blue teeth and all." Nick laughed and handed money to the woman.

"Nice to see you, Nick. Your mom and dad were here earlier."

"So that's where all the raspberry pie went," Nick said. "Shoulda known to beat my dad to the raspberry."

"How's school?"

"So far, so good."

"So I see." She nodded toward Kasia.

"Better have two coffees to wash it down."

They slid into a space vacated by another couple at one of the waiting picnic tables. The concern over blue teeth aside, Kasia ate with obvious pleasure.

At the first sound of Eleanor's voice, the pie turned to cotton in Kasia's mouth.

"Do you mind?" Eleanor slid onto the bench opposite them. "Hello there," she said, as if she just recognized Kasia.

"Sure thing, Mrs. Roderi." Nick shifted their plates to make room at the table.

"Thanks," she said, still looking at Kasia.

"We'll keep your place for you while you order." Nick didn't seem to notice that Kasia didn't even lift her eyes in acknowledgement.

"You and your friend don't need my company," Eleanor replied.

Eleanor smiled again and edged away toward a group of older people sitting at the other end of the table. Uncomfortable, Kasia kept her head down, even though Nick tried a few times to get her attention. The silence between them grew. "Cat's got your tongue?" he asked. Then he blushed, "I can't believe I said that corny thing—something my grandmother used to say to me."

Finally, Kasia looked up. "We have a similar expression in Poland: *polknelas jazyk*—Did you swallow your tongue? Anyway, no, I was just digesting the pie," she said, scraping the last of the blueberry pie from her plate. Behind the food and past the beer tent a country and western band was warming up. Nick took her hand, and they walked over to the small knot of a dozen young people waiting under a sign: Hayride.

Climbing into the tall wagon was a trick in itself for someone as short as Kasia. After a few futile attempts to get her leg up and over the back fender of the wagon, she let Nick pick her up and toss her gently into the waiting hay. Kasia was surprised at the sweet sliver sting of it against her skin. As more young people arrived, they shifted around in the bed of the truck to make room. Nick introduced Kasia to some of his high school friends.

Just at dusk, a man in a battered tennis hat and suspenders came along leading two dark brown horses to the wagon. He swung up into the driver's seat and turned back to face the riders. "No smoking of any kind allowed. And keep your arms and legs inside the wagon. That's about it for rules. Ready?"

"Careful of the bumps, Mr. Wescott," someone said. Kasia registered the man's name.

"This trip's not for the faint of heart. Just grab onto the person next to you if the going gets rough." He winked and looked around the wagon as if counting heads. "Almost forgot. Jim there has the hat." Someone in the front of the wagon held a fireman's helmet aloft. "It's two bucks a person, three a couple. That's a special sweetheart deal tonight only." He laughed again and tugged the reins and clicked the team into motion. At first, the horses plodded and a rocking carried them out of the fairground and toward a dirt road.

As the wagon gained speed it soon glided smoothly through the tall grass away from the lights of the picnic and into the cool, dense woods behind the fairground. Kasia shivered slightly from the change in temperature; Nick unrolled a blanket from his backpack and wrapped it around her. Like most of the other young couples, they lay back in the straw and looked up studying the sky. Kasia was aware of Nick's blueberry breath, his arm around the back of her shoulders. When she realized he was not going to do anything that she might object to, she relaxed and let the gentle movement of the cart carry her into the pleasure of the night. Voices and laughter from the other passengers floated toward them on the cool night air and reassured her that they were not alone. The canopy of trees darkened until she could not see beyond Nick's face.

"Small towns are like that. Everybody knows everybody else and sits down wherever there's space. Mrs. Roderi wasn't being rude." His voice was quiet and even.

"I know that."

"As soon as she sat down, you changed completely."

"I didn't mind that she sat with us."

"Sure seemed like you did."

"I think she saw some of her friends and went to sit with them. Anyway. No biggie." Kasia practiced one of the slang expressions she'd heard about campus.

In the silence between them, someone worried out a tune on a harmonica. The light reedy sound filled the evening air with longing and sorrow as the notes threaded their way through the branches overhead, rustling the leaves that had already begun to change color. Nick let the conversation drop. Exhausted by the grueling work she'd done to catch up on her studies, Kasia felt herself relax. Yes, this was good. She needed a little fun in her life, to balance the work and worry she'd had since her trip to Fenston. Instead of speaking, she snuggled as Nick drew her close in the fragrant bed of straw. Kasia lay in his arms feeling safe and far away from her troubles. For the second time, she fell asleep with Nick beside her.

Earlier that evening as Nick and Kasia walked away from the pie tent, the air, as if bedeviled by some unseen spirit, rustled the stained paper plates on the tables and one of the Styrofoam cups toppled, emitting a dribble of whitened coffee.

"Such a nice boy," Athena offered of Nick. "Raised right."

"He'd be a good one for her." Eleanor offered. "Smart but not smart-alecky."

The women could have interchanged their lines or discarded them entirely, as they each knew what the other would say. But that was not their way. They needed to say things that went without saying because there was so much that begged to be said which neither of them would give voice to. Athena might have said, "We should have known that she'd find her way over here." And Eleanor might have answered, "Sooner or later, this whole mess will blow up and there will be hell to pay."

A short distance from the food tent, only seconds after Kasia had paused to look back for the second time, something else happened of interest to Athena and Eleanor. The women leaned toward each other, clutched their outdated pocketbooks, peering into the darkening space along the row of such mild amusements as a late summer evening allowed. The two might have looked slightly malevolent as the shock of recognition played across their features.

Blinking their eyes, the women nodded to each other as they noticed one figure step out of the walkway from the parking area into the growing shadow of the dunking tent. For just an instant before she emerged fully into the light of the midway, they had the sensation that they were seeing double. Simultaneously, they recognized Alice Darling.

Had she moved into the lane between the pie tent and the tables three steps sooner, Alice would have brushed the shoulder of the half-sister she had never seen. Did not know existed. A moment earlier and

Betty Tomkins, standing at the counter in the beer tent and looking out into the night, would have noticed the two heads of striking blonde hair. Anyone passing might reflect on two very similar smiles that gave the impression of easy surprise and pleasure. Someone else might muse on the way two women of different stature, nineteen years apart in age, can in the right mischievous light, look like twins. A moment earlier still and Edna Welbert might have imagined that she gazed across the pie stand counter into two pair of eyes the same odd blue flecked with bits of darker gray.

Instead, Kasia and Nick, hand in hand, walked unknowingly away from the place where fate would inexorably draw her. But not just yet. Alice Darling looked toward the path, toward the space where the hay riders and wagon awaited the darkness and their driver. Instead, she sauntered toward the pie tent in the more clearly lit front of the fairground. In the few moments the chance meeting did not take place the swirling air stilled, as if giving the night another chance at the ticking Big 6 wheel. Athena and Eleanor shivered but did not speak of what they had seen, and Betty did not remark on the uncanny likeness of the two blonde daughters of Ben Darling.

Alice took a seat in the pie tent. She put the three pilsner glasses she'd won in the penny toss on the table and turned to the selection list now reduced by not only raspberry, peach and coconut custard, but blueberry as well. She sighed and said, "I guess it will be Dutch apple." Athena and Eleanor made their way through the crowd to Alice's table. Athena waited for her to take the first bite. "Did I poison you?" she asked.

"Great as always," Alice smiled.

"Tom Miller's favorite," Eleanor added, with a wink toward Athena.

"Hear anything from your mother?" Athena's voice was casual.

"Not for a while."

"Any idea where's she's gotten to this time?" Eleanor smiled indulgently at the thought of Hattie the wanderer.

"According to her, she was signing up for duty as a bat counter in Canada."

"Never knew she liked wildlife," Athena laughed.

"Did she say when the drill would be over?"

Alice finished the pie and looked up at her mother's friends. "What about her? Even for Mom, this has been a long silence. But you know how she is when she gets away, she forgets everything else."

"Of all people to catch the travel bug at that late date?" Eleanor mused. "Seems like once she got to going places, she just can't stop."

"I'm all for it." Alice poured milk into her coffee cup. "Everybody needs to get away from time to time. If you see her first, tell her I said hello." She put the plastic fork down on her plate and pushed away from the table.

After Alice left, Athena sighed. "I keep hoping she'll find someone."

"She's always been a loner."

"Yes, she—" Athena stopped abruptly. Then her voice faltered. "Not always, I guess." She stood still, digging a tissue out of the sleeve of her white shirt. "Nope. Not always. Her and Gordie. We were all beside ourselves that they spent every waking minute together. Couldn't keep them apart."

With that, the old wound that had been so long buried in Athena's heart ripped slightly and for a moment she was absent from the evening, from the talk with her friend. Her body sagged as she recalled the grief when the uniformed officer drove into the lot before Westcott's. She'd seen him through the window and began to scream her son's name.

"Now it seems so awful—trying to put the brakes on them. We should have let them—I've even thought that maybe there would have been a baby of Gordie's to love. Kids, we thought, what do they know? But maybe they sensed that there wouldn't be much time."

Understanding the way sadness could overtake Athena, Eleanor led her friend back to their table. Eleanor felt her own sorrow climb into her lap, the heft of a small body against her ribcage. Neither woman spoke. Instead, they sat looking out into the vastness beyond the small town where their lives had played themselves out into late middle age.

Harmonica music came and went as the air moved indolently. "Life is strange, the way it tugs and shuffles. You think you're going one way and before you know it you've ended up someplace completely different." Eleanor sighed and rubbed her forefinger across the oilcloth table cover. "All the philosophy and prayer in the world can't prepare us for what any ordinary day might bring."

"Full of surprises. Wait till Hattie gets back," Athena said.

Again the wind stirred the bushes at the edge of the lighted area. The chill night had begun to loosen the leaves on the fiery maples.

"Oh, Hattie, where are you? The woods are on fire!" Eleanor wailed in mock dismay, relishing her private allusion to that other salesman.

•

Chapter 25

At summer's end, the slow and sleepy Hapwell campus ratcheted up as students scurried between classes, sports, jobs and meals. Kasia had not noticed Nick standing by the door of the library until he called her name. "This is your last chance," he said.

Confused, she looked up. "Last chance?"

He nodded solemnly. "Last opportunity."

"I know what last chance means," she replied tartly.

"This is it, then. Your last chance."

"For what?"

"You don't even know what I'm talking about, do you?"

"Guess not."

"You're not from here so—"

"You mean a foreigner? Just watch it. You know I'm a citizen. Unless you consider Connecticut a foreign country."

"Let's start again." Nick backed down, sensing he had hit a nerve.

She smiled.

"We go on a date and you don't fall asleep on me. Your last and, I'm sorry to say, final chance will be tomorrow. Nothing sleep-inducing like a dark night and a hayride. I want to stack the deck in your favor."

She noticed how flushed his face was. "Where?"

"Can't be a movie; you might conk out before the credits. Or a concert. Too soothing, soooo. It's washing cars. Let's see what you can do with that."

"A date—washing cars?"

"Okay. Maybe you could crawl into a backseat for a quick nap. But I'll keep an eye on you to make sure you're too busy to nap."

"Washing cars? As if I don't have enough schoolwork."

"Science club car wash. Saturday. Proceeds go to fund a bird sanctuary."

"Some date."

"Afterwards, we can clean up and if you haven't dozed off, a bunch of us are planning to drive over to the Crystalle Palace for ribs."

"Maybe I'll fall asleep in my plate after all that activity?" Kasia simulated a loud snore.

They were both laughing when they had to rush off. "Pick you up at 1:30," Nick called over his shoulder.

Kasia was surprised that Nick asked her out again after the picnic fiasco. First she bolted down a plateful of pierogi and an immense slab of blueberry pie; then she embarrassed herself by being rude to that witch from the store to the point that Nick noticed it, and finally after she came out of her snit, she fell asleep in the hayride while every other couple seemed to be making out. When she woke and realized they were almost back to the fairground, she was so mortified she remained speechless. Even though Nick laughed and brushed the hay out of her hair and jacket and kissed her goodnight, she counted the evening an unqualified disaster. Sure she'd seen the last of him, she'd almost felt relief; after all, his Fenston connections might prove uncomfortable for her. Then why had she looked for him on the campus every day, hoping they'd eventually bump into each other? And why did she feel so happy that they had?

That evening, B.J. was sprawled on her bed anguishing over chemistry homework and chewing the split ends of her ponytail when Kasia returned from her last class. She dumped her books on her desk and took a yogurt out of their tiny fridge before she sat down at her desk.

B.J. gazed up. "You look pretty spunky for a Friday afternoon. I'm beat. This book is even more confusing than the teacher. And my lab partner is a nitwit. I'm going to fail out."

Kasia laughed. "Sure you are. Just like you did last year, Dearie Dean's List."

"Seriously. I have to study all weekend just to catch up with where I should have been on Monday. And then it starts all over again."

"Not me. I'm not touching one book until Sunday. I'll work all day if I have to, but I need a break."

"How did the Zoo test go?"

"Okay, I think. I didn't finish the extra credit question, but I think I aced the rest."

"Plans?" B.J. asked, shifting the heavy book to her pillow

"Yeah. Washing cars."

"And I'm going to the ballet."

"No seriously. I'm helping with the Science Club car wash."

B.J. looked up, a smirk on her face. "Let me guess. This was not your idea. Right?"

"But it sounds like fun."

"Another guess: Mr. Muscles from *over yonder*." She nodded in the direction of Fenston.

"Yes again." Kasia felt her annoyance growing as she started to sort through the piles of clothes heaped on the chair by her bed.

"Romance with a capital R."

Kasia felt her face growing red. B.J. really knew how to get to her. "I don't understand why you have to be so mean about Nick. He's really a very nice guy."

B.J. sat up straighter and put the book across her knees. "I didn't know I was being mean. Just saying what I think. So sue me."

"That's what I'm talking about. I just don't get it. Every time Nick's name comes up, I feel like I have to defend myself. And him. What do you have against him anyway?"

"Absolutely nothing. It's just that I don't like seeing you throw yourself at some hick."

"That's not fair. I'm not—there I go again, defending myself. If I want to spend time with Nick, I will. And you can just mind your own damn business." Kasia was fuming. Once she let herself get whipped up, she felt justified to continue. "Anyway, I don't see you introducing me to anyone. I like to have a social life, even if you don't."

"Who said I don't?"

"I've been here since you came back to school, so I know. You haven't been out once. I guess none of the guys around here are good enough for you. All hicks, right?"

"Locals. Townies. Hicks. Whatever. I'm here for an education. And to play hockey. I don't have any time left over for romance." She trilled the last word caustically.

"That's bull."

B.J. leaned over and took the remote from her nightstand, checked her watch, and flicked on the television. In the time they'd been roommates, certain events had become ritual. A rerun of *Gilligan's Island* started and the Professor and Mary Ann hid in the woods to kiss, only to be discovered by Ginger. The roommates laughed companionably, breaking the tension. Kasia moved to sit at the foot of B.J.'s bed for a better view of the tiny screen. At the commercial break B.J. put her head down and began reading.

Kasia, still prickly from their conversation said, "If you have time to watch television and hang around the lounge, you have time for a social life."

B. J. leapt up from the bed as if she had been stung. The textbooks tumbled to the floor with a thud. She crossed the room in three long strides, grabbed her sweatshirt and slammed the door behind her so hard the roller shade flew up and rattled around the rod. Kasia stared after her in disbelief. Until that moment, B. J. had seemed a most placid person.

Kasia replayed the scene in her mind. Surely, nothing she said was strong enough to trigger B. J.'s response. Maybe it was something different in English, Kasia thought. Or it could be the work. Recalling the pressure B.J. put on herself to achieve in sports and academically, Kasia decided that when her roommate returned she'd apologize.

Chapter 26

After changing her outfit six times, Kasia still wasn't satisfied. Why did all her clothes looks like something out of refugee footage on CNN? And how was she to cope with hair that hung flat and plain as a shower curtain? Through a slather of magic mud, she peered at herself in the bathroom mirror and realized that she had developed a huge crush on Nick Morgan. The problem inherent in dating someone from Fenston plagued her. Why couldn't life ever be simple? Why couldn't she fall for some guy from Philadelphia, or better yet, Ohio, someone with no ties at all to the quagmire of her family?

Everything seemed to be going wrong. She and B.J. fought over little things. What had started out as a perfect roommate situation had become a nightmare made worse by the knowledge of how good it had been. She had ruined their friendship with her hasty temper. And now this—falling for a guy who could only mean more trouble of the Fenston variety.

Despite her misgivings about dating Nick, Kasia's heart raced as she washed the mask from her face, curled her long hair, donned the seventh outfit—jeans and a green hooded sweatshirt—and started for the car wash. Hoses, soap, buckets and rags littered the side yard of the science building waiting for the crew to assemble. As soon as he saw her coming, Nick waved a mop and pointed to three cars already lined up waiting their turns. Soon Kasia, Nick, and the others were industrious and wet. Guns and Roses pulsed while they worked under an unclouded September sky.

"Watch out for this one," Nick said, pointing to the car approaching their station. "We would have to get him."

"Who is it?" Kasia asked.

"You're lucky you don't know. Chemistry. Dr. del Ray. If he's half as picky about his car as he is about our quizzes, we'll be here all afternoon to get it right for the measly ten bucks."

"He's the one B.J. is always complaining about."

"I feel sorry for her if she has him for intro. He thinks everyone is preparing to be a research chemist, even if they're only taking the basic course. He runs around the room saying—" Kasia joined in with the one word exhortation she had picked up from B.J.'s complaints about Chemistry class and mimicking her professor— "Method. Method. Method."

They stopped the chant and averted their smiles when Chad del Ray stepped out of his car. A short man with a receding hairline addressed by combing all his remaining hair forward on his head to a small pointed triangle above the space between his eyebrows, he wore corduroy cut-offs, black high top sneakers and a T-shirt that proclaimed him an expert tree hugger. True to Nick's insight, del Ray bent to scrutinize Kasia's progress with his dirty tires. Pointing out spots she'd missed, he said, "Are you the cause of my best student daydreaming when he should be working?"

Kasia looked quickly up at Nick, who either hadn't heard or was pretending he hadn't.

"Must be someone else," Kasia stammered.

"I have my suspicions." He bent again to inspect her effort. "Don't give him too much of a hard time. He'll need all his wits about him for the exam next week."

Kasia had been formulating her reply when suddenly a long piercing siren wailed and everyone stopped what they were doing to look up. "No problem. They're practicing drills and alerts at the firehouse," Nick told them. "Every fall they have an actual burn—some old building that's beyond saving—to test the company's readiness before winter sets in. I think that's next week."

Escaping from del Ray's gaze, Kasia moved to the next car in line, brandishing her steel wool and soapy rag. Satisfied with the job, del Ray paid Nick and drove off.

"I haven't been this dirty in a long time," Kasia said as the last car, an immense station wagon with a rusty tailpipe, gleamed under their polishing cloths. "It'll take me hours to shower it off."

"Fifteen minutes. I'll pick you up for lunch at the Palace. Don't want Pete and Rich to hog all the ribs."

"I don't think I ever met anyone who thinks about food as much as you do," Kasia said. "I bet you even dream a menu: hamburgers, pizza, pie."

"That's not what del Ray thinks."

Kasia reddened. So he had been listening to her conversation with his teacher. Suddenly she felt a happiness she couldn't account for. They'd spent the afternoon working hard and getting dirty. They hadn't even talked very much. Yet she had this feeling of being where she belonged. Everything with Nick felt so easy, so right.

Sitting across the booth from her at the Palace, Nick touched Kasia lightly but deliberately on the hand. Both the intent and the tentativeness pleased her. After the car wash he had changed into fresh jeans and a blue button down shirt worn thin at the collar but carefully ironed. He told Kasia more about the farm, his family—parents and nine year old Caroline. "Caro," he said with a mock serious tone, "a spoiled brat." Kasia pictured his mother standing in a kitchen ironing his shirt, his father at the table drinking coffee from a big green mug and reading to her from the newspaper. Stung with jealousy, she studied Nick's handsome face for something not to like. She failed.

"Sounds perfect," she said. And meant it.

"The folks are okay."

"You don't sound very convinced."

"My dad, anyway. My mom. Well, she's got her own ideas about how the world should run. Her way. If you know what I mean. And if things don't go her way, watch out."

"A woman who knows her own mind," Kasia joked.

"Not so easy for the rest of us sometimes," was all he'd say to clarify his comment.

Full and weary, they drove through Fenston along the road where they had first met on their way back to school. Riding closer to him than she had earlier, Kasia said, "Can we stop again where you showed me that first day?'

"The overlook?" Nick's response was quick and warm.

"Yes."

This time the climb seemed shorter and less steep as Kasia followed Nick on the path. Her sneakers held the ground and she was just slightly out of breath from trying to match Nick's steps when they reached the top. Nick had carried the blanket from the truck and they sat on it, shoulders touching as they looked down at Fenston. The slightest hint of fall mottled the treetops.

"I was going to suggest coming here, but I thought maybe you'd be tired from the car wash. It seems kind of special because of that day we met."

"I'm determined to keep my eyes open." Laughing, she looked at him, bug-eyed. Then she peered down into town below.

"Funny, isn't it?" Nick followed her gaze to the cemetery. "Every time we go there my dad says the same corny thing: 'Cemetery's on the prettiest hillside in Pennsylvania. People are dying to get in.'" And we all laugh.

She smiled, but her eyes scanned the town below, studying the view intensely.

"Looking for anything in particular?"

"Now that you mention it—the store. And your barn. What about those other places?"

"You want me to go through the whole town and tell you who lives where? I don't get it."

"Like for instance, where does that Mrs. Roderi live?"

"Remember you asked me about the quarry," Nick pointed to the dark ridge on the opposite hill. "I told you it's called Eddie's Folly? That's the Roderi place. Just follow the road back from the stone works toward the street and you'll see their house. Pretty much hidden by trees, but you can see the roof and some of their junk cars in the back."

Kasia looked down steadily as if trying to figure something out.

Nick looked at her quizzically. "Anything else, Ma'am? Why are you interested in the Roderis?"

"Just curious."

"Na-ha. You don't ask idle questions. And the way you acted at the picnic when she sat down by us. What don't I know? What's going on? She seemed to know you."

"I met her the day I ran out of gas. I stopped at the store and she was there—" She stopped.

"And—"

"Forget it. It's nothing."

"I don't think I can." Nick spoke slowly, a grudging, melancholy tone to his voice. "Del Ray's on the money. I think about you all the time. Then I go over and over our conversations and well, I don't know how to say this, but something isn't right. The way you acted at the picnic. It just didn't seem like you. Other things too. Sometimes when you don't think anyone is looking, your face is so sad." He put his arm around her, as if to soften his words.

Kasia drew away from him on the blanket and let his arm slide off her shoulder. "How do you know what I'm like? You've only seen me a few times."

"That's true. I don't know the answer. But I feel like I've known you forever. Maybe you think I'm a hick. I'm so clueless that I wouldn't know what's up. But you'd be wrong. I wish you'd tell me what's bothering you."

Kasia read such intensity and honesty and concern in Nick's face that she turned away. Then all the feelings that she'd been contending with alone surged in her and she thought she'd burst if she didn't tell someone. Very softly, she said, "Okay. But you'll be sorry." Immediately, a feeling of relief flooded through her. Then worry. "When you know, you'll see lots of people in a new light, me included."

She sighed and took a deep breath, but when she began her voice was steady and quiet. Kasia spoke of her childhood, the father she'd loved who disappeared when she was eight years old, her mother's death and Hattie, the friend who had seen her through the most traumatic time of her life. At some point, Nick shifted around; instead of sitting side by side, he was in front of her, his face full of empathy. She put her head down as she continued, but he lifted her chin and touched her tears away with his fingertips.

By the time she had finished, the sun balanced on the rim above Eddie's Folly and Nick's face was inches from hers. He waited a few moments and then bent toward her and took her in his arms.

She tried to pull away, but his embrace was firm. Relieved, she re-laxed. Her mouth trembled. "You know what that makes my father?"

"Yes." Nick answered. "But—"

"A bigamist. Can you imagine? I stood right down there and looked at the grave of Ben Darling and it all came crashing in on me."

"You mean—"

"When I saw his name."

"You didn't know—" Nick sounded confused.

"Of course not. Would I have come if I had?"

He drew back. And exhaled a long breath. "Wait. Let me get this right: I brought you up here the first day we met and made some wise-crack about your local relations and you saw your father's grave. And that's when—"

Silently, she nodded.

"I'm so sorry. Oh my God. I'm sorry."

"What for? If I didn't find out then, it was only a matter of time."

In the distance, trucks hummed on the interstate. There was a breeze and a number of small thuds in the woods behind them. Kasia flinched.

"Apples falling." Nick pointed, then dropped his hands into his lap. "There must be more to it than that. Some explanation. I knew Ben Darling when I was a little boy. He was a terrific guy. It's hard to be-lieve—" Nick stopped and put his arm around Kasia again. "You came here to find Hattie Darling?"

"Yes. But we knew her as Hattie Beste. Crazy as it seems, now that I know how she tricked us, I thought she was the most wonderful person in the world. My mom's loyal friend. And mine. I imagined that if I could find her, maybe I could learn about my parents, more than the few vague memories. She had to know something, things an eight year old wouldn't pick up on or recall."

"What did she say?"

"Never got to see her. She's away."

"Right! I heard she's away on a trip."

"Now that I know about her and my father—" Kasia wiped her face with the back of her hand. "Anyway, I can't decide what to do next. I don't even know if I want to see her. But then the next time I think about it, I want to confront her."

"It's hard to believe she'd do something like that."

"You don't believe me?" Kasia's temper flared.

"Of course I do. But she's always seemed kind."

"Seemed. I thought so too. I was wrong."

Kasia relaxed. Her tears stopped.

"I can't imagine what you're feeling. But me, I'd have to have it out with her. It's the only way I'd be able to deal with it."

"That's why I was asking where everyone lived."

Nick nodded.

"Which house is Hattie's?"

"Everyone calls it the Beste place. Her parents lived there—and her grandparents and on back. It's the oldest house in town." Nick pointed beyond the first hill of the Crystalle ridge to a large gray colonial with red shutters in the shade of two large horse chestnut trees. "May be the prettiest too. There's a pond in back. Summers, they'd put up a fish flag. That meant the pond was swimmable. All the kids in town learned to swim there. Mr. Darl—I mean your father—would come out sometimes and horse around with us. Strong guy. Used to be a Marine or something."

"Yes, he was." Then Kasia was quiet for a moment thinking of the shabby row house in Connecticut where she and her mother had lived, had waited through the tormenting heat and poverty of that last terrible summer for her father to return.

Nick took his arm from around her shoulder and lay back on the grass, looking up at the sky. He tugged Kasia back toward him. He hitched himself up on his elbow and studied her face. "You've really had some hard stuff." His voice was tender.

Kasia didn't want to cry again. She needed to be strong, to carry out her plan. She swallowed hard. "I wonder how long she'll be gone? How will I find out when she gets back? I absolutely won't ask that witch Eleanor. She didn't even want to admit that Hattie lived in Fenston."

"Simple." Nick's face brightened, as if he finally would be of help to Kasia in this quest. "Alice will know."

The mention of Alice's name flooded Kasia with a long buried memory. One evening she and her mother and Hattie were in the backyard of the house in Connecticut. It was before Piotr arrived. Her mother and Hattie sat on the porch steps watching Kasia practice hopscotch.

They spoke softly, then they grew quiet. Beyond the yard and the vegetable garden the summer noises of their alley—cars and music and people talking in Spanish—rose up, comfortingly ordinary. Fireflies hovered and disappeared.

Suddenly, Hattie was beside Kasia explaining a game she used to play with her own daughter, Alice. Statues, she called it. Laughing, her head back, her auburn hair swirling around her neck and shoulders, Hattie took Kasia's hands in hers and twirled her around and around in the summer twilight.

Kasia liked the game. With her mother watching from the near darkness, she and Hattie spun and whirled, feeling the night air damp and sweet on their faces. Revolving as they could, they spun away from the orbit they shared. From somewhere in her own spinning Hattie would call out the word *statue* and Kasia froze, inventing attitudes of grace and fear and surprise wherever she landed.

With Nick's words and that memory, something new entered the equation. Kasia, the vengeful orphan, froze once again, this time stunned by the knowledge that living in the pretty gray house just a mile away was the sister she had never known.

She thought of Hattie. Then pictured her father splashing in a country pond with a group of children. Jealousy, grief and longing rose like bile in her throat when an idea started to form, like the answer to a question she had not even thought to ask. A word formed on her lips. And another. Soundlessly, she ran her tongue across them, tasting the blend of sounds. Had she spoken aloud? She glanced at Nick but he was looking away, unaware.

She said, "Yes, Alice." Then he did look over, pleased at the reaction to his suggestion.

"Alice," she said again, as if making up her mind.

The other words were silent. So precious she was holding them inside herself, learning their syllables. Together the words formed a scene on the screen of her imagination: *Alice. My sister. Revenge.*

Chapter 27

Eddie walked through the arbor examining the vines, feeling the slight pop of the grapes' sweetness with the pressure of his fingers. In a few weeks, they would be ready. He would harvest and press them and have the best homemade red wine in the county. *The Collected Poems of Wallace Stevens* was open before him to page 255; he leaned over the picnic table and quietly but slowly tested the words, uttering them three, then four, then five times:

> *The law of chaos is the law of ideas,*
> *Of improvisations and seasons of belief.*

The pages fluttered in the wind, and he looked down again and steadied them with his hand, staining the pages.

In the week since Eleanor's fall as she showed signs of recovering, he had begun to relax. But he knew he was kidding himself. Like past patterns, she'd almost seemed back to herself, then something would set her off. Her obsession about the child at first was constant, as if once having given voice to her loss, she could not stop. For a few days, it seemed to lessen. But he knew well enough that this was only a hiatus.

When he saw Frederick Chrissman's car coming toward him, Eddie felt a small thump of panic in his chest. He walked over to the driveway and motioned his friend to the parking area behind the house. Suddenly, Eddie was second guessing his meddling into Eleanor's past.

Frederick bounded from the car and shook Eddie's hand with a warm priestly grasp. Eddie drew his old friend with him toward the farmhouse. He hadn't imagined Frederick would come in person. What if he had not been home? Eddie stopped halfway through the backyard just out of earshot of the kitchen. "Before we go inside, I want to tell you that Eleanor has no idea that I was looking for information about the baby."

Frederick's eager, friendly gaze changed to one of confusion. "I thought you said she was—is—upset about it."

"Absolutely. But I didn't want to get her hopes up about finding anything. Not until we did."

"Makes sense," Frederick said. "And, as it turns out, just as well."

"Oh." Eddie studied the other man's face. Behind him, he could see into the bright kitchen where Eleanor was working at the stove. It occurred to Eddie that Frederick might have come at dinnertime on purpose. He remembered the quiet dinners he had eaten alone in the rectories where he'd served and realized that they had not invited Frederick in more than a year.

"I was right about where the child would have gone. All the parishes in the diocese sent their babies to the Marian Nursery. No exceptions. But there was no baby brought to the nursery on August 10, 1955. Not one. And none in the two week period on either side of that date. An anomaly, according to Mother Susan Rafter. During the 1950s they averaged about five children a month, but none during that four-week period. I had her dig farther, and she said there was not one baby from St. Bartholomew's Parish during the entire month."

"How can that be? Eleanor was certain of the date. Six weeks later she was already at Stella Maris."

"If it had been better news, I would have phoned. But since I thought it might be upsetting, I decided I'd better tell you in person."

"I appreciate your help and concern." Eddie had the feeling Frederick was lingering, then he too smelled the aroma of the dinner Eleanor was preparing. "You'll stay of course. Eleanor will be glad to see you. You might just cheer her up. We had a young fellow staying with us for a bit. For a while, that took her mind off the baby. He and his sister went to stay—"

"Let me guess—with Gloria."

Eddie laughed. "You are correct."

After a half-hearted demurer, Frederick followed Eddie into the kitchen and surrendered to the warm enveloping blandishments of Eleanor Roderi's roast beef and peach pie.

Still beautiful despite some added girth since the last time Fredrick had seen her, Eleanor held up her floury hands to brush her long hair away from her face with the back of her wrist. The pale skin around her gray eyes crinkled in accustomed smile lines. "I must have known that if I made a fine meal, the Lord would provide the guest."

Frederick recalled the days and months after Eddie and Eleanor left the religious life, the scandal, titillating gossip that spread like the scent of incense from pew to pew. Eleanor was pregnant, ready to give birth, and they had to leave. Eddie had seduced a string of young nuns. The two of them had been into witchcraft and were caught and banished by the bishop. On it went, one scenario after another. Once, before they left, before anyone knew about the connection between the novice and the chaplain, Frederick happened to see them together at a religious festival. They were standing with a group of children waiting to board a bus. Though engrossed in the task of collecting tickets and checking off names, they were an island unto themselves. As he walked toward them he sensed the immense heat of their combined lust and beauty. And within himself, a longing for something he'd never experienced arose. When the word went out that they had left together, he recalled that afternoon. Nor was he surprised all these years later—in the way Eleanor looked toward Eddie and he smiled at her, at the way he took the silverware from her hand to set the table, in the slow way she still teased out his name—by the longevity of their love.

After the meal, Eddie took out the grinder and ministered to the antique espresso machine his parents had brought back from their wedding trip to Italy. Frederick said, "It's been so wonderful. This evening. A real gift. I hate to ask another thing. But—" he nodded his head toward the alcove between the dining room and the living room. Sheet music and recipes and newspapers were piled on the closed cover of the baby grand; the bench was the resting spot for a number of unfinished needlework and sewing projects. In a few minutes the space was cleared and Eddie sat at the keyboard and began to play.

"I must have sensed that you were coming," Eddie said. "I've been playing a lot of Chopin lately."

Frederick smiled that Eddie had recalled his favorite piece. Eleanor drew him to a comfortable chair and handed him a thimble of anisette and set a small white cup of thick, fragrant espresso on the table at his side.

As Fredrick sipped and listened, Eddie's music flooded him with longing. He glanced around the room, every surface filled with mounted stuffed creatures, bric-a-brac. Generations of Roderi family photos smiled down on him. Behind the piano, the wallpaper had buckled and was coming away from the wall. In such splendid disarray, two talented and loving people had passed their lifetime. A part of his fussy, priestly sensibility shuddered to think of the stacks of magazines he had glimpsed on the porch, the dingy dishtowels with which Eleanor had swiped her counters, the spider webs in the corner untamed by anyone as careful and fastidious as Mrs. Metz, his housekeeper.

The music floated around him. Eleanor had perched on the edge of the bench next to her husband. Frederick closed his eyes and thought about the way life moves away day-by-day and the evening he would have spent alone. Imagining the rooms of his rectory, perfect as a stage set. Empty and perfect. A place where it must appear a life is being lived. But was it? He felt a welling up within himself and was grateful that Eleanor and Eddie seemed to have forgotten, in their connection to each other, that he was in the room. Despite all the years of sermonizing and public speaking, he would not have trusted his voice not to betray the sorrow and longing he felt, the ache for something utterly human and fleeting.

It was past midnight when Eddie walked the priest out to the car. Despite the August air, cool and moist on their skin after the heat of the parlor, the men lingered saying goodbye. "You're troubled, Eddie."

"Yes. I don't know where to go next with this thing."

"Whether to tell her you made inquiries and what you came up with?"

"While I was playing I could feel Eleanor there beside me. She's the most true, substantial thing in my world." Eddie's voice creaked. "I can't bear to see her in such agony. Who would have thought—after all this time—"

Frederick knew to wait until his friend could bring himself to articulate his reservation.

"I feel so disloyal even thinking it, but—" Again, Eddie broke off.

He put his hand up and ran it through his hair. Frederick looked away. "The idea came to me—what if, just what if, there had never been a child at all?" He exhaled fiercely. "I can't imagine how I'm capable of such a thought. But there it is."

"That would be one explanation. Learning there was no record. Of course you'd wonder."

Eddie felt relief that his friend understood.

"I've been a priest for a long time. I don't have to tell you, just when I think I've heard it all, something comes along to challenge it. But this."

Eddie nodded, relieved that Frederick understood. "How could it not be true? Why would—"

"I don't know." Eddie looked back at the house, as if appealing to Eleanor for clarification.

"Could there be another answer? Something we haven't thought of. Maybe she was sent somewhere else? Or she forgot the date? Many possibilities."

"The problem is what should I do now? Every time I think of it—"

"I've been puzzling it out all evening. You're probably not going to like my suggestion."

"I'll consider anything."

"You need to see Joe McGill."

The image that sprang to Eddie's memory was of the smug, self-satisfied young priest, a teacher at the seminary Eddie had attended. A man most of the seminarians disliked and feared.

"He has a heart condition. Like me. Had surgery a few months ago. He's living at St. Simon's."

The name of the place where Eddie had spent six years preparing for the priesthood brought back those long ago times with a sweet pang. "He's teaching?"

"You really have to keep current with diocesan changes. When vocations diminished they turned the place into a home for old and cranky priests. Time hasn't improved him. He's a curmudgeon and it will be a long trip. But he's still sharp. He was at St. Bart's in '55 and has a steel-trap memory about his parish. He may have the answer."

Unwilling to part, the two old friends stood listening to the night. Deer slid into the tree line, calling to each other in their high grieving voices. Somewhere at the edge of the swamp across the way a loon echoed confusion and longing to a great applause of wings. Standing in the driveway in front of Frederick's sensible Ford, Eddie looked across the drive at Eleanor's old pink monstrosity, the car that had given her so much pleasure. The contrast seemed somehow a symbol of the life he'd chosen. He was overcome by the bond he felt with his old friend, faithful through all their differences.

Frederick climbed slowly behind the wheel and Eddie strode toward the house. He swept his arms wide as Frederick backed slowly down the driveway. *"Lux et veritas,"* Eddie called. When he reached the back porch, Eddie threw a switch. Hundreds of tiny colored bulbs illuminated the backyard and the deck. White lights traced the graceful, knobby branches of the birch trees casting generous shadows on the grass and intensifying the color of the first fallen leaves. Red bulbs traced the roofline of the shed behind the house. Blue and green blinkers twined the porch posts. Frederick's beams blinked a weak response to the gaudy panoply of Eddie's farewell.

A spasm squeezed Frederick's heart while he drove home. As it mounted he didn't know if he could prevent himself from pulling off the road and calling for help. But he drove on, parked the car, and entered the rectory. When the pain lessened, he understood his reaction as disappointment. He undressed and brushed his teeth and hung his clothes in the closet. He knelt on the floor beside his bed and began his evening prayers—not the required daily office, but his own meandering invocations as he revisited moments throughout the day and back into time, lighting on a scene recalled from childhood, a joke, a bit of wisdom, a thought he'd had about the article on images of Mary and womanhood he was writing for *The Catholic Light.*

Frederick thought again about the flow of energy between Eddie and Eleanor and the home they had made, an accidental monument to history, hope and theater. He recalled how they sat across from each other, their heads inclined as if including him in their expectation that the next moment might be filled with wonder.

Soon an egregious thumping resumed in his heart. He forced his attention away from it and back to the prayers. Sweat blossomed warm then cooled on his skin. Concentrating, he mentioned every living being he could think of and then his own pitiful wants. Since his first heart attack eight years earlier, he had known it would end this way. Giddy with pain and excitement, he knew he should phone for help but couldn't think why he might want to.

McGill came into his thoughts. Had he mentioned the old priest? He said a quick prayer for him as he imagined days at St. Simon's stretching before him. Eventually that would be his own fate too, unless he could endure the pain a few more minutes. Surely he'd lose consciousness and go beyond it. Was doing nothing a sin? If it was, he hoped he'd be forgiven. Nauseous, his flesh clammy, he forced himself to push the pain to the edge of his consciousness.

Frederick's head felt heavy and he leaned his cheek on the nubbly white spread, recalling that as a child he had knelt in that same position to pray before sleep. Then his mother's voice spoke to him out of the darkness. It did not concern him that he couldn't understand the words. The *sh-sss-sii-shhh* sound helped him recall the way her mouth formed the syllables of their evening prayers.

The small seam of light coming from under his door gave him the sense that all was well, that someone beyond his room was looking out for the world, for his friends, for him in his sinfulness, sorrow and longing.

Chapter 28

On the drive into Scranton, Eleanor and Eddie told Billy and Tina about Sister Gloria and her place, where they would be guests. Harmony House turned out to be a large red brick row house, anonymous among many on the long city block. When Sister Gloria stopped hugging her, Eleanor turned to draw them into the conversation. "These are my dear friends, Tina and Billy Fallon. New in the area. Eddie and I entrust them to you until they can get on their feet. I know you'll be glad they're with you," Eleanor said in her precise and calm way.

And with that, Billy and Tina, now dressed in clothing supplied by Eddie and Eleanor, morphed from the poor unfortunate homeless kid and his stripper sister to a brother and sister, friends of respectable and well-loved people in the community. People who just happened to need a place to stay for a while. Billy knew by the way Sister Gloria looked them over that something had happened between her and Eleanor, but they had exchanged information and he and his sister were the beneficiaries.

Sister Gloria had taken them on. She smiled and led the way to their rooms. Eleanor and Eddie followed, commenting on how good the place looked. "Praise the Lord and pass the mashed potatoes," Sister Gloria giggled. "We've got some dynamite sponsors. This year we were able to fix the plumbing. Now we won't have to hike to the outhouse in the middle of the night."

For just a moment, Billy took her seriously. Then she opened the door to a bathroom so new it still smelled of paint. "At the moment, there's nobody in the other two rooms that share this bath. You two'll have to christen it." Everything amused Sister Gloria.

At the door, Eddie and Eleanor said goodbye. "We'll pick you up at noon on Sunday so we can catch up and have the day together," Eleanor said. When they turned to leave, she teared up and Billy felt his hands hanging at his sides. He wanted to put his arm around her, but held back.

"Here," Eddie said, thrusting some papers into his hand. "Don't get rusty on me. See you Sunday."

"By then, you'll be ready for a real meal," Sister Gloria added.

The high ceiling and fan kept the room cool, despite the brutal weather that had settled into the area the week before. Big and airy and quiet, soft blue walls with white curtains, a room to himself right next to Tina's, the shelter was nothing like Billy had imagined. He'd never lived in a city before, even a small one, and opening his window and looking out into the street below brought instant entertainment.

His bed was the bottom of a double decker. Sister Gloria had explained that normally families only got one room, but because of Billy and Tina's ages and low demand for shelter during the summer months, they would each have a room. If another family with a boy of similar age showed up, they would share the room. Billy didn't know what to think about that. He was lonely during the hours Tina was at her new job and might like someone around. Depending on the person. He wasn't sure.

Once he settled in and unpacked—laying the other pair of jeans and the shirts and socks and underwear Eleanor had insisted on buying him in the top drawer of the dresser, he put his comb and toothbrush on top, leaving four drawers and the nightstand empty. From his duffel bag, he withdrew his last few possessions: a tiny travel chess board, a copy of *Catcher in the Rye*, a tablet and pencil, a bright blue bandana, and a harmonica, all gifts from Eddie. At the bottom of the bag lay his newest acquisition, also a gift from Eddie, brand new, still in the case. Billy slipped it from the pouch and palmed the pocket watch, appreciating its heft and gravity. He set it on the dresser and sat on the bed and looked at it. Then he got up and put it back into the box and stashed it under his clothes in the drawer.

Sister Gloria tapped at his door. "Dinner in fifteen minutes," she said. For the first time in his life, Billy felt special.

As hard as it had been to think that Eddie had been a priest and Eleanor a nun, it was even more difficult to square the image of the woman dressed in cut off jeans and a Smurf T-shirt, running shoes and white socks with his notion of nuns. Sister Gloria defied age. Her blondish hair was chopped haphazardly around a heart-shaped face dominated by gray green eyes swimming behind large red-framed glasses. In contrast to Eleanor's soft, slow voice, Sister Gloria cackled a laugh at the end of most of her sentences.

"Lucky you came when there was a lull in the action. Afternoons are quiet around here." Indeed, the sitting room—furnished with two overstuffed sofas, a loveseat and four chairs, a television and bookshelf against one wall—where they met and the kitchen she led them through were empty. "House rules," she said, handing Tina and Billy each a copy of the small booklet. "Read 'em and weep," she laughed. Then her tone shifted. "You can let me know at breakfast what jobs you'd like. Anything's negotiable, except cleaning up the bathroom after yourself. Gluey drains just don't hack it around here." Again the laugh.

On closer inspection, Billy's room contained some amazing accoutrements: a boom box, an easy chair with a floor lamp next to it and a small desk. He looked at the papers Eddie had given him and saw that they were postcards addressed to Eddie. The other side read: NG1–F3. At first Billy didn't understand. Suddenly, he recalled Eddie's words as he thrust the paper into his hand—"Don't get rusty." Each card bore a different chess puzzle.

Smiling, Billy went to his desk, pulled out the chair, and began to lay out his board. He moved Eddie's knight to the third rank, to comport with the card. Then he puzzled over his response, weighing and evaluating, moving various pieces to test them out against Eddie's opening, but always keeping his finger on the piece. Finally, he moved his pawn from D7 to D5, exhaled and lifted his hand from the board. He could imagine Eddie clasping his hands together as he looked across the board to examine Billy's move. He could hear the short whistle of breath as Eddie decided what he would do next.

When he reported for dinner, a woman and three little kids were seated at the dinner table, and a high chair was pulled up beside it. Another woman stood at the counter next to Sister Gloria, cleaning celery and chopping carrots into small strips. A steady stream of talk flowed between the work area and the table as Tina and Billy arrived in the kitchen. On the counter, a sliced ham waited. When the aroma hit Billy, he realized how hungry he was.

During the time he had been with the Roderis he had begun to appreciate food, not just to fill himself up but to savor the taste of a dish well-prepared. Throughout his childhood, he had subsisted on a diet of Twinkies, Cheerios, SpaghettiOs, and sandwiches—Fluffernutters, peanut-butter-and-jelly and cold cuts. Now it seemed like he was always hungry. He felt saliva flood through his mouth in answer to the tangy scent of the ham.

Hands swaddled in enormous gray mitts, Sister Gloria opened the oven and took out a casserole of baked macaroni and cheese. "Gang way, hot stuff coming through." She slid across the room and planted the dish on a trivet in the center of the table.

The two boys stopped racing matchbox cars between them and looked up. "Justine and her kids, Alley and Mark. Helen and Bobby." Sister Gloria pointed her wooden spoon at each as she introduced them. "This is Bobby's sister, Gloria-Two." She planted a kiss on the head of the bald baby in the highchair, who responded with delighted gibberish. "Everybody, meet Tina and Billy. We're first names here," she said as she motioned them to seats at the table.

The room fell silent and they bent their heads. Sister Gloria even made wisecracks in her prayers. "God, thanks for this hot kitchen, this food which I hope we made enough of, these hungry souls, and the new showers. We need all the help we can get. Anybody else have something to say?"

A small voice that belonged to Helen spoke. "Gloria Two got her first tooth. Thank you."

Mark, who had stopped the car race in deference to the prayer, said, "We went to the pool today. Thanks."

"And are having ice cream. Thanks," added Bobby, looking up at Sister Gloria mischievously.

Billy looked around the table—Sister Gloria in her odd costume, the other women, the children, Tina, dressed in a tan skirt and brightly colored blouse, scratching absently at the remaining cluster of poison ivy on her wrist—and realized it was a room full of women and children, and he was the closest thing to a man in the house.

Chapter 29

Balancing her packages two on either side, Kasia hurried toward the student activity van at the back of the parking lot. During the hours she'd been inside the mall the weather had turned warm. She lifted her hair away from her sweaty neck and loosened her sweater. Then she quickly stowed her bags on the floor in front of her.

"Buy enough?"

"Nu-huh."

Gudrun smirked. "I don't know how we got separated. One of us must have wandered off. Bargain coma, I guess. You forget everything else."

"I looked for you—"

"Me too."

"Great sales. Wait'll you see this." Kasia pulled a purple turtleneck out of one of her bags and a pair of button front Levis from another. "How about you?"

Laughing, Gudrun poked her hand into one of her bags and felt around. An identical pair of Levi's emerged. "We were probably in next door dressing rooms."

"Aren't they cool?"

"But I have to stop. I'm spending too much. Every week I'm buying something else."

"Check this out," Yvette, almost hidden behind an enormous pile of shopping bags, squealed as she held up a blue suede jacket and matching cashmere scarf.

"Cool." Kasia fingered the soft fabric and held it to the light to appreciate the color. "Must have cost a fortune."

Yvette raised her eyebrows in response. "What do you think? It's not a K-Mart special," she said, pleased to use the punch line of one of the jokes going around school.

"Fashion show over?" Mary corkscrewed in her seat and peered into the back of the van. Then her sweet tone shifted. "Buckle up right now. New clothes and all—you wouldn't want to be a hood ornament, would you?"

During the fifteen-minute ride from the Viewmont Mall, Kasia glumly began to total her purchases and mentally revisited her bank account. Like Gudrun, she'd been spending wildly. Nothing she brought with her from Poland seemed suitable for the life of a college student in America. In her old clothes she had felt self-conscious and nervous as she looked around at the other students. Shopping was the only solution. Each week, she and Gudrun and Yvette were at the head of the line to take the shuttle to the mall so they could add to their "acceptable" wardrobes. Unlike Yvette, who seemed to have unlimited funds and craved luxury items, Kasia bought only things she felt were absolute necessities, shopping store to store for the best bargains. Still, the purchases added up. Now she was facing a difficult problem. As soon as she understood Piotr's complicity in keeping her father and Hattie's secret she wanted to break off her relationship with her uncle. But she needed the check he sent. She'd have to figure out some way to make money on her own.

When the bus pulled into the Mitchell Hall lot, Mary said, "Looks like somebody's company's cooling his heels." Kasia leaned over to look out the window. Nick was tossing a Frisbee with two of the guys from the next dorm. He had taken off his sweater and his hair was mussed and sweaty. *Handsome*, Kasia thought. *So, Mary knows that I'm seeing Nick. No such thing as a secret around here.* A little shoot of pride flashed inside her.

Nick stopped playing when he saw the van approaching and peered inside trying to locate her. When they stopped, he slid open the door and laughed at the sight of the young women amid a plethora of shopping bags. "I thought you'd be studying and I'd rescue you and take you out for dinner," he said as he took the bags from her and held her hand as she jumped down from the van. "And all this time you were being a mall rat?"

"Mall rat?" Kasia said. "Doesn't sound very nice."

"People who hang out at the mall. Fluorescent tans. Long arms from carrying too many packages. You know the type."

"I was just there for a little retail therapy," she said, repeating the phrase B.J. had used earlier. "Shopping makes me hungry. Where are we going?"

"I don't know if I should tell you. You might not want—"

"Anything would be fine." Kasia handed him two of her bags and started for the door.

Nick followed. "My house," he said.

"Huh?"

"I knew you'd say that."

"All I said was 'huh.'"

"But I know what it means."

"What?"

"What what?"

"What do you think I meant?"

"Looks like you got mail," Nick said as they passed the mailboxes in the lobby.

Kasia snatched the letter postmarked from Poland and shoved it into her bag.

"My competition?"

"My uncle." She paused at the elevator, then punched the button.

"You know—my mom and dad and my sister. My house." He resumed their previous conversation.

"Sounds good."

"Really?" Nick's voice brightened.

"Why not?"

"I didn't think you'd want—"

"Are you inviting me or warning me? Maybe you don't really want me to come and you're projecting your feeling onto me."

"Thank you, Dr. Freud." Nick smirked. "Are you trying to psycho-analyze me? I took Psych 101 last year, remember. I'm miles beyond that."

Kasia opened the door to her room, relieved that B.J. was out. When she turned to take the packages from Nick, he bent to kiss her. Her arms went up around his neck. They stood embracing for a few minutes.

She brushed her cheek against his. "What time?"

"Now."

A tweak of anxiety coursed up the back of her legs and reflected in her expression.

"That's more like it," Nick said. "A little jitters—just the right reaction."

"From your description, I know they are great. But still—"

"Like I said. Wouldn't be normal if you didn't feel a little nervous about meeting the folks."

So this is where we are, Kasia thought. They hadn't even slept together, yet they were at a threshold. Nick's parents wanted to meet her; obviously they thought she was important in his life. Or maybe it was different in America. Maybe you didn't have to be exclusive or deeply involved for the parents to invite you for dinner. So much about life as an American college student was confusing. Who could she ask? She thought of Mary. She didn't want Mary to know so much about her life. Besides, Mary's advice would probably be rendered in such oblique idiom that Kasia wouldn't understand it anyway.

B.J. Suddenly Kasia longed for one of their heart to heart talks, those long meandering nighttime discussions that had no focus, beginning or end, but that were so satisfying. The talks that had ceased with the big argument. Since that night they had kept all their discussions on a superficial level. She missed B.J.'s wit and friendship, her common sense advice.

"Twenty minutes?" she asked.

Nick nodded. "I'll be outside with Fred and Jim. Twenty minutes, tops, right?"

Quickly, she unpacked her things and put the letter with the growing packet of similarly unopened envelopes on her desk. The importance of the dinner grew like a haywire experiment in a petri dish while Kasia showered and dressed in her new jeans and turtleneck.

She brushed her blonde hair and caught the sides back with butterfly clips. She fussed at her makeup, first applying it, then scrubbing it off to start again. She settled on blush and lip gloss only.

By the time she spritzed on some Coty Musk she'd bought that afternoon, the prospect of her visit to Nick's house had grown into a frightening monster. What would they think of her? Would she disgrace herself and forget, as she occasionally did, the English word for some common thing? She pictured herself passing Nick's father the sugar bowl and saying "Salt?"

Was the sweater too tight? Would the button front jeans pop open when she sat? Should she eat a lot or a little?

An eight-year-old waving pompoms greeted them. "Kasia, this is Caro, the bratty little kid I told you about," Nick winked.

"Big shot."

"Squirt."

"I'll get you for that." Caro grabbed his arm and swung around. He lifted her foot off the ground as she squealed in pleasure.

"Are you a cheerleader?" Kasia asked.

"Midget football."

"That's a really nice outfit," Kasia said.

"We're getting ready for the first game on Saturday afternoon. Wanna see?" Her short blue and white skirt swirled around her thin legs as she kicked and bellowed, "TWO-FOUR-SIX-EIGHT, WHO DO WE APPRECIATE—THE LAKERS, THE LAKERS, THE LAKERS!" Then she spun forward into a cartwheel and landed in a split at Kasia's feet and beamed in anticipation of their appreciation.

For Kasia, finding her way back to what her life would have been like if her father hadn't disappeared, if her mother hadn't died, if she hadn't gone to Poland to live for ten years, was just that simple. She had been exactly Caro's age when she left Hartford. Kasia felt tears behind her eyes, remembering a little of that time. She forced them back. Maybe she could satisfy her curiosity through Nick and Caro. She might see what her life would have been like if she'd had a normal family.

"Cool jeans," Caro said to Kasia when she finished the cheering. She spun around a few times and then stopped to look Kasia up and down. "I like your hair, too. Mom says mine may not stay blonde when I'm older. If it doesn't I'll put bleach on it. I like skiing. Do you?" Caro's rapid-fire chatter reminded Kasia of the afternoon she met Nick.

"I've never done it. But I think it would be fun."

"Come on." Ignoring her brother, Caro led Kasia around the side of the house to the deck where a table was set for dinner. Nick followed in amused silence. Kasia stood listening to the child's detailed description of her third grade classmates and looking out over the farm, the distant circular hay bales glinting in the late afternoon sun.

Nick's mother held the kitchen door open for his father, who carried an immense wooden tray piled high with serving plates, pitchers and condiments. His mother's face was animated and friendly. She held out her hand to Kasia and his father did the same, saying, "Welcome." The word diminished in the air and no one else seemed able to say anything more.

Kasia felt her face warming under the gaze of Nick's parents. They were young, Kasia thought, much younger than she expected anyone's parents to be. Nick's mother said to call them Grace and John. Would she like some iced tea?

She had avoided this scene so many times in Poland. Whenever she found herself dating anyone for a period of time, when the era of meeting the parents began, she broke off the relationship. Kasia had been certain what she was about, and her plans for the future didn't include getting involved and losing the focus of her dream to go to America.

The other thing that held her back from being absorbed into someone else's clan was harder to accept: How would it feel to be in a family, even an unhappy one like Georg, her last beau in Poland, had described? She could only imagine dragging some guy home with her to meet Uncle Piotr, how uncomfortable and stiff they would be. The thought stung her with self-pity, shame for having a strange life. Somehow she had let herself forget those old fears when Nick asked her to meet his parents. After all, Piotr was on the other side of the ocean. He didn't know what she was doing and she intended to keep it that way. Since she learned of his treachery, she recalled that he had sent her mother to America against her own will. He was the past that she could do nothing about, part of what she would banish from her mind, forgetting him completely. Now she would make a life for herself.

Feeling like a bird with a wounded wing, she looked around at this very regular, very American family. Speechless. If she could have given language to her thoughts, she would have said, "Yes, I will have this for my own." Instead she smiled and said yes to grilled chicken, candied sweet potatoes, salad and sweet corn.

"Our own corn and greens," John said, smiling at her with the same guilelessness that she loved in Nick, as if all the pleasures of the world had been universally agreed upon and he was offering them to her.

"I thought you'd talk really funny but you don't," Caro offered.

"Me too," Kasia said, and everyone laughed.

Kasia did not call anything by the wrong name. The words were there whenever she opened her mouth. She looked out toward the driveway where she and Nick had first met. His family was as kind and accepting as he had been that first day. When she complimented the chicken Grace asked what kinds of food she missed most from Poland, and John voiced an interest in the country's public transportation system.

After dinner while John and Grace went into the barn to do chores Caro and Nick and Kasia did the dishes. Kasia peered around the kitchen, curious about the way Nick's family lived. The room was large and bright, obviously the center of family activity. Caro's schoolbooks were scattered on the counter, a tablet open to a page of half-completed homework next to them. Off the kitchen, she glimpsed a washer and dryer and freshly ironed shirts hanging in a row. Beyond the kitchen, the living room's pale yellow walls and blue rug, the chintz overstuffed sofa and loveseat, the framed family photos on the breakfront, spoke of care and modest comfort.

Everything about their life seemed organized, easy. Nick's mother worked part-time as a receptionist in a local doctor's office and his father farmed and during the winter worked the road snow crew. Though not lavish, their home was attractive, and Kasia had the sense that the dinner she had been invited for would have been the same without her, perhaps with the exception of the chocolate cake.

The only odd moment of the evening came when Grace answered the phone—a long conversation about whether she could find people to help picket something the following week. Kasia tried to listen, but Caro absorbed so much of her attention that she was only able to get snatches of the exchange. When Grace hung up the phone, she came back into the room smiling, just as John's mood had shifted. He looked up as she entered and remarked, "The cats sharpening their claws, Grace." She gave him an evil look and they both retreated to the kitchen for some heated whispering. Kasia wondered whether Nick would talk about it, but by the time he drove her home, taking the back roads slowly so he could stop along the way to kiss her, his parents' quarrel had slipped from her mind.

Though neither Kasia nor Nick had forgotten about it, they had spent the entire evening without once referring to Kasia's Fenston situation. As Nick pulled up in front of the dorm, she realized it was the perfect time to ask him a favor.

Chapter 30

"OK. Don't get all steamed up about it. I'll wait here," Nick said. He took his chemistry book from the floor and began to riffle through the pages. "Have to review six chapters—a cumulative test next week." He had parked the truck under a maple. An orange leaf fluttered onto the windshield, where it waved at them.

"I'd prefer if you just came back in a half hour."

"That's where I draw the line. I'll wait here."

"Okay," she said reluctantly.

"Okay," he echoed.

But she did not jump from the truck. "Nick, do I look nice?" She ran her hands over her hair.

"Good enough to eat." He laughed. "But I thought you were going there to get revenge. Does it matter how you look?"

"Think you're smart, don't you?" she answered. But her attention was already moving up the long drive past the line of trees catching the morning sunlight to the house beyond the curve, the edge of the deep porch just visible.

When Kasia started up the drive, Nick got out and caught up with her a few feet away. "Good luck," he said and patted her shoulder.

Kasia hoped the door wouldn't open so quickly after her knock; she'd counted on last minute inspiration for what she would say when she finally met her sister face to face. "I'm Kasia Darling," she'd say, her voice powerful and authoritative. She'd relish the look of consternation, fear, and disbelief on Alice's face. Through the window on the porch, Kasia glimpsed polished floors, deep sills, soft colors, and beyond that a curved dark wooden staircase and an archway into a formal dining room, a colored glass chandelier. She imagined the scent of some indefinable yeasty sweetness, as if the house had absorbed a hundred years of baking bread.

Footsteps. The door opened. "Alice?" Kasia asked, her voice much shakier than she would have wished. She took in the tall thin angular body clad in red silk pajamas, black velvet flip-flops.

"I'm Alice," the woman responded, crossing her arms in front of her. She wiped sleep from her eyes.

Kasia blinked and stuttered. A small sound—something like a giggle—escaped from her lips. She blushed, furious with her own lack of composure. Except for the difference in their stature, the sisters were startlingly alike in coloring and features—blonde with high cheekbones, well-defined chin and arched brows. Alice wore her blonde hair short, feathered back from her cheeks with fringy bangs. Kasia noticed the large hands and short, square nails.

"What is it?" Alice spoke casually, as if she did not notice the similarity.

"I'm Kasia."

Alice continued to look at her, holding the door in a way that suggested exclusion or suspicion, though her face and voice betrayed neither.

The confrontation was not going as Kasia had planned. Kasia found herself somehow unable to figure out how to proceed. Alice's composure, her intractability, was not what Kasia had expected. She felt her face flush. Futilely, she waited for a response. "Kasia. Kasia *Darling.*" She paused. The lack of response, lack of curiosity was aggravating. Blinking back tears, Kasia looked right into Alice's eyes and held them. There was a protracted silence while she waited.

"What's this about?" Alice asked as nonchalantly as if she expected Kasia to try to sell her Avon cosmetics.

As much out of frustration as anger Kasia kept her eyes clasped on Alice's face as her pupils hardened to the density of nail heads. "Kasia. Your sister."

Kasia thought she had readied herself for almost any kind of scene, from tears to a door slammed in her face. Instead of surprise or curiosity, Kasia read anger and wariness in her sister's face. Why was Alice studying her like that? Staring at her face. The next moment Kasia felt her legs shiver and give way beneath her as the edges of the world started to turn black. Alice stepped out onto the porch and took her arm to steady her just as she started to crumble.

Alice steered her to a chair. "Put your head between your knees. Breathe."

Kasia did. Wracking tears prevented her from speaking.

"Just take your time. Breathe." Alice demonstrated the breathing she wanted Kasia to do. Her voice was clinical but soft.

Kasia started to speak. "My father. Your—" but her voice quivered and the corners of her mouth twitched involuntarily. Struggling for control, she looked at Alice, who held out her hands in a gesture of patience. After a minute, Kasia began again. "My father—your father. My father—" she said weakly, as if Alice should be able to construct the whole picture from those few words.

"You mean Ben Darling?"

"My—" Kasia nodded.

"He was your father?" Alice asked, her voice surprisingly cool, the complete opposite of Kasia's passionate weeping. Alice's apparent detachment made Kasia all the more upset. How could she be so calm?

"Yes. We lived in Connecticut. I just found out about it because I came here from Poland. I saw in the cemetery." Kasia's English deteriorated with the frantic pace of her thoughts and the grief of what she was saying.

"Just like that. You came here to find him?"

"Not him. I came looking for Hattie. I didn't know anything about him being here, their being married—" she broke off again; the words drew her back to the scene at the hilltop cemetery—the tidy fence marking those inside who belonged together, the certainty of Hattie's place beside Ben—an image that still had the power to hurt her.

Alice grew agitated. Finally, Kasia had said something that surprised her. She ran her hands through her hair. "Hattie. My mother? How does she figure into this?"

The thought was suddenly audible between them, though Kasia hadn't meant to speak it. "You knew? About him? About us? You knew!"

"For a while before he died." Alice looked at her little sister.

"About father. About me?"

"Yes. Something. Not a specific thing. I knew something was going on."

"But how?"

"I knew there was someone else. Someone he cared for. I found out when I was seventeen." She paused. "My best friend was killed in Vietnam."

"Gordon Wescott." Kasia uttered the name she'd seen on the service marker in the cemetery.

"Yes. Gordie." She shook her head. "I was devastated. My father was working away. I knew I wasn't supposed to call him when he was away, but I had to. I knew where he stayed. Who his friends were at Precision. I called the place—um," she searched for the name, "the Idle Away, the hotel. He wasn't registered. Then I called Precision—"

Kasia looked confused.

"The company he worked for. And they didn't know where he was either, said they thought he was still in Pennsylvania."

"That doesn't prove anything." Kasia found herself defending her father, though she knew long ago Alice's fears had been well founded. She herself was the proof that there had been someone else.

Alice grew more agitated, as if reliving the events buried for eighteen years. "I just put two and two together. After that I kept my eyes open. I noticed that he went out every night. 'Getting some air,' he'd say. I followed him a few times over to Crystalle to the pay phone he called from. Like clockwork. What else could it be but another woman? Any other phone call he'd make from home, right? It was already such a horrible time for me. I couldn't believe that Gordie was gone. Then my father—"

Kasia was quiet. It was Alice's turn to compose herself. "It still hurts," she said, her voice low and weak. "I felt like I lost him too. How could I ever believe him again?"

The sisters looked at each other. Alice looked away, struggling to continue. "But my mother. Did she know about you and your mother?"

Kasia nodded. She reached tentatively for her sister, then dropped her hand. In the silence she heard the silvery wind chimes at the edge of the porch ping softly.

"She never told me anything?"

By the time Kasia had finished telling her part of the story, from the day her father left to Hattie's life with them in Hartford to Piotr's arrival, Hattie's sudden departure, her mother's death and her life with Piotr in Poland, a curious calm had overtaken her, as if telling diminished the events' power over her. Each time she shared the story, it became a little easier, and she felt a little less shame.

Now Alice's breath came in big gulping sounds, not crying exactly, but inhaling as if she were trying not to. Kasia had the sensation, one she felt grudgingly, that she wanted to comfort her sister. After a minute, she reached out her hand again as Alice had done for her and patted her on the shoulder.

"It's so strange," Alice said. "I wanted a sister more than anything in the world. An only child—I still remember praying—"

"Me too."

Suddenly Alice's face shifted from sorrow to anger. "She knew all the time. Mrs. Sweetness and Light knew. And never a word. 'Alice, I've been meaning to tell you there's a little sister somewhere who looks just like you.'"

"Maybe she thought she was doing the best for everyone," Kasia heard herself excusing Hattie.

"When my father—our father died, what prevented her from telling us? I quit my job in California to come home and be with her. Inexplicably, she left—gone for months. Had us all so worried. We couldn't figure out what was going on. I never till this minute knew where. She refused to discuss it. Now I find out that she was in Hartford while I was left here to grieve alone.

"Dad used to beg her to move with him, but she couldn't even leave town. I bet you didn't know that about her. Housebound, some people call it. Agoraphobia. Couldn't leave Fenston. Weeks sometimes she wouldn't even go out of the house. Then suddenly dad dies and she's cured. She's off for months, even after I moved back home. I never understood it." Alice spoke slowly, as if clarifying, understanding more with each word.

"Now you do?"

"Maybe this explains some of it. But why didn't she tell me before she left? It would have made so much more sense." Alice's face darkened with anger and confusion.

Kasia stopped for a minute to think. Why had Hattie kept them apart? She would have loved to have a sister, even across the world. How much it would have meant to know she was not alone. The shadow of something dark crossed her imagination. She balanced her desire to have family against how she would have felt to know that her father had been a bigamist, a common Tarzan. "She might have been protecting him."

"Did your mom know?" Alice asked.

"Yes. No. I mean, I don't know."

"You couldn't tell?"

"I was so young—just eight when she died."

"Yes, of course. I forgot." Alice sat heavily in the chair facing Kasia.

"I just remember how worried I was that she was so sick. At night I would think about what I'd do if she died and he didn't come back. I understood the word 'orphan.'" Kasia gazed around at their surroundings, taking in the deep porch, the beautiful old house, the long sweep of driveway and the lawn, the enormous old trees. "Our life was not like this." Kasia glanced around. "We were very poor. My mother always worried. We ate what we grew in our backyard. There was never enough of anything, that summer. Then Hattie came and it was better."

"When my mother appeared, how did they—?"

"Hattie and my mother—seemed like friends—" Kasia broke off, obviously trying to remember. "Did they both know? I was too small to understand much beyond the facts that my father had disappeared and my mother was dying. What did I know?"

"This whole thing is crazy. My mother knows there is another woman and doesn't do anything about it until my father dies. Then she heads to Connecticut, the scene of his crime, and moves in with the other woman and her child."

"The strangest part is that she came when we needed her. I guess you'll have to ask her why. I've wondered whether he told her about us, about mother's illness, before he died." Kasia heard in her own voice that she still wanted to think the best of Hattie.

"He died suddenly, right in the middle of a conversation. She thought he had fallen asleep."

"We'll never know what happened unless we ask her."

"Don't think I won't," Alice said, her voice now calm and steady.

Kasia recalled her Hattie, the loving friend of her childhood, and questioned whether the picture was more imagination than memory. That image didn't correspond at all with what she was hearing between Alice's words. Clearly, theirs was a difficult relationship. How would she ever sort out the truth? She had come to Fenston to get some kind of emotional touchstone, a foundation she could revert to when she needed a sense of her own history. So far all she'd found was quicksand. And more lies.

Full of rage and pain, Kasia had wanted to hurt someone else, the person who had benefited from those sun filled summer swimming days, lived in the big house, the person who had enjoyed the pie tent every summer and never questioned the privileges she had. Kasia had gone to the Darling house to tell Alice about her father's bigamy and her mother's deceit. Now that she had accomplished her mission, she felt herself curiously unsatisfied, as if the thing she had sought evaporated just as she touched it. She didn't want to and tried to talk herself out of it, but Kasia felt a deep sorrow for Ben Darling's other daughter as she realized she was not the only one who had been wronged.

The beautiful house, the porch, colorful with its brightly cushioned Victorian wicker, the tendrils of plants hanging from each pillar, the fields and orchards below, did not offer much comfort. Strange to think that her sister, living in America in this beautiful place, was no happier than she. She remembered her mother's attempts to make their old Hartford house pretty—the china she searched for and bought one piece at a time at the Salvation Army, her delight when the old wallpaper didn't bleed through the white paint in their tiny bathroom. Kasia could hear her mother's raspy wheeze as she painted. And occasionally, her singing.

Oddly, she could imagine herself inside this life as well. She could see Hattie working in the garden at the side of the house, trailing the bean runners up the trellis or leaning back on her heels to examine the hollyhocks and peony bushes, her face expressing the same satisfaction in growing something as it had in their backyard in Hartford. Kasia looked through a wither of purple wisteria vine toward the side meadow—apple trees heavy with fruit. Hattie lived here. Her father had lived here too. He had awakened each morning to this sky, this air, these trees. Each day, each moment, he had moved farther away from the part of himself that she held onto. She would never locate him.

Alice seemed to read her thoughts. "How could father have done this terrible thing? How could he have hurt so many people?" she asked, but her voice was far away and unable to reach Kasia. Despite her attempts to thwart its growth with her rage over what had been done to her, Kasia felt a blossoming inside herself whenever she thought of Hattie.

Walking toward the truck Kasia wore an expression of sorrow and wonder, as if she'd forgotten Nick had been waiting for her. She shrugged off his consoling embrace without speaking. He followed her lead, then started the truck and backed out of the driveway. After a minute he asked, "Where to?"

"I don't care. Just not back to the dorm. Here. Can we stop here?" she asked, indicating a road into the lake. Her voice was devoid of the gravity Nick expected.

"Sure," he said. The smell of cedar carried on the air along the lake. The yellowing branches of larch trees and the rushes in the swamp reflected in the calm water. Kicking through the decaying carpet of evergreen needles, Kasia walked aimlessly, preoccupied with her thoughts.

"Let's sit." Nick took her hand and pointed to the old structure jutting out over the shore of the lake. Kasia nodded. He dusted flaking paint from the top step for them to sit. Barn swallows chittered overhead and twitched their forked tails at the interlopers.

"What is this place?" Kasia asked, looking around.

"A dance pavilion. Been here forever. In the old days, it put Fenston on the map. People used to come from all over for dances. My parents told me about it. Hasn't been used in years. Falling apart, but every time someone mentions tearing it down to make room for something else, the old-timers act like it's the Taj Mahal or something. I guess most of them had their first dates here."

"Must have been nice," she said. *A long time ago,* she thought.

Immediately the Hattie of her imagination sprang to mind. Young, with an old fashioned party dress and her hair, a lighter brown, hanging long and loose. Music and a warm gauzy light surrounded her. She was alone, looking out over the railing of the pavilion at the moonlight dusting the tops of pine trees across the lake. When he touched her shoulder, her dress swirled around her legs. She smoothed it down with her slender arms. Kasia knew the man was her father, though she could not see his face. He took Hattie's hand and they moved onto the floor, where he encircled her back with his arm. She lay her cheek on his chest and they danced in the night scented by trees and lit by the gold lights overhead. It was all so easy to imagine.

Nick was giving her time to get around to telling him what had happened with Alice.

"Dances. Summer nights. I bet a lot of people fell in love here." She stopped for so long Nick didn't expect her to say anything else. "I can understand why they don't want it destroyed. People need to hold onto something, anything at all associated with their history." She sighed deeply. "Just look at me," she said. The suggestion of a sob followed her words.

"Want to talk about what happened back there?" Nick asked. Tentatively he touched her hand, then put his arm around her shoulder. She did not push it away. Instead she leaned into its shelter and warmth and tried to imagine something lovely, the pavilion filled with music and dancing couples, the sound of the lake water lapping the shore.

"I like her. I didn't expect to, but I do."

"Alice's what, seventeen years older than you?"

"Nineteen."

"You look a lot alike."

"Weird, huh? Everyone always thought I looked just like mom. I guess not. But like father, she's tall."

The conversation appeared to sooth Kasia.

"We agreed to meet again. And she said she'd let me know when Hattie came back. She suggested we just show up together and confront her."

"How do you feel about that?"

"Not sure. We both have the right to some answers. Strange, but she seems angrier than I am. Somehow talking to Alice—I just felt—I think I'd like to see Hattie alone. Still—"

"I know you're tough and think you can handle anything."

"I am?" Kasia said, her tone incredulous. "I seem that way to you?"

"Sure you do."

"I don't feel like that."

"Come on, Kasia, think of the way you chased down that guy who tried to steal your backpack at the airport. That really took guts."

"Yes. But that was different. It happened so quickly. I reacted, that's all. With this situation, I have to think everything through and decide what to believe, how to act. Most of all, I need to figure out what's driving me to know all the details."

"Don't let too much of your psych class get mixed up in this," Nick said.

For the first time all afternoon, Kasia laughed. "Yeah. It's easy to be in the textbook. Read all about it. Forget it's really me, my life. But there are things I need to know. Now I'm not even sure who knew what when."

"Does it matter?"

"Yes." Kasia paused. "Well, no." She shook her head. "I don't know. That's one of the things I have to figure out."

"Don't decide anything right now. Relax and look at the water," Nick said. He rubbed his hand lightly across her shoulders.

"That feels so good," she said. "Get your studying done while I was in there?"

"Not much. I'll crack the books tonight. What about you? Homework?"

"I'm caught up, except for comp. The draft of our next assignment is due Thursday. An essay on an unusual experience. Let's see. What can I write about? Do you think meeting a sister I didn't know existed and finding out your missing father was a bigamist, now dead and buried in his other wife's family plot, would qualify? Maybe for extra credit we could arrange a field trip to see the evidence."

Chapter 31

The purple shrouded altar was filled with enormous floral arrangements. Eddie and Eleanor found seats in the third row, squeezing in between the nuns from the elementary school and a group of teen-aged boys. Before the service started, the organist and soloist rendered the *Ave Maria, Dies Ire,* and *How Great Thou Art.* Sitting back in the pew, Eddie closed his eyes and allowed the music to draw him back to his time as a priest, the pleasure of celebrating the mass, of feeling at one with a community of people in the intensely beautiful worship. Beside him, Eleanor fidgeted in her purse and withdrew a wad of Kleenex. She blew her nose and then slid forward to her knees, the beads slipping through her fingers as she mumbled the decades of the Sorrowful Mysteries.

McGill was one of fourteen celebrants at Frederick's Requiem Mass. The old priest—Eddie calculated that he was at least eighty—looked alert and fit as he strode from the sacristy to the altar. Standing in a line behind the altar, priests of every size and age, color and mien, all dressed in opulent purple silk vestments deeply embroidered with golden thread, regarded those who had come to bless the life and spirit of the departed. One of the young priests circled the casket at the front of the church and moved down the center aisle swinging the ornate brass censure before him. The air filled with incense.

Distracted by his own thoughts, Eddie had lost his concentration on the ritual prayers until the consecration. At the moment of transubstantiation, the priest held aloft the host and the congregants held their breath in witness of the miracle before them. Pew after pew of mourners filed to the front of the church for communion. Some held out their hand to take the host. Others allowed the priest to place the host on their tongue. Neither Eddie nor Eleanor took communion. When Eddie left the priesthood, he had been excommunicated—forbidden to partake of the sacraments. Later, Frederick and some of his other old friends tried to convince him to seek a dispensation so that he could remain in the church. He had refused, explaining that he had known what he was doing and would suffer the consequences. Eleanor, though not technically precluded from participating in the church's rituals, elected to follow his lead.

As the communion line continued through five verses of *Panis Angelicus, Bread of Angels* Eddie contemplated Frederick's life, the impact his humility and charity had made on so many people. Eddie liked to think that had his own life not taken such a radical turn he would have been as good a priest as Frederick.

A sudden flutter of jealousy passed over Eddie as he watched the old priest deftly quaff the last drop of wine, cleanse and cover the chalice. At the end of the mass the congregants stood, waiting to be sent forth. McGill's surprisingly vibrant voice sang out, *"Ita Missa Est,"* dismissing the mourners.

In the recessional that followed Frederick's casket, McGill passed within inches of Eddie and Eleanor, then paused, looked back in recognition. It was enough for Eddie to consider it the sign he had prayed for. On the drive home, they were silent. At the corner of Standard and Main, they both noticed but did not comment on the office building occupying the site of the Esso station where she'd changed her clothes, their names, their life that night so many years before.

Tears spilled over and Eleanor sobbed quietly. Eddie drove slowly, then pulled into a shopping center parking lot and stopped the car. He knew without words that she was thinking about her lost child again. He looked at her tenderly and held out his arms. The late morning sun shimmered across the blacktop. People came and went, the parcels of their lives borne heavily or lightly. Eddie searched his heart for words that would heal her. "You have to accept the past. Offer yourself the same love and forgiveness you'd give someone else."

"But how can I? I don't understand how forgiveness works for something this terrible. And what about penance?"

"It will come to you. Maybe you've already begun and haven't realized it. Think of all the good work you do for others. Redemptive work."

"You make it sound so easy."

"I don't mean to. Nothing important is easy. You know that, dear heart? It's a glorious untidy world. A world we can't tame. We just have to do our best—day by day." Feeling more helpless than he ever had, Eddie touched his wife's face with fingers once refined with the subtle ways of forgiveness now coarsened with the layering of years of work and life.

The next day while Eleanor was at Wescott's Eddie phoned the diocese office for the phone number of St. Simon's. The old priest, sounding hearty and lucid, remembered Eddie. Not at all surprised by the call or the request, he said Eddie was welcome to visit anytime.

Chapter 32

Eleanor stood at the door watching Eddie's car recede. Without his solicitude she was going to have to figure this thing out herself if she was to get on with her life. And she so wanted to do just that. She was tired of the concern and worry on his face.

With still an hour before she had to leave for the store, Eleanor found herself tidying up a little here and there. She wandered into a seldom-used space, the narrow room off the dining room. Once it had been a study for the kids to do their homework and projects for Scouts and the FFA. Years of detritus littered the long table and hung from the shelving over it. Every surface was covered with materials, from old shingles waiting to be painted and stenciled to a waist-high snarl of grapevine in the corner, an easel and oil paints, pastel bales of nylon netting. Clearing off a spot on the corner desk, Eleanor sat for a moment. Her thoughts were so far away from the present that she hardly noticed her hands at work separating a multicolored clump of needlepoint yarn. She felt, as she had almost every moment, a burden in her soul so intense that she could feel it like a palpable presence, a fist-sized knot in the center of her chest.

The harsh light overhead illuminated the curling photos and yellowing newspaper clippings pegged to the wall at her right. She studied them slowly, looking carefully at each one, trying to imagine why they concerned her. How had she allowed the Pardford Fair in 1980, where she won first place for her tomato relish, to consume her thoughts? How could she be the woman who had raised children, taken top honors when she graduated from college? How could those children have made projects of plaster of Paris and paint and tree bark, taken piano lessons and danced in spring pageants? All of it so real, so engaging at the time. How could any of this life that she had been the center of taken place without her going mad from longing for that first baby?

More than the pain she felt for that loss, a pain more searing than it could possibly have been when she first gave him away, she was stunned by shuffling through the artifacts of the life she lived when she was not looking. And now, obscured by her guilt and pain, a life she could hardly remember.

Eleanor reached up and lowered the shade. The bright skeins of yarn, the photographs, the vines, the netting, the paint leapt back into shadow. Still the room seemed bright. To blot it out she closed her eyes, but thought she could still see seams of light through her lids. From the stacks of fabric on the shelf above her she pulled a remnant of old cotton and draped it haphazardly over her head. The movement dislodged the pile and piece by piece it fell slowly onto her lap and the desk in front of her and the floor. Eleanor didn't move. She felt foolish. But immediately that thought was replaced by another—Stella Maris came into her mind. She tried to pray, but her thoughts were a swirl of images from that long-ago time.

The metal loops clicked along the rod decisively as Ellie jerked the curtain around her cell, obscuring the view but not the sounds from the row of identical beds where the nine other novices tidied their spaces too. Quickly she dressed her narrow bed the old way, the way she was shown the first day at Stella Maris. The bottom sheet smooth across the mattress, tight and tucked as swaddling, pulled taut with the corners folded deep. When she lifted and snapped, the clean swath billowed above her. Almost alive, without weight, the top sheet hovered then settled into the outline she so easily imagined.

Suddenly, there he was on the bed. The white fabric creased and wrinkled around the contour of his body. Despite the fresh sheet scent of sun and bleach, she smelled him—sour, smoky. Her palms skidded across the material smoothing and molding until she touched the gap between his legs, between their bodies as they merged, between his fingers pressed flat as he held her above him, his cheeks against the pillow, his dark, accusing stare. Waiting.

The draft of air pulled from her window as the door opened had awakened her that night, the first time her Uncle Dan came calling. She startled and sat upright in the bed, struggling in the dark to see. The house was still. Upstairs her mother and grandmother slept in their uneasy truce. She could picture them, her mother with her face turned to the wall, while in the next room her grandmother, her false teeth smiling in a water glass on the bedside table, breathed hoarsely, the air rushing in and out of the cavern of her open mouth.

He shut the door behind him, and the curtains settled back against the screen. Her room behind the kitchen, once a pantry, still smelled of yeast and sugar. She could make out the blurry corners of the room and his shape as he approached her. "Shush," he said, "It's only me." The sickly darkness of his breath and when he got closer, the singed odor of his sweat, made her stomach rebel.

Later, counting backward after the birth, she calculated that she had gotten pregnant the first month. Sex with Uncle Dan became a regular part of her life that summer. He came prepared with a condom. Holding her fast to the bed, he fumbled it on with one hand, sliding it down like a glove over his penis. Occasionally it slipped off as he tried to enter her tight refusing body. She didn't fight or cry out, for he had whispered how he would hurt her so much worse if she did.

If she told on him, he would blame her. "Ellie. Sweet little slut," he whispered into the side of her neck, "you think nobody knows what you dream of at night. I'm here because you want it. What would Gran say? What about Sister Noreen? Would you be her pet if she found out what you dreamed about? Sweet little slut, don't worry. I won't tell."

Everything innocent about the world changed. Her family, the old shoe into which she trod in an unexamined and uncomplaining way, suddenly drew from her surprising anger. About that same time her body began behaving badly. Some days she could hardly get out of bed her legs pained so. And low down between her legs there was a kind of twitch and thrum, a current. Not all the time, but often enough that she wondered at it, pressing her fingers tight there into the notch of folds. Her breasts ached too.

191

Late at night her body was electric. She didn't understand. Images of people touching and holding each other fluttered behind her closed eyelids. When bad thoughts came to her she moved her hands over her own body, pressing here and there to erase them.

Uncle Dan seemed to know what part of her was calling out. Where and how to touch. Understanding what they were doing was wrong didn't help. Hating herself more than she hated him didn't stop her from wanting him. She'd lie tense as a tuning fork listening for his quiet step outside the door to her little room behind the kitchen. His visits continued through the summer. Then one night he lifted the cotton gown away from her legs and felt the small hill of belly forming. "Ohh," he said, and his penis deflated. "Oh, oh."

When Billy arrived in their life, something shifted in her. Seeing his quest made her realize that there was another part of the equation. It was not just about her guilt. Somewhere a child had grown up, now a child of middle age, whose life was linked with hers. Had he wondered all these years about the woman who had given birth to him and then sent him away? She had been aware all that time of her own pain but she never considered his. What of that other pain and longing? How had she lived each day, each minute knowing there was a child she should have loved and cared for? Wasn't that the worst sin of all?

Chapter 33

There was an unusual gravity in her voice when Sister Gloria called. She explained that Kandy had showed up at Harmony House looking for Tina and Billy. Harmony was a safe house, a shelter for those who sought refuge from harassment or harm. Its location was a secret from all but the residents and those who had to know in order to keep the place functioning. Tina sobbed apologetically as she confessed to giving Kandy the address. She simply hadn't understood the danger.

"Think I'll head down there with some honey. Put my mind at ease. Good chance to see Billy too." Eddie seized the excuse to be away from home for a long stretch.

"Remember that monkey, what did they call it?" Eleanor said as he readied to leave.

"Sailor."

"Those eyes. It looked at you like it knew everything that was going on," Eleanor said.

"Reminded me of some of the illustrations of the Hindu Monkey God, Hanuman."

"Those two were bickering over it like it was a child."

Eddie tried for levity. "A classic case of monkey in the middle." He gave the smile that always followed one of his puns.

Ignoring it, Eleanor asked, "Is that creature at Harmony too?"

"Yes. When Billy got on the phone he couldn't stop talking about it.

He's wild for Sailor. Said it's smart as a person. Anyway, Kurt took off with all her money. Some agent." Eddie pronounced the word as if it were an obscenity.

"I think you spell it P-I-M-P. Imagine marrying something like him. Talk about desperate."

"While I'm there, I thought I'd spend the day in town, make the rounds of the secondhand bookstores, see what's turned up."

"Goodie. What we really need around here is more books." Her voice dripping with mock sarcasm, Eleanor swept her arms around the room, each wall filled with bulging bookcases.

"Don't expect me before dinner." He kissed her and looked into her face, relieved to see her eyes clear of pain, at least for the moment. Disquiet though he was about deceiving his wife, maybe by the end of the day he'd be able to offer her some solace.

Billy, Sailor and two younger boys were in the back-yard, a tiny rectangle of dirt and matted weeds, a city oasis featuring a swing set and sandbox, a foreshortened basketball hoop, a gas barbecue and a large picnic table, all surrounded by tall privacy fencing. To the delight of the three boys Sailor, dressed in his white suit, the hat perched jauntily just above his left ear as it had been the first time Eddie saw the animal, was swinging overhand, his long arm span propelling him quickly along the top crossbar of the swing set. When he reached the end he turned and balanced on the side rail, holding on with one hand and swinging the other as trapeze artists do, awaiting adulation. He hopped up and down and blew kisses to his fans, then shimmied up the pole and began the show again. When he saw Eddie approaching he stopped mid-swing, to hang by one dexterous hand as he saluted with the other. The boys hooted in pleasure.

"Eddie," Billy said, surprise and delight evident in his voice. "Wait'll you see this." When he withdrew the harmonica from his pocket the monkey stopped, climbed down from the jungle gym and stood next to Billy. Positioning the harmonica against his lips, Billy tooted out a short three note ditty and Sailor began to dance, an awkward bobbing up and down, keeping time. Clearly, Billy was no longer the withdrawn, frightened kid Eddie had first encountered.

Eddie found Gloria in the basement cleaning fish over a newspaper.

One of Harmony's benefactors had returned from a fishing trip with a trunk full of flounder, which she was rapidly turning into neat meal-sized packets. She wielded the knife with knowledge and ease, surprising Eddie. Reading his thoughts, she said, "My grandfather was a great fisherman. He taught me to bait the hook and clean the catch. Never know when little bits of knowledge will come in handy."

"Now you're singing my tune," Eddie said, and they both laughed. He picked up another knife and a large fish.

"You're the Renaissance man, all right," she said, leaning back and swiping her wrist across her forehead, wiping back the tumble of hair. "Latin scholar. Chess champ. Fish cleaner."

"Everything okay here?" he asked.

"One blessing after another," Gloria crowed. "No sooner do we get a freezer than another fridge appears out of nowhere. Then the fish. Sure bet we'll have them filled in no time." She pointed to the two new appliances, one white and the other almond, against the far wall of the tidy basement.

"Uh-huh. I meant with the security."

"No problem."

"Sure?"

"Sure as anyone can be about anything. I won't kid you. I take every breach seriously. Some of the women who come here are running from some bad actors. But Tina told only Kandy. Kandy told no one. They're both here. You and Ellie can stop worrying."

"Ellie," he said softly, tasting the unfamiliar syllables.

"Oh, I forgot," Gloria laughed. "El-an-or." She pronounced every syllable. "By the way, did El-an-or ever tell you about the time she and I almost got the heave-ho from the convent?"

Torn between wanting to hear even one story about Eleanor's time in the convent and his sense of the day getting ahead of him, the latter lost. "No," he said, inviting Gloria to reminisce while they cleaned fish.

"The place was so large and grand and confusing," she began.

Gloria and Ellie, like most of the girls, had come from simple homes, not places with three parlors and a kitchen as big as most houses. They loved to explore. A few times they almost got caught in the rooms reserved for the professed sisters. One day Ellie had been polishing the floor in the hall. Gloria was in the kitchen on the other side of the door when she heard her friend singing. She had only intended to open the door and tease her, tell her that sister Martin de Pores sent her out to tell her to stop. Ellie was on her knees with polish rag, flipping it from side to side like she was beating it up. Gloria could hardly see her face. The sun streamed through the high windows and the long hall puddled in sunlight gleaming the glossy wet of polished wood.

"I ripped out of my oxfords—how we all hated those old nunish shoes—and was in my stocking feet before she knew what I was doing. I hiked my habit like Ellie's, tucking the hem into the waistband the way we did when we were scrubbing so the skirt wouldn't get wet. 'Ellie,' I said, 'watch this.' And I ran a few steps and glided. She was on her feet in a flash. We skated that hallway for God knows how long, habits flying behind us. Starting from opposite ends of the hallway, we'd run to get up a good speed then slide on stocking feet the rest of the way, passing each other mid-skate. We were trying so hard not to laugh or shriek. It might have gone on all day, heedless of our duties, except Sister Martin de Pores on her way into the storeroom to inspect my work caught a glimpse of us and put a stop to it."

"Did you really almost get expelled, just for that?"

"Remember the old days, Eddie, the way the orders were ruled. There were so many vocations that they could dispose of a few at whim. We could have gotten the boot for much less. Mother Athureen really laid into us. But she gave us another chance." Gloria giggled. "And look where it's got me—here in a dungeon cleaning fish." Her obvious joy belied her words.

"Ellie," Eddie said again, pronouncing the name of the novice he'd fallen in love with. Suddenly a flood of images of his wife as she had been when they first met flowed across the screen of his memory, and he was reminded about his real mission for the day.

Chapter 34

Resting grandly on a hilltop over-
looking a valley of pine trees and a patchwork of meadows, St. Simon's
Seminary and Retreat was built as a facility to train priests when the
church had better prospects. Eddie's experience of the place had been
during that happy era for the church when vocations flourished and
the order could afford to be selective. In those days the halls thronged
with seminarians scurrying to classes, their eager young faces engaged
with the ideas of the time. Often to the delight of their religious parents the top students in the local colleges entered the seminary—much
like an exclusive club.

By the time Monsignor Wilbur McGill traded in the iron grip over
his parish for an easy chair with a view, the seminary had assumed its
new function. He had joined a dozen or so other elderly priests in the
immense structure. Announced by the housekeeper, a sturdy woman
dressed in an outfit so austere Eddie wondered if she belonged to some
obscure order which had not heeded Vatican II to modernize their
habit, Eddie was ushered into the high-ceilinged newly refurbished
gymnasium. The basketball hoops had been removed and the wooden
floor covered with strips of rubberized padding on which sat various
exercise machines. McGill was rowing fiercely, pulling the oars toward
and away from himself rhythmically, his stringy muscled arms and legs
pumping.

"Welcome back to the old place. Now you'll get a chance to see

197

what you spared yourself by leaving." McGill disembarked from the machine and took up 25-pound arm weights and pumped them up and down expertly. His face was red with exertion and hard to read, but Eddie thought he saw loneliness and genuine pleasure to have a distraction in the old priest's fierce gaze.

It occurred to Eddie that McGill had known he was coming and had arranged to meet where he could show off a little. He waited patiently, making small talk until McGill took a towel and pointed toward a door.

"Looks like you could use a workout." McGill pointed to Eddie's middle.

"Lots of changes." Eddie deflected the comment.

They took chairs opposite each other in the small sitting room. McGill's skin, still slick with sweat, looked grayish in the dim light. "Much as I'd like to believe so, I don't imagine you're here to catch up with me," he said after wiping his face and draping the towel over his shoulder.

Eddie nodded and started to speak, but McGill held up a hand to silence him. The imperious priestly gesture aside, Eddie felt sorry to see the man, once the terror of the diocese, the pastor no young priest wanted to serve, still so needy.

"Ever since you called, I've been trying to come up with the answer to the question: Why would you want to see me? Why is that, Edward?" He looked Eddie over. "You know everyone was astonished, even dismayed, when you left. Of all the men who passed through here in those years, I think we all would have agreed that you would be the last one we would have thought. You had such a future ahead of you. Your name was on the bishop's short list, you know, for an appointment to Rome."

Eddie nodded. He tried to speak, but McGill interrupted him with another wave of his hand. The crone who had greeted him came to the door and he nodded. She ducked out and returned with an ornate tray carrying the elements of high tea, beautiful English china set, tiny cakes, transparent slices of lemon. Eddie surmised the opulence was for his benefit.

McGill sighed dramatically. "But it was not to be. You made your way in the world and judging by what—I don't know except a feeling

I had when I saw you the other day—it's not been any better," he hesitated, "or worse than what the rest of us have come to."

Refusing to be drawn into the game, when the priest stopped talking this time Eddie didn't attempt to speak so McGill couldn't interrupt him for the third time. Instead, he let the silence lengthen as he looked around the room.

The monsignor began again. "So, does it have to do with me? Or rather with me as I currently am? No. What would you care about that?"

Keeping his face as blank as possible, Eddie stifled his desire to wedge a few words in between McGill's harangue.

"Then it must, if my grasp of syllogism hasn't completely abandoned me in my dotage, have to do with my seemingly predictable and lackluster life as pastor of St. Bartholomew's Church in Harley."

Eddie controlled his face to hide his surprise.

"Yes. I'm warm. I knew it. The next question is—excuse me for rushing along, but I'm so anxious to see whether I'm right in the little mystery game I've played these past few days that I can't help myself. Useless old priests have so few distractions; surely we can be forgiven for relishing them when they come our way."

Eddie had forgotten just how much he disliked McGill on the few occasions their paths had crossed. That old antipathy surged in him. He willed himself to keep his demeanor calm, his hands flat and relaxed.

"The next question I asked myself is what is the connection between Edward Roderi, that used to be priest who went against his vows to disgrace himself and run away with a little nun half his age, and me."

Eddie felt the irritation mount. McGill relished his advantage. Clearly, he hoped to provide Eddie with an opportunity to exercise humility. "And all at once I knew it must have something to do with her. The connection is Harley. Kellow. Right?"

Finally McGill, having scored the points he wanted, letting Eddie know he understood exactly why he had come, refused to go any farther. To continue would save Eddie having to explain about Eleanor's baby and ask what had become of it. But McGill, master of the pound of flesh, sat back in his chair, ready to hear from the no longer Father Roderi.

The white-hot rage that coursed through Eddie's body alarmed him. He tried to force his mind away from the conversation with McGill, concerned that it had enflamed him to the point that he would drive erratically. "That son of a bitch," he heard himself say as he lost the battle over his emotions. "That pretentious, officious, unctuous, smug, elitist, misogynistic bastard." The litany pouring from Eddie gave him momentary release from the fury.

"If you wait long enough, everything you expect to happen in life eventually comes to pass," McGill had said. "And that's a promise. I expected this visit right after you left. What man wouldn't need to know? Felt a little disappointed when you didn't show up. Then I surmised that either she'd figured it out herself or hadn't told you."

A car directly in Eddie's path blared its horn. Realizing he had wandered over into the oncoming lane, he forced the wheel sharply back. "That obnoxious, paternalistic, officious sycophant," he mumbled.

But was McGill also a liar? Eddie scoured his memory for every tiny detail she'd told him about her recollection of her pregnancy and the birth of the child. She was unclear about just when she had conceived. Though she was tiny, a belly formed and her breasts swelled and hardened, but clothed she had not looked pregnant even when she went into labor. The labor was intense and short. They administered a drug, she didn't know what it was, but she was unconscious for the actual delivery. The last thing she remembered was the searing, tearing pain and a mask pressed against her nose and mouth. No cry. No glimpse.

"Myra came up with the idea of telling the girl that the baby was taken away by adoptive parents. A grandmother's prerogative. I thought it best not to interfere."

"What happened to the child?" Eddie asked dully, articulating the question he had come so far to ask that he hadn't noticed the answer implied in McGill's responses.

McGill stared at Eddie as if he weren't quite bright enough to get a good joke. Then he laughed.

The sound of the laughter filled Eddie with a murderous rage. Or maybe it was that he was finally aware of the punch line which McGill took his time delivering.

"There wasn't any baby. Never was. Hysterical pregnancy, I think they call it now. There are even shows about it on television. Back then,

I'd never heard of it. The mind convinces the body that it is pregnant and the body obeys, showing all the symptoms. Even though there was no pregnancy, it was clear that she had been promiscuous. 'Teach her a lesson,' Myra said. Let her think she'd actually given birth. The result, as you know, was that the girl entered the order. Where, of course, you found her. The question has always been for me, as I had this extra insight into Ellie Kellow, who seduced whom?"

For the second time that day Eddie thought of Ellie as he had first seen her, nervous and intense, with those immense purple eyes, the deep intelligence of her face and her modest, self-effacing grace. He bolted from the chair, feeling as if he'd been pinioned there for hours. For once catching McGill off guard, he strode from the room, leaving the housekeeper who had been standing just outside the door in his wake.

In the empty hall he turned right, but had no recollection of the layout of the huge structure. At the end of the corridor he found himself at the entrance to the chapel. He remembered the heavy double doors, the inlaid brass and scrollwork. Inside he could hear a deep voice toiling though a prayer. Eddie stopped and thought about prayer but could not bring himself to go inside. His heart pounded. Nearby someone was preparing food and the smell of burnt toast assaulted his stomach. If he didn't breathe fresh air soon, he was certain he would pass out.

Suddenly like a missive from his unconscious he turned, his body seeming to remember more about those long ago days in that place, and without conscious direction from his brain he walked past the chapel and to the left and out of the side exit of the residence. He staggered until his eyes accustomed themselves to the bright sunlight.

All his senses were ablaze with fury. Even the sight of the green pastures plush with cows, serene and beautiful below, couldn't soothe him. Following the walkway around the side of the building, he found his car and sat for a moment in the driver's seat, readying himself for the ride home and wondering whether what he had learned would bring his sorrowing wife any peace.

Chapter 35

B.J. knelt over the tub. Stacked on the floor and in a laundry basket atop the toilet seat were cups, plates and glasses. Enormous swells of foam edged over the side of the tub and slid to the floor. The shower was running. The bathroom floor was covered with towels and clean dishes drying. Amid the clatter of dishes, running water and the tinkle of silverware, she had not heard the door open. Kasia swatted little bubbles that floated up from the frothy water.

"What's this?" Kasia shouted.

"Guerilla dishwashing." B.J. closed the tap. "Just invented it. Found a few glasses under my bed. Then some more on the closet shelf. One thing led to another. I decided to gather up all the dishes. Way too many to wash in the sink. So—" B.J. let her logic speak for itself— "guerilla dishwashing."

As she scraped and sudsed each plate, holding it up to the shower spray until it was free of foam, B.J. repeated Spanish phrases in various voices, echoing the words that came from the boom box in the corner. *"Habla espanol, senorita."* She affected a macho swagger voice into a plate held like a mirror in front of her. *"Muchas gracias, senor,"* she simpered, a kid with a missing front tooth. *"¿Tiene algo en negro?"* a high-pitched girlie voice asked as B.J. held an imaginary blouse up to her chest. *"Un billete de ida y vuelta,"* the deep heavy voice of a jock requested. Then in the cloying tone of Mrs. Mercado, the Spanish teacher, *"No comprendo. Repita, por favor."*

A smile crossed Kasia's face. She and B.J. had avoided talking about their argument, but they had come to a rapprochement a few days earlier when the Fenston events had forced Kasia to her breaking point. They had been walking silently to Sunday supper when Kasia started to shudder as though an enormous chill had descended on her. She stood still unable to walk another step.

B.J. steered her off the path to the Union and onto a bench in the memorial garden. "Come on, Kasia. Talk to me. What's happened? It can't just be about—"

Kasia began to sob uncontrollably. B.J. waited, then patted her friend's back.

Slowly as her tears subsided, Kasia recounted all that had happened since she arrived at Hapwell. Telling B.J. about her parents, her discoveries in Fenston, the existence of a previously unknown sister, was hard, but each word brought her a lightening of spirit.

"That sucks," was B.J.'s pronouncement—the label she placed on everything displeasing, from too much homework to the revelation that her hero, Woody Allen, had been having an affair with his stepdaughter.

"Yes, it really, really sucks," Kasia agreed. Somehow the word itself, the way it encompassed so much emotion and yet kept it handleable, made her feel better.

"Can I help?"

"How?"

"Anything you can think of, I'll do."

"That's just it. Nothing can make any of it better. It's just something I've got to live with, I guess. Every time I think about it I get furious. Can you imagine? My father had two wives. Bizarre, yes. But I can accept it. But that Hattie knew it all the time. And Piotr. How could he? What a traitor."

"Yeah, that double sucks." B.J. could be such a comfort, Kasia thought. "Maybe even triple sucks."

Over the days since they had the argument they had both worked to steer away from troubling topics. Kasia was careful not to discuss Nick around B.J. For her part, B.J. didn't mention the argument or her quick extreme reaction. The days when they were icily polite to each other had made them both realize how lucky they'd been in the room-mate sweepstakes and how much they would lose if they allowed small differences to come between them.

"Maybe—yes, there is a way you can help me. I want to put Piotr out of my life completely. The money from my mother's house pays my tuition and board. But Piotr sends me spending money. I haven't been cashing his checks. I'm still okay for the time being. But soon I'll have to figure out something."

"I'll give you what I can—" There was no more room on the drying towels, so B. J. stood and hung four coffee cups from the shower curtain hooks.

Kasia laughed. "I don't mean I want you to give me money. I want you to help me find a job."

Now Kasia stood in the doorway admiring the wonderfully unorthodox dishwashing. Then she began to repeat the phrases herself in her best Sophie voice, mixing the Polish hard g's with a kind of Spanglish chirping. "You have test tomorrow?" she asked.

B.J. ignored the question and motioned for help with the epic washing. "Get that file organizer off my desk. See if you can slip the big plates into the slots to dry."

Kasia obeyed. "Works great!" she said. B.J.'s ingenuity never ceased to amaze her.

"*¿Comprende?* Spanish test?" she asked again and handed B.J. another stack of dishes. "It's amazing there are any plates left in the cafeteria. Smuggling one or two out every day, it adds up. If everyone in all the dorms had this many, we'd be eating out of our hands."

B.J. stopped washing long enough to make a bowl out of her cupped palms. "Please sir, more gruel," she whimpered shyly in a Cockney accent.

"But why are you washing plates we're going to bring back?"

"Return groaty, crud-covered, smelly, disgusting plates?"

"A Spanish test?" Kasia persisted.

"*Si, senorita.* How d'ju know?" B.J. nodded sheepishly as she held a cereal bowl under the shower stream.

"*Naturalmente.* Ours was last week. Plus, what do you always do to prepare for a big test. Housework, laundry, letters, anything but study. *¿Es verdad?*"

"So be smart. But I won't tell you about the great job I heard about today. How do you say 'coincidence' in Spanish?"

"Yob. Did you say 'yob'?" Kasia's eyes sparkled.

"Maybe I won't tell you."

"*Lo siento.*"

"Okay. Tomorrow at one go over to the vet clinic on Prospero Street. You know where that is, don't you?"

Kasia nodded.

"Mrs. Talbott will tell you what's involved. A vet tech. Part time. Flexible hours. I think it's primarily taking care of the animals in the kennel, but a few hours a week you have to help Dr. Pryal. And the best part is you can walk to work."

"A miracle worker. How did you find out about it?"

"Wish I could say I had anticipated my roomie's problem. Actually I saw Mindy Talbott at the laundromat. She asked if I was interested. It's good money and flexible hours. But with practice and away games, I couldn't take on anything else. Anyway, it's yours."

"Laundry too? You, my dear," Kasia switched her most exaggerated Transylvania accent, "have made my day."

"Yeah. Saturday morning. I wake up at nine and you're long gone. Are you sure you're really a college student? Nobody else around here is up until noon. Where were you?"

Kasia ignored the question. She wasn't ready to talk about her encounter with Alice, so she started to dry the clean dishes and stack them in a box. "How are you going to get these back into the caf without getting in trouble with Mary?"

"The commuter lounge is dead on Saturday night. I figure we'll wait until dark then just leave the box on a table and someone will find it and take it up to the kitchen."

"Great idea. Wait. Did you say *we?*"

"We. As in 'you and me.' Our dishes, remember? You made just as many trips to the dorm with a dish of food hidden under your jacket as I did. Remember all those extra chocolate puddings?"

"Okay," Kasia said reluctantly.

"By the way, you got a call."

"Who?"

"Guess."

"Who?"

"Guess. If I talk to him a few more times, I'm going to start calling him *Tío* Piotr."

"Good. Let him be your uncle. I don't want to claim him anymore."

"He's frantic that you haven't called him. 'Vat isss she doinggg?'" B.J. imitated Piotr's voice. "'I know she isss busssy, but please ask her to phone me.' He sounds really pitiful. I actually felt sorry for him."

"Well don't. Let him worry. I'll talk to him when I feel like it. What did you tell him?"

"Same as always. I said you were out. For once I wasn't lying. I told him I didn't know where you were." B.J.'s voice was small and echoey as she leaned into the soapy water and trawled the bottom for overlooked silverware. Her long legs dangled over the edge of the tub.

B.J. pulled the plug and watched the dirty water swirl down the drain leaving Cheerios, lettuce leaves and bits of unidentifiable goop in its wake. "Yuck. Much more of that and I'll give up eating entirely." Sweatshirt and jeans completely soaked and wet hair plastered to her cheeks, she made her mad scientist face.

"*¿Esta loco?*" Kasia handed B.J. the cleanser and sponge.

"A phone call before ten, wicked. So since I was up anyway, I figured I'd get a few things done around here. Were you in the library?"

"Tell you later," Kasia said, and she would. Having friends like B.J. and Nick, friends she could confide in, had made all the misery in her life bearable. Yes, after dinner and their replacement raid on the college's dishes, she'd tell her roommate everything. Soon she'd have a job and one more part of her plan would fall into place.

Chapter 36

The lopsided, heavy box of dishes clanged and rattled as they hurried across the campus, 5'1" Kasia on one side and 6' B.J. on the other. By the time they were twenty yards from the Union they were laughing so hard as they imagined the consternation on the janitor's face when he discovered a small kitchenful of crockery and cutlery that they had to put the box down. Shushing each other, they waited to see if they heard any voices.

A man came out of the building, his hands in his pockets and head down. Whoever it was seemed lost in thought. He stopped under the lamppost and took something from his pocket, fingered it and then put it back. B.J. and Kasia froze as he passed within ten feet of where they were hiding. They recognized Doug Martin, a guy who was on the seven-year plan at Hapwell, taking the minimum courses each semester for fulltime student status. He bragged that he hadn't set foot in the library since freshman orientation. The instant he walked away a light leapt onto the lawn in front of them. "Doesn't she ever go home?" B.J. whispered, pointing to Mary Turkelson's second floor office.

"She must be watching the door. Thank God she didn't see us."

"Right. The shit would definitely hit the fan if she found out what we were up to. What a hawkeye. Did she have her deerslayer hat on?"

"Shush," Kasia begged. "I have to pee. If you make me laugh, I'll lose it."

B.J. smirked.

"Just remember, you got us into this."

They took off their sweatshirts and folded them around the dishes to cushion the sound. Then they hoisted the box again and moved carefully around the rectangle of light and toward the building, into the door and down the steps to the commuter lounge. B.J. leaned the box against the wall to free Kasia's hands so she could open the door.

When they stepped inside, the lounge at the end of the corridor was not in the total darkness expected. The door to a storage room stood open. Inside a small table glowed in the light of a lantern. They were already past the door when Kasia recognized Yvette. Kasia backed up, pulling B.J. with her. "Hi. What are—"she blurted. On the table was a large baggie filled with marijuana, a scale, and a pile of smaller baggies.

Too late to shield what she was doing from view, Yvette echoed, "Hi." Her delicate, manicured hands leapt to her lap.

"We didn't know anyone would be down here," Kasia said as she and B.J. balanced the box between them.

"Neither did I," Yvette said, regaining her usual composure.

B.J. was silent behind Kasia, though her roommate knew by her breathing that she was holding back. B.J. slid the box to a table. She walked over to Yvette and looked down at the table. "If I were you, I'd take this someplace else. Like off this campus completely." She turned away sharply before Yvette could respond. "Let's get out of here before we get a bad rep just being with her." B.J. walked out the door.

Kasia glanced at Yvette's expression of smirking bravado. "I'm not going to tell you your business, but you need to use better judgment," she said.

"Or what?" You'll turn me in? I don't think so."

Just the tiniest threat tinged Yvette's words, but enough to make Kasia shudder as she recalled her visit to Yvette's room a few weeks earlier. *Oh my God*, thought Kasia, *that's how it happens. How you become a client of a drug dealer.* Would B.J. believe it was only that one time, only because her world was falling apart? Would anyone believe her? She doubted it. She felt Yvette's eyes boring into her back as she followed B.J. out of the building.

Drawn into the cleaning frenzy that followed the clean-dish-return caper, Kasia wet a cloth with soapy water and wiped down the night tables and desk surfaces. Moving her thumbnail furiously, she scraped up chunks of cheese and gluey circles where cups had stuck. "Every day it's some new thing," she said.

B.J. listened attentively to the account of Kasia's encounter with Alice as they worked side by side piling all their textbooks on the desk and slotting tapes into cases. "You have to just let it go. Don't let all that family crap get in the way of your classes."

"That's easy to say."

"I know. But try to keep the focus on yourself. It's their problem. You're not to blame for any of it. You're the innocent victim. Don't let them hurt you any more than they have." B. J. was great at pep talks.

Kasia stopped scrubbing and looked over at her roommate. Then she put down her cloth and went to hug her. "Beej. You are so great! Just having you to talk to—"

B. J. shrugged the arms away. "We've gone this far," B.J. said, a little embarrassed by Kasia's emotion. She threw in a wad of dirty paper towel, then closed the drawstring of the second full green plastic garbage bag. "Might as well go completely white tornado and change the beds." She tossed a set of clean sheets to Kasia.

"Sure." Kasia agreed. The cleaning reminded her of days in Poland with Sophie, the satisfaction they had taken in gossiping about Piotr's messy ways.

"Do you believe that Yvette? She's like an accident waiting to happen. How could she deal drugs? In a public place, no less," B.J. said.

"Maybe she figured that nobody would be in the commuter lounge or that hallway on the weekend."

"I don't know what will go down first, her getting busted or Gunnar finding out that she's been seeing four other guys on the side. How dumb is that on a campus this size? Sooner or later his English will be good enough that he'll understand the jokes and gossip."

"I wonder if he knows she's dealing?" Kasia asked.

"Doubt it. He's really a nice guy. Just a little dumb. I talk to him sometimes in Little Hall. We have class right next to each other. Guess he's not doing so well in English. I told him about the tutoring center."

"I hope he goes. If you get too far behind, there's no making it up."

"What about us? Worried we're going to get in trouble for having too many dishes in our room. Meanwhile, she's dealing drugs. I knew she was wild, but nothing like that."

"I didn't figure it out either," Kasia said. She remembered the night she'd gotten the grass and pills from Yvette. At the time she'd thought of it as a friend who just happened to have something that would help her relax. She really needed to feel better. "A little sample," Yvette had said. Only when she saw Yvette preparing the drug buys did she put that statement together with the epic shopping sprees. The money. "I just wish she'd quit before she gets busted."

"How did we get so much trash." B.J. hefted the bags as if to weigh them. "Must be ten pounds each. I'll take them down."

While B.J. was gone, Kasia opened her desk drawer and took out the packet of unopened letters from Piotr. Arranged in no particular order, twenty or so envelopes. She slit one open and scanned it. Dated August 15, it was full of news from Poland—worker unrest, the rumors that the next prime minister might be a woman—something he knew she'd be particularly interested in. Piotr was mildly distressed that he hadn't heard from her in a week. "I hope you are studying hard, *Malutka* but…"Without reading to the end, Kasia refolded the letter and put it back into the envelope and threw it and the rest of the letters into the empty wastebasket.

When the room was completely clean, Kasia replaced bedraggled Lulu next to Tweetie Bird on the pillow. The doll's cottony hair grew in sparse clumps—the rest of the celluloid head bald with pinholes where the hair had once sprouted. B.J. had christened her Chemo Baby. The lace trim of her petticoat hung below the faded red peasant dress. Beneath the dress, the white cotton of the doll's torso was hardly discolored and the red heart stitched over the left breast was still bright.

Tired from their toil, the roommates studied for an hour and then went to bed. Kasia had enjoyed the work. Suddenly lying there in the dark talking, she felt the contentment of someone who has suffered and finally come to a place of ease and rest. B.J. made her feel so normal, so average. She could almost think of herself s a real American college student with ordinary concerns until the old questions intruded.

When another confidence was finally revealed that night in the dark Kasia was completely unprepared. She had begun to fall asleep thinking about Nick, the little V of skin beneath the collar of his blue shirt, when B.J. spoke again. "Kasia, you awake?"

"Mummmm," she answered. But something in B.J.'s tone made her take notice. "What, Beej?"

"Nevermind."

"What?" Kasia sensed something. "Come on, what, tell me."

"It's just that—" B.J.'s voice got lower with each word, "I know you have a lot on your mind, but I've been worried about something—"

What, Kasia thought, problem could Ms. Perfect have? A great family, a zillion friends, Dean's list, and a letter sophomore year for hockey. "What?" The lack of sympathy in her own voice surprised Kasia. She softened. "Come on, B.J. I've told you the whole mess of my family life. Now it's your turn."

B.J. cleared her throat and started, "The problem is—"

Kasia waited.

"It's weird."

"You're telling me about weird."

"Whew," B.J. exhaled in frustration. "Remember the night we had the fight?"

Kasia felt her face flush in the dark. "I've been meaning to apologize. My fault. Completely."

"I bet you were surprised when I flipped out."

"I don't even remember what I said. Whatever it was, I must have been really out of line."

"Don't you get it?"

The clipped syllables alerted Kasia to something. "What, Beej? Get what?" Kasia tensed, hearing something painful and complicated in B.J.'s voice, a wistfulness she didn't associate with her self-assured friend. Thinking back to the way B.J. let her tell her painful and complicated story in her own time, she waited.

"About guys. Dates. Remember?"

"Yes."

"It's just that—"

"What? You know all this groaty stuff about me and we're still here. Did some guy trash you? That's why you don't go out? Whatever it is, you'll feel better if you talk about it." Kasia wondered as she said that, whether she really wanted anyone else's problems. But she wanted to be as good a friend as B.J. had been to her.

"Just that—"

"You're gay?" Kasia said the first thing that had popped into her mind to fill in the blanks. The word squatted between them as darkness drew its comforting curtain around them. Kasia heard a shudder and then the unfamiliar sound of B.J. weeping. Kasia struggled to find her voice. "Is that some kind of a big deal or something?"

"Maybe. I'm a jock. Never even had a date. Guys aren't interested. I must give off some gay vibe or something. I'm so worried. I didn't tell you—If you knew, you might not want to room with me. I would have told you before but I'm just figuring it out myself."

"Do you think I'm some kind of an old country born-again? What's the big deal?"

There was a long silence between them. Kasia held back. She'd let B.J. decide where the conversation would go next.

"Time for some serious zzzzs." B.J.'s usual confident tone—almost.

"Beej?"

"Huh?"

"Anytime you need to talk—"

"Okay."

First a sister Kasia didn't know she had. And now B.J.'s possibly being gay. *What next,* she wondered, turning again in bed and repositioning her pillow and enjoying the luxury of fresh sweet smelling sheets.

"Thank you." B.J.'s voice was uncharacteristically so small and childlike that Kasia imagined it could have come from the pillow next to her, from Lulu's chipped and much kissed lips.

When Kasia heard B.J.'s breath move into the even measures of sleep, she got out of bed and took the letters from the basket and put them back into her desk drawer.

Chapter 37

Nick watched from the library window as Kasia climbed the hill from town toward the campus after her first day of work in the Ausland Animal Clinic and Kennel. When she saw him, she brightened and waved for him to join her. "The smell just about knocked me over," Kasia reported. "And the noise. I think all those little dogs in the back kennel must be in competition—whoever stops yapping first gets to eat last. The three minutes after you put the food into the bowls is the only silence of the day. I was tempted to feed them every half hour just to have some quiet."

"Sounds awful," Nick commiserated, rubbing her shoulder. "Tell me again why you are working when you don't have to?"

"I don't want to be dependent on Piotr."

"Didn't he take care of you your whole life?"

"That's different. I was so small I didn't have a choice. And I didn't know then that he was hiding so many things from me. Now that I do—that changes everything."

"Admirable." And she read the word in Nick's expression as well. "How can I help?"

"Let me complain," Kasia smiled engagingly. "I need to. I just get frustrated. Some of it's fun. I love getting to let them out into the run. There are three cocker spaniel puppies who are so adorable."

Nick put his arms up, inviting her to snuggle. Instead Kasia bent her face down to her sleeve and sniffed. "Don't even come near me. I smell like dead dog."

"How nice," Nick laughed. "Now I really want a hug!"

"I'll shower and meet you in the library."

The scene with Nick repeated itself on Thursday. Kasia admitted that the work had, if anything, gotten more odious. "I finished early with the kennel stuff today. There's an old trailer at the back of the property. The vet tech who quit used to live there. Then some kid broke in and was squatting in the place." Kasia shivered in disgust. "He asked me to straighten it up a little. The place was a total wreck—mice turds everywhere and a scuzzy cot with smelly old blankets. Dr. Pryal was hinting around that I should move in and save my board fee."

"Did you tell him you were strapped for money?"

"Yeah. Serves me right, huh? He said it was a shame nobody was living in such a nice spot—quiet and private. Of course, he would pay me less too. Fat chance. I wouldn't even put my lunch in that refrigerator. I opened it and the smell was even worse than the rest of the place. Stuffed with rotting food."

"Gross!"

"I just closed it up and walked back to the run and watched the dogs playing. That's the last time I'll finish my work early."

On Saturday the Hapwell campus blazed with red maples, oak and birch trees, each making a seasonal statement. Along the drive the school flags welcomed the homecoming crowd. Kasia hurried from the clinic for the hockey field on the back campus, the centerpiece of the campus weekend celebration. B.J. and her teammates had been practicing for days to perfect their offense against their traditional opponents, the Sparks of Montiel College. For the first time in twelve years, Hapwell had a chance to win the first game of the season.

Nick had saved her a front row seat in the crowded bleachers. Beside him Caro, delighted to be at a college function, bobbed her small head in time with the action of the cheerleaders on the side of the field. Her blonde hair was caught up in twin bunches above her ears and decorated with small blue and white pompoms. She had insisted on wearing her own cheerleading uniform and her legs twitched in imitation as she studied the moves of the older girls.

Kasia slid in next to Nick with five minutes to spare. He tried to explain the rules and how the game was played. Clad in plaid hockey kilts and blue sweaters, the team swarmed onto the field in the afternoon sunshine. The crowd roared as the young women ran the length of the field warming up and waving their sticks in salute. B.J., easily the tallest player on the team, jogged to the cage and adjusted her leg and chest pads. Her face intense and focused, she pulled the protective mask in place and took her position inside the goalie cage. Kasia stood and gave her roommate the high sign.

The centers moved into position and began the ground sticks configuration to begin play. Hapwell got control of the ball and moved it quickly down to the other goal. One of the wings smashed it, the sound sharp in the afternoon air. The ball careened toward the opposing cage. The goalie blocked. Kasia lost sight of the ball, but suddenly it flew toward the cage again and scored. The crowd screamed in delight at the good start to the season's opener.

Kasia, Nick and Caro leapt to their feet with the rest of the spectators at each goal. The opponents were fierce in their stickwork, and at the last minute the teams were tied. The ball moved again toward B.J., who stomped out of the cage as far as she could to defend, counting on her wings to support her. The ball roared toward her and she lifted the stick and caught it in midair and sent it smartly to an offensive player. It was a strategy they had practiced and their work paid off. The ball moved quickly downfield and the goal went in before anyone seemed to realize what had happened. The Sparks' goalie twirled in fury and disbelief.

With thirty seconds left on the clock the Sparks seemed dispirited by the defensive blunder. The ball dribbled toward B.J. so slowly that she blocked it with her leg. Hapwell had won. B.J.'s teammates threw down their sticks as the final seconds ticked away. B.J. whipped off her mask. Suddenly she was surrounded by teammates hugging and pulling her toward them in a huddle of delighted shrieks.

By the time they caught up to B.J. she had peeled off the pads and hung a towel around her neck. Her hair was matted and sweaty where the mask straps had pressed, but she was electric with the effort and excitement of play. Gunnar joined the others in the crowd. Smiling broadly, he stepped forward and patted B.J.'s shoulder in praise.

"I figured if we could start out strong, they'd d fall apart. And they did," B.J. said. "We really wanted this game. The whole team pulled together—" Her cheeks were ruddy with effort and excitement. The short skirt showed off B.J.'s strong shapely legs.

On the way back from the hockey field Nick, Kasia and Caro walked the long way around the campus through the woods and along the shore of the pond. They stopped on the small wooden suspension bridge that hung over Foster Creek. Caro ran ahead to the college green shouting the cheers she'd learned. She threw down her hands and punctuated the phrases with a series of cartwheels across the lawn. "How did work go this morning?" Nick asked.

"We had three surgeries. One of those dogs was really heavy," Kasia said, rubbing her right shoulder. She rolled her head around trying to loosen up her muscles. "I had to help lift him up on the table. He must have weighted seventy-five pounds. Then Dr. Pryal got an emergency call and I had to hold Fluffy while he answered it."

"Why don't you quit if it's so awful?"

"I would quit in a minute if I hadn't already paid $18.00 for the smock. And I really need the job—"

"Maybe you should reconsider the thing with your uncle."

Kasia gave him a withering look.

"Whenever you talk about him, he sounds like a really great guy."

"Had me fooled, too."

"There could be some explanation for what he did. Something. If you don't ask him about it, you'll never know."

"Please. I can't let myself depend on him just as if nothing has changed."

"Just a suggestion."

"Actually the job's not that bad. Most of the time I can block out the noise. And I love feeding the dogs. But today. I just wasn't ready to assist at an operation. That's all. We got the dog up on the table and put him out. No problem. But when he made the incision, I almost puked. He thinks he's on *General Hospital* or something when he's doing the procedures." She stopped and dramatically displayed her upraised forearms as if she'd just scrubbed. "Then he turns to me and says, 'Why don't you close up?' And leaves me there with an unconscious dog, guts smeared everywhere—"

Nick winced in sympathy at the revolted expression on Kasia's face.

"Would have served him right if you hurled on him, splattered his pants and shoes."

"Yeah," Kasia said. "I didn't think of it or I would have let myself. When he came back, I must have looked pretty green. He told me to go outside and get a breath of fresh air."

"Never mind. I've got some good news for you, little miss." Kasia smiled at the pet name he'd begun using. "You know that road trip you've been wanting to make? How about tomorrow?"

"What about your chem test?"

"For once del Ray took pity on us. Postponed—until Wednesday because of homecoming."

Kasia said, "You, my dear, are a prince."

"And."

"And? What else?"

"We're going in style. Asked my dad to use the car and he said okay. Air-conditioning and everything."

"I'm psyched."

"It's a long ride. I'll gas up the car and get a map. How about we leave at 7?"

Caro ran toward them. "Come on, you guys. I want you to watch me." And she was off again, her thin legs surprisingly strong and elastic in the jumps and twists.

"Talk about hurling. One of those cartwheels would have me on my knees," Nick said, pride evident in his voice. "That little rug rat is something else."

"Terrific jumps. I think you'd make the college team," Kasia called to Caro. She quickly reviewed the condition of the room, then asked, "Do you want to come up and check out my room while I change for the barbeque?"

Caro bounced her delight.

"I'll be here," Nick said, joining a group of people stretched on the lawn in the sunshine.

Kasia admired the girl's determination. She thought of one of the entries in her old journal, one she had made when she was Caro's age: *Mrs. Anney told me that I should do my best, even when I'm sad.* Caro always made her think back to those days in Hartford when her life was turning on itself. Even so, she'd tried to heed Mrs. Anney's advice.

She could recall the classroom and her desk, her books, the smell of the lunchroom at the end of the hall—something like turpentine and mashed bananas, a comforting smell. One little memory. One day in all that time. But it might lead to more. Why did she have so few recollections of her life?

Caro was impressed with the dorm room arrangement. She bounced on both beds, inspected the toiletries and looked in the refrigerator. When she spotted Lulu on the bed, she asked, "Whose is that?"

"Would you believe it's mine? Lulu. She's very old. She was my mother's doll a long time ago."

"Lulu?"

"My mother called her that. *Lala* is the word for doll in Polish. Maybe that had something to do with it."

"Lulu, the lala," Caro said, obviously pleased with herself as she carefully repositioned Lulu next to Tweetie.

Inside the Student Union, B.J. was the center of excited attention about the play that had clinched the game and won the championship. Nick handed Kasia and Caro glasses of punch and spread a napkin filled with ginger cookies out on the palm of his hand for them to select one. Gunnar was still at B.J.'s elbow. Later as they left the building at the end of the party, they passed him and Yvette in the stairwell. Gunnar was looking frustrated as Yvette gestured excitedly, her quick little hands circling him like small birds, diving, pecking at his chest. Kasia passed without their noticing her.

That night as the roommates were heading to the library, Kasia said, "You must be so excited."

"Feels great. We were so close last year. It super sucked when they scored two goals in the fourth quarter. We just couldn't come back. With this win under our belts, we could go all the way to district champ."

"I see Gunnar's become a hockey groupie."

"He's great. But I don't think he knows diddly shit about hockey."

"Oh?" Kasia said, a little question in her voice. "You and he have been hanging out together?"

"He's my tutee."

"Since when?"

"Since last week."

Kasia laughed. "Really?"

"Part of my work study. I have to tutor him in lit. He's totally confused about the stuff they're reading. It's crazy. The poor guy can hardly get through a menu and they put him in Hamm's class. Impossible. Week one—straight into Melville. Gunnar didn't get it at all. Our first session he asked me to help him." B.J. mimicked Gunnar's deep voice. "*Bartleby the Scrivener.* He called it *Bartleby the Sribbler.* I was trying so hard not to laugh."

"Doesn't he have a cool voice? He sounds like Spock," Kasia said.

"Sweden's not exactly Vulcan, but it might as well be. He's so totally clueless."

"I can't imagine Spock jumping around all excited like Gunnar was today."

"They call that school spirit," B.J. retorted.

Kasia raised her eyebrow. "Anyway, Beej, you did great."

"Yeah. But now I have to do some serious catching up. I haven't cracked the chem book all week."

"Ouch."

"Yeah. Double ouch."

"May the force be with you." Kasia held up her fingers, then blushed as she realized she'd mixed up her sci-fi sources.

Chapter 38

"About time." Athena hurried around the front counter of Wescott's Dry Goods and General Merchandise to hug Hattie Darling.

"Things a little boring without me?" Hattie laughed. "I missed you too."

Athena put her finger to her lips. Almost a whisper, her voice had an edge that made Hattie draw back. "Don't want Will to see you just yet. No time for chit-chat." Athena took off her white apron and put it on the hook behind her. "Keep the counter for a spell," she called loudly. Then she led the mystified Hattie through the door to the kitchen of their living quarters at the side of the building.

She picked up the phone and called Eleanor. "Hattie's here. I'll wait." Then she turned to Hattie. "El's on her way over."

"What's going on? Why couldn't I stop to say hello to Will? I don't get it." Hattie sat at the enamel top table and gazed distractedly around at the open hutch, the rows of clocks that Athena collected. In the deeply familiar place a harbinger broke the silence a few seconds before the others striking the hour, alerting them that even as they sat there time was leaving them, moving away each second. Hattie wrung her hand. "Tell me. I know something's wrong?"

"When El gets here."

"What? What? Something with Alice?"

"Alice is fine. But about Eleanor. Before she gets here, I want to prepare you. El took a tumble down the hill into her quarry. She's pretty scratched up."

"She fell?"

"It was raining. Slippery. And she fell."

"What was she doing in the quarry in the rain?"

"You'd have to ask her. But I wouldn't encourage it. She's been acting kind of strange lately."

"One of her black moods?"

"Worse than usual. Much worse. I talked to Eddie about it the other day. He listened like he knew something was up, but he wouldn't give any specifics."

"That's Eddie. You can get a stone to talk easier than him if he's not ready."

"Eleanor didn't even tell me about the fall. Showed up here Wednesday for work looking like the loser in a cat fight and acted as if nothing was out of the ordinary. Only way I knew what happened was Clem blabbed. Seems he saw her fall and rushed over and saved her."

"As long as El's okay."

"Want some tea?" Athena popped up again, filled a red enamel kettle and set it on the stove. Her white button down shirt was tucked into her rolled up jeans and she wore boating shoes without socks.

"I can't stay long. Haven't even been home yet."

"Where did you go this time?"

"Trout fishing in Canada." Hattie smirked.

"Eleanor will be here in a minute." Athena looked at Hattie, then examined her more closely. "Some vacation. You've got bags under your eyes down to your knees."

"No lectures, please. Just stopped to let you know I'm back. I brought this for you," she said as she pulled a bottle from her canvas bag. Inside the clear liquid a stalk of buffalo grass winnowed in the light. "I remembered how you and Will like vodka."

"*Polish* vodka!" Athena stressed "Polish" and looked sharply, opening her mouth as if to say something more, just as the door flew open.

Clad in black tights and a long yellow shirt, her hair piled on top of her head and secured with a yellow pencil, Eleanor looked like an overwrought bumblebee. Her face and neck were pocked with scratches. She was breathless, her cheeks bright pink from exertion. For the moment Eleanor had forgotten her own cares and was focused on the problem at hand. "Did you tell her?"

"What? Tell me what?" Hattie said, her voice rising with each word. "What's happened?"

Athena reached for Hattie's hand. "Not Alice. But something has happened. We were worried about how you'd take it."

"Three weeks ago, I was tending the store while Athena and Will had a date—" Eleanor began solemnly.

"For God's sake, El. Don't give me the preamble. Just blurt it out!"

"Okay." Deflated, Eleanor looked to Athena, who nodded back. "Okay. Kasia has come to Fenston looking for you."

"Ohhh," Hattie exhaled—a sound as if all the air had left her body. "She's here. That explains—"

A collective sigh rose from the three women as they looked at each other. After a short silence, three voices at once moved across the known and the unknown of Kasia's appearance in Fenston. Hattie gasped, "Oh my God, that poor kid. How can I face her? How can I make her understand that what I did, I did for her and for Anya?"

Her friends tried to comfort her. "You were just trying to help. Surely she'll understand."

"I can't imagine her pain," Hattie wailed.

"Wait just a minute. Let's back up." Athena held her hand up to silence Eleanor and Hattie. "What did you mean, 'that explains'—explains what?"

"Forget it."

"No. Absolutely not. If there is something else, something you haven't told us—now's the time. We'll help if we can. But we need to know everything."

Hattie looked into the faces of her friends. A sob tore from her. Athena rose and brought a box of tissues from the kitchen counter to the table and placed it in front of Hattie.

The words came in a disjointed torrent. "I'm just relieved. I got there. I waited and waited. And she never appeared. All day. In the evening. Late at night. I waited. And she was gone. There was nothing I could do. I stayed another four days. I saw him. But not her. I couldn't understand. So I came home—" Hattie reached for another tissue as Athena and Eleanor looked at each other in confusion.

"Who? She? He? Who? I sound like an inept bird caller." Athena tried for a bit of levity.

"Kasia. I waited outside and she never—"

"You *were* in Poland?" Athena whispered, incredulous. "I can't believe it. It just flashed into my mind as you walked in the door: *She was in Poland.* And the vodka—"

"Yes." The word came slowly, as if drawing itself out painfully. "Yes. Yes. Yes."

"But why?" Eleanor handed Hattie a cup of tea. "Maybe you want something stronger?"

Hattie looked at Athena, then at Eleanor. "I'm too tired. Wait. Eleanor knows about Ben? Did you tell her?"

"She already knew."

"But, how—" Hattie glanced from back and forth between her two friends.

"I knew from the start," Eleanor began.

"Skip it. That's not the important thing—" Athena broke in. "Kasia. You went there looking for her?"

Hattie nodded.

"How did you know where to go?" Athena asked.

"It's been so long," Eleanor added.

The two women studied Hattie as she struggled to decide where to begin.

"Ten years," Hattie said. The look on her face wrenched the hearts of her friends. "I always go. Once a year, I fly to Poland, rent a car and drive to Warsaw. From the store across the way or sitting in the café on the corner I can see the house. Then I wait. I see her coming home from school. With her friends. I watch her playing. Growing up. I see Piotr growing old. His face wrinkling like my own. Yes. I guess you would say I go to spy on them."

"How many—" Eleanor stopped mid-sentence, as if seeing Hattie for the first time. "You okay? You really look terrible."

"That's what I said," Athena added.

"I do feel pretty rocky. Probably jet lag." Hattie shrugged off their concern and continued, "Nine times now. I don't know why but I had kept the address from when I had written to Piotr for Anya."

"But why? Why did you go all that way?"

"Hard to explain. The first time, I just needed to make sure they were okay. The next year, I couldn't stop thinking—wondering. I kept going back. It gave me some comfort. I had to give them up, but at least this gave me a small connection to two people I loved."

"And this time, she was gone and you were worried." Athena gave a short laugh. "I guess that's what you call irony. You go there to see her just as she arrives here looking for you."

"Reminds me of 'The Gift of the Magi,'" interjected Eleanor. "The de Maupassant story about—sorry, the O. Henry story—"

"At least you won't have to travel halfway around the world when you want to see her again. Just a short drive."

"What?" Hattie caught her breath and wiped her eyes again. Her friends were laughing. She didn't get the joke. She looked from one to the other—the old friends who had been her strength in the turmoil of her life. "Kasia?"

"She's a freshman at Hapwell."

"Here?" Hattie's voice echoed her features—a complexity of terror and joy.

Nodding, Eleanor gave a short burst of laughter. Athena cracked the seal on the bottle of vodka and placed three small juice glasses decorated with red-ribboned black Scotties on the table in front of them.

Chapter 39

Relieved that Alice's car was not in the drive, Hattie pulled her suitcase from the trunk. She remembered Ben returning from a trip, the exhaustion in his face, the weary curve of his shoulders as he walked up the porch steps. She opened the front door and walked into her house. Time to think, that's what she craved most, but how could she focus when she was so tired? Now she would be forced to tell Alice about Ben's other life and Kasia. How could she explain her own complicity without causing a terrible rift?

She was tired. Tears of exhaustion and frustration sprung into her eyes. She dropped the suitcase in the foyer and walked through the rooms of her old house, letting the place itself, its persistent presence in her life, soothe her. She had missed her home.

She walked into the living room and stood in a rectangle of light from the French doors looking out onto the late summer meadow, recently hayed for the last time. The room spoke to her of everything she had at one time hoped her life would be. The certainty of pale green striped wallpaper, the history of the old chandelier which had been converted from kerosene to electric by her grandparents, the cleanliness and clarity of its sparkling chimney glasses. In the center of the dining table, exactly as she had left it, sat a large wicker basket filled with dried roses and asters, wheat and grass. She remembered gathering and drying the flowers, selecting the basket and studying its composition. In the kitchen a half-eaten store bought apple pie covered with a tea towel stood on the counter, next to her Limoges teapot and a rumple of linen napkins.

She had been away too long. Suddenly she felt tired and sick. And sorry. She couldn't even solve the problems she had with Alice. What made her think she could do any better with Kasia? Recalling old arguments that left her confused and shaken and guilty somehow, Hattie thought again how difficult it would be to tell Alice about Ben. Secrets revealed. That wasn't always the answer.

Hattie knew she was coming to the end of an emotional journey; her inexplicably strained relationship with Alice might not survive. Figuring out how she could keep the knowledge of Ben's deceit from Alice had forced her into more falsehoods. Their relationship had become as difficult to navigate as her travels to Poland.

Since she left Hartford she had tried to figure out how much to tell, who to tell, and when. As much as she moved the thoughts around, like so much bulky mismatched furniture crowded into a small room, the answer was always unsatisfactory.

Chapter 40

Bobby and Mark had turned out to be pretty neat little kids. Despite the six year age difference Billy played with them, burying McDonald's action figures in the sandbox and digging them up again to begin another civilization. Tina had started her job. Every day she dressed in one of the outfits Eleanor made for her and left for work in the gas company office run by one of Eddie's friends. Most of all Billy and Sailor adored each other.

Whenever Billy came out in the garden to play with him, Sailor performed. Spinning and jumping, the big collar of his shirt flopping around his simian face, Sailor ended on a back flip, then jiggled up and down chortling madly and applauding himself. When the show was over Billy lofted Sailor to his shoulder. He carried the monkey over to the picnic table where they sat facing each other, Billy on the bench and Sailor cross-legged on the table before him. Sailor made Billy laugh with the see-, hear- and do-no-evil poses Kandy had taught him.

Billy recounted to this wise, accepting friend everything about what had happened at home before Tina left—how she had begun to stay away longer and longer and then one day after much slamming and screaming, she came into his room where he had been pretending to sleep and told him that she had to go. He spoke longingly about the time he stayed with Eleanor and Eddie, explaining their strange house, music books and the animals that lined the walls. To the recitation Sailor responded with one of the dozen or so facial expressions from his repertoire. Billy's favorite was when Sailor cocked his head to the right and rolled his eyes upward. He looked like one of the saints in the holy pictures Eleanor had tacked to the walls around the house.

The monkey was an ideal best friend. Billy felt safe enough with Sailor to talk about how he had pretended sometimes that he belonged with Eleanor and Eddie—that they had found each other and somehow they would stay together as a family. He imagined days of going with Eleanor on her errands, their long strange conversations—so engrossing at the time but impossible to recall in much detail later—his evenings opposite Eddie over the chessboard. Just when it seemed the world had stopped and he came to rest in the perfect place, just when he imagined it couldn't get any better, Eleanor found Tina and things changed.

"Not that I didn't want to find her," he confided in Sailor, who sat raptly listening, studying Billy's face. The monkey either knew what Billy was saying or responded to the shift in tone of voice, because he raised his eyebrows in waiting for the next part of the sentence. "—but I had gotten used to being there." His tone indicated that he considered it silly to be feeling homesickness for somewhere he'd spent such a short time. Yet there it was. He missed Eddie and Eleanor and his room with the squirrel watching over him as he slept.

As if to say enough of this self-pity, Sailor got to his feet and tugged Billy's arm up and down, indicating that he wanted to dance again. Billy laughed and slipped the harmonica from his pocket. He was teaching himself a song; the notes were fading from his mind. Forcing himself to concentrate, he allowed the air to flow out of him and into the sweetness on the other side.

Chapter 41

As they moved north, the trees grew darker, their sere leaves sparser than in Pennsylvania. Snuggling back into the comfortable contoured seats of the car, Kasia said, "Nice."

"I think so. But my parents never use it. My mom practically refuses to ride in it. Says it's ostentatious. She doesn't want anyone in town to know we have such a fancy vehicle. My father takes it out once in a while."

"Did they change their mind after they bought it?"

"That's the problem. Nannie and Grampie gave it to them—a twenty-fifth anniversary present last year."

"Some present." Kasia admired the impressive array of dashboard amenities.

"They're loaded. When I was little they were always coming by with stuff, but my parents didn't go for it. Actually my mom more than dad. My grandparents even tried to put a down payment on a house in Crystalle when I was born."

"Wow." Kasia'd seen the palatial houses in Crystalle, the upscale village next to Fenston.

"One of the first houses over there. I'll take you by and show you sometime."

"Your parents didn't want it?"

"Sounds great, doesn't it? But my mom thinks if you take stuff from them, they've blackmailed you. My grandmother's really social. The story goes she was furious when mom dropped out of college and married a townie."

"But they kept the car?"

"My mom was all ready to send it back. Then Grampie had to go into the hospital. Then he died. Mom sort of forgot about the car. It just sits in the garage, except when Dad takes it out to charge the battery." Nick pointed to a gauge. "Two years old and less than three thousand miles."

Kasia caressed the buttery leather seats. Her hand came away with something bright; a sparkly film covered her palm and fingertips. As the light shifted she noticed the same twinkling stuff on the carpet, as if fairy dust had been shaken inside the car.

"What's that?" Nick asked.

"Some kind of sparkly stuff. Powder maybe." She dabbed a bit on the tip of her nose and made a funny face at him.

"Wonder how it got there?"

Towns streamed past, and Kasia glimpsed the roofs and windows and backyards of hundreds of homes through the trees. Beyond, she knew, there were still more homes and shops and businesses—immense buildings where the work of cities turned its back on travelers. The map open in front of her, Kasia traced the long snake of Rt. 84, thinking how many times her father must have traveled between his lives—two wives, two daughters, between she and her mother and Hattie and Alice—over this same route. She gazed into the windows of other cars—people moving fast alongside their car, destinations etched into their faces. One back seat was filled with balloons and streamers. In another, two old people concentrated on the road before them, the wife as attentive to traffic as her husband clutching the wheel. She imagined that like her, everyone was rushing toward Connecticut and some revelation of time past.

Sensing her reflective mood, Nick tried to distract her with chatter—tales of Fenston, the kind she normally delighted in. He recounted the small plane that had landed again and again at the strip outside town and everyone's shock when the state police surrounded the airport in advance of one landing. Someone on the ground must have alerted the pilot and his mysterious, wealthy passenger. As the plane flew low over the still valley some of the bags they frantically jettisoned burst and showered the cows and fields of Nick's farm and their neighbor, old Mrs. Newberry out hanging clothes in her yard, with precious white powder.

"What was it?" Kasia asked, imagining a sugary snow in mid-June.

"Drugs. They had been flying in drugs from Mexico."

"Really? In Fenston?"

"See how smart they were. Who would have expected it? They'd been getting away with it for years."

Kasia's feeble sigh was not the reaction Nick had hoped for. "Nervous?" he asked.

Yes. She had imagined herself walking up to her old house so often. But this close, another thought hovered near her. "What if we can't find it? I was so young when we left."

"Don't worry." He sounded more confident than he felt when he thought about a big city's intricacies. He'd been to New York and Philadelphia with their swirls of underpasses and highways. He switched on the radio of his father's Lincoln Town Car. Static. "Pick a station," he said.

She played with the knobs and soon their rushing capsule filled with music. Kasia had to concentrate to think above the mindless words.

When she saw the sign for Hartford, she felt a tightening in her chest. Nick was about to ask if she knew which exit to take, but her tension stopped him. How would she know? "Why don't we stop for a coke?" he suggested.

"I'm worried that I won't know where—" But they were on the ramp moving in the orderly flow of cars.

"No sweat." Nick touched her hand reassuringly. "We'll ask. Did I tell you how pretty you look today?"

Kasia had dressed almost formally in a skirt and stockings, little brown shoes and a scarf around the shoulders of her cream colored sweater, as if she were going to visit a fussy maiden aunt. Nick had never seen her in anything besides the short skirt she'd worn the first day he found her along the road or her jean and T-shirt uniform, or her work clothes. Suddenly her determined little schoolteacherish otherness touched him as he realized these were the clothes she had brought from Poland.

The woman in the McDonald's couldn't help. Neither could the gas station attendant. Or the cop they pulled up next to. "Gordon Street. That's a new one on me." He shook his head good-naturedly. "Lived here my whole life. But it doesn't sound familiar."

"It's a small street. Only one block," Kasia said, averting her face, her accent thicker than Nick had ever heard it. When she looked up, Nick noticed that she was about to cry.

The cop saw too. "Just a minute. Pull over there." He indicated a side street. He steered the cruiser in behind them and picked up his police radio. After a moment he walked over to their car. "Desk doesn't know either," he said suspiciously, looking past Nick to Kasia. "You all right?"

She nodded. "Just worried. We've come a long way," she said.

"Pennsylvania." He'd noted the license.

"Poland. She used to live here when she was little," Nick added.

"What other streets do you remember?"

"None." Her face burning with shame and frustration, Kasia shook her head. Then she did remember something—a clue. "I went to Webster School."

"Now we're getting somewhere. Webster School. You're on the wrong side of town." He grinned, happy to be able to solve a problem so easily.

"Back to the highway?" Nick asked.

"Nah. Better to follow along Prospect here." He pointed back to the wide street they'd turned off. "You'll come to a big shopping plaza, turn right just beyond that until you come to Duncan. It'll be a good two miles to Duncan. Turn left. The school's about five blocks down."

And there it was. As they drew up to the building Kasia had a sense of the room, of winter afternoons, of the pressure of Mrs. Anney's reassuring hand as she leaned over the desk to encourage her. She almost trembled with joy at the sight of the double doors, the playground, the high arched windows of the old building. Just as she had left them. They pulled up and parked on the quiet Sunday street.

"Do you think you know the way from here?" Nick asked after a few minutes.

She nodded confidently. "Down the street." She pointed ahead. "I'll know the turn when I see it."

He drove slowly, watching the roadside as if his attentiveness could assist her in finding her way home.

"Here," she said. "Turn here." And there was such gladness in her voice that Nick felt grateful that he was with her.

Alertly, she pulled her body forward. "Yes, this is right. I remember that house with the colored window." She pointed to a large gray house with a circular stained glass window in the front door. "And that firehouse. Yes. This is right." She flushed with each recognition.

But when they turned finally onto the small street where Kasia had expected to find her home, there was a long brick and stucco office complex. "It's Gordon," Nick said, looking up at the street sign. "Maybe the next block."

"There's only this one block," Kasia voice rose frantically. "But I know this is it."

Nick drove slowly down the empty street. Swirls of dirty leaves shot up as they passed through an intersection, Sisson Ave. Kasia gasped, "There's the Stop and Shop where we went. It has to be back there."

"We'll ask." Nick eased the car to the curb in front of the building before they realized the store was closed. He exhaled in frustration, then touched Kasia's cheek. "Do you know anyone who lives around here? A neighbor? One of your friends?"

Kasia shook her head.

He started the car and turned around in a driveway and headed back down the short block, thinking that perhaps they'd gone by too fast and the house was farther back. As they passed the brick building, Kasia read the sign, "Molton Dental Associates." Then she stopped, a catch in her voice. "300–360 Gordon Street." On the other side of the street a long low building with a curved driveway and parking lot along one side was revealed to be a nursing home.

They drove slowly down the street. Then Nick turned the car around and started back. An elderly man towed by a large German shepherd crossed in front of them. Nick parked the car and got out. Kasia followed.

"Excuse me, sir," Nick said, exhibiting his best Fenston manners. "We're looking for—" He stopped. Now that they knew where the house had been and saw that it was no longer there, what were they looking for?

"Wasn't there a row of houses over here?" Kasia pointed. "Ten years ago."

Up close the man looked friendly enough, but the dog leapt and pulled at the leash as if annoyed at the interruption in their walk.

"Stinger, hold on," the man said to the dog, with little effect. "Stinger!" He smiled at Nick and Kasia as if including them in his predicament. "Can't chat. Stinger makes the agenda. Sure. A whole bunch of rundown row houses probably built when the typewriter plant first started up, I'd say. Real eyesores in this part of town. Most likely bought out for the dental place. That's about it. Can't stop progress." He smiled again and trotted off behind Stinger.

A deep shudder seized Kasia's body. There it was. Gone. The porch. The silver maple. Her house. Gone. Not just her house, but the whole street of row houses, twenty or so families gone. An eyesore. Was that how people thought of them? She pictured her mother fussing with her old crockery, scrubbing the porch furniture, staking pole beans and tomatoes in the little backyard. An eyesore.

She could not hold back the tears of rage and frustration as one more sliver of her past, almost tangible in its promising closeness, melted away before her eyes. Her house with its old wallpaper and wood floors, her room at the top of the stairs, the garden where her mother had grown armsful of flowers and vegetables while she played. Her house, the one backdrop in the world where she could situate the increasingly fuzzy memory of her parents. Where the yeasty, slightly tart smell of her mother's body would call back what she'd lost. Their porch, the sidewalk where their last photo was taken. Their holidays and everydays.

She wanted it back. She needed a place for those meager memories, the locus of her childhood in the indifferent world. Without a touchstone, even one as ephemeral as an old house an ocean away, she'd be lost. Realization fluttered before her like a ream of blank paper luffing in air. How could she find herself now that the life that really belonged to her, the place that was somehow contained within the small row house on Gordon Street, was gone? Gone.

Nick parked the car and tried to comfort Kasia. Her pain was all the more real to him because he'd had so little in his own life. Empathy drove him to try to imagine life without his parents' constancy, the house where they had always lived filled with every thought and wonder of his being, a town full of people who had been the enduring wallpaper of his world. He'd had moments of frustration and anger with his family. Like when his dad wouldn't let him go to Syracuse. Instead to save money he made Nick live at home and attend Hapwell. Even though his grandmother offered to pay for any school he could get into. And he certainly resented how easy Caro had it, so few chores and so much attention. Recently he'd been angry when his mother had begun to imagine herself custodian of the public morals and was canvassing the town trying to get people to picket the strip club in Wiggins. Things he had considered crises, like when Caro cried and hid in her room when their parents argued, or when their father called his mother's crusade the Women's League for Decency and their mother slammed the bathroom door and wouldn't come out even when it was time to leave for the movie—all his own troubles seemed paltry, any complaint so unworthy.

Nick simply couldn't imagine what Kasia was feeling. He loved her and didn't want her to suffer. He had intended to help and this was what came of it. A fiasco. Again unwittingly he had led her to something that would cause her grief. Like the afternoon in the hillside cemetery, he had intended to please her but his actions had brought new torment. Why had he not left it alone, allowing her thinking that a trip to Hartford was out of the question? She would still have her thoughts and memories about her childhood without knowing that it had all vanished.

When her tears stopped, Kasia opened her little purse and dried her face on a tissue. Then she straightened her skirt and repositioned her purse in her lap. A small hiccup in her voice, "Aren't I a fun date?" She looked over at Nick and tried to force a smile.

"The funnest," he said, trying for a light tone.

They were quiet for a time.

"The prettiest, too," he said, running his hand across her shoulder.

"He said our house was an eyesore." Kasia sounded defeated.

"Urban renewal," Nick offered weakly. "It's not just here. All over the country. They go in and demolish old places and put up new high rent buildings in their place. They've even tried a few things like that around Fenston."

They were silent on the drive out of Hartford as Nick concentrated on finding his way back to the interstate and navigating the sudden traffic. The sky was gray and rumpled as old laundry, and soon it rained lightly. When they were on the open highway, he peeked over and saw with relief and some amusement that Kasia was asleep.

She dreamed of an Easter afternoon in the flat in Warsaw, and her basket sat waiting on the sideboard while she helped Sophie ready the holiday dinner. The steamy kitchen was full of good smells. Pots atop the stove gurgled. She was small and had been given the task of removing the butter from the special small Lenten lamb mold onto a china dish. She stood on a chair, a towel around her waist as she carefully dipped a knife in warm water and cut around the edges of the form, then turned it quickly onto the waiting plate. She felt the solid release in one flawless motion as the weight transferred to the plate. Proudly she lifted the tin and looked down. But instead of the golden lamb of sweet butter, there was a large yellow moth, its wings thrumming the air. Afraid that Sophie would be angry with her for such a mistake, she plucked the butterfly up and stuck it in her mouth.

The next moment she was sleeping on the couch in the parlor. It was twilight and the small bell over the front door rang announcing Piotr's arrival. She stirred, but couldn't wake up. Then she felt the clean fresh air he carried into the house as he came toward her and leaned down to kiss her forehead, his customary *buziak,* the butterfly kiss. *"Malutka,"* he said, "Wake up. Don't waste your life in dreams."

She awoke with the imprint of her uncle's healing lips, soft as wings against her brow. And Nick, solid and warm, beside her.

Chapter 42

The voices were far away. Billy paid them no heed. He and Sailor were engaged with the business of learning a new song: "Sailor's Holiday." Later he would wonder how he had so soon forgotten that the world required constant vigilance. Survival skills. But for the moment he moved from note to note, satisfied to follow the re-imagined sequence of Eddie's song, reclaiming it as he went along.

Mark and Bobby stopped playing in the sandbox and joined Billy and Sailor at the picnic table. Bobby took a stick and beat time on the bench beside him and Mark pumped his foot up and down in time. It was the same phrase: *What shall we do with the drunken sailor? What shall we do with the drunken sailor? What shall we do with the drunken sailor early in the morning.* Billy fingered out the melody and Sailor, as if he understood the words, cavorted and twirled across the grass. There was a breeze but the sun was warm and they had found a safe place, one with a backyard and other people who needed some peace too. Their music blocked the voices now rising in the room at the front of the house. The kind of voices the boys had each grown up listening to. The sharp, stunning syllables of anger.

Sister Gloria had no time to worry about how the man had gotten into the house when she found him going through the second floor, opening each door and closing it again when he discovered the room did not contain what he had come for. Her rubber flip-flops slapping the bottom of her feet as she raced down the hall, she caught up to him and firmly put her hand on the knob of the door he was about to open. "You'll have to leave here," she said, keeping her voice calm and low. "Only residents are allowed above the first floor. If you are looking for someone, just tell me who and I'll have them meet you downstairs."

She smelled his thick cologne mixed with alcohol, a scent that spoke of masculine victory. Ignoring her, he tried to twist the knob with her hand still attached. Despite the shoot of fear she felt, she stood her ground. "I'm sorry. You'll have to leave. Now," she said, raising her voice slightly.

Down the hall a door opened. Justine peeked out. "It's okay, Justine. No problemo." Her inflection didn't change with the Spanish phrase, a code for *call the police*. Wordlessly, Justine pulled her head back into the room. Gloria only hoped that the cops would arrive soon, as she knew that behind the other shut doors on the hall there were women afraid to come out, each imagining that the embodiment of her worst fears stood in the hall with only Sister Gloria between them.

"Don't make me hurt you, lady." The voice was higher than she had expected, with an accent she thought of as western, right out of the movies. Moments after he spoke, another door opened at the other side of the hall and Kandy stepped out, her face a mask of resignation and despair. "I think Kurt's looking for me, Sister."

The man motioned Kandy toward him.

Sister Gloria said, "Go back to your room, Kandy. When he's downstairs in the sitting room, you can speak to your visitor." She stared straight into the fellow's face, refusing to let his eyes move from hers.

"Okay," he said finally. "I don't want trouble. Just to see you and Sailor."

Gloria turned and led him down the stairs, with Kandy following a short distance behind.

Gloria agreed to fetch Sailor from the garden. Reading the situation and wondering how to handle this security issue, she left Kandy and Kurt in the sitting room, him perched on the edge of a La-Z-Boy underneath the oil painting of praying hands and Kandy sitting opposite him on a chintz wing chair.

Gloria knew the statistics, the high percentage of abused women who eventually return to their abuser. All Sister Gloria could offer was the possibility of a different kind of life; she could not force anyone to accept it. She whispered a quick entreaty to the Lord that Kandy was not about to make that mistake.

Gloria retrieved Sailor from the backyard and carried him into the parlor. She placed Sailor in Kurt's outstretched arms. He fussed with the monkey, cooing over it and rubbing the fur of its back with short deft strokes. Sailor preened at the attention and nuzzled his face against Kurt's neck.

Kurt smiled at Kandy, his voice thickening with a kind of sweetness. "Go to Mommy." He lifted Sailor across the coffee table and handed him back to Kandy. She seemed surprised and pleased at this inclusion—at Kurt's acknowledging her place in Sailor's life.

She's falling for it, Gloria thought; *he's reeling her in like an unsuspecting flounder.*

"Thank you, Daddy," Kandy said, her voice soft and childlike. She smiled coquettishly and twirled around and around, the monkey clinging to her in a frenzy of happiness.

Yes, Gloria thought, *it's over. He's got her.*

When he heard the siren Kurt startled, glaring around at Gloria and Kandy and then to the door. As if recalling that he was in a city after all and sirens were a frequent occurrence and had nothing to do with him, he seemed to relax a little.

Billy, Bobby and Mark came in the back door in pursuit of Sailor. As they got to the archway between the kitchen and sitting room, the boys watched Sailor being handed across to Kandy, their ecstatic spin. They heard the siren and then the footsteps on the porch.

Justine had crept silently down the steps, worried about what had happened to cause Gloria to speak the code words. She crouched on the low landing and looked through the banister at the scene. When the policeman knocked at the door, she turned to answer it.

Sister Gloria, who had stood as if frozen from the moment she heard the siren, started quickly for the door as well. "I'll see to this," she said, trying for nonchalance, but Kurt's face morphed from the mask of congeniality he'd worn since he allowed himself to be led into the sitting room. In a flash his hand flew to his pocket and came away with a small silvery gun, dwarfed in his large palm. Justine was the first to see it. She screamed.

"You didn't have to, Kandy," Kurt said, his voice filled with hurt and anger. The tiny movement of his finger filled the room with a deafening noise.

The bullet appeared to hit Kandy in the back. She spun around again as if to continue her dance. Her face, lively and happy a second before, shifted through confused and frightened and finally settled into a blank stare.

Sister Gloria said "Dear Jesus" and reached out her hand as if to steady Kandy, whose knees buckled. She fell backward, toppling into the seat of the couch.

Pinioned behind her, but still smiling, Sailor loosened his grasp around her shoulder and jerked it up alongside his face, imitating Kurt's motion of pulling a trigger, but more dramatically, as if schooled by old movies. Sailor's keen little eyes looked around the room, taking in each face for a mere second.

"I'm okay. I'm okay," Kandy said. And miraculously, she was. The bullet had passed through the fabric of her shirt but had not hit her.

"I'm sorry. Sorry. I didn't mean—" Kurt fell to his knees beside the couch.

"*EEG, EEG,*" Sailor cried, the meaningless sound managing to convey all he knew about betrayal and pain. He slid from behind Kandy's shoulder. Blood soaked the front of his white shirt. He put his hand over the place where the red pulsed from him. His eyes, full of surprise and sorrow, stopped when they found Billy's. There they lingered, then dulled.

Chapter 43

It had been one of the most difficult days of Eddie's life. In no hurry to return from his audience with McGill, he had taken the side roads, traveling slowly through the perfect fall afternoon to let his thoughts catch up with the knowledge he'd gained. Once again, trying to ferret out some information about Eleanor's past, he had stumbled onto something so disconcerting he wished he'd left well enough alone.

Should he tell her he'd been to see McGill? Would she be able to accept the knowledge that the pain she'd borne for so long was based on a trick of her own body and her grandmother's vicious deceit? In her fragile state, could she bear the deliberate hurt of it, even now?

The route he'd chosen brought him past Class Acts, where a new marquee, *Delicious Kandy Kane Opening Tonite,* barely registered.

Finally, as even the slowest road leads to the place one must return to, he steeled himself for the task before him. As he passed Wescott's and the blinker light at Fenston corner, he could see Athena standing at the counter, ringing someone up. He saw Phil Newberry get out of his car and take a paper from the metal rack on the store's porch and open the door. The normalcy of late afternoon in Fenston fortified him.

Just as he turned into their driveway, Eleanor raced toward him in her pink car. When she saw him she laid on the horn and gestured wildly. He backed up and waited. "Get in, Eddie, for God's sake, get in," she cried. Her face was flushed and her hair flew around her head in an untidy swirl, as if set in motion by some frightful energy. He felt her kinetic heat as he slid into the passenger seat.

While they drove, Eleanor, passing and honking until she reached the interstate and had complete range of road before her, told him what little she knew. Kurt had found the notepad on which Kandy had written the address of Harmony House. She'd torn off the top page. When he realized that she'd taken Sailor, he softly penciled over the paper until the address was visible in the white indented areas.

Kurt had gone to Harmony House to claim his woman and his monkey. He would get them back, convince Kandy that he would settle down and not ask her to dance again. Baring that, he would leave her and take Sailor with him. He didn't, he cried over and over to the police and anyone else within earshot, mean to hurt anyone. The police barging in startled him and he reacted before he realized what he was doing.

A policewoman answered the door and verified that they were the people Sister Gloria had called. Kurt had already been taken away. Eleanor gasped when she saw the blood pooled on the floor. Sailor was still on the sofa covered by an afghan. In the kitchen, Sister Gloria tried to comfort the residents, who were all terrified and realizing that it could as easily have been one of them.

Sister Gloria rose and motioned Eddie into the hall. "They just left the monkey. What should I do with it?"

"I don't know," Eddie answered. "I don't know anything anymore."

The boy hadn't spoken since Eleanor and Eddie collected him and Tina and Kandy from Harmony House and took them to Fenston. The police had plied all the witnesses with questions—most of which seemed useless and redundant, as two officers themselves saw the shooting as they entered the house. One had leaped forward and seized the gun from Kurt, who seemed stunned and docile. Amid the consternation of the scuffle, the others yelling, cursing and praying, the boy stood silent, his arms at his sides, staring at Sailor's body, which had fallen back onto the sofa. Kandy's moaning and self-recrimination continued as they piled into the car. Eleanor, after making sure that Gloria and the others would be cared for, did her best to comfort the woman who clutched onto her, sobbing and thrashing.

Eddie sat at Billy's bedside until he fell asleep. Billy's empty stare tore at Eddie. The boy looked beyond Eddie to the squirrel, then closed his eyes. Sensing that he was not asleep, Eddie kept his silent vigil, puzzling over the day's horrific events. How was it that however much he wanted it to be, his love was no protection for anyone? This was the most difficult and persistent lesson of his life.

When Billy's breathing became regular, Eddie turned out the light. Feeling useless and tired, he walked past the door to the kitchen, where Eleanor and Tina and Kandy sat over cups of tea, their backs curved in question marks of shared supplication. Tina was recounting how she and Kandy had met, the friendship they'd had. "I thought I was helping her. And look what happened."

"You did help," Kandy said. Then she sobbed and buried her face in her hands. "I would never have gotten away from Kurt without you. Even today, I was ready to go back. A few nice words and I was his slave."

Eleanor said, "Maybe you can think of it this way. Sailor died so that you could really be free."

Kandy looked at her in gratitude. "That might help. If I can remember that something good came out of his death."

The solitude of blue air enveloped Eddie as he left the porch. He wandered past the apron of light from the kitchen window into the deep scent of decaying leaves, past the orchard to the place where years before he had persuaded Eleanor to let him build the bomb shelter, much to the amusement of his neighbors.

Inside the piles of supplies—tins of food and blanket rolls, first aid kit and moldy and decayed clothing. He'd given up the project one afternoon when Eleanor had asked, "How many people will it hold?"

"The five of us. Easily," he'd replied, imagining the twins and their little brother, Eleanor and himself.

"Would you really be able to live like that—alone in the world? How will you turn the others away?" With her simple question, he realized that unless there was room for everyone, the bomb shelter would be useless.

This mute reminder of his effort to use his knowledge and industry to keep safe those he loved mocked him. Life mocked him, teaching him the same lesson again and again. In the forest at the edge of his world, darkness gathered and spun, deriding him with the sense of his own impotence and foolishness.

Despite the cool air, sweat gathered on Eddie's brow. Suddenly, he felt old and the vain toil of all his days settled into his bones. How many more disasters would come of his best intentions? He had tried to salve Eleanor's grief—to what end? Thinking he was delivering Billy to safety, he had led him and others into danger and loss. How had his love caused still more despair? How had he thought that he could cocoon those he loved against the world's evil?

Heartsick, Eddie evaluated the shambles of his life. In the sparse moonlight he could make out the small swell of ground where they might have entered the shelter if bombs fell. That summer, as he feverishly worked to complete the shelter, he had felt the buzz of their aerial approach. Instead, sorrow came in the form of another lost child. On a seamless golden afternoon, Athena and Will's son Gordie had been killed in the swamp of Vietnam.

The misperceived threats Eddie'd guarded against had kept him busy while the real ones approached just at the edge of his vision. At work shoring up false barriers, he only looked up in time to see the harm had come from a different direction.

Chapter 44

After the long disappointing trip Kasia couldn't wait to take a shower. She felt dirty, somehow tainted by the word that still echoed in her ears, *eyesore*. This was one time she wished she didn't have such a good command of English.

Colored light streaked the area in front of her dorm. Too small to be a fire truck. An ambulance? Was someone sick? Had there been an accident? They parked and hurried closer, then realized it was a police car, its bubble light circling in the twilight, coloring the branches of trees and the faces of students lining the walkway.

Kasia shivered in the chill air as they approached the door of the dorm. A uniformed man stepped in front of her and said firmly but politely, "Nobody goes inside. We're conducting an investigation. Shouldn't be long." He nodded toward the clump of students, indicating that Kasia should join them.

Gudrun in sweatpants, a towel wrapped around her head, waved her over. To Kasia's question she shrugged, "Don't know. We were on our way back from swimming, and they wouldn't let us in."

"You must be freezing." Kasia nodded to the towel.

"The icicles in my hair will have to thaw before I comb it. But I'm more bummed about the study time. I just went swimming to wake myself up before I begin studying anthro. Now I'll have to pull an all-nighter. Any NoDoz?" Like the rest of the international students, Gudrun struggled to tailor her English to that of her fellow students.

"Drugs," someone behind Kasia whispered.

"Really?" Another voice.

"What else? Everybody knows—"

"Shushh," whispered someone in the back. "Forget about what you know or think you know—want to be called up in court?"

"Look," Gudrun said. The front door of the dorm opened and Clem Tompkins and a state police officer led two figures from the building. The first walked boldly, his head up, his tight rebellious face clearly visible. Doug Martin twisted and squirmed in Clem's grip. Behind him a small figure, face averted, walked slowly, a swath of soft blue bathed in the red splash of the police flasher. Kasia recalled the day Yvette leaned toward her in the van and showed her the prized cashmere scarf. Glamorous even as she walked toward the police car, Yvette lowered her head into its soft folds to shield herself from view. Still there was a gasp when the crowd realized who it was. They stared at each other in confusion.

"Yvette," one girl smirked. "Must be drugs."

"Shush," another said.

"We don't know for sure what this is about," Gudrun said in defense of her friend.

Kasia turned when B.J. appeared at her side. "Just finished practice. What's going on?"

"Looks like someone's in trouble," Kasia said, noticing again how heavy her accent was whenever she was nervous.

"Yvette?" B.J.'s voice was flat, inflectionless.

"Surprised?" Kasia guarded her tone of voice. No use accusing anyone. Still, how would the police have known? Someone must have told them about Yvette and her business.

"Don't look at me," B.J. said, as if Kasia had formed her suspicions into words.

"Who's looking?"

"I don't go for the drug stuff. But I didn't rat her out. If I'd thought about it I might have, but I've been too busy."

"Did I say anything?"

"No. But I know what you were thinking. Who else did they get?"

"A guy. I think it's that Doug."

"He's a loser!" B.J. poked Kasia on the arm to get her attention, then pointed across to a figure at the edge of the growing crowd. Gunnar stood apart from the others as Yvette was helped into the police car. His baseball cap was pulled down obscuring his features, his hands in his pockets. He was surrounded by some guys from his dorm.

"Don't you want to talk to him?"

"And say what? Your girlfriend is a waste?"

"Well, no. But maybe just that you know this must be hard for him."

"Not with all those guys around. Besides, I'll see him tomorrow. We have a session before he takes the grammar test."

"I thought you saw him on Tuesday?"

"We added Monday and Friday."

"You must be in the money. I thought you couldn't fit anything else into your schedule?"

"A freebie. Just until I get him caught up. You wouldn't believe how much progress he's making." B.J. looked across at him. "I just hope this doesn't affect his concentration.

"Mummm." Kasia hid her smile.

A state policeman leading a dog emerged from the building and the waiting students were let in. "Looks like you came up lucky," B.J. said, pointing to Kasia's mailbox, the only one in the row that had a package inside.

She thought immediately of Piotr and the strange, disquieting dream she had in the car on the way home came to her. But when she picked up the parcel she saw that it was a small department store box with only her name written on the top. She flopped on the bed and slid her nail under the tape to open it. Inside there was a dense soft aluminum foil packet wrapped in a blue water silk scarf.

Three photos fell from the folds of the scarf. The year 1955 was written on the ridged edge of an ancient black and white snapshot, and someone had printed along the bottom, *Ben—the catch of the summer.* Standing next to a rowboat, her young father's face reflected an unclouded joy. Almost forty years ago. Young. Happy. There was nothing in the picture that Kasia could connect with her father. The unlined face before her might have been one of the boys on the campus.

The second, a color photo dated 1978. *Eddie, Ben and Will trying out the new equipment* read the notation on the back. Three men hung dramatically from the side of a fire engine, their free hands outstretched. Ben was in the middle. In this older face she recognized a line of alertness across the forehead, the way she remembered him looking at her with his eyebrows drawn together in concentration, just a hint of something around the eyes, something she couldn't have summoned until prompted by the photo. Then she recalled it fully, the look that came to mind when she thought of him. It was like finding something she hadn't thought she'd lost. Swirls of memories and feelings clicked in.

The final photo must have been taken close to the end of his life. The date was smeared—1980 or maybe '82. *Yankees Trip.* He was one of a group of men seated on bleachers. *I was born then,* Kasia thought, *and here was my father smiling and happy in his other life with Hattie and Alice and their friends—going to baseball games and fishing, talking to his neighbors and friends as if nothing had happened, as if I didn't exist. All the while Mother and I were home waiting for him.*

There was no note. She was grateful to Alice, she guessed, or Eleanor—whoever had sent the pictures.

"What's in the box?" B.J. asked when she came back from showering.

"Photos."

"I mean in the package."

Kasia hefted the silvery packet she had forgotten about and found it dense and soft. She peeled back the foil.

Her eyes gleaming with pleasure, B.J. said, "Brown stuff." Their expression for anything chocolate. "Outta sight. Who—"

Kasia plopped onto the rug, her back against the bed. B.J. joined her and she spread open the foil packet between them on the floor.

"Fudge. Walnuts, too."

"Oh, yes. Yes. Yes." Kasia moaned at the first bite and held the package out to B.J.

"So where'd you go anyway? Dressed like that, you weren't at a car wash. Or is that a secret too?"

By the time Kasia had recounted the lost Hartford afternoon, they had eaten the entire batch of fudge and washed it down with four Diet Cokes. B.J. groaned as she licked her finger and blotted up the remaining flecks of walnut from the sticky bottom of the foil. "Go figure. Almost everyone else around here wants to escape and forget about life before college and it won't let go. The other day in anthro Dr. Dwyer brought in a newspaper article about this kid who's trying to divorce his parents. He asked how we felt about it. Lots of kids said they could relate."

"At least he has parents," Kasia said.

"You, on the other hand—" Then B.J. stopped, realizing what she was about to say. No parents. Hard to imagine.

"No, go ahead. What were you going to say? I'm so confused I don't know what to do. Say anything. I'll listen."

"Sure?"

"Yeah. Sure. Whatever."

B.J. looked squarely at her friend. "I hate to see you bumming like this. Seems like every time you settle down, something else comes along to upset you."

Kasia nodded, willing herself not to cry. B.J. could be such a comfort, capable of putting into words exactly how Kasia felt.

"All I'm trying to say is, maybe you should give it a break. Concentrate on school. On your own life." She studied Kasia to see if she should continue.

"And," Kasia asked impatiently.

'Seems like you have lots of good stuff going. Nick."

"Ah-ha. So now Nick's good for me?" Kasia said triumphantly.

"As my old granny always said—" B.J. screwed her face into a croneish grimace and made her voice a cackle. "Handsome is as handsome does. He seems like a nice guy, kind and all. And you're doing great with the classes. Don't let that other stuff pull you down."

"Yeah," Kasia answered. "Easy for you to say. But I'll try."

"Just a thought," B.J. said as she picked up the foil and licked away the last smears of brown.

"Gotcha." Kasia echoed one of B.J.'s favorite retorts. And she slumped back fully nourished by friendship and fudge.

Chapter 45

The following afternoon, the door to her room didn't budge when Kasia turned the knob. She tried again. She put down the bag of apples and pears Nick had brought her and stood there calculating how long it would take her to round up the janitor and wondering where B.J. had gone. She'd told Kasia she'd be studying in the room all evening. *"Colera jasna."* She bit the curse between her teeth.

"Just a minute." B.J.'s voice came from inside just as the lock clicked and the door jerked open. The bags toppled and apples and pears rolled across the floor, settling here and there against furniture and piles of laundry. Kasia thought she heard another door shut. The room was dark but for a candle on the nightstand and a seam of light showing from under the bathroom door. She heard the toilet flush.

"Somebody in there?" she asked.

B.J. was wearing an oversized Phillies T-shirt and underpants. On her hands and knees she crept around gathering pears and apples into the uplifted hem of her shirt. She stopped and took a bite of apple. "I take it you got fruit instead of fudge?"

Kasia noticed a pair of glasses with round metal frames next to the candle. "Beej?"

"What?"

"Who's in the bathroom?" They both listened as the shower came on.

B.J. sighed. "Gunnar."

"Gunnar?" Kasia pronounced the name incredulously. "Your tutee?" She took in the unmade bed, the dark room, the snarl of cast-off clothes on the floor. "Late session, I guess."

B.J. refused to look up. "Don't go all Tammy Faye on me, Mrs. Morality."

"Didn't take him long to forget Yvette." Kasia refused to let the focus slip to her.

"They were broken up weeks ago. He dumped her as soon as he found out what she was really like."

"Wonder how that happened?"

"Don't think I told him. He walked in on her and Doug. He was totally schizoid when he showed up for our session. He told me the whole thing." B.J. chewed thoughtfully for a minute. "He's a really sensitive guy. We were just studying Lit."

Kasia felt herself smiling, but didn't want to let B.J. off the hook so easily after all the grief she'd given her about Nick. "Must have been some homework session to require soap and water."

"Shush. He'll hear you." B. J. stood and hobbled around the room picking up stray articles of clothing from the floor and piling them next to the apples in the middle of her unmade bed.

Kasia sat on the desk chair watching. "I think I'll have a little talk with that Tarzan when he finishes primping."

"Please," B.J. begged, her expression of supplication comically overdone. "Please go away for a while. Just until he leaves."

Kasia considered the request until she heard the water switch off. "You owe me one," she said and ducked into the hall.

"Honest to God, I don't know how it happened," B.J. explained later that night. "One minute we were sitting on the floor going over Marvel's "To His Coy Mistress." In a precise English accent she recited, "'If we had worlds enough and time.' He was leaning over to follow along. His hand landed on my leg. You know, like to brace himself. Then I started to feel something weird in my, well in my—" She pointed toward her crotch. "*What*, I thought, *is that*. Just then Gunnar started running his other hand up my back and I turned all runny and weak inside, like I'd just blocked a shot and couldn't get my breath."

"Yeah, I know that sensation."

"You do?"

"Like your skin is hot all over and tingly and wanting to be touched. Like you are opening up and just waiting for him to breathe on you and you'll melt. You feel like your skin is turning blue and shrinking or something."

"That's it! How do you know?"

"Do you think you invented sex? But I have this puritanical roomie, and so am forced to take my love life elsewhere. Not some cushy bed in a quiet, private room."

B.J. ignored the barb and considered the description. "Yeah, your skin gets all wet and hot. Then. Oh, m'God. It just kept going. We were all over each other."

"It's like that sometimes," Kasia remarked wisely, glad that for once her knowledge was superior.

"I don't even remember locking the door. There was no stopping us. We're lucky it didn't hit us someplace else. "Imagine—library *infla-grante*," she cackled.

"Or on the floor in the cafeteria."

"Yeah. I'd be like, 'hold my tray while I—'"

"I'm afraid to ask. Did he? Did you? Use something?"

"I'm not completely daft. Of course."

"Came prepared, huh?"

B.J. switched to her faux Polish accent. "Kiss my wrinkled dumpa."

Dupa," Kasia corrected. "It's *dupa*. And I think I'll leave that to Gunnar, if you don't mind."

"Whoa." B.J. shivered, recollecting their lovemaking. "That boy is dangerous. I better stay away from him if that's the best I can control myself."

"Yeah," Kasia said. "Fat chance."

On and on B.J. went. She couldn't say Gunnar's name often enough or stop expanding on the bliss of their lovemaking. In the darkness Kasia rolled her eyes, but she was relieved to have something else to think about besides the awful situation in Fenston. She couldn't imagine what the next day would bring. Kept awake by worry, she gladly suffered the endless description of B.J.'s pyrotechnic orgasms.

"And the other thing—Kasia, are you still with me?"

"Yes."

"You'll never believe it."

"Try me."

"Gunnar dropped the dime on her!"

"Dime? Like the money?" Would she ever learn all the American words?

"Turned her in. Yvette. He ratted her out. He was fed up with the stuff she was pulling, so he called the cops."

"No kidding. He must have really been mad at her."

"Yeah. That too. But I think he was sick of so many kids getting wasted all the time."

"A good Samaritan." The irony in Kasia's voice was lost on B.J.

"You got it."

Despite her preoccupation with her own problems, Kasia recognized some opportunities for herself in B.J.'s new situation. "Does this mean Nick and I can—?"

Before they went to sleep the roommates worked out a system whereby they honored the locked door by disappearing for an hour and returning, no questions asked. Kasia forced herself not to mention B.J.'s former anguish over her ambiguous sexual orientation, a topic that seemed buried in the fast receding, far distant past of September.

Chapter 46

Suddenly more tired than she could ever remember being, Hattie left her suitcase where she had dropped it and climbed the stairs. She passed Alice's open door, the large room in a comfortable disarray of clothing and books. Since Alice's car was not in the drive, Hattie knew her daughter wasn't home.

She paused and inhaled the particular scent of her own old house, the place she had lived in and loved. The pale green walls of the room, a soft hue Alice had chosen when she returned to live with Hattie, gave the room a sense of serenity and comfort, feelings that had eluded Hattie for the past few weeks. Love for her daughter caught in her throat. She knew Alice would find out about Ben, about Kasia, about her mother's duplicity. *I will fix this thing,* she told herself. *I will make it right again.*

Inside her own airy spacious bedroom, familiar objects called to her as she passed them: perfume bottles on a glass tray, the wooden jewel box Ben had made for her when she was pregnant with Alice, the handmade Amish star quilt and soft mauve blanket at the foot of the high poster bed, her bedside table, books and magazines with little post-its marking something that had interested her. She felt the past close around her and tried to allow herself to be calmed by it.

Every movement required her complete attention. Her feet felt leaden and she longed to throw herself onto the bed and sleep. Determined to bathe and put on fresh pajamas before she allowed herself to rest,

Hattie drew a bath and shook a handful of lavender salt into the water rushing into the immense clawfoot tub her great-grandfather had proudly installed, then invited the town in to see.

As she bent to enter the bath, she caught her reflection in the large mirror behind the door. *Thin,* she thought. *When did that happen?* Her legs seemed longer, her arms narrow and spare. After all the pastry she had consumed on the trip, she couldn't have lost weight. Then she realized she hadn't eaten a real meal in more than a week—her appetite, like Kasia, had gone missing. Even when she went to Wanszawienko, the café near Piotr's house she had loved in the past, the fruit rolada and her favorite cream filled makowiec didn't tempt her.

Lying back in the tub, she soaped a cloth with Dove and washed, moving her hand over her shoulders, feeling the tension and knots drain out of her. Her mind flitted from image to image. She tried to bring it back, to make it float on the water. Clearly traveling alone was more of an ordeal than she could cope with. Whatever else, she was glad not to have to go to Poland again. Somehow she would find Kasia and tell her everything. She would make her understand. Both of them—Kasia and Alice. She would explain exactly what had happened and they would realize that she had made the best choices she could.

Forcing her thoughts away from the problems that would confront her soon enough, Hattie closed her eyes and drifted in time and saw the kind strong face of Piotr as he had looked the first night they made love. That night, now more than ten years ago, in the living room of Anya's house, was with her as strongly as if it were happening now.

As soon as they met, Hattie was aware of the sexual tension between herself and Piotr. She felt shamed by her own emotions. How could she be feeling sexual attraction when Anya lay dying in the room upstairs? She felt skittish and embarrassed around Piotr, hoping he did not recognize her attraction to him. One night Piotr had given Anya her evening medicine while Hattie tucked Kasia in and heard her prayers. When Hattie came downstairs she noticed that the tree lights had been left on. She went into the living room to unplug them and found Piotr sitting in the dark.

Piotr asked her to sit with him a moment. In the soft lights and primal scent of the Christmas tree they talked about Kasia's day, their hope that Anya's suffering would soon cease. Piotr took Hattie into his arms and held her, stroking her face with the tips of his fingers. She felt anew the pebbly texture of the old green sofa against her bare skin as he laid her back against the pillows. Unconsciously she had preserved the memory of his touch, the tender questioning look in his eyes as he entered her. Until that night Ben had been her only lover. Despite her nervousness, she and Piotr seemed to know intuitively what would please each other.

For the month that followed, their lovemaking was as easy as breathing. Often they held each other long into the night when neither of them could sleep. Nothing could be done for Anya. She would die. Kasia would be alone. Once she had tried to talk to Piotr about Ben, to find out what he knew of Anya's missing husband. It was one of the few times Piotr exhibited a temper. "Look around. She's dying in this dreadful place—this hovel. And he disappears. About him, what more needs to be said."

Hattie leaned forward and added more hot water to the tub. Piotr was so real in the reverie that she felt herself parting to welcome him. Her breath was rapid as she touched herself. How could she have left such pleasure? That she had done so still astonished her. Then she'd think of Kasia and Alice, how much the truth would have hurt them both. Recalling one of Eleanor's long explanations of karma, Hattie wondered whether this was hers—to love deeply and lose the person she loved. It had happened with Ben and then with Piotr. What did she have to learn in order to be allowed to have the love she craved?

By the time the water had started to cool, Hattie felt pleasantly drained of tension. She submerged herself in the tub to wash away the remaining bubbles and opened her eyes, studying the linden trees outside her window; their golden oval leaves caught in the bright rectangle of light as the sun moved behind Crystalle Ridge, casting a gaudy Technicolor glow around her. *Still daylight,* she thought. A day that stretched from Warsaw to Fenston, encompassing an extraordinary gambit of emotions.

The enamel was cool against her skin when she lay back again. She looked down past her breasts and the slight swell of her belly, beyond the two bony plates of her knees to her toes. Then quickly back.

Something about her right breast. Inverted somehow. She put her hand to her breast. With a slow steady pressure that reminded her of the first time a boy had touched her there. She recalled the deep nougaty smell of the woods where they had played at each other's bodies. She must have been thirteen or so. And joyous and fearful at the insistence of her own longing. With her wrinkled fingertips she felt the soapy slide of her own skin along her breast. The small knot, a turgid hardness centered just above and to the right of her nipple.

"Oh God," she heard herself say, suddenly upright. Her hand now quick and forthright as it registered again the presence of the lump. Despite the tepid water, she had begun to sweat as she lifted then lowered her arm, turned on her side, knelt back on her haunches. In each position, she verified the lump. Water sloshed from the tub as she thrashed about. Repeatedly she brought her hands to her breast—first the left hand, which easily reached across and had first felt it, then the right, awkwardly pulling back her elbow and twisting her hand to fully encompass the offending breast.

More fiercely, angrily, she clasped herself, grabbing and pinching her own flesh as if chastising it with frantic examination. She sobbed and felt a mass of corresponding fear in her belly—some trenchant thing had grown inside her without her knowing.

Suddenly Hattie Darling, who had cried aloud so infrequently that she did not recognize the sound of her own grief, was shrieking. She splatted again into a sitting position; the water shot up around her, soaking her hair and face. Then she quieted and sat in the lukewarm water and put her hands to her face, then back to her breast again. Clasping her breast between two hands, she roughly squeezed it and dug her fingers into the tissue, seeking again the tiny hard piece of matter that would change everything, the place where her body had turned against her.

She pressed her cheek against her raised knees and wrapped her arms tightly around them, making herself as small as she could. Powered by a relentless animal howl, her breath thickly moving in and out, clotted with tears and snot and fear.

When the bathroom door flew open, Hattie didn't seem to notice. Then Alice was on her knees beside the tub, calming her. "Mother, what? What is it?" But Hattie could not be comforted. Her words were somewhere else, hidden in the part of her life where they might do some good, where their utterance made sense. To Alice's alarm, Hattie sobbed and huddled and would not let herself be helped up. Alice leaned across the tub and soothed her mother as she would a small child who didn't understand the basis for her fears. Finally Hattie's tears subsided and she looked up pleadingly.

"What is it, Mother?" Alice whispered. "What?"

For the first time, if she had not been incapable of seeing beyond her own terror, Hattie might have read in her daughter's face the small child love that had layered over with irony and will. Then she grasped her daughter's hand and placed it on her breast and moved it slowly across the skin, rubbing her fingers back and forth on the spot where the offensive bump lay until she saw recognition leap into Alice's eyes.

"Oh. Oh, Mom," Alice said, her voice going dry around the paltry syllables of their relationship. But Hattie knew what she meant.

Chapter 47

Eddie eased his body onto the bed so as not to disturb Eleanor. He closed his eyes and waited, but sleep was as elusive as hope. The soft air moved about him. Eddie tried to make himself construct a difficult chess problem, imagining the board spread out in front of him, focusing as he placed the pieces and visualized the gambit he might employ. Sometimes it worked and he fell asleep trying to figure it out.

"There's more, isn't there?" Eleanor whispered. He felt the long stream of her exhalation rush across his cheek. "I mean, not just the shooting. Something else?"

He turned to her, and for some reason recalled the apt Spanish for double bed: *cama matrimonio*. It was the nest where he and Eleanor had hatched their plans, conceived and delivered their children, and enacted and comforted each other in their deepest passions and despairs. "Yes," he whispered back, a habit formed when the house was full of curious children and only in the time before sleep could they talk things over at length.

They waited out the silence, like worshippers at a Quaker meeting, certain that when the time was right to speak, someone would. Eleanor touched his bare shoulder lightly, her fingertips tracing the bones underneath his flesh.

"There's no way—" he began, then faltered. "Since you told me—" he began again.

"It's about the baby?" she said. Her inflection carried the question.

"Yes." He trembled, hoping that he would find the way to tell her that would cause the least pain.

"All night, I knew there was something more. Some way it all connected up. It had to." Beneath her words, Eddie listened to her voice, surprised at its firmness and calm.

"There was no baby," he whispered. He wished he could call back the words, but what good would that do?

Feeling her grief spring from his eyes, Eddie recounted his visit with McGill, every detail except the old man's venom, the pleasure he'd gotten from informing Eddie that he'd known all the time.

Eleanor lay still next to him, listening. He could tell by her breathing that she was not crying. When he spoke about the treachery of her grandmother, she drew in her breath as if to speak, but didn't.

Finally, when he finished, she said, "Hysterical pregnancy," as if weighing the words.

He waited for her to speak again.

"Do you remember a long time ago, I told you my family wasn't family in the sense we think of, you and me? You didn't understand. But when I left Harley, I left it behind—all the ways they hurt me and each other. I went to Stella Maris, blindly searching for a new life. I found it, not there in the convent, but with you. Still, if I hadn't been there we would not have met."

Eddie smiled in the dark, remembering.

Eleanor shifted in the bed and a whiff of her sweet talcum reached him. He took her into his arms. She shifted her weight and settled her cheek against its accustomed space on his chest, allowing him to massage the back of her left shoulder.

"Once that happened, out of one thing came something better. I knew that my life had changed—I had somehow been delivered. And tonight, for the first time, it all makes sense. All that pain was for something."

Eddie tried to follow. "Tonight?"

"Billy came into our lives on the most difficult day of the year for me. That day, I began to feel the loss even more strongly. I thought I'd go mad from grief. I thought it was about the baby. Had you half crazy trying to figure out what to do to relieve me of that old pain." Her breathing became shallower—then she sighed, as if letting something sink in. "But there never was a baby. Instead, in self-defense my body had contrived a way to get me out of a terrible situation."

Eddie, amazed at the complexity of his wife's analysis, smiled to himself.

"Just like now. I thought Billy's coming here was about the baby. But it was about Billy. Maybe it was always about him. About preparing for him. Waiting for him to appear."

"We love him, don't we?"

A rustle in the bushes beneath their window told them the deer were tasting their rhododendron.

"If family's not the place and people you're born into, it has to be something else—where you find your deepest self. People veer into the orbit of your life mysteriously. Somehow, they're yours. You can either turn them away or accept them as your family."

Eddie knew at once what she meant. Billy had come to them—not just to Eleanor, but to Eddie too. Focused on their own worries, they had almost refused the gift of his presence in their lives. Eleanor's preoccupation with that long ago pregnancy and Eddie's caring for her had nearly made them miss the point. There was a child—Billy. He was the child they needed to care for and nurture.

"So he stays," Eddie said. The prospect thrilled him. "What about Tina?"

"Tina and I talked."

"Oh." Eddie's voice had a question.

"Everything that happened aside, she knows she's not ready to care for Billy herself. She's barely eighteen, no skills, no education. She loves him very much, but she's lost too. Before she can take charge of him, she needs to find her own path, not play mother."

"I imagine she has some wounds of her own to tend."

"Gloria and I will put our heads together and find something for Tina and Kandy. They'll be support for each other."

"She's willing to leave Billy?"

"She's full of guilt even with the thought of leaving him. But I think she'd be relieved if he could stay with us."

Eddie said, "We'll call Bill Ferris."

"A lawyer?"

"We need to do this right. He can take us through the paperwork. I seem to recall from some work I did with Sister Gloria—there are steps. He has to be declared an emancipated minor. Then he can say who he wants to live with."

"Tina seems to think that their mother and stepfather won't be a problem," Eleanor said.

"Seems logical. They haven't even filed a missing persons for him."

"This has been a terrible setback for him. He was just beginning to trust again. To use his voice. It will take time, but we might even be able to get him to speak again."

Eddie knew his wife was right. He felt himself immersed in the idea so completely it was as if he had slipped into a bath of warm healing water. His wife's voice, full of plans and tasks, came to him from far away as he formulated a few ideas of his own and drifted into the calm lap of sleep.

Eddie returned before anyone had stirred. "Rosy-fingered dawn," he smiled to himself as the first rays of sunlight pointed him back to Fenston. Gloria had not been surprised at being awakened so early or at his errand. He was sure that she would not have discarded anything important to Billy without checking with them first. She helped him gather Kandy and Tina and Billy's belongings into the car.

Hanging the Do Not Disturb sign on the door to his basement workshop, Eddie began his task. He covered his worktable with a fresh sheet of paper. As he worked, one part of his mind totally engaged in the process while another played over the days of pleasure he and Eleanor had ahead of them as they brought Billy back from his terrified silence. Eddie imagined winter evenings playing chess, checking over the boy's algebra homework, listening to the tales of school and friends.

Painstakingly he ministered to the object before him, the tangle of sinew and bone, flesh and blood, as he removed the skin. Exertion showed in his face, yet Eddie felt rejuvenated by purpose and effort. The whole process would take weeks, if he worked steadily, allowing for the necessary time between steps. He was grateful to Sister Gloria, who had carried the body to the basement and kept it overnight in her empty new refrigerator until she could figure out what to do next—perhaps burial on the Roderi farm.

Later he would need Eleanor's skills as a seamstress. The white jumper, shredded and stained beyond salvation, would have to be fashioned from memory. The body was almost perfect, the small entry wound would be easy to conceal. Hands, as artists the world over knew, would be the hardest part. But he would recreate them, each finger and nail, exact and perfect.

He shifted the light over his table until it illuminated the untouched head. As he studied its harmony of features, he imagined how the re-done face would emerge. Fragments of old hymns came to him. *"Panis Angelicus,"* Eddie murmured over and over, thinking ahead to the day that he could reunite Billy with his friend. He would position the monkey upright, his hand raised in a salute. Sailor. Smiling.

Chapter 48

Hattie referred to the lump as *the nubbin* when she called Athena and Eleanor an hour after she had discovered it. Since then she had used that one word exclusively, as if by naming it something other than the lump, the mass, the tumor or any other quasi-medical term, she could diminish its gravity. As if mastery of a thing lay in naming it, she had reached back into the world of happy endings, easily vanquished challenges, and chosen a word from childhood. A cute, diminutive and unthreatening word lifted from the world of books about rabbits and gardens and children without cares. Whether the nubbin was malignant remained to be determined. Beyond the phone calls and arrangements handled so adeptly by Alice, there were long swaths of time.

The nubbin had superseded all thought about what had come to light while she was away. If this were any ordinary homecoming, Alice would have flown at Hattie with a thousand questions. Did Hattie know that Kasia had come? That she was at Hapwell? That Alice had met her? Even without those explosive revelations to deal with Hattie's homecomings were always fraught with difficult readjustments, as mother and daughter were at once pleased to see each other and at the same time worried about how difficult the other's presence would be.

But the discovery of the lump forced everything else into stasis. Alice occasionally dipped into her pile of unsorted complaints. Everywhere she moved her mind her thoughts were pocked with emotional bombs, none of which could be exploded now.

Instead, Alice did her job—triage. Preparing for the worst, she called every person she knew who had worked with breast cancer to ask about treatment options. Competing opinions drove her into the medical library only to find that even the recognized experts in the field didn't agree. Mastectomy, radical and otherwise, lumpectomy, radiation, chemo, both? Her mother, in this one instance, would look to her for reassurance and guidance on the medical front. What could she tell her?

The night before the definitive second test, Athena and Eleanor came by for a visit. Alice was relieved to have them stay with Hattie while she did some grocery shopping and paid bills. But once out of the house, she couldn't wait to return. As she pulled two bags from the back of her car, she glanced toward the house. Under the domed kitchen light the three women huddled in their customary positions around the table. Her first instinct was gratitude that Hattie had such support.

Alice stood in the kitchen doorway a moment before they realized she was there. On the table sat a teapot covered by a quilted cozy in the shape of a doll's skirt, beside it a half-empty bottle of Anisette, Eleanor's answer to all life's joys and sorrows, and three sticky shot glasses. Hattie was describing the compression mammogram. She gestured a large oval on the table in front of her, cranking wildly with her other hand. "She squeezed my boob inside that thing till it was as thin as a taco and as long as the state of Florida." The three, including Hattie, hooted with laughter. Hattie wiped her eyes and caught Athena's glance. "Might as well laugh," she said.

Alice felt the old jealousy rise in her. As long as she could remember, her mother had Eleanor and Athena. Through all the good and bad—Gordie's death, the wild escapades of Eleanor's brood, Eddie's calamitous business decisions, Ben's absences and death—they had come together in support of each other. Unlikely friends. Athena with her sharp tongue, her blue jeans and workboots, her store and late night walks, her crazy collections of rescued treasures. And gypsy-clothed Eleanor—more brains than MIT and less common sense than a kindergarten class. Her half-built, half-decayed house and operatic life. Anyone looking at the two would conclude they had little in common with Hattie, the graceful, gracious widow in the big house on the hill.

Yet the scenes of their friendship had been one of the enduring facts of their lives.

Alice tried to force envy from her heart. She should be glad her mother had these friends. But it was always Eleanor, Athena and Hattie. Hattie moped all day no matter how Alice tried to distract or entertain her. But just let Eleanor and Athena show up and she exuded pleasure. She had them, and Ben when he was there. Worse still, Kasia regaled Alice with stories of the Hattie that had showered her with love too. *What about me,* Alice wanted to know. There were so many people in Hattie's life that Alice didn't even get crumbs. Hattie didn't seem to need anything at all from her only daughter.

The next day, Hattie submitted to all the tests without complaint. Alice noticed her mother's hands shaking as they sat in the overcooled lounge awaiting the results of the second biopsy, as the first had been inconclusive. "You're shivering, Mom," she said.

But Hattie shrugged and pulled the rumpled blue cotton gown up around her shoulders. "I'm fine. Just a little chill," Hattie said, almost defensively.

Alice felt the response as a rebuke. Dimly she remembered a time before they had started misunderstanding each other. So long ago—at eighteen she had left home because she thought she'd feel less lonely with strangers. Yet here she was back in Fenston living in the old farmhouse with her mother. Before she returned she had vowed to make things different. But she didn't understand what had happened between them and knew even less about how to change it.

After a series of disappointing love affairs, Alice's loneliness had increased. She'd begun to wonder what kept her in Fenston. But now that her mother needed her, how could she leave? Mixed into this turmoil she could not shake the thought that her mother had known all along about Ben's other wife and child and not told her. How could she contend with that longstanding and grievous deceit on her mother's part? The worst part was that all this time, she had not known about her little sister.

Kasia drifted into Alice's thought. The spunk it took to walk up to their front door. The quiet, gutsy way, betrayed by only the slightest tremble in her voice. She had insisted that Alice hear her out, even after she'd almost fainted. Alice longed to turn to her mother and tell her how much she liked Kasia.

Instead, silent, side by side, they had waited for over an hour. Alice had admired the skill of the technician who had taken the X-rays efficiently and quickly, aware that the pressure on Hattie's breast was painful. Alice looked over at her mother, who was pretending to read *Good Housekeeping*, her glasses perched on the edge of her nose. The silvery snake of roots down the middle of her auburn hair shimmered in the light from the overhead fluorescent.

Mother and daughter looked up when the door opened. Alice caught her breath at the love that welled up within her heart. She glanced at Hattie, who had dropped the magazine onto the table, snatched off her glasses and struggled to refocus her eyes. She looked dim and trusting as the technician smiled beyond them at the wall and said, "The radiologist has a few things to go over with you. Can you follow me?"

A vague mewling sound came involuntarily from Hattie. She put her hand up to her cheek and looked around. "Why, all right," she said, as if unsure what she was doing there.

Alice reached out to help her mother to her feet, but instead found herself foolishly weak and without words. She steadied herself. An interview with the radiologist—she knew what that meant. *Some nurse,* she thought, as together they walked to the office at the end of the short hall.

Chapter 49

The rapping woke her at eight a.m. Kasia looked across to B.J.'s empty bed. Practice. She remembered it was Monday and rolled over, glad that she wasn't a hockey player. But the noise continued. Finally she got up, stepped over the soda cans and crumpled foil from the night before and opened the door to find Mary glaring at her. "Dead to the world? Don't you have class?"

"Spanish at 11," Kasia said. Then the scene with Yvette and the police came to her. She tried to wake herself up enough to be cautious when the inquisition started.

Mary backed her into the room. "That gives you a little time to tidy up this hovel."

Kasia waited for the purpose of Mary's surprise visit to emerge. It didn't take long. "Where the hell were you yesterday?"

"Out with a friend." Kasia heard the defensiveness in her voice. Surely Mary didn't think she had any connection to Yvette's dealing.

"If I may ask?"

"With Nick Morgan. We took a long drive," Kasia said, hoping the mention of squeaky clean-cut Nick would dispel any of Mary's suspicions.

"Aren't you full of surprises? Long Sunday drives. Unexpected relatives showing up." Mary walked over, pulled out the desk chair and settled in with the air of someone who could wait for the right answer. Looking at the jumble of papers on the desk and shaking her head, she tugged the short purple vest over her waist and fiddled with a pencil.

"Relatives?" Kasia's thoughts flew to Piotr as the name issued from her lips. Had something happened? With a sense of unease for the second time she recalled the dream, his soft kiss on her forehead.

"Not Poland. Haven't heard any more from that neck of the woods, which leads me to believe you've squared things away."

The stack of unopened letters from Piotr was in the partially opened drawer Mary leaned on. *Please,* thought Kasia, *please don't let her look down.*

"No. I had a visit from your sister yesterday."

"My sister?" Kasia heard her voice creak.

"Your sister. She was frantic—looking all over for you. I found her going through the carrels in the library."

"Frantic?" Kasia wondered whether Mary's account could be accurate. She was surprised at the pleasure she felt that Alice would come to see her. But frantic?

"Corralled her in my office and calmed her down. Must have talked for an hour nonstop. I got the lowdown on the whole family scene. Weird enough for Ripley."

Kasia found it hard to imagine Alice talking to anyone for two hours. Then she recalled the night she and the other student landed in New York, the epic diner feast, and Mary's uncanny ability to get even the shyest of them to become a storyteller. "But why was she looking for me?"

Mary would not have her conversation flow challenged by Kasia's question. "She's one terrific gal. Promised I'd give her a jingle when you turned up. But with all hell breaking loose around here last night—I assume you heard about that—it slipped to the back burner. She's on her way over right now. I told her I'd hog-tie you to a chair until she got here. Meanwhile, why don't you get cracking on this sty before you entertain visitors."

By the time Alice arrived Kasia had rearranged the detritus to Mary's satisfaction, while the evil taskmaster grilled her about her long lost sister. No, Kasia didn't know where Alice worked, except that Kasia thought she was a nurse. Yes, she lived at home with her mother. About thirty-five. Kasia cooperated with the inquisition, eager to keep Mary off the subject of Yvette. When Alice arrived Mary turned uncharacteristically quiet, but she lingered in the doorway well beyond the time Kasia thought appropriate.

When they were finally alone, Kasia turned to Alice and said expectantly, "She's back?"

"Yes. Four days ago. But that's not why I'm here."

Kasia felt a prickle of anxiety when she recalled Mary saying frantic. "Four days?" ·

"I know I said I'd let you know. But something happened."

"What?" Kasia's voice sounded gruff, even to herself.

Alice had intended to give Kasia the news gently in her best nurse-talking-to-the-family voice. Instead she put her hands up to her face and sobbed out, "Breast cancer."

The word drew a thread of pain like a nerve up Kasia's back. She sat heavily on the bed and pulled Alice down beside her, putting her arm over her sister's shoulder. Alice stiffened and immediately regained her composure. She recounted the chaotic days since Hattie's return in the same detached, clinical way she had told Kasia about Ben. Remembering her feelings around her own mother's illness, the waves of fear and refusal and numbness and fury washing over her, Kasia's heart went out to Alice. When Alice paused, Kasia said, "Have you told her I'm here?"

"No. I don't know why. Maybe I should have, but it didn't seem like the right time. She doesn't need any more stress."

"Of course. That can wait," Kasia said. "How bad is it?"

"We're waiting to find out. If it hasn't metastasized, the surgery won't be as extensive. But there'll probably be radiation and chemo to follow. I'll let you know right away. Even the best case scenario, it's not an easy thing." Alice was readying to leave, though Kasia had more questions.

Kasia followed her sister to the door and for the first time saw the pain and tension in the face still startling in its likeness to her own. Impulsively, Kasia leaned her head against Alice's shoulder and put her arms around her for the second time. Alice didn't soften. Neither did she pull away.

Kasia stood in the pale blue hallway. She had dressed in her good clothes, the outfit she'd worn to Hartford. Absently, she hiked her sagging pantyhose and tucked the back of her blouse into the waistband of her shirt. She waited to be summoned. The dank, helpless smell of the hospital hallway made her feel small and afraid, drawing her back to the days and nights of her childhood, the growing array of medications on her mother's nightstand.

Kasia felt bile surge up into her throat. She struggled not to vomit. Hearing voices, she peeked around the corner. Eleanor in clogs clacked toward her and touched her shoulder. "Here," she said, drawing Kasia to a bench beside her, absently winding the long black and silver hair that had come undone from her chignon over her ears. "Collect yourself. It's not a pretty sight. She's weak."

"Did they find out—"

"Wasn't as bad as it might have been. But I won't kid you. It's serious." Eleanor's eyes were moist.

"Maybe I should come back later." Kasia felt relief flood through her as she imagined passing through the large glass doors of the hospital and out into the fall evening. Walking, then running as fast as she could away from the building, across the parking lot and into the trees beyond. She wanted to run from all the sadness, from Hattie, from everything that she had never wanted to know about her father. From illness. From death. From the memories of her mother's last days.

"She wants to see you. But you can only stay a few minutes." Eleanor stood and drew Kasia to her feet.

"Is Alice with her?"

"She went home to change. She'll be back this evening to stay the night with Hattie."

Kasia drew in her breath.

"You okay?"

"I don't think so."

Eleanor's eyes brimmed over behind her large glasses. "I know this must be difficult. So much conflicting emotion. So many questions. Eddie says when it doubt, just let your heart speak. It'll know what to say."

Kasia felt her teeth chatter.

Eleanor put her hand on Kasia's. "You can do this," she said. "Just go to her. The rest will follow."

When Kasia timidly nudged open the door and saw the groggy smile, she felt Hattie's warmth, her comforting presence, around her. Hattie, her Hattie, older and smaller than she had remembered, but still Hattie with her auburn hair and lively brown eyes, looked up at her from the pillow. Hattie wriggled the fingers of her left hand in welcome. The right side of her chest and her right arm were heavily bandaged. She looked uncomfortably balanced on the bed, with something beneath her keeping the bandaged side elevated. Kasia glimpsed a tube running into a clear pouch of yellowish liquid.

"Have you really come all this way to see me?" Hattie said, her voice weak but surprisingly clear. "Sit here. I want to look at you."

Kasia waited for her heart to speak. She hoped for the word that would help them both understand why she was there. But Eddie had been wrong. Inside her there was only a chill, windy silence.

She took the chair at the side of the bed and her legs began to jiggle involuntarily. She was a little girl again, terrified and confused by the illness of someone she loved. Hoping Hattie hadn't noticed, she put her palms flat on her thighs to steady them. Beyond the bed, a machine drew spiky lines across a screen. Nearby, another whirred softly.

"Don't worry. I'm not in pain. Just a little woozy from the medicine."

Still unable to speak, Kasia tried for a smile.

Hattie studied her face. "Do you remember playing Clue?"

Kasia visualized the box open on the red kitchen table, the colored markers shaped like Hershey Kisses, the various marvelous instruments of destruction against the lavish painted backgrounds, rooms with curtains and secret passages—all so clear in Kasia's memory. She recited, "Colonel Mustard in the billiard room with the candlestick."

"I've thought of it so often since those days in Hartford. Even then when we played, I thought of the mysterious way we'd come together. I tried to find an answer that would harm no one. Again and again I reasoned through every decision. Should I have done this? Said that? Always the same unsatisfactory answer."

"You should save your strength. Don't talk about it now."

"No. I must. I should have told you long ago. You and Alice. I need to talk about it."

Kasia voice was soft but firm. "How long did you know—about us?"

"The answer to that changes. I thought I knew nothing about Ben—your father's—life on the road, nothing really. Later, I came to think I must have unconsciously understood some shorthand he'd used, because as soon as he died I went looking. Of course there were clues, but I didn't put them together. Alice would say I didn't let myself know. Maybe she'd be right. Ten years now, and it's still as confusing as the day I drove up to 321 Gordon Street and sat on the porch. You brought me a glass of water. Do you recall?"

Kasia nodded. Her trip with Nick, that terrible afternoon, returned to her. "The house. I went there. Our house—the whole street—gone." Kasia choked out the words. "We met someone on the street and asked. He said they tore them down. All the houses. 'Eyesores,' he called them."

"It's all right. You can cry," Hattie comforted her.

In the silence between them, the humming, the soft tapping of footsteps along the hall.

Finally, Kasia asked, "Why did he do it?"

Hattie shifted in the bed.

"I'm sorry. I'm upsetting you. I should go."

"Please. I've needed to have this conversation for so long. Please stay."

Kasia waited, unable to say anything more. She felt the place inside herself where the confusion and anger roiled. Her silence refused it a way out.

"Little by little, from what your mother told me, I pieced it together. You know she loved him very much. It's hard still for me to say this, but I think he loved her too. Their lives collided like two stars gone off course. I was so angry. I wanted revenge. He had no right. But later as you and your mother grew to mean so much to me, I came to understand a little bit."

"And Piotr?"

"With Piotr I found out for myself that you can love two people. Then I understood a little more what Ben must have gone through."

"Why did you leave us?" They both heard the hurt little girl behind Kasia's words. The old wound tore. Both were close to tears.

The door opened for a nurse carrying a clipboard. "Mrs. Darling—" she looked down as if to verify the name. "Don't overdo it with visitors. You need to rest." She cast her efficient smile toward Kasia, who quickly got to her feet and slipped her bag over her shoulder.

"Of course," Kasia said, wiping her eyes on the back of her hand.

"Just a few minutes more," Hattie pleaded.

"These pills will let you know when the time's up." She shook two pills into Hattie's good hand from a tiny pleated paper thimble and lifted a cup of water to Hattie's mouth.

Hattie waited until the door closed again before she continued. "Leaving you and your mother, leaving Piotr, was the hardest thing I've ever done. Far more difficult than going there in the first place. Everywhere I looked, any action I took, was bound to cause hurt. I measured it out and thought my leaving would be best. But like blaming Colonel Mustard, I couldn't know for sure."

Kasia was doing the exact thing she'd sworn not to. She could see how exhausted Hattie was. She stood by the bed and touched the uncovered hand. "I'm so sorry this—"

"No, dear one. I'm sorry. So very sorry. How long I've waited to be able to tell you that." Hattie rubbed her thumb along Kasia's hand, lingering over the ring with its bright stone. "I don't want you to answer now, but to think about whether you can forgive me?"

"Forgive?"

Hattie's words had begun to slur and she struggled to keep her eyelids open. "Will you come back?"

Hattie was already asleep as Kasia whispered, "Yes." She stood at the bed for a while watching the machines perform their small particular miracles.

Chapter 50

Dazzled by the variety and volume of foodstuffs on the shelves of the immense Price Chopper superstore in the Scranton plaza, Kasia found it hard to locate the things she'd need to make the dinner she'd promised the Morgans. Hoping to distract her from what was taking place with Hattie, Nick had asked her to fix some of the Polish food she'd told him about. He volunteered to help. Now he pushed the cart behind her, patient while she examined six brands of sauerkraut before selecting one. Similarly, the meat counter filled with cuts displayed on blue Styrofoam trays and identified by names she didn't recognize presented a challenge. Only the thick mottled ropes of kielbasa and the basket full of loose golden onions and garlic reminded her of shopping trips in Warsaw.

The ordeal of the checkout line, queuing up behind towering carts and crying babies, housewives scanning *The Star,* and children grabbing at tiers of candy bars—so unlike the small shops where aproned clerks scurried behind the counter as the shoppers held their baskets up to receive their goods—reminded Kasia of her foreignness. Had she never gone to the market with her mother? She tugged Nick's face close to hers and whispered, "Now I know what I'll write my compare/contrast essay on—the difference between grocery shopping in Warsaw and in Scranton." She looked down at the meager contents of her cart and again scanned the crammed and colorful aisles.

"So we'll count this as research, not an afternoon that we completely deserted our studies," he said. Kasia loved that about Nick; whatever they were doing he could find some good part.

When they'd finally stowed the bags behind the seat of the truck Kasia sighed in satisfaction. Nick switched on the radio and smiled. "Maybe you should check the list one more time. It's a long way back." As she ticked off the ingredients, Kasia felt her confidence returning. She knew the recipe for Bigos by heart, having made it a thousand times. She'd chosen a dish she felt sure would impress Nick's mother.

"Everything but the vodka and red wine," she said.

"My dad has both. I told him what you needed to make your secret recipe."

"Then we're set." Kasia said, eager to begin the first stage of preparation of a dinner that would take place two days later. After the first day of cooking, the meat needed to rest so that the unusual, complex flavors of the various ingredients had time to work together.

Nick proved a fine sous chef—attentive, interested and willing, if not particularly skillful. She showed him how to test the meat she had put into the freezer to make sure it was firm enough to slice in thin strips. Tears springing to his eyes, he uncomplainingly peeled and minced the onions and garlic.

The air in the kitchen, full of their laughter and industry, drew the rest of the family. Grace interrupted her phone canvassing for picketers for the assault on Classy Acts to locate a covered casserole dish. When John wandered in from the garage, where the scent of frying onions had reached him, he volunteered to run over to Wescott's for caraway seed, the only spice the dish required that Grace didn't have on hand. Nick filled the sink with soapy water and dirty implements. Hovering at Kasia's elbow, Caro watched each step as closely as if she expected a test to follow. Finally Nick suggested she could be a participant rather than spectator if she'd wash the dishes as they used them.

When the first step of the meal was finished and cooling before they could cover it and put it in the refrigerator, Nick and Caro and Kasia made peanut butter and banana sandwiches, which they ate in the den watching a football game.

The industrious and ordinary day pleased Kasia. Without much ado, the Morgans had shifted and shuffled and made room for her at their table. Worried about what they would think of her, but sure that they'd find out through the Fenston grapevine, Kasia had given Nick permission to tell her parents about her connection to Ben and Hattie. That conversation was a scene she tried not to imagine. She thought of the Morgans as the typical family, people who took care to keep their own lives uncontaminated by tawdriness. A case in point was Grace's continuing campaign against Classy Acts. Kasia worried that John and Grace would discourage their son's friendship with someone like her, someone with such a strange past. On the contrary, they seemed, if anything, warmer and kinder to Kasia, including her in Caro's cheering events and inviting her along when they drove to Binghamton to see Grace's mother.

In the two weeks that Hattie'd been home from the hospital, Kasia had visited her faithfully every other day. As if by unspoken agreement, they talked only of pleasant things. Kasia listened, amazed at how much Hattie recalled from those days in Hartford. Triggered by Hattie's reminiscence, she began remembering more herself, filling in small gaps. The blessing of memory sustained her. The big questions—how Ben and her mother had gotten together, where he had been when he wasn't in Hartford, were left for another time.

The week after her surgery, Hattie started making trips to the hospital for an eight week course of radiation and chemotherapy. From the first day she was terribly ill, nauseous and weak and pale. Usually Alice met Kasia at the door, eager to have someone other than Athena and Eleanor to talk to. The sisters, big and little, stood together looking into each other's worried face for reassurance. Alice had taken a leave from the hospital so that she could be with Hattie through the course of her treatment. Worriedly, she recounted the day's events.

When Mary stopped her in the cafeteria Kasia noticed Mary's hair had been cut and permed, and it seemed as if she wore a bit of blusher and lipstick. Typically no-nonsense, she let Kasia know she was aware of the situation and offered to help. "If you have trouble getting over there, give me a jingle. I can drop whatever I'm doing long enough to play chauffeur."

And so on the days B.J.'s car wasn't available, Mary drove Kasia to Fenston in her green Neon. Suddenly finding the time to be away from her college duties, she waited, chatting in the kitchen with Alice while Kasia and Hattie visited. Once, when Alice and Mary's conversation drifted into the sickroom, Kasia and Hattie were startled to hear Alice giggle in response to something Mary had said. Hattie paused, listening. Then she smiled. "I'd almost forgotten that laugh."

Covered by an embroidered cloth, the end table near the chair held various vials of medicine. Hattie looked worse each time Kasia visited; like the trees outside the October window, she was gradually losing her vibrancy. Seeing Kasia's alarm, Alice had explained that the treatment would make Hattie sick in the short term, but that her long-term prognosis was very good.

The minute Kasia arrived Hattie waved her in, extending her good hand to clasp Kasia's. She didn't let go for a very long moment. Far from the operatic confrontation Kasia had rehearsed, her afternoons with Hattie were spent sharing only the pleasant memories and skirting the looming topics. The fondness that had bound them ten years earlier returned. Hattie loved hearing about Kasia's studies and campus life, her misadventures in pet care.

Widening patches of scalp, blanched and vulnerable, showed against the remaining long hair, gray at the roots. Hattie's shoulder-length auburn hair fell out in clumps. One afternoon when Kasia arrived, the rest of Hattie's hair had been shorn. "Too much of a contrast—those long hanks next to the bald spots. And dyeing it seemed like such a bother." Hattie patted her head tentatively, as if verifying what had happened. "Besides, the wig will fit better. Alice is a pretty good barber, don't you think?"

Jealousy took Kasia's breath away. Yet she understood. Alice was, after all, the real daughter. How foolish she thought herself, how useless and peripheral. Of course Alice, a skillful, competent nurse, should be the one to care for Hattie. Kasia wondered which of her own fantasies she was fulfilling by spending so much time in Fenston. Hattie had Alice, after all.

A haircut, such a simple thing, tore away at something hard and deep inside Kasia. She wanted to be the one, the final one, the necessary one. The one who got to cut Hattie's hair—just as Hattie had drawn the comb through her own hair and trimmed her bangs.

Before she found out that Piotr had lied to her for all those years, she felt she was central to him. Now she was worse off than before she left Poland. On the edge of other people's families—the Morgans, B.J.

and her folks, and now Alice and Hattie—she felt more an orphan than ever. A person without anyone who loved her, without memories or hopes that she belonged. No matter where she looked, she was reminded again and again of her losses.

Even Piotr, probably engrossed in the work of his business, his evenings in the flat in Warsaw, had forgotten about her. When Kasia thought of him it was always winter twilight. After dinner, in his cardigan sweater and cloth slippers, he'd read the paper and drink a glass of sweet tea, then check her schoolwork. Carrying his street shoes from the mat inside the door, he'd place them on a folded piece of newspaper and brush away the day's soil. His mouth formed in the deep oval of concentration, he'd moisten a piece of cotton, open the small round tin of paste polish and shine his shoes before replacing them, side by side, ready for the next morning. Recalling the fussy ritual she'd despised in Warsaw brought tears to her eyes. Even Piotr had been able to let her go without much thought. Her face burned with anger and shame to be such an expendable, unlovable human being.

One day, Hattie recounted what had led up to her arrival that summer in Hartford. "When Ben died, I was devastated," she began, taking a sip of tea and settling back on the sofa. "One minute he was there beside me, the next I realized he was not breathing. Suddenly, he was gone. And not just away on one of his interminable business trips. For a while after the funeral, I was numb. Then I started to do what people said would help me get over his death. Readying his clothes for the Goodwill, I found an appointment card for a Dr. Doran. The time and date of the appointment were written under the name Darling. I couldn't believe that Ben had consulted a cardiologist.

"That started it. That little card. I became obsessed with the thought that I had never really known very much of Ben's life when he was away from me. I knew him here, in Fenston. But what of the other part of his life, all the time he was away? All I knew were the little anecdotes he told when he came home, and as the years went by they were fewer and fewer. I don't think you can imagine me then, how infrequently I left Fenston—or my house, for that matter. Suddenly everything I didn't know about Ben's life tormented me. Where had he stayed? Washed his clothes? I'd never even asked him. Where had he eaten his meals? Alone, I assumed at the time. How could he have died leaving so much of his life unexplained? I became completely focused on what I didn't but should have known. Finally, though I seldom drove anywhere, I got in the car alone to follow some dim strange idea that I would find peace with Ben's death if I could understand more about his life. Little did I know where it would all lead."

Kasia watched Hattie's expression as she spoke. Even though every word was the revelation Kasia had waited for, when she saw the fatigue etch itself on Hattie's face, she said, "You're tired. Why don't you stop? We can talk some more next time I come."

Hattie shook her head. "This is good for me. I've carried it too long. I must say it. Like the cancer. I need to get it out."

Kasia nodded. The air was still and she smelled the mustiness of a fall afternoon as she waited for Hattie to pick up the thread of her thoughts and continue.

"When I got to Hartford, there was one mystery after another. The doctor's office at first said the card was not Ben's. When I argued, the nurse showed me in the book that the appointment was for someone named Anya Darling. But why would Ben have had her card? What had caused the mix-up? I wanted to think that the nurse was covering up her own mistake, putting someone else's name in Ben's timeslot. But *Darling*? Then the owner of the hotel where Ben stayed said that he hadn't roomed there in years, when I knew it had been less than a month before. So many things didn't add up."

Hattie sighed, a look in her eyes as if she were no longer seeing her own surroundings, but was alive in the memory of that confusion. "In the end, I found you and your mother in the phone book."

"It was that simple." Kasia's voice quivered.

"How to account for what came next? That I would end up moving into your house. That you and your mother would come to mean so much to me. That I'd repeat Ben's life of deceit. Fall in love again, first with you and your mother, and then with the brother of my husband's other wife. It all sounds so impossible, doesn't it?" Hattie's eyes glistened with tears. "A real soap opera. But that's what happened."

Kasia could feel her breath catch in her throat. This. Just this was what she'd needed. It didn't sound impossible at all to her. Deep in her mind and heart, she realized every word Hattie uttered was true. A sigh escaped her, and she felt the world lighten.

Hattie glanced at her. "This must be hard for you to hear." She blinked back tears. "I would have given anything to spare you."

"If you really loved Piotr, you did give up everything. You could have been with him."

"I wanted it. But that happiness would have cost too much sorrow."

"All of this. It's what I needed to know." Kasia stopped, thinking again about that moment on the hillside, the sight of her father's grave.

They talked until the pole lamp blinked on in the side meadow and the shadow in the house came to life: Ben, the man who had allowed himself to think he could love two women in two worlds without hurting anyone, was very near—a comforting presence.

"Your mother said that she believed that Ben had sent me. And who can say that in some way, some mysterious way, he hadn't?" Hattie whispered. "I have so little certainty. But one thing I know for absolutely sure is that he loved you both very much. Another is that his love for you did not diminish his love for Alice and me."

As Kasia was readying to leave, Hattie pointed to her closet. "Over there, can you get something for me? Top shelf."

Covered in old-fashioned paper—pink white sprigs—the small box felt familiar in Kasia's hands, reminding her of something just at the edge of her consciousness. A shard of memory tugged at her as she laid the box next to Hattie.

"Now dear one, this is for you, something I've been saving but never expecting I'd finally be able to give to you. Open it."

Inside Kasia found neat rolls of fabric, dozens of them in various sizes, all carefully wrapped and tied with ribbon. When she touched them, the scent of lavender rose from the box and she was transported to her mother's bedroom.

"This was hers," Kasia whispered, not trusting her voice.

"Yes. Some she brought with her from Poland—see the white there—the skirt of her communion dress. But most of it she collected in Hartford. She had hoped to make you a quilt with it."

Kasia couldn't stop her hands from diving in and fingering the small bundles. Some she opened, undoing the bows her mother had made. With each parcel a memory blossomed—those memories that she had never been able to summon. "I remember this," she said, holding up a swath of peach silk. "Her good blouse." And a vision of her parents holding hands on the sidewalk in front of their house came to her. A sheaf of faded blue flannel carried her to her mother's bedside and she could see them reading and laughing. A long strip of tattersall cotton saw her screaming with delight as her father, his strong arms clad in that fabric, hefted her onto his shoulders. Each piece of fabric gave Kasia another little buried fragment of her past. The touch and smell of the old bits of fabric had unlocked a flood of memories.

Suddenly Kasia wanted to be alone with her thoughts, with all the scenes recreating themselves in her memories. They proved that she was not, as she had feared, an unloved, unlovable person. Hers had been a childhood filled with joy and the love of both her parents.

Chapter 51

After the big bust, drugs were essentially nonexistent at Hapwell. Either Yvette and Doug had been the only two dealing or the others had been frightened into inactivity. Rumors circulated, but no one seemed to have any concrete details. Gudrun reported that Mary had gone into Yvette's room and packed up all her stuff but wouldn't comment.

For the first week or two, people expected something more to happen. Slowly, students settled back into their studies. Yvette seemed to have been all but forgotten. Kasia hated to think of her in jail somewhere with no one to visit her. She had done something wrong, but she was alone in a foreign country. It just didn't seem right to carry on as if she'd never existed.

One night as they drove home from Hattie's, sensing that Mary was in a particularly mellow mood, Kasia questioned her. Mary let out an exasperated sigh. "A real surprise. We screen applicants, but some rotten apples slip through no matter how careful you are. They say you have to watch out for the quiet ones. Proved true in this case."

"But what happened? Did they go to court?"

"Between us?"

"Of course."

"Sent her packing. Police agreed to it if she'd leave voluntarily. I think they put a hold on her visa so she can't come back into the States. For all I know she's wiggling that little butt all over Paris by now. Her parents didn't understand what all the fuss was about. Good riddance."

Kasia recalled the last time she saw Yvette snuggled into her blue cashmere shawl. Now she'd never get her wish to marry an American and spend her life in the States.

Mary switched back to her favorite subject, Alice. "She's some woman, your sister. Been through hard times. Can't be rushed or crowded. Lucky for me, I'm not going anywhere."

Mary's comment did not surprise Kasia. Just hours before, when Hattie had asked Kasia to fill her water pitcher, she had surprised Mary and Alice in the kitchen. They weren't kissing, exactly, but leaning into each other as if preparing to. Surprised at how happy she felt to see them together, *sure,* she thought, *sure*—love explains the new softness in Alice, and Mary's sanguine mood and new hairdo.

"Mind a little detour?" Mary asked as they drove through Fenston corners. "If I don't get some chocolate peanut butter ice cream soon I'm going to start mooing. Since we're within hollering distance of the best dairy in the state—"

"Great. Where?" Kasia had eaten only one meal, a combination breakfast and lunch, a bowl of Lucky Charms with Diet Pepsi instead of milk and half of a soggy bean burrito she'd found in the back of their tiny refrigerator. Ice cream was her favorite dinner entrée.

"Wiggins Dairy Bar. You mean to say your tour guide Nick hasn't taken you there yet?"

Presiding over the crowded parking lot, atop a tall pole positioned between ruddy swollen udders, a ten foot black and white spotted cow rotated in the crossed beams of spotlights, the creature's big eyes opening and closing ecstatically. A dozen or so people were lined up for ice cream. Mary ordered a double chocolate peanut butter on a sugar cone. After scrutinizing the list of thirty-seven flavors, Kasia opted for one scoop of pumpkin and one of something called Charlie Brownie, chocolate ice cream with chunks of brownie and walnuts.

While they sat enjoying their treat, on the other side of the road about 100 yards down an enormous neon sign sprang to life. "What's that?" Kasia pointed.

Mary looked at her watch—"Nine P.M. Must be that girlie place all the locals have their bustles in a bunch over. Bold as blazes and twice as brassy."

Kasia looked mystified.

"Classy Acts. How's that for hyperbole? Big-boobed nitwits doing the hoochie-koochie for a bunch of guys with hat sizes bigger than their IQs. Some class."

Mary must have been at least mildly curious herself, because instead of turning left back to the school she headed toward the light source and drove ten miles an hour down the steep incline into the parking lot and past the windowless building with the flashing marquee.

LAST NIGHT: THE CUPCAKES
FOUR GIRL REVIEW

As they drew alongside, the ice cream in Kasia's stomach soured as she recognized among the handful of cars a distinctive Lincoln, one she knew had been driven recently to Hartford. She forced herself to blot the image from her mind.

Chapter 52

Fortunately B.J., snowed under by homework, planned to chain herself to the desk for the whole weekend the big dinner was to take place. She was happy to let Kasia borrow the car in exchange for a promise of leftovers.

After struggling through the zoology chapters Kasia put the finishing touches on the final draft of her process essay about her recent experience assisting Dr. Pryal as he removed what seemed like hundreds of porcupine quills from the mouth of an astonished and inadequately sedated Irish setter. She had divided the ordeal into the steps required for the essay, making sure logic prevailed and careful that her descriptions were sufficiently informative. She did not go into the part where the dog had nervous diarrhea on the examining table or the hysterical children, the dog's owners, who kept running in and out of the treatment room while they worked.

At the Morgan house all went as planned. When Kasia lifted the cover from the casserole that had been refrigerated for two days, the aroma was gorgeous. The table was set. The garnishes of chopped dill pickles, fruit compote, horseradish and sour cream were ready. She removed the foil and put the baking dish back into the oven under the broiler to brown.

Just as Kasia finished whipping the potatoes with fresh parsley, baked garlic, milk and butter, the apple of discord fell onto the center of the oak trestle table in the pleasant dining room of the Morgan home. The messenger who provided this particular omen was returning three large signs with the words CLASSY ACTS in the middle of a red circle with a slash across.

Eddie Roderi, who Kasia knew from his visits to Hattie, stood respectfully at the Morgans' front door, signs in hand, explaining to John Morgan that although he and Eleanor weren't interested in such entertainment themselves, they had a strong belief in the constitution and in the rights of other citizens, however misguided and banal their tastes, to seek whatever entertainment was not specifically forbidden by the law of the land.

Grace had showered after mucking out the stalls and was dressing for dinner. Droplets of water from her wet hair fell on the shoulders of her blue shirt as she hurried toward the door. She stopped short when she saw Eddie. Warming to his topic, he began explicating the historical, philosophical implications of freedom of speech. When Grace had heard enough to get the gist of his position, one she found particularly foolish, if not selfish, she said, "But you were a priest."

"Don't hold that against me, please. I've done my penance—all these years of farming and minding my own business should count for something." Eddie tried for a light tone.

"Don't you care about the youth of our community?" Her belligerent tone increased in volume.

"Depends on what you mean by 'care.'"

"Do you want our young people living with that sinfulness next door?"

"What I want doesn't matter. Fact is—we've all lived next door to iniquity. If not one sin, then another."

"But—"

"Eleanor didn't feel right about just taking down the signs and destroying them, so she sent me over to explain."

Grace narrowed her eyes and glared at him. "You won't change your mind? Everybody in town is displaying them."

"Fraid not." Eddie looked as if he truly regretted causing upset. "El and I are firm on it. Sorry to keep you from dinner. Smells wonderful." Eddie looked at the table set for five and gave Kasia a wink.

"What can you expect?" Grace huffed after Eddie left. "They raised the worst pack of brats in this county. Getting into every imaginable version of mischief, and the two of them just ignored most of it." She looked around for someone to second her outrage. Then she moved toward the bedroom, eager to complete her interrupted toilette. "Must have been some priest," she muttered.

Kasia recalled the film of glitter on the dashboard of the Morgans' seldom-used car, the sighting of that same car in the Classy Acts parking lot.

"Just a minute," John said, his face set in a stern expression. "Grace, have you been going around plastering people's lawns with those posters without their permission?" he asked. His voice contained something hard, something Kasia saw Grace and Nick and even Caro respond to.

"Just a few places. Where people weren't home."

"The Roderis weren't home?"

"I didn't actually—" But she was drowned out by a metallic bleating from the kitchen.

John and Nick, Grace and Caro all got there before Kasia. Smoke billowed up from the burners of the stove. "The Bigos," she cried. In all the excitement of Eddie's unexpected visit, she'd forgotten that the meat was browning under the broiler.

John flipped off the stove, grabbed two hot pads and pulled out the casserole. The meat on top was black and the sauerkraut dry and brown as straw. The kitchen had filled with smoke. Caro started coughing.

The smoke alarm continued its shrill warning. "Shut that damn thing off," he barked to Nick. "And open the door."

"Oh, no," Kasia cried, surveying her masterpiece.

"Is it bad?" Caro asked. "If it's ruined, maybe we can have peanut butter and banana sandwiches," she added hopefully. For all her eagerness to help in the preparation, Caro was not looking forward to eating the strange concoction.

Grace was at Kasia's side. "Don't worry. It looks lovely," she said, surveying the blackened mass. "Give me a minute with it. I think we can salvage the bottom," she said, scraping away the blackest parts with a spatula. When she pried the top layer of unrecognizable char away, the meat and cabbage underneath bubbled delectably. Unharmed.

"Now everybody grab something and head for the dining room and close the door behind you," John ordered, hoping to trap the smoke in one room.

Obediently, they took their places at the table and silently passed the food from hand to hand. John got up and lit the candles, joking about more smoke than fire when he struck the match.

All that work, Kasia thought, *spoiled at the last minute.*

Caro was the first to pronounce in a surprised voice, "This is good. Mmmm."

"I'll say," John said, and began eating in earnest.

"The flavors are so unusual," Grace offered, discretely shoving a few shreds of charred meat to the side of her plate. "I'd like this recipe."

Nick smiled across at Kasia and gave her the nose wiggle, their sign that things were more than averagely amusing.

A welcome calm enveloped the table. The first tentative, meager helpings they had put on their plates were replaced by heartier servings. John experimented, mixing the meat dish with a little of all its accompaniments, the pickles, sour cream, and horseradish.

The doorbell rang again.

"Any more surprises, Grace? Take out any billboards?" His voice was still edgy.

Kasia imagined their private scene later that night, when their guest was gone and the kids in bed. Nick had told her that his parents' infrequent arguments had accelerated in volume. "Pissers," he called them.

Nick rose. "I'll get it." Forks lifted, they all looked up, as if they expected something more from Eddie Roderi. There was a bit of muffled conversation and then a new tone in Nick's voice as he said, "In here, sir." He ushered the caller toward the dining room, where they sat enjoying the meal.

The next moment Kasia gasped and dropped her fork. She bolted from her chair to run toward the tall stooped man with the sad eyes. *"Wujek,"* she cried.

Without even thinking about how furious she was, she grabbed the man and kissed him hard and long. "It's my uncle Piotr." Her voice was filled with wonder.

When she recovered from the shock of seeing him, her grudges and anger nudged the happiness out of her voice. "What are you doing here?"

Chapter 53

Kasia was grateful to Nick and his family for their efforts, but every conversational foray ended with a weighty silence. Piotr stood at the door, refusing to sit at the table. Obviously, his English had suffered in the past months. Creaking out a few rusty polite words, the hard endings of *g*s and *t*s over-pronounced, he attempted to conclude the obligatory small talk while Kasia struggled to extend it.

She needed time. All the imagining, all the planning for her confrontation with Piotr, the way she would tell him off, bring him to his knees with supplication and regret, the way she would stun him with her knowledge of all he had conspired to keep from her. The image of his sorry face as she banished him from her presence forever fled just when she needed most to recall each exquisite detail of her well-deserved retribution.

Instead, she could not get past the fact of him, his face creasing with the effort of pleasantries, the way his hands hung defenselessly at his sides, the glimpse of his gray cardigan beneath the camel jacket, the foreignness of him, so infuriating, so familiar, so beloved.

"What's this about," she demanded when the door closed behind them. Struggling to rekindle the flame of her anger, Kasia refused to look at him.

"At least you didn't forget Polish food? Bigos, wasn't it?" Piotr asked in Polish.

"Don't change the subject," she said, and slid into the passenger seat of the rental car. "What do you think you're doing here?" Kasia spoke in rapid English.

"To be honest, I don't know." Though heavily accented, his English was perfect.

"That makes two of us."

Refusing to acknowledge her retort, he continued, "My niece abandoned me without warning or explanation." He stopped his flippant tone, sighed, then began again more swiftly. "Many years ago when your mother and I had a misunderstanding and she put me out of her life, I allowed her to do it. For weeks I've been thinking about what is going on with you. I made that mistake before, and you see how much she and I lost. I would give anything to have those years back. This time I decided I'd try something different."

"And what was that poor-me-I-can't-speak-English act back there?"

"Forgive me."

"So it was bogus!"

"Bogus? I don't know the word. But I was playing dumb. I wanted to talk to you alone. Maybe some other time we can spend an evening with your boyfriend and his family."

"How did you know—?"

"Your roommate is a real *gadula,*" he chuckled.

"Chatterbox. Yep. that's B.J."

"She and her friend were studying when I arrived. After a long time—I think they were deciding whether I was dangerous or not—they even let me in the room." His eyes grew wide with mirth. "They were worried that I wouldn't find my way here, so they came in the car with me."

"What a pal," Kasia muttered.

"She told me to tell you she'd used her other keys and took the car. I said I'd make sure you got back."

The evening air was chill. Kasia drew her sweater around her. Above them, stars spun like grains of coarse salt thrown against the night. She breathed in the smell of Fenston, of Morgan's farm, of the woods across the street, the pungent, cedary, good-dirt smell. She held her breath and steadied herself. Then she took another long breath and looked back toward the Morgan house, the silhouettes of Nick and Caro clearing the table. Her worlds collided.

"Naturally I was curious about the people who had kidnapped my niece. Now that I've found you and seen for myself that you are not being held captive, forced to endure ugly, painful tattoos from head to foot, I'm ready to hear your explanations. Indulge me. I'd like a glass of tea and some dinner. Do you know somewhere?"

Sitting on the edge of the pink Formica vanity sink in the pine-scented ladies room of the Red Bird Diner, Kasia readied herself, dawdling, drawing out the moments before the crescendo, the delicious self-righteous finale she was orchestrating in her imagination. If Piotr thought he had questions, wait till he heard hers. She checked her watch. Ten minutes, okay!

She slid into the corner booth across from her uncle, blew the paper from a straw and poked it into her Coke. An enormous black fly spun in the crevice of the window, with a surprisingly loud buzz. Kasia watched the futile attempts to gain air.

Preoccupied with the fly, she could not believe the words she heard rolling from her lips. What was wrong with her? She hadn't begun her speech about his duplicity. Before she could call it back, she had blurted something that had nothing to do with Piotr or the family secrets she'd uncovered. Instead she'd told him everything she knew about the situation around Classy Acts, Grace's obsession with family values and closing the place down. She recounted her discovery of John's car in the strip club's parking lot. "I was so fooled," she wailed. "I thought they were the ideal family." Shaken, she stopped, still reeling from what she had blurted out.

Piotr agreed it was sad. And terribly confusing. "But, *Malutka,* is this what you've been doing here? You had to come all this way to find out that people are not angels?"

His face was kind and his voice soft, the tone he had used when she was little and came to him for answers. How had she allowed herself to forget his calm, thoughtful presence, his willingness to help her? Even if he did lie to her, she could still love him, couldn't she?

"But Nick's father in that place? Gross."

"Do you think when you have children that everything else goes away, all the feelings, all the dreams and desires? In that case, I'm glad

I'm not a parent. Being perfect is too big a responsibility."

"And his mother running around trying to change things she doesn't even understand?"

"It's natural to want to warn others away from danger, especially the harm you most fear for yourself."

"It won't work." She thought of Eddie's visit.

"Certainly. But she must try. That's how she sees her responsibility."

Kasia was silent.

"They are fine people—like me and you—struggling to do their best. It's a untidy and difficult world. Sometimes no matter how we try, we fall short."

Was he was talking about her father? Now, after all these years when he would discuss nothing about her life in Connecticut, was he finally going to explain things to her?

Trying to rekindle her anger, she turned and watched the fly. "I'm not saying 'perfect,' but—"

"Let's talk now about how you've dismissed me from your memory, precisely as I worried you would. See, what I most feared came to pass. But first," he motioned the waitress to the table, "unlike some people who had a feast tonight, I've had no dinner at all."

He ordered scrambled eggs and toast and more tea. Kasia asked for a dish of rice pudding. The fly soared up again and the waitress leaned across the table and snatched it expertly with one hand. "Last of the season, I hope," she said, smiling.

"So we were talking about mistakes. Over the past two months, I convinced myself that letting you come here was another mistake. You wanted it, but did I have to allow it? Was I wrong?"

When Kasia took a breath and started to respond, he held up his hand.

"Why? The past. I forced your mother to leave Poland when she didn't want to because I thought she'd have a better life in America. I was wrong. That error cost me so many years with her. When you insisted on going, this time, I thought, let her decide. Wrong again?"

"And Hattie?"

"Ah. And Hattie. So you remember Hattie."

"Of course."

"Think about it. With Hattie, a different way. Letting someone

I love turn away from me. Already two times—the same mistake. I couldn't forgive myself another one. That's why I had to come and find you. Finally, I learned that letting go too easily is even worse than holding too tightly." His voice trembled with remembrance and regret. "It seems old-fashioned to your generation, but Hattie, well, she was the love of my life."

"But when you found out about Hattie and my father, what could you do?"

From sorrow to lack of understanding—the shift of emotions in Piotr's face confused her. "Find out what? What does Hattie have to do with your father? He was gone long before she got to Hartford."

"You couldn't just ignore all that had happened, the lies, the way she came to us," she stammered.

"I'm now not following," Piotr said, his forehead creasing with an attempt to make sense of her statements. He switched into Polish.

So he had not learned his lesson. He continued to treat her as a child. "Don't pretend to me." Kasia's face darkened. "Did you think I wouldn't find out? Am I terminally stupid or what?"

"What a terrible thing. I never, never thought you stupid. Not for one minute of your life. Headstrong perhaps—my fault, probably. But not stupid. How could you say this thing to me?"

"But Hattie—"

"Hattie. Hattie. So far in the past. Do you mention her to hurt me? She went away and that's that. I didn't understand it. Still I don't. But it was her decision. Maybe I should have tried harder to make her come with us. I was hurt and didn't ask enough questions. In the middle of so much else, can you blame me?"

Kasia forced her thoughts back to that sad time, Hattie's leaving and soon after that her mother's death. In those long quiet days in the house as she and Piotr prepared for the trip to Poland, the snow wrapped itself like an obscene bandage around them. There was nothing to do, no air in those quiet rooms, no light with its pleasant tricks to comfort her. They were disposing of the past, shedding the possessions that had made up the background of their life.

Piotr's expression told her he was remembering too. When the food was placed in front of him, he stared down as if it had offended him. The waitress hesitated. "Isn't this what you ordered?" she asked, rifling the pages of her pad with the eraser end of her pencil.

"Yes, yes, it's fine," he said. When she walked away, he took a sip of water and paused as if thinking about whether he would say something. "I wonder. Was it so obvious that I loved her? I knew she loved me too. Suddenly she said she was leaving. Without so much as an explanation. I didn't understand it. And still I don't."

"You couldn't have wanted her to go to Poland with us once you knew."

"Knew what?" he demanded. Still he did not pick up his fork. Kasia watched his face as he reviewed every grief and memory of the months before her mother died, every confidence he and Hattie had shared. "What was there to know? Hattie was kind to you and Anya. I had feelings for her. I thought she did too. I must have been mistaken. For her own reasons, she needed to go. I just had to accept it."

Could it be that he hadn't found out about Hattie and her father? That her rage, the unread letters in her drawer, all the times she forced herself not to remember his kind face or the *buziak* moth wing kiss on her forehead, she had wronged him? Could it be that he hadn't connected her coming to Pennsylvania with trying to find Hattie? That he didn't know the woman he loved was three miles away, recovering from cancer? Had Kasia hidden her plan so well? Could it be? Then relief and recognition bloomed inside her. "You don't know, do you?"

"What, Kasia, know what? Talk to me."

"Eat," Kasia commanded, pointing to the untouched plate cooling in front of him.

For it was clear at last. Hattie had left Piotr and gone back to Fenston, given up the chance for happiness with him, to protect Ben's daughters. Kasia's heart swelled with the hope that at least some of these sorrows could be rectified.

Everything that had happened to Kasia in the three months since she arrived at Hapwell blurred together with her past, and began to make sense. The tombstones on the hill, Hattie's nubbin and wig, the other daughter of Ben Darling, schoolwork, the vet clinic, the missing eyesore house on Gordon Street, Nick's grandparents and the grudge car—there was so much more she and Piotr would need to puzzle out together, now that she finally understood where she belonged.

Piotr loved her. Knowing that, Kasia felt the strength in herself that everyone else already recognized. The one thing she had needed slipped quietly into her life. Wherever she went, she knew that her uncle's love would follow. She would always have a home.

Another fly staggered like a tear down the pane. "We'll talk," she said. "But now, eat. You'll need all your strength." The glass cast back the double image of their faces and beyond that the terrible, fragrant American night she would teach him to love.

About the Author

The Season of Lost Children is part of The Fenston Trilogy, which traces fifty years of the interwoven lives and friendship of three women in a bucolic Pennsylvania college town. While *The Season of Lost Children* focuses on the life of the eccentric former nun Eleanor Roderi, *A Trick of Light* chronicles the heartbreaking discovery and redemption of Hattie Darling, the only daughter of the town's first family. Pearlsong Press will also publish *From: Oz*, which recounts the exploits of Fenston's shopkeeper, Athena Wescott, and her late life affair with...well, you'll have to read it to find out.

Poet, translator, playwright and novelist Karen Blomain holds an MFA from Columbia University. A university professor, she has conducted multi-genre writing workshops around the world. Ms. Blomain is married to the writer/photographer Michael Downend. They have nine children and fifteen grandchildren (so far) and live on The Hill in Scranton, Pennsylvania, Blomain's hometown.

About Pearlsong Press

Pearlsong Press is an independent publishing company dedicated to providing books and resources that entertain while expanding perspectives on the self and the world. The company was founded by Peggy Elam, Ph.D., a psychologist and journalist, in 2003.

Pearls are formed when a piece of sand or grit or other abrasive, annoying, or even dangerous substance enters an oyster and triggers its protective response. The substance is coated with shimmering opalescent nacre ("mother of pearl"), the coats eventually building up to produce a beautiful gem. The self-healing response of the oyster thus transforms suffering into a thing of beauty.

The pearl-creating process reflects our company's desire to move outside a pathological or "disease" based model of life, health and well-being into a more integrative and transcendent perspective. A move out of suffering into joy. And that, we think, is something to sing about.

Pearlsong Press endorses Health At Every Size, an approach to health and well-being that celebrates natural diversity in body size and encourages people to stop focusing on weight (or any external measurement) in favor of listening to and respecting natural appetites for food, drink, sleep, rest, movement, and recreation. While not every book we publish specifically promotes Health At Every Size (by, for instance, featuring fat heroines or educating readers on size acceptance), none of our books or other resources will contradict this holistic and body-positive perspective.

We encourage you to enjoy, enlarge, enlighten and enliven yourself with other Pearlsong Press books, which you can purchase at www.pearlsong.com or your favorite bookstore. Keep up with us through our blog at www.pearlsongpress.com.

Fiction:

The Fat Lady Sings—a young adult novel by Charlie Lovett

Syd Arthur—a novel by Ellen Frankel

Fallen Embers (Book One of The Embers Series)—paranormal romance by Lauri J Owen

Bride of the Living Dead—romantic comedy by Lynne Murray

Measure By Measure—a romantic romp with the fabulously fat by Rebecca Fox & William Sherman

FatLand—a visionary novel by Frannie Zellman

The Program—a suspense novel by Charlie Lovett

The Singing of Swans—a novel about the Divine Feminine by Mary Saracino

ROMANCE NOVELS & SHORT STORIES FEATURING BIG BEAUTIFUL HEROINES:
by Pat Ballard, the Queen of Rubenesque Romances:
> *The Best Man*
> *Abigail's Revenge*
> *Dangerous Curves Ahead: Short Stories*
> *Wanted: One Groom*
> *Nobody's Perfect*
> *His Brother's Child*
> *A Worthy Heir*

by Rebecca Brock—*The Giving Season*

& by Judy Bagshaw—*At Long Last, Love: A Collection*

Nonfiction:

Fat Poets Speak: Voices of the Fat Poets' Society—edited by Frannie Zellman

Ten Steps to Loving Your Body (No Matter What Size You Are) by Pat Ballard

Beyond Measure: A Memoir About Short Stature & Inner Growth by Ellen Frankel

Taking Up Space: How Eating Well & Exercising Regularly Changed My Life by Pattie Thomas, Ph.D. with Carl Wilkerson, M.B.A. (foreword by Paul Campos, author of *The Obesity Myth*)

Off Kilter: A Woman's Journey to Peace with Scoliosis, Her Mother & Her Polish Heritage—a memoir by Linda C. Wisniewski

Unconventional Means: The Dream Down Under—a spiritual travelogue & memoir by Anne Richardson Williams

Splendid Seniors: Great Lives, Great Deeds—inspirational biographies by Jack Adler